BLACK
MAGIC

I0675006

David Nottingham

First published in 2025 by Blossom Spring Publishing
Black Magic Copyright © 2025 David Nottingham
ISBN978-1-917938-03-7
E: admin@blossomspringpublishing.com
W: www.blossomspringpublishing.com

Acknowledgements

Niina Marni. I acknowledge the land I live on and where this book was written and mostly set is the traditional lands of the Kaurna people and that I respect their spiritual relationship with their country.

To my family always: Mick, who inherited my virtues and not my vices; Jac, who gifted me with grandchildren and thereby a touch of immortality through bloodline and name; and Hayden and Rhys, whose manifest uniquenesses act as an enchanted elixir for one allergic to banality and conformity.

To Werner, Manuela, and Ina, many thanks for the support and encouragement. Writers need readers, and the earliest ones remain valued memories. To any and all other readers, gratitude and hopes that you enjoy reading my imaginings as much as I delighted in transforming synaptic visualisations into word paintings.

Countless thanks to all at Blossom Spring Publishing — notably Laura, who transformed my simple cover ideas into eye-catching art, and Pam, who converted a multitude of typos and literary sins into a readable novel. Without you my authorship would forever remain PDFs on a flash drive in a box at the back of a cupboard. You rescue my characters and plots from paupers' burials in a forgotten graveyard.

To all of my numerous lecturers, with gratitude for sharing your expertise: there is some of each of you in my scribblings. Any perceived errors are carefully-considered poetically-licensed choices; any genuine ones are mine alone.

1

The phone rang. I spent twelve years eight floors up in a city-based office designed and managed to ensure the firm's lawyers, myself included, could concentrate on making a great deal of money for the firm's partners, myself not included. Twelve years hardwires certain habits into the subconscious, one of which was ignoring ringing telephones.

Early in the morning, still half asleep at my desk, I daydreamed and listened absently to the annoying noise punching its way into my consciousness until I realised if I didn't take the call, nobody else would. While the idea appealed, it also spelt doom for a struggling one-man legal firm in a regional town. I picked up the handset and pressed the flashing button.

'Good morning, Miller Legal.'

'Is that Mister Miller?'

Not, I realised, considering my opening greeting, *a particularly intelligent question*. Then I worked out I hadn't identified myself. My bad, and I decided to be polite.

'It is. Van Miller.' Civil, succinct, and informative. An improvement on pretending to be my non-existent office staff until I found out whether I should continue in the same vein, change into managerial mode, or hang up. All three were well-practised possible options.

The voice, when it continued, was professional clipped acerbity, conveying less warmth than the remnants of my tea. 'My name is Emily Parsons. I'm the personal assistant to John Picino.' She switched into a tone dripping with breathy reverence, 'The Attorney-General of South Australia.'

That grandiose pronouncement marked the precise moment when the pleasant and uneventful morning went into freefall. Experience, common sense, even the familiar nervous frisson tingling coldly along my spine were warnings I normally would have taken notice of. I don't remember why I didn't simply bring the conversation to a stop before it started with a polite farewell and a disconnection, but what I do recall, vividly, is being enveloped by an insistent almost visceral sensation I should.

My greeting sounded grander than the reality. Miller Legal was me full-time, Maya part-time, and a cleaner, Karen, who waved brushes around three times a week to offer clients an enhanced impression of the place. I'd been a lawyer for fifteen years, having previously served as a police officer for ten, Maya was a newly qualified lawyer who acted as my researcher and general dogsbody and occasionally had the opportunity to practise what she was trained for, and Karen was on loan from the medical practice in the other half of the building.

I owned fifty percent of the property. One of the four neighbouring doctors, Alexandria Miller, surname not a coincidence, owned the other fifty percent and all of me. Maya owned a middle-aged cat, an ancient Toyota sedan, and a new and expensive mountain bike. My previous employers owned a nine-storey building in the middle of Adelaide and filled the top floors with a multitude of lawyers. I grew increasingly disillusioned with defending people for whom, in a sane society, public executions would have been reinstated. The pressure of long hours and a growing moral malaise brought on a small but not ignorable breakdown featuring a few days I couldn't remember. Alex, demonstrating considerable presence during my cognitive absence, made life changing decisions for both of us.

She was working in the Emergency Department at the Royal Adelaide Hospital and finally decided the bruises on her cheekbone, the third set gifted by patients who decided the cure for stupidity was self-medication using tablets mixed up in a bucket in a shed, qualified for the enough-is-too-much-already label. That final conclusion, coupled with my anxiety attack, convinced us to abandon our high-pressure soul-destroying slaveries and begin again somewhere less stressful. I took over a struggling one-man firm in the rural river town of Murray Bridge from a post heart attack retiree and spent much of my office time formulating wills while she bought into the medical practice and occupied her working hours preventing their activation.

People we knew considered the romantic coupling of the legal intangibility and medical precision as unusual, if not highly improbable. Alex had the answer for their perplexity. 'Doctors surgically remove lawyer's consciences and then lawyers return the favour by defending us against malpractice suits. And we can tell each other the deep dark secrets about our work and we're protected from any criticism by lawyer-client or doctor-patient confidentiality. It adds spice to our lives.' The funniest part of it was many believed her straight-faced assertions, but the truth was our professional lives were as deliberately detached as our private lives were inextricably intertwined.

We had a much renovated late-nineteenth-century house overlooking the river, my impractical but enjoyable BMW Mini Cooper, Alex's family-sensible four-wheel drive Toyota, a dog named Judge with more genetic origins than brain cells verging on setting a record for canine longevity, and a son Rob who, like most of his peer group, was in early high school educationally and late preschool emotionally. The upside of our new existence was we all seemed to be ageing at a considerably slower rate than when we were speeding towards destruction in the fast lane. Mostly, I ended up less tightly wound and far more relaxed. As I answered the phone, I didn't know it but everything was about to change.

John Picino! We were at university together. I left the police and enrolled in law. He had a degree in economics and worked as a minor politician's PA for a few years before deciding law was a more suitable option. We met on day one, semester one, and hit it off immediately. Partly due to the closeness of our ages, a few months either side of thirty, and also because we were the only two in our year with any noticeable knowledge of the world.

Everyone else was still pissing high school tap water or private school Evian and trying to get laid. We were much more grown up than them although one look at the female contingent and that approach seemed an excellent plan. I was a born-again single after cohabiting with another cop who, as she left, declared my decision to change careers to be totally irresponsible and stupid. Picino, Giovanni by baptism, Gio to his family, and the more culturally-inclusive and professionally-pragmatic John by choice, remained free and was exploring his options. His cavalier attitude to life and loyalty was to become my problem.

He was studying law and politics and I was studying law and the anatomy of a fellow legal student, Eva. Sometime around halfway through second year she decided John was a more suitable option. I was aiming at practising law in the public interest and John had his eye on a politically-connected career in his own interest. Righteous struggle and penurious anonymity versus amoral luxury and status. Eva went with the money, fame, and bullshit.

Picino and I exchanged blows in the UniBar, and never spoke again. As far as I was concerned, the situation could last forever but listening to Emily's private-school-implanted articulations, I had the feeling I was in for a disappointment. I was right.

'Mister Miller, the Attorney-General' — another indrawn venerating breath, *was Picino boffing her?* my far from irrational question, considering the subject and tone of her exaltation — 'was wondering if it was possible for you to make an appointment to meet with him.'

I debated asking why the state's Attorney General, a title I heard from others he'd long coveted and now apparently liked his adoring minions to use regularly, sought to meet with me, a simple country lawyer, but decided it would be a waste of time. She probably wouldn't tell me anything anyway and, unless John Picino had changed a lot in the last few years, she wouldn't know.

He always was a secretive bastard. He was staking his claim on Eva for three months before I found out about them and we, he, she, and I, spent most of our time together, both at uni and outside. Did I want to talk to the treacherous prick? Basically no! Still, Emily, despite the initial professionally-mandated intensity, sounded nice, her voice inducing reminiscences of a secretary at the firm I'd harboured unrequited lustful thoughts about. I figured I might as well hear her out; I should have known better.

'The Attorney-General says it's extremely important and urgent.' Well, at least I was right, she had no idea of why he asked to see me. Important and urgent is legalese for I'm trying to convince you I'm well informed and extremely is adding stress to counter the possibility of incipient failure. If I were a beginner, it might have worked but at legal-speak, Picino-pidgin, and protective secretarial ambiguation, I was a polyglot. Whatever he sought from me wasn't for the hired help to know about. Part of me was intrigued, the other ninety percent longed to hang up. Emily was still talking. Reminded of observing the fondly-recalled secretary's undulating progress across the office I knew I could have listened all day. Reminded of Picino trampling across my life I knew I should have stopped listening immediately.

'Please would it be possible for you to come into the city for a conference? Preferably today?'

It was necessary to clear something up before this became ridiculous. 'Emily, you don't mind if I call you Emily, do you?' She murmured something vaguely assentive, or not precisely dissentive. I went on.

'Emily, you, and he, do realise I live and work in Murray Bridge. It's about an hour to an hour and a half out of the city, dependent on traffic. Meaning a two and a half to three hour round trip' — plus the two minutes it will tell him to go and... well, no, I didn't finish the suggestion — 'and I have my own practice to run here. If you could give me an idea of what...'

'No, I can't, but He,' the capitalised deification implicit in her reverent tone, 'said you could bill us for the time and travel expenses, a full day was what he said, and he'd be extremely grateful if you could please come. He said it's something best discussed in person, not over the telephone'.

I checked my diary and all I found was a will update, something Maya could handle in her sleep, and I did need to pick up a couple of things from a friend in the city. Yes was the obvious answer. But something in me kept saying No! If Picino required something from me, it would be something I didn't want to give him. Guaranteed.

Besides, he'd lost our punch up; perhaps he was after round two. He owned the police force and maybe he and a few friends would be waiting to even the score. Or maybe he was desperate to give Eva back. According to the social columns and legal profession gossip, she was an extremely high rent legally-qualified trophy shown off by her important husband at social functions and election campaigns.

I realised I was being silly. And evasive. And unfair to Emily who, despite the expensive speech patterns, sounded nice. Also, as a wage slave, she wasn't to blame for her boss being a complete shit.

'He said please and he'd be grateful and would pay for my time? Are you sure we're talking about the same John Picino?'

'Mister Miller, look…'

'Yes, alright.' He was sure I was going, I was sure I was going, but I wanted to put up a semblance of a fight for my own self-respect. 'Is two o'clock acceptable for *l'avvocato gentiluomo*? At his office?'

'Two is perfect but not at the office. Do you know where Il Palazzo di Napoli is?'

As it happened, I did and said so. One of Picino's cousins owned it and they were clannish, making it the obvious choice for a confidential meeting. What was unclear was why we would be having one. But if curiosity was one of my weaknesses, another was well-made Italian food.

'There's a private room upstairs. He'll meet you there. At two, yes?' I said yes yet again and we hung up. I was fairly sure I was first but not by much. I was uncertain whether Emily either understood my Italian or if she did would have approved my less than venerational reference to the ungentlemanly lawyer she worked for, but I was sure she must have discerned from my sardonic tone he was unlikely to be on my Christmas card list. I wondered if she'd pass that on as she relayed my acceptance of his unwelcome invitation and decided it was doubtful. Her tone hinted at admiration, denoting a deficit of common sense. Her misplaced emotion would probably edit any report, which, when you worked for a nasty piece of work like Picino would indicate, if not necessarily common sense, then a well-developed sense of professional survival. I hoped she wasn't involved with him beyond the office; she sounded nice and, as the old proverb went, if you lie down with dogs you get up with fleas.

Redacting the unpleasant imagery, I made another tea and progressed to thinking about the morning's events. I function more effectively with a brew to sip between meditations. The tea was delicious; I make it with leaves and filtered water and only use the best brands. The thoughts were far less palatable; I think with caution and assume only the worst. Alex, when in medico mode, exhibits a professional and caring bedside manner offering no hint to her patients of the latent vulcanism lurking behind the big brown eyes and warm smile. She knew about my short and unpleasant relationship with

Picino and was going to go ballistic. Best to get it out of the way first. I rang next door, she was free. Twenty seconds later she was in my office. Fuming. Burning brightly would be more accurate.

We'd been to a friend's birthday party the night before and both of us drank too much. Part of the following argument was a result of the morning-after blues, some was Alex's natural hot bloodedness, but most of it was my illogical decision to agree to Picino's inexplicable summons.

I could perceive no good reason why I did, but I had, and I needed to live with the aftermath of my choice. Part of which was Alex was no longer talking to me. She had, at length. When she finished tearing at my liver she stormed out and I pitied any patients she saw that morning.

I was sitting and sipping, the echoes of the Hellenic bomb-bursts reverberating in my aching head, when Maya walked in. She sat in my clients' chair and looked at me. When I said nothing, she waited a minute. For her, a demonstration of extreme patience.

'You know Van, from outside it's sometimes hard to tell from the noise if you and Alex have been arguing or making love.'

Maya lived in a tiny granny flat at the rear of our two-acre property and probably overheard her fair share of both. When she began working with me, Alex invited her to stay there and they became friends. Maya and Rob didn't hit it off the same way. My opinion was he found her tomboyish athleticism and energetic intellect a bit threatening, and her views on his predilection for, as she put it, stupid computer games and voluptuous airheads, signed, sealed, and delivered the failure of any relationship beyond silent disdain. The women remained close despite such a setback, and Maya's connection to two-thirds of the family allowed her a degree of latitude with her comments. Still, her comment crossed an unspoken line: if she'd been wrong, I would have said something.

Alex's passions were often loud, and she tended to speak quickly, occasionally lapsing from her near-perfect English into a bastardised and often crude version of her second language in frustration. Unless the listener understood Greek-flavoured English, which Maya didn't, the expletive exhortation instructing immediate departure and the emotive one inviting immoral debauchery are almost indistinguishable. I noticed Maya was smiling, I did the same. It took effort. Between the hangover and Alex's operatic fortissimo, my head was sensitive. All the way down to ground level.

'Alex tells me you're meeting with the Attorney General, John Picino. The Liberal MP. She says he was once a friend of yours. Then she used a word for him I need to look up later. Something in Greek, sounds rude.'

I said the word and she nodded; I told her what it meant and she laughed. Alex, the convent-educated doctor, whose middle-class parents were from the genteel suburbs of Athens, occasionally acted like a peasant from the slums of the Athenian dockside. I found it funny, even a mite sexy sometimes. Her parents did not. Alex's mother was typical Greek, loud and totally devoted to her family. Her father was a successful businessman who owned shopping centres and blocks of units. Serious money for sure. Alex may have been small and trim but the rest of the family were the opposite.

My parents lived an hour south of the city in Victor

Harbor, a quiet coastal town except on long weekends and school holidays when the invading tourists destroyed the quaintness and serenity they drove there to enjoy. Retirees like my father and mother flocked there in droves to live in imitation of the local penguins, who occupied nests in an artificial council-built environment. The oldies did the same, presumably and hopefully minus the noisy and often public mating rituals.

Maya's family lived upriver in citrus country. They grew oranges and practised being anti-intellectual. They were amused when she visited to have a qualified lawyer selling bags of mandarins in the shop, guaranteeing her home visits were rare and short. To avoid living in the city, she visited countless country lawyers asking about jobs. Most had nothing available; those who did she rejected for a variety of undisclosed reasons I assumed were all linked to racism, sexism, or both. I interviewed her by asking her to research something giving me headaches for a week. Within an hour it was found, downloaded, printed, collated, and foldered on my desk. She was hired. Two days a week.

Soon she was in every day handing out free advice to the community, especially the Aboriginal population with whom she shared about twenty-five percent of her bloodline and, something she pragmatically failed to tell them, about five percent of their spiritual beliefs. Many of them hired me to represent them which worked out well if you discounted the free tea, coffee, and biscuits I was supplying. Over a couple of years, we developed a casual and easy camaraderie where no questions were out of bounds. Including the unspoken ones I was being slow to answer.

'Yes, I'm meeting with John Picino. No, I can't tell you

what it's about because I don't know yet. And no, it isn't for public dissemination until I say it is. All clear now?'

'Nearly. Can I come?'

'To the city or the meeting?'

'Both.'

'No and no. Someone has to do Mrs Barrett's will and the meeting is by invitation only. Sorry.'

I wasn't but I do know how to mollify women who don't like being told no despite the evidence of what happened after I'd argued against Alex's strongly-worded observation suggesting I ring multiple-expletives Picino back and tell him to single-expletive himself. Maya took it well, if flouncing off to the bathroom in deafening silence can be described as such. It was an improvement on five minutes of heavy-calibre-machine-gun Greek. Same message though.

I was preparing to leave when my mobile bleeped. A text. From Alex. She was only about three metres away in a straight line but there are some things, apparently, more effectively transmitted through an impersonal medium. Three parts to the text: I love you anyway, drive carefully, I'll send you a list of stuff to pick up in town. That was the sequence it arrived in; I had the feeling the order of importance considering recent events might be one-eighty degrees about. I grabbed Nurofen and a bottle of water for the road; as I left the office Maya was still sulking in the rear.

I figured a drive along the freeway with soothing jazz, a blend of Miles, Evans, and Coltrane, would, as it always did, relax me. But the day, and I, were different, my equanimity was in total disarray. About three minutes into the journey I pulled over, took three Nurofen, and switched to Deep Purple's 'Made in Japan'. Sometimes only an oral dose of painkillers and an aural dose of sensory overload can do the trick. Fifteen minutes later, it had. The Mini was designed for fast comfortable driving and the sound system was loud, clear, and punchy. Later I'd make it up to Alex and Maya; for now, I had John Picino and city traffic to look forward to. I figured the day could only get better. Hope though, as I knew all too well, is akin to prayer: beseeching an unhearing uncaring cosmos and waiting in vain for a favourable response.

2

As I entered the restaurant a tidal wave of memories came flooding back. The smell of heated garlic and other taste bud enticing spices was a three-course meal in itself. I remembered the first time I tried Italian food. Not far from where I now was, in the company of a girl whose name I couldn't recall. She took me to an eatery much like the one I was walking into and later she took me home and showed me how Australian girls, like their cooking, lacked spice. When she left a month later, she informed me the same was true of Australian men. I had no idea what she meant; I was born in England.

My mother was a passable cook at best: her meals were Anglo-unadventurous in every way. Nourishing enough, but incurring the culinary excitement of a white-bread cheese sandwich. From the first time I tasted genuine Italian food and later progressed to the courageous cuisines of other nations including Greece, which led me to Alex, unadventurous food and women to match lost any attraction.

Alex's family meals resembled a hedonist's wish list. The noise, smells, and festival vigour of the whole event contrasted strongly with the meat-and-veg blandness of my family's mealtimes and the quiet, almost silent concentration on the task of digesting the stodge. Alex's view was that the only thing the English ever cooked properly was Joan of Arc and then only succeeded because they used French ingredients. I may not always have gotten on well with my in-laws but going to their house to eat was worth all the hassle I endured as an outsider. And Alex was a great cook, what she did with lamb would have the woolly martyrs granting her forgiveness for their deaths.

Standing inside the doorway of Il Palazzo di Napoli was a promissory tingle to the senses. It was a pity I was there to meet Picino, otherwise I'd have taken a seat and prepared for transcendence.

His cousin, who I remembered as soon as I saw him, also recognised me. He waved politely and pointed to the stairs at the rear. I went up with the sensation of ascending a scaffold. There were four doors; each, I knew, led to private dining rooms. Once, long ago, Picino told me the local mafia often met there to plan their criminalities. I was never certain if he was having me on, but somehow, considering why I was there and who I was meeting, it seemed a possibility.

I'd found a two-hour park a short walk away; if Picino had anything even remotely suspect in mind or even if he didn't, I could easily be back in the car with an hour and three quarters in hand. Since meters don't refund, the cost would be included on his bill. I'd already added twenty percent to my normal hourly rate for the aggravation his call caused me with Alex and Maya. Another few dollars would be barely noticeable. Petty, I knew, but profoundly satisfying.

As I climbed the last few steps I slowed down, took deep breaths, tried to get into a less confrontational frame of mind. All it did was slow the ascent and make me sound like I was unfit. I sped back up and reached the landing as one of the doors opened.

Looking at me was the smiling face of John Picino; looking back was my unsmiling one. He waved his arm indicating I should enter. I did, and as the door closed behind me, I realised we were there alone. *Outstanding*, I thought, *if I hit him again there were no witnesses*. Then I realised I was sounding like a villain in a bad mafia movie. Must have been the garlic-drenched odours, or the history of the place, or perhaps Picino's black clothes, or his slicked back black hair. Or all together. Or, more likely, my lingering suspicion he wished to replay our last face-to-face encounter. As, if I were being honest, did I.

Instinct told me to turn and leave. Curiosity, and an unwillingness to lose face not to mention being forced to concede the argument with Alex, kept me in place. We shook hands, he warmly and politically-practised, me coldly and lawyerly-professional. No funny handshake, I noticed, negating one nagging suspicion I'd harboured concerning his rapid ascension.

He was still smiling, although behind the gleaming teeth I could sense hesitation, something I'd never associated with him before. Whatever this was, it was important to him. Giving me an edge, helping me relax a little. And decide to increase the twenty percent addition to his bill to thirty. I may be honest but, at heart, I was still a lawyer with his own practice. I could justify it later as a tax refund; sounds more elegant than vendetta.

Still without speaking, unusual for such an extroverted narcissist and another signifier of his uncertainty, he pointed to the set table by the window. Feeling more in control than earlier and recovered from the marital tiff and the chaotic traffic I left city living to avoid, I sat. After a short pause he did the same. I may have decided to stay but it wasn't going to be me making the first move. Looking at him directly with a gaze he seemed unwilling to return, I waited and watched. He blinked first.

'Donovan.'

'Giovanni.'

The use of each other's unedited names was a standing joke at university. My mother named her apolitical son with a voice like an asthmatic foghorn after a sixties protest singer she'd seen live many times and possessed countless recordings of. Picino's mama named her enthusiastically amoral one after a saint she'd talked to many times in church and collected innumerable pictures of. The unintended heavy irony had been the cause of much amusement both to us and our friends. It melted some of the ice with its resonances of our less conflictive days, but not enough for me to get the ball rolling. It was his party and his family restaurant: he could serve the entrées.

'I hear you got married.' The familiar mocking tone was still there; there'd been a time when I'd found it likeable and funny, then came a time when I didn't. The aversion was still in place and in excellent health.

'Typical Picino. Trying to make small talk. You were crap at it then and it seems you still are. What do you mean, I hear? If you've gone to the trouble to get me here then your department has given you my life, chapter and verse. Skip the small talk and get down to why I'm here. If not, in ten seconds I won't be.'

'Typical Van. Impatient and to the point. Well, you're right, I do know everything, I employ seriously capable researchers. I even know you still play tennis, competitively as it happens, with more skill than you used to have when I chased you all over the court. I hear you've won trophies. I didn't know you were into that sort of self-affirmation.'

'I'm not, but it's part of the game and I go along. It was always you who enjoyed showing off your boasting mugs. You even married one of your trophies, you probably tell people you won her in a fight, and you came out on top. I tell you, John, if it makes you feel like a success then go for it. Unlike you though, I only display the things I won honestly. What is it they say, enjoy your wins and walk away from your losses? Except, if I remember rightly, you couldn't. I see the scar's been fixed; did you get asked too many questions you couldn't answer?'

I could see my digs were annoying him, which was the aim. He bounced me all over a tennis court in those days, but if we ever faced off across a law court now, he'd be the one on the run, something he was all too aware of. He may have achieved high office and become the anointed consigliere to the parliamentary dons, but I was the superior lawyer. He spent his years playing political games in a make-believe world and I'd spent mine practising legal manoeuvres in the real one.

His sharp dig about trophies was the sort of tactic he excelled at. A quick stab into a vulnerable area. But he'd been surrounded for years by sycophants who gave him the match point even if he lobbed the ball into the net, and I wasn't one of those any more than when I'd knocked him half senseless all those years back.

By reminding him I knew the real truth about that day I, far from indicating any lingering upset over Eva's selfish defection, was able to use it as a thrusting blade of my own, deflecting his snide barb and aiming it straight back at him. It gave him a clear understanding of where our relationship was now. And to be truthful, in the absence of any chance to hit him again physically, then to do it psychologically was an excellent substitute.

His only defence against unpleasant truths: change the subject and become aggressive. Like the Picino of old, he used it as I was certain he would. I knew him too well for his tricksterism to confound me. Irritate, though, was something else again. I had a burning need to move the meeting forwards but he, the impatient Picino of times past, highjacked the next step.

'While it might be fun to catch up on old times, there are more pressing matters to discuss. But before we do, are you recording this conversation?'

'No.'

'Are you sure?'

I looked at him in an I've already answered that sort of way. He raised his hands in a peace gesture. 'Sorry, I forgot, you don't like it when people question your honesty.'

'No, I don't. If you owned any, you might understand why.'

He stood up, bit his lip and walked to the other side of the room. My barb had hit home whatever genuine feelings he may still have possessed, I could see that. Was I sorry? Was I hell!

He'd changed in more ways than the years older. There was an earnest attempt at genuine bonhomie in his voice I knew from past and professional experience was part politician, part lawyer, part Picino, and part play-acting. It was as put on as the expensive suit, the pretentious accoutrements, the cheery smile, the smoothed-out speech patterns. The rough edges, once admirable, replaced by a veneer of respectability and polish, which wasn't. It was a persona he lampooned in our student days, a viciously accurate disdainful dig at such pomposity. Now, I suspected, the disdain had morphed into custom, the play-acting into reality. What he'd once laughed at was what he'd become. I would have found it sad, if I cared enough to give it currency. All-too-familiar petulance break over, he came back to my side of the room. 'Do you want to eat?'

Damn right I did, but there was no intention of being there for long enough. Nevertheless, I was after a drink and said so. He went to the small bar and poured me a generous glass of what looked like and turned out to be an expensively smooth whisky. I sipped as he sat down. In my head I was counting; he had two minutes and I was gone. But first...

'John, are you recording this meeting?' I owned the gear but I hadn't thought of it and what I might have required was in my office. Unlike me, he employed people to do those things for him and I wouldn't put it past him to play dirty with me. He might be an Honourable Member and all that palaver now, but I knew him when he was a double-crossing bastard and they, like leopards, don't change their spotty fur hats for haloes. He shook his head emphatically and seeing it didn't satisfy me, said, 'No. You have my word.'

I tried not to laugh and nearly succeeded but I knew he could do earnestness at will, so...

'John. Minister. Mister Attorney General. Signor Picino, this is for the tape, capisce? If you're recording this and haven't told me or you tell any lies at all during this meeting, I'll sue you into bankruptcy and, for dessert, ring Eva and tell her about Sophia Natuzzi.'

The shock showed. 'How do you...?'

Words failed him, something I could probably have sold tickets to and made a killing. I had no intention of answering. Alex's gossipy friend knew someone whose daughter's bestie was Picino's horizontal hobby. Women talk. Politics, law, and sex in Adelaide. Small, small world. Big, big fun.

He recovered and in his response, I caught a glimpse

of the old Picino. 'Now instead of your bleeding conscience making you fight legally with Queensberry rules you punch people below the belt with rumours.' But it was no rumour and he knew it as he knew I'd do what I said I would. Eva would have killed him. Or made him wish she did before his mother or Sophia's brothers found out.

'I swear there's no one listening or recordings being made. Van, I promise.'

I believed him. Mostly because he believed me, the rest due to the feeling that our meeting was not something he desired but needed. And I wanted to know why. I told him to get on with whatever it was. He poured himself a drink and took a large gulp, put the glass down and turned to look me in the eye. It was what he used to do when we were having a serious discussion back when. I knew the evasive preliminaries and retrospective animosities were over.

'Your researcher, she's Indigenous, isn't she?' I must have looked surprised. 'It's important, believe me. I'll tell you why in a minute, but I need to get there my own way. You do some work for the Indigenous community up there in the bush and I guess they trust you. There's rapport?'

'Some, yes. Obviously, I'm not one of them but Maya is and we try to help where we can.'

He said nothing but I knew how he felt about do-gooders and conscience-followers; he didn't need to. All he showed was a slight curl of the lips. To someone who knew him well it was louder than a shout and more informative than a speech. I'd evidently answered his question, though.

'Alan Fenwick. Senator Fenwick. You know who I mean?'

Of course I did. Me and everyone else in the country. The conservatively religious senator for South Australia who achieved immortality by dropping dead as the Senate were sitting and at the perfect moment for his departure to be live on camera. The entire country was talking about it six weeks back. Then some minor Royal committed a scandal and dead pollies were old news. 'Not forgotten, more like no longer front page,' I added.

'Not front page, no. But far from forgotten. His widow, Veronica, is kicking up a fuss. Apparently the first post-mortem found no cause of death. She demanded another one which came up with the same result. Poor bastard got sliced and diced twice but with no outcome to compensate for the indignities. As a qualified doctor, even one who hasn't practised for a long time, she doesn't believe it and as a widow whose husband had a record of perfect health, she wants answers. But not the ones she was given. It seems a lot of people kick off and leave no traces of why, he's one of many but she isn't accepting that. I know she's into her fifties but she's still hanging in there. Think MILF Barbie. Definitely appealing and popular with it, especially in the north of the state and around Parnham where both he and she were considered for sainthood. She's pornogenic, personable, and politically connected, also a close friend of the PM's better half. She, and her cause, are not going away. That's problem number one.'

I was confused. 'What do I...?'

'Patience, Van. Not your strong point but for now it needs to be.' A tad hypocritical, considering he'd interrupted me to pass on the critique, but since I had no intention of hanging around long enough to become seriously bothered, I let it go and let him go on.

'I didn't say the number one problem, I said problem number one. Different thing altogether. There's a list, so hang in there. Okay?'

I nodded and sipped. As part of a large firm, I sat through many drawn-out information sessions and developed a long attention span. What I had to do was prevent my antipathy to the speaker detracting from my listening and retaining abilities. The whisky was helping, as was the notion of making out my invoice.

'Problem number two. A Chinese consortium is bidding to purchase a property. Bilden Downs Station, it's got cattle or something equally rural. Christ only knows, I never watch Landline let alone visit such places. Anyway, the Chinese want to buy it, the current owner is seventy plus and wants to retire, and with the money on offer he, me, you, and all our combined extended families, even your acquired-by-marriage Greek nation-state, could retire in comfort. It's to be run as a working cattle station with a sideline as a quiet country retreat for stressed-out Chinese businessmen: embassy workers, Bank of China employees and all those types. Away from the city, lots of open country, cows, horses, nights under the stars, alone with the desert, all the holistic horseshit people seem to think enhances their lives. Sounds awful but I'm told there are people who find it comforting.'

He smiled the sort of dismissive smile he used to when someone liked something he disdained. I recalled seeing it often and still didn't like it. He could see my reaction; the smile vanished.

'The locals have been promised the supply and maintenance contracts, the nearest town, Parnham, stands to gain greatly from being near the place, and Fenwick, who has friends in the cattle business up there supports, sorry, supported, the idea completely. Used to visit often and was popular with the locals. Absolutely no downside, all good. Yes?'

He watched to see my response. Since his query was rhetorical, there was none.

'Unfortunately, no. Many of our pollies, federal and state, are against the whole thing. Racism, you know the "don't want loopy Chinamen wandering around threatening the idyllic lifestyle of rural Australia" sort of hateful rhetoric, and by the way that's part of a speech made in public by a Parnham local. Obviously, I left out the rude words and paraphrased the rest. All of it is unapologetically xenophobic and nationalistic, the old White Australia Policy resurrected. Fears about foreign ownership, financial invasion, and all the other inward-looking drivel. The town, the federal pollies, and our home-grown parliament in this state can't reach an agreement and it's all up in the air. And that's number two.'

Bloody hell, I was thinking, we're only up to two. Already it was enough to bring about a localised civil war, conflicts with a bad habit of spreading far beyond the sites of origin. All it took was media attention and mass ignorance. I could see why as a politician, he was concerned and as the Attorney-General, he was involved. What I still failed to see was why I should be either. He carried on before I could ask.

'Problem number three. And here, my friend, is the start of where you come in and why you're here. Well, nearly why. I'm getting there, trust me. The Traditional Owners also don't want the Chinese taking over what amounts to a sizeable lump of what they consider to be their natural heritage. Any guesses from the consulting expert on such things as to why?'

'There are probably two or three ancient and important sacred sites on the property and they're worried they'll lose access to them or worse the atheistic Chinese will imitate the Western Australian mining industry and remove them altogether.'

From the expression on his face, I realised my informed guesswork hit dead centre. Sacred sites discussions cause contention. Most of the sites under discussion are genuine and their protection truly a cultural right and spiritual necessity. But not all; there have been isolated instances where underlying motives with less admirable aims including money were present, and those occasions attract the most publicity and are the ones the doubters recall every time the topic comes up. My lingering cynicism regarding any untoward manipulations of the issue wasn't completely unfounded but there was no way I'd share my feelings with Maya. Despite her avowed lack of spirituality, she felt deeply about other people's rights to their beliefs, especially those she saw as her blood-kin. As, it seemed, did some of the Parnham locals.

'Only one, but it's considered important. The old man who owned the place gave the local community open access and refused to allow cattle or anything else near it. The Chinese give no similar guarantees. They said maybe but not particularly convincingly. What could be easily solved with a few minutes' diplomacy has turned into a major deal buster. Half the town want the sale and half don't. Fenwick was pushing for it and had a few others backing him but with him gone, it's all in doubt.'

Like me he knew that was not necessarily an end to it. I threw in, 'Doubt isn't finished, only delayed.'

'Absolutely. The pro-sale crowd is lobbying heavily.

The lovely widow was involved in and is continuing her husband's work, using her popularity and come-and-get-it smile to drum up widespread press coverage for the cause and her whisperings in the PM's wife's ear, not to mention his political pragmatism, have him intimating, if not yet declaring, support for the cause. Heavy hitters want this to happen. Fenwick's sudden exit slowed it down but may not have stopped it dead. No pun intended.'

'Alright,' I said, 'let's see if I understand this. Fenwick's pet project was to help turn this place into a Chinese wellness centre and make the locals rich. The townsfolk, especially the business owners, want it, the PM and other pollies want it, but a few locals and the Aboriginal community are opposed to it because of the sacred sites, and the racists don't want it because — well, they're racists. I can see why you need someone with the right cultural knowledge and connections to help but you have dozens of those on tap. You pay their wages and can tell them what you want. With me that's not the case. Again, will you tell me why the bloody hell I'm here?'

He took a long swallow of whisky and looked straight at me.

'I don't want a person with cultural knowledge and connections. I need a lawyer with them who is someone I can trust to help me do something I can't do in my position and not tell anyone he's doing it. Which narrows the field considerably. I need you for this and I'm asking you nicely for your help. It's something a social-crusading lower-case-liberal do-gooder like you should be jumping at.'

He paused. We were getting close to the point where I said yes or no and I suspected no might be a serious problem for him. I was mulling over his description of me and feeling inclined to believe that, for once, his words signified genuine admiration and not his habitual sarcastic contempt. I looked at him and nodded, a small movement not meaning yes, I'll do it, but yes, I'm still listening.

'Fenwick's exit — there's been an accusation of murder. Someone has, anonymously and in writing, claimed he was killed. The letters are handwritten, they can't be traced to a computer, and the writing is block letters and completely generic. Looks like early primary school writing and handwriting experts say it was probably done to make it unmatchable because everyone's block letters are essentially the same. I'm not sure about that but it would certainly make proving who wrote them difficult.'

He paused; we were getting to the tricky part. If there was a politically sensitive aspect to why I was here, it was what came next. There are a number of areas where the elected rulers prefer to tread carefully; I was curious to learn which one caused him to clandestinely consort with his avowed enemies. Which was probably a collective with a long membership list but, in this instance, was limited to yours truly. Didn't I feel blessed?

'The accused murderer is an Aboriginal man named Henry Day. He's about seventy, lives in Parnham, has hardly ever been out of the town. He needs a defence lawyer, an effective one, and he has to be found innocent. Legally and above board. For everyone's sake.'

Which was where I came in. I was a perfect fit although not yet a willing participant. He had more work to do before I might consent, and he knew it.

'We, me, and those I represent, want this man exonerated completely. By a reputable lawyer. One with credible connections to the Aboriginal community and a reputation for involvement in social justice issues. I can't be seen to help at all although, obviously, if I can, I will. It's political, what with Fenwick's widow's connections, the current state of Indigenous issues overall, and other things we need to discuss.'

I was shaken. But I saw his point. The state government, as represented by him, preferred being seen as objectively and equitably dispensing justice meaning they required someone like me to fight the good fight they didn't want to be seen losing deliberately yet had more to fear from winning. The idea of becoming involved wasn't an attractive one, but it was possible the accused would only accept someone with my connections; all others might have trouble gaining his confidence. Fine, I was an ideal candidate. But... 'If Fenwick died in Canberra, live on air as it were, and with no cause found, why is anyone even considering making legal moves against an old man who was half the country away from where it happened?'

'Van, whoever sent letters to the PM's office and a truckload of other places said Fenwick was killed by magic. A Kadaicha man, namely one Henry Day, current location Parnham, sang him to death. Black magic, if you can believe such a thing in this century. I need you to defend him. And win. Because once Fenwick's widow and the press hear about this... well, you can work it out for yourself. Okay, Van, yes or no? And, if it helps... please.'

Please? From Picino? A memorable first. I wished I'd been recording; I could use it later to convince the many who simply wouldn't believe it possible. Me included.

3

By the time I was out of the suburbs and in the Heysen Tunnel, I'd relaxed enough to start breathing. The whisky's effect was well and truly worn off, which was a disappointment; the angst of meeting Picino again also faded, which wasn't. I drove at a slow speed in the left lane with the music off and thought. I'd accepted an unwinnable case and would be widely unpopular for doing it. Mostly at home, which was an hour away. I needed to work out how to deal with it.

I was unable to predict what possible charges the courts could bring against Henry Day, but I was convinced they'd come up with a legal loophole loose enough to push him through and tight enough to use as a noose. A popular politician with religious connections and admirable aims was dead and someone was about to be accused of his murder despite the legal requirements of means, motive, and opportunity being non-existent. The legal process was designed to allow for pedantic last-minute variations covering unforeseen necessities; it was clear he'd be charged but there were no hints as to what with. Also evident was I was going to defend him but not how.

As I passed the Hahndorf exit, I made a decision. It was obvious and incontrovertible. It was necessary to ignore the politics: Fenwick's vindictive widow, the Chinese connection, the fortunes to be made or lost by the townspeople of Parnham, the nation's propensity for unreasoning racism, and even the contentious and newsworthy topic of sacred sites and land rights. All of it had to be put to one side, and simply focus on proving the man innocent. While, naturally, sidelining the distant possibility he might not be.

My first move, place my doubts on hold and demonstrate that any charges laid were nonsense and it was impossible to kill someone using magic. Doing that would involve offending Indigenous spiritual beliefs, opposing the religious nutters and racists who were ready to believe in magic and were convinced all non-whites were guilty of something even if they weren't sure precisely what, convincing state and federal pollies their valued colleague hadn't been murdered and his popular, attractive, and sympathy-inducing widow with the highest of political connections was chasing moonbeams without intimating lunacy, and attempting to come up with an alternative and acceptable explanation for his inexplicable death.

All within the limitations of a one-man firm going up against government lawyers with unlimited resources, the Australian public, the Chinese consortium, the Parnham residents, God's followers and for all I knew their deity himself, and anyone else who decided to join the fight. I'd take them on one at a time, that was the answer. As I pulled into the driveway, my first challenge was waiting for me. If I survived her, I figured, the rest would be easier. If not, they wouldn't matter.

I did what I always did when we disagreed; I put my arms around her and held her close. As before, it worked. She held my hand as we walked into the house where I found Maya perched on a stool in the kitchen. Alex handed me a mug of tea; she knew me too well and I was dying for one; Italian restaurants might serve wonderful food but like their French cousins have never heard of tea let alone included it on their menus. For them it was coffee; spelt near-identically, café versus caffè. It was the same with tea; té and thé when they occasionally deigned to acknowledge its existence. Their loss. There was a reason the British Empire outlasted the Italian and French ones; fortified by mugs of it we all moved into the lounge and sat. I sipped and tried to appear calm as they stared at me expectantly.

I told them it all. Minus the part where I threatened to out Picino by telling his wife about his recreational activities. It was blackmail which is firstly highly illegal plus both women would consider my use of it as unprofessional and unethical. Not to mention what I'd threatened to reveal was told to me in confidence, something Alex would be more than a smidgen annoyed about. Therefore, that particular interaction remained undisclosed. I'm not a coward but I know when and how to act like one.

I gave them the gist of the letter disseminated too widely to be ignored and reminded Maya that since we didn't have Henry Day signed up as a client, yet we weren't supposed to know about it. Be careful, okay. The advice got me a look. I was close to mid-level on the list of those graduating law; she received several awards and finished in the top three of her final year, something she liked to remind me of matronisingly each time I dared to sound remotely patronising. Alex always took her side.

It took a while to run through it and neither of them interrupted. They both watched me until I finished, then looked at each other. Alex spoke first.

'Why are you doing this?' She frowned. 'It's a recipe for disaster. Picino knows that. He probably has surprises waiting that won't be ones you'll like.'

Now I knew she was still annoyed at me. Her anger took two forms. Either she shouted and talked rapid-fire with Graecisms peppering every sentence as earlier, or she spoke unhurriedly and pedantically as then. Both are intense. I liked neither when I was the target.

'The old man is going to be accused whether I'm involved or not. Yes?' They nodded.

'Between the political pressure and all the other stuff there will be a lot of effort expended to find something to nail him with. The law can be manipulated and you both know that. Somebody needs to be there for him and it has to be someone who cares about the various issues driving this. That's why I said yes. Plus, I know Picino.'

Damn right I did. I hoped he might have changed, becoming a minister and securing his current portfolio. But he hadn't. 'I watched him today. Still the same person he was years ago and I can read him like a book. And he knows me and thinks he can foresee what I'll do, how I'll react. Alright, then on the surface I need to appear to do what he expects. But I'll also do what I must to win. But I need you two supporting me to do this. Otherwise, I can't do what I have to.' I looked at each of them in turn. 'Well, are you with me?'

Alex got up and gave me a hug and a kiss. She might not have liked what I was involved in but it was clear she agreed it was the right thing. Morally and ethically, we were always on the same page. On other things we weren't even in the same library. As she went back to her seat, Maya spoke.

'Well then, what now?' No discussion, straight to the point, support assured. Cool, I thought.

'I need all you can find on Fenwick, the town, the Chinese bid, superstitious magic, any media reports on what's happening, and anything else helpful you think of. In the next couple of days, we need to fly up there and talk to the old man. But we can't until he contacts us. Once Picino's local contact has suggested us, we can move. Offer our services. Get moving. I'm going to talk to people and try and get my head around the politics.'

Picino could have been playing a game; I wasn't sure. But there were more important issues to concentrate on than any political conspiracies coalescing in dark corners. My once comprehensive but now debilitated familiarity with the Criminal Law Consolidation Act would be an excellent place to initiate the reinvigoration of my somewhat neglected professional development.

'I need a refresher course on homicide. It's been a while and I have to try and work out what they're likely to come up with. Singing Fenwick to death, perhaps by subjecting him to hours of hip-hop' — a scathing look from the only avid fan in the room — 'might pass some people's pub test but it would be a bastard to find any precedents in law. If something pertinent is hiding in the any of the statutes, whether ours, some other state's, federal, or in another jurisdiction altogether, I'd prefer to know about it before hearing it in court from the prosecution.'

I yawned and Maya took it as a hint. It hadn't been, I was wrecked. She left and I followed Alex to the bedroom. She suggested I could do with a shower. We took one; apparently, I was forgiven. My best intentions, it seemed, outweighed my earlier mistakes, whatever they were. I wasn't sure. I was also unsure about the case and tried not to think about it for a while. Alex made sure I succeeded.

Next morning, I drove to the office and by the time I unlocked, Maya was there. She wheeled her bike to the back room and had the kettle full and heating before I turned my office computer on. She handed me a tea and disappeared into her own office. I went through to the back into our small storeroom and read the labels on the packing boxes of books sitting there since I moved in. Rural lawyers rarely need to read up on law. Until now I hadn't, especially since Maya began doing my research.

This was different. What she knew about murder statutes might be more than I did but it wasn't as much as we required. I found the box I was after and ripped the tape off the top. A few minutes later, I found the books I was after and was back at my desk drinking tea and thinking where to start. Since none of the books seemed a more suitable choice, I decided to begin with the Act and progress outwards.

Three hours, four mugs of tea, and a packet of biscuits later I was thoroughly sick of legalistically- tortured prose and firmly convinced I was right. You could be charged with almost anything in this state and the conditions for a murder conviction were many and wildly varied, but absolutely nowhere was there any serious provision made or even hinted at for taking action against someone who threatened, intended, or even confessed to causing death by magic, nasty thoughts, or any form of spells, curses, incantations, magical amulets, voodoo dolls, black masses, or anything not containing physical elements of causation scientifically subjectable to evidentiary examination.

In short, murder, whether through ill-intentioned singing or any other supernatural means, wasn't only not awarded much space in the legal books; it was, I'd discovered, notable for its unremitting exclusion.

One weighty tome I recalled trying to avoid while at

university to the detriment of my grades — it turned out the lecturer wrote it — did contain a minimalistic reference to the topic in an appendix. It pretentiously, interminably, and categorically stated that superstitious beliefs didn't belong in a legal system practised by a civilised society in the twentieth century. Concluding I could extrapolate the statement to include the twenty-first, I further determined, from the author's learned opinion, that seeking to accuse my client of murder by voodoo, in any form and whether home-grown or imported, wasn't going to get the state's prosecution case out of the starting gate.

I knew Picino would have known that even before his extensive research staff confirmed it. The same question nagging at me since the previous night was still in my head: why was he concerned that any sort of charge could be formulated? Someone somewhere was thinking faster and more effectively than I was, not necessarily a world first. It was essential I go faster: catch up then go around them. Lateral not literal reasoning was the go. Trained as a cop and a prosecutor, I tended to research and reason in mostly straight lines, but I knew someone who was neither and therefore didn't.

I knocked on Maya's door and went in. Her printer was grinding away and the pile of printouts on her desk was impressive. I sat and waited until she stopped typing and turned her attention to me. For nearly fifteen minutes I ran through my findings. Describing a non-result may sound easy but it takes time if it's done properly. We both spoke legalese and there was no need to slow down for her to catch it all. When I stopped talking, she only asked one question. The same one I failed to get my head around, and it sounded equally ludicrous when she asked it.

'Why are they bothering to give this desk space? It's not covered in law, totally unprovable, and is extremely likely to turn into a joke and embarrass them.' She made a face in agreement with her words. 'It doesn't make sense.'

She was right; it didn't. Instead of focussing on how to prove Henry Day innocent, I'd be more effectively using my time attempting to evaluate why anyone should want to. Clearly, there was something going on behind the scenes Picino might not be aware of.

I required a break from brain-straining law books and to hear her take on it all in more depth. I offered to buy her lunch and we tossed a coin, pub or café. The pub won. In my opinion, legal conferences produce their best results when conducted over a pint accompanying a hot lunch. Maya always agreed, especially if the firm was paying. She picked up her pile of printing; we were used to working lunches and knew places to sit in the pub where prospective clients and the incurably nosy would leave us alone. I drove; even if she had her car I would have driven. I told her many times it's not her driving, it's her car. I didn't think she believed me, which made two of us.

The Bridge was our usual choice. The food was good, if basic, with a wide range of beers, for a country pub anyway, and there were quiet corners in the dining area where two cagy lawyers could hide. Maya and I were sprung there once talking intensely and the old biddy who spotted us felt it her duty to inform Alex during her next check-up. She now sees a different doctor and while Alex didn't spell out her response, I knew my wife well enough to fill in the blanks. Both of us hate gossips and the information I used and abused about Picino's love life shows only one of us is one while the other only threatens to be. Maya found our uncovered romance amusing and the next time we saw the chatty old duck in the street she held my hand until we were past her.

We ordered at the counter and I fetched drinks from the bar. We were in a corner behind a potted plant and out of sight of the other diners. I took a welcome drink and looked meaningfully at the stack of paper. Maya grabbed the top page.

'Fenwick. He'd been in the senate for eight years. He represented South Australia, lived in Adelaide, with a second home in Canberra, and there were social ties to some cattle station owners in the north where Parnham is, it's somewhere in the middle of the area. He visited several times a year and was almost universally loved. As is his wife — sorry, widow. By all accounts, and there are many, he was religious, fond of publicity, a great bloke, dedicated and hard working. No health problems until… well, until…'

For many Indigenous people, death was not a favourite topic. I waited; we'd been there before following a funeral of a client. She would get over it then discuss it as if it wasn't important to her. It was, though and, like always, she did.

'No one wished him gone, in any sense. Including the local Indigenous community. They liked him and he did a lot for them. This, even if it's true which it isn't, makes absolutely no sense at all. In many ways his passing disadvantages almost everyone in his district if you ignore the sacred site issue which upset people but not enough to want him out of the picture. Anyway, Parnham. In between Coober Pedy and Marla, so a thousand klicks give-or-take north of Adelaide. Founded late eighteen hundreds as a support base for the local cattle stations. It's on the highway and there's a slip-road meaning it gets some of the through traffic. There's a fifties-era concrete-block motel, a roadhouse, a caravan park, a supermarket that's smaller than our local deli, a community centre slash meeting hall slash occasional church used by everyone for everything really, a pub that's perpetually on the verge of going under, a post office that's no longer staffed but has a post box that's emptied twice a week, and enough houses to fit the two hundred-odd inhabitants plus twenty or so unfit for habitation. Oh yes, there's a rubbish dump and an airfield.'

What she described was a typical outback dust bowl nothing hanging on by its fingernails. A situation rectified by Chinese ownership of Bilden Downs Station which was close enough to benefit the town and far enough out to allow the imported convalescents to avoid the inherently white, and innately prejudiced, locals. Whose attitude to the Asian influx did not, it seemed, extend to not taking their money. That they wanted. What they didn't want was their presence.

'Apart from the mainstream racism, there's a small religious group in town, about twenty, called the Australian Christian Alliance, part of an Eastern-states cult with members in high places, who don't want atheists and communists moving in. It's not selective, they don't like the RCs, Prods or Muslims or for that matter my mob either. Socially selective and insular crowd. Never made any trouble but never formed any friendships either. They live on the edge of the town well back from the highway. A possible problem, do you think?'

I couldn't see why and said so. 'A small group of conservative fundamentalists would have nothing to gain by Fenwick's death or any fallout from it. Ignore them for now, worry about it if we find we need to later. Go on.'

'The Chinese. A bunch of business types led by a high-flying international banker named Lao. They appear to want what Picino said, a self-supporting business venture where stressed suits can decompress. The Yanks have dude ranches, in Europe there's health spas, we have pubs and beaches. Same thing, different surroundings. Again, there's no benefit to Fenwick being out of the picture: the opposite is the case. They're still pushing for the sale and are even bending on the sacred site issue. Only a slight give but it's something.'

She shuffled through the last few sheets of her pile and found the one she required.

'Last but probably not least there's death by magic and Henry Day. He's an old man: desert country hard life seventy, not city grandpa rest home seventy. In his picture from about ten years back he looks somewhere between eighty and card-from-the-King time. By now — God knows how he's still upright and breathing. Maybe a portrait in a cupboard.' She laughed. Behind the mirth I could see the tinge of embarrassment: jokes about age and death were not usually her style. Between us they were extremely rare; that they existed at all was indicative of our friendship and trust. In any other company they were absent.

'Speaking of which: magic, there's not much serious info around. A few crap exploitation movies and authoritative books mostly written by those who saw an Aboriginal person once and now know everything about them.' Not, I knew, her favourite people. 'Nothing worth reading or trying to use.'

She seemed to be done but it was something often

seen before; Maya is totally comfortable with researched material but hesitant to put her own thoughts forward. I wasn't sure why but I suspected it's a family thing. Having met them and seen the interactions, it was a safe bet their highly intelligent daughter was ignored in favour of the more straightforward sporty and sweaty rural labourer types. She paused for a few seconds then took a breath.

'I had a thought. At Adelaide Uni, there's a lecturer my friend used to talk about; apparently, she knows more about magic in our and other cultures than anyone. She's written or co-written books and articles considered the definitive texts in overseas unis and a couple here have them on their reading lists. I have her name and contact details and one of us should go talk to her. Shall I give her a ring?'

'Yes, great idea.' She looked pleased and I knew my hunch had been right. 'Then I think we should enquire about flights to Parnham. Did you say it has an airstrip?'

'Yes. Dirt but long enough for most small planes. The Flying Doctor and the vets use it.'

'Right. Go and get things moving. The lecturer and flights and whatever else. I think I should talk to the woman at the uni and we should go to Parnham together once we get the call from Picino's local there. Fancy a day in the outback?'

From the look on her face, she did. Being included actively seemed to please her. It would be interesting to talk to Henry Day, I'd never met a sorcerer before, unless you include the Greek Orthodox priest who was at my in-laws one night for dinner and talked my ear off about religion, specifically my lack of it, through all five courses. The guy looked like Merlin's evil twin with his long beard, black robes, and twitchy eyes. Unlike the Welsh wizard, though, his magic failed; this sheep remained lost.

4

The Murray Bridge Airport, far more grandly named than the rural dusty airstrip reality warranted, was a few minutes' drive from the town. At eight in the morning, a light breeze travelled unhindered across the open paddocks and sliced through my coat. I went back inside the building and looked through the glass at our transport.

I didn't like flying in small planes. Three wheels, two propellers, and one pilot. No hosties or whatever the PC term was for those who brought my drinks and food when I flew, and almost definitely no parachutes or life rafts. I never saw the sense of them; flying from Adelaide to Melbourne or Sydney, the only water you cross is the river my house overlooked, and a pilot would have to be unbelievably skilled to land a 737 on even the straightest stretches. The toy we were about to go in looked as if it could land on a suburban street. Our pilot was Gary, who looked like one of the characters on TV soaps who spend most of their time on the beach causing the girls heartache. I asked him about landing on roads.

'Sure. Well, a long one anyway. Often do. Sometimes there's nowhere else to put down. Less holes than paddocks.' He laughed. 'Less sheep and cows usually too.'

Usually? Comforting? Not! He wasn't finished.

'I can land this anywhere. Don't worry. You'll get to fly again afterwards and if I do my job properly so will the plane.' Bad taste pilot humour exhausted, he went off in the direction of the men's room as I went off in the direction of Maya. She wasn't looking worried; people her age usually weren't, being ten feet tall and indestructible. Only older and worldlier panic merchants like me tended to think about crashing and dying of hunger and thirst in the outback. She appeared excited.

When I asked, she said, 'I am. It's the first time I've been in a small plane and I've never been so far north before. Cool, eh?'

Right! Cool? I was a lawyer, not Indiana Jones. All he was afraid of was snakes, which reminded me, they have them in the outback too. The day was not improving.

Maya and Gary caught sight of each other and the air between them started to heat up. He offered to carry her bag and she handed it over with a smile as I was left to carry my own. We all went out into the cold wind and climbed up a fragile staircase into the plane. Each footfall made the plane rock, my nerves doing the same. I could blame no one else, flying to Parnham was my idea; driving there would have taken all day each way. The plan was to arrive before lunch, talk to Henry and be back by dark. I'd be happier once we were airborne, then I could sneak some liquid fortification from the flask in my bag. Doing it at the strip would have been a public admission of my nervousness. Also, I might have to share and it was a small flask.

With a light cloud of dust rising behind us we lifted off. Maya was up front next to Gary and alternating between staring out of the window and watching him doing his pilot thing. I took a gulp, replaced the flask, and settled down. And recalled the previous afternoon.

Picino called at three. He told me to give him a number that wasn't my office or personal mobile. I gave him the number of Alex's surgery and told him to wait a few minutes. I was sitting in a spare room at the rear of the medical part of the building when the receptionist put the call through. The door was closed and we were secure, which is what I told him when he asked using exactly those words. I laughed and told him he was being paranoid.

'Well, Van, yesterday I would've agreed with you. Today, however, things have changed. I'm not in my office; I'm in the office of a trusted friend and using a prepaid mobile bought by someone else. I suggest you do the same, then no one can get the idea I'm colluding with such an enemy of the state as yourself. Not a long way from that topic tomorrow morning the accusation, Henry Day, magic spells, all of it, will be front page and heading the television news programmes. Someone has spread the word. You have my promise it wasn't me and I've no idea who it was and if it turns out to be someone in my department, they'll be processing speeding offences in an isolated regional shithole until they retire. After I tear their throat out with my teeth. That's the first of the day's problems.'

He loved lists. I remembered the fact from the previous day and our student group projects. I had the feeling he should have been an economist; then I remembered he used to be. His thoughts were organised into lists, columns, and tables. Mine were disorganised into chaos, fate, and hope. How did we ever become friends?

'The second is the DPP, which as you know is connected to my department but totally independent of it or any other political entity, seems to have found something to charge the old man with. They're being tight-arsed and close-mouthed about it which means they haven't nailed it down yet but my guess is it's in the area of threats and victimisation to the point of causing intense stress possibly leading to health issues and, in his case, self-induced termination. That's a quote from one of my people who knows someone over there; needless to say, it's non-attributable and you and I are currently talking about our student days if anyone happens to find out we met. Bottom line, though, there's pressure to place Henry in the frame if they have to construct the frame themselves to achieve it. Even if they don't convict, they'll get him into a courtroom and ruin his life.'

The Office of the Director of Public Prosecutions, known acronymically as the DPP and acrimoniously as several other things could, as I knew well, be bloody-minded. The tax-funded body and I met many times in courts and across conference tables. Its lawyers claimed they performed their functions impersonally; there was no malicious intent, personal bias, or political influence, and their hardline administration of justice was for the benefit of the people they served. Somehow impartial detachment made it all worse. Nasty, vicious sadists I can understand; public service sociopaths confuse me.

I knew they were a legal necessity but how they on occasion disregarded the boundaries of their remit was at the core of my dislike. Their mandate in law to act independently of the political machine was fine in theory; the separation of powers formed a core principle of systems of government like ours for centuries, the delineation of those who instituted legal statutes and those who interpreted them. However, in practice, adherence to the independence was sometimes more a sly manipulation of legal semantics than strict observance. Dealing with the DPP was likely to be nasty. For me, let alone a rurally-raised elderly pensioner with intellectual limitations.

'Did the old man phone or write to or otherwise

contact Fenwick or his office? It would be next to impossible to prove he scared someone to death from his living room.'

'True, it would, and the answers seem to be no, no, and no. He doesn't have a phone, home or mobile. He doesn't even have a television; apparently, he's old fashioned and technophobic like most old farts. My old man can't even — anyway, no to all. I agree, what it means is he couldn't have frightened him. Which, unfortunately, helps the case for the use of magic, not harms it. And that's where the next problem comes in. The word is out in Parnham and of the locals are getting aggro. Have you heard of the ACA, the Christian group?'

I said yes and waited for him to give me the bad news I could easily make a good guess at.

'They're creating trouble. They went round and threw rocks through Henry Day's windows, and were threatened with violence by a crowd of other residents who may not favour the local Aboriginal community much but are even more hostile to imported fundamental loony Christians. Big punch up, police from Marla and Coober Pedy called in mob-handed, several arrests, and Henry Day taken into protective custody. It happened this morning.'

I went to interrupt to ask about Henry, but he got in first.

'Henry Day is safe at home with a police officer playing nanny. Ian Basham, Senior Sergeant. Ignore the name, he's fifth generation Aussie and about six and a half feet tall. Not to mention armed. Your client is safe. I know Basham, he's a top bloke. His suggestion, and I agree, is you get your client out of there and somewhere safe as soon as. Fly up there' — he cut off my protest — 'we'll pay for everything in the end. Not sure how but we'll get the dollars from one place or another, perhaps slash a few pensions or raid a super fund.' He laughed; I didn't.

'So, make him safe before any god-drunken half-wits decide to even the score, whatever score they think there is in their mad brains anyway. We use a crowd called Company Air; I'll give you a contact to talk to there. They're discreet and rarely ever crash; it's why they get our work. Your turn, anything new on your front?'

I gave him a quick rundown on what we found and could tell from the lack of response it was all stuff he already had. We were getting ready to hang up when I heard a phone warble at his end; he asked me to hold on while he took the call. A minute later he was back.

'Right, more bad news. The widow Fenwick has upped the pressure on the PM and he's spoken to the Premier and offered as much legal assistance as might be required. Canberra lawyers, and probably many others across the nation, are scouring the law books to find anything capable of being manipulated into a charge against your client. I gather the believers in magic spells have decided in the absence of any other cause of death, Henry Day's hands-off conjuring must be the culprit. I used to think at least some of my political colleagues were intelligent, I might need to review my position considering all this.'

It hadn't taken long for the witch-burners and suchlike to go into crazy mode. The twenty-first century and the crazies were trying to drag us back to the sixteenth. The press wouldn't swallow any of this but they'd blow it up; they weren't paid to believe, their daily bread was earned by stirring the shit and they do it more than well.

'Van, by tomorrow night, Henry Day will be a cultural

hero, a centrefold for racist hate, and a murderous evil wizard who summoned up demonic forces to protect a pagan sacred site and murdered a local saint. Poor old bastard probably has no understanding of what it's all about. You need to find out if he does and try and let him know what's happening. Good luck with both. Van, I know you and I have our differences and I know you don't totally trust me but take my word for it, I'm in your corner even if I have to be seen to stand on the far side of the ring. Alright?'

I said yes and we hung up. I never liked his sporting metaphors. I think his use of one was to show he was genuine. He probably was but if there was one thing I knew about Picino, his genuineness was subject to constant change to suit his own benefit. Therefore, I didn't completely trust him; I might prefer to but our past made it complicated. The historical cherchez-la-femme was only part of it; the rest was that everything else about him irritated me. Not least that we were talking again.

Besides, all this new information was more important. What started as a simple case of a few religious and racist cranks waving flaming torches was turning into a full-blown scythe, cudgel, and pitchfork equipped medieval witch-burning with my client, and me, standing in the ring of flames. Hyperbole aside, the airborne shit was truly about to connect with a multitude of fans and I was the one nominated to hold the only raincoat. The problem was I had no clue as to where it was or even what it looked like: finding it was going to be a challenge.

A week earlier I told Alex I was bored with wills and divorce settlements; right then I'd have been happy to go back to daffy old ladies disinheriting wayward sons and vindictive ex-wives financially castrating ex-husbands in a heartbeat.

An hour later, my office phone rang. This time it was, probably unsurprisingly, the DPP. A Monica Derwent. Lawyer, public servant, and clearly another meticulously articulate product of one of our convent style production-line schools for young ladies or those who wished to appear to be one. Her enunciation may have been a delight; her news was the opposite.

'Mister Miller. My name is…' and she went into her introductory spiel which sounded rehearsed to the point I began to suspect she was reading from a cue card. I let her complete her rap, sipping my tea and laughing silently over the day's newspaper cartoon: it was funnier than usual or maybe I was in the mood to be easily amused. Whatever, when the noises in my ear stopped, I started.

'Ms Derwent' — no huff of disapproval, she was definitely a Ms which fitted the voice and manner perfectly — 'what can I do for you?' If it sounds a mite servile and willing to please; it wasn't and I'm not. It's a standard legal greeting basically asking what it is we're going to argue about.

'As it happens, I'm calling to pass on information my supervisor felt you should be made aware of.'

Translation: the law mandates I must be given what she was about to share but making out as if she was doing me a favour was more to her liking. I pitied her boyfriend; sex must have been given out like a benediction with gratitude expected at the end of each stroke. I'd met a thousand like her, worked with a few, and constant contact with all diseases, even occupational ones, brings immunity. Another sip, God I love Earl Grey, and a short wait while she figured out I knew what she was appearing to say and what she was truly saying and then...

'Your client is, I believe, a Mister Henry Day of Parnham. Is that right?'

'That seems to be where we're at.' Me being careful; this game allows me to drink my tea and earn money at the same time but until I held a form with his signature on it, he was my client in name only. For the time being, I was being circumspect. It's a pretentious term for lying by omission; the use of it as a word provides proof you have a well-developed vocabulary while the use of it as a concept provides proof of nothing legally binding. No direct answers, especially over the phone. Seems to be equates to maybe, maybe not. Or, in the legal vernacular, no comment.

'Are you aware that Mister Day is the subject of a legal enquiry connected to the death of Senator Fenwick?'

'Yes.' If I had to work at this, so did she. And that one was safe to answer. Since most of the state's legal profession were probably aware, for me to be was unlikely to cause any problems.

'We have questions for Mister Day and one of our people will be going to visit him in a couple of days. Obviously, as his lawyer, you need to be there unless you give us permission to talk to him in your absence.'

When hell freezes over, love. 'No, I think not, Ms Derwent.' Same thing? Yes? No?

'What do you suggest?'

I had to give her something. 'How about I fly him to Adelaide and then I can talk to him when I need to. As can you. Does that sound like a workable solution?'

'Please wait a moment.' Silence, a click, then the sort of hold music likely to have made Beethoven say prayers of thanks for his deafness. Come to think of it, it was Beethoven. In the same way the Simpsons is Shakespeare.

Click! 'Mister Miller, that's fine with us. Furthermore, since it makes everybody's life easier, we will cover any costs incurred on your part in transferring Mister Day to Adelaide and with his accommodation.'

That worked. Damn, did it work or what? I intended to have him stay at a friend's house, and I was going to look up the Air BnB rates and double them. More rewarding in a number of ways, the plane flight was being funded. I suspected the devious hand of Picino pulling strings but however it came to be, my bank account's health moved from incipient morbidity into remission. The didactically-inclined Ms Derwent was still rattling on...

'... if you could let us know where he's staying, we could arrange a time to speak to him with you present and appropriate to us all.' Yeah, Monica, not to mention legally required, which you hadn't.

She said goodbye and hung up. I called Maya in, refilled my mug, sat comfortably, and reviewed it all with her. She laughed about the flight being paid for, looked worried when I told her about Henry's house, offered to speak to the local police as soon as we were finished, and appeared concerned when I mentioned the ACA.

'Van, the small group is a part of a wider sect. In Sydney they have hundreds of members. They hold rallies and are connected to influential people. Senator Ranley is one of their patron saints.'

Great! Helen Ranley, the red-haired racist fruitcake and her fascistic ideologies would be an added problem we could do without. Her views on race issues were well publicised and intelligent people found them somewhere between infantile and repulsive. But she had powerful allies and a loud political voice.

'If she enters the fight against Henry Day, then the adverse publicity and right-wing invective will ramp up to uncontrollable levels.'

Maya smiled. 'Maybe, but all those who believe they're nothing more than racist rednecks and rural simpletons will take our side by default. They might not necessarily believe Henry is innocent, but they won't want him to be tried by a medieval star chamber formed by the likes of Ranley's neo-fascists. As many will be for us as against. It could get interesting.'

I recalled Maya's ironic comment as the sound of the engines changed and the desert appeared to be getting closer at an alarming rate, figuring if we survived what was looking like our imminent crash landing, we would soon get to discover just how interesting it might get. I took another belt and replaced the flask in a side pocket of my travel case next to the prepaid mobile I asked Alex to purchase last night. I'd sent Picino the number and given it to Maya. Elements of this case made me nervous but the liberally-minded conscience of long ago was far too rarely offered the opportunity to go out and play: it was raring to run. Rocks through windows were nothing new to me; I'd argued acrimonious divorces, both sides, and in my previous existence defended walking defects who considered property damage a legitimate form of dissention. Also, racism was an integral part of most of the cases Maya talked me into taking on.

But magic spells and inexplicable deaths was new territory. I spent part of the flight looking out of the small window at old territory and wondering what I was getting into. After a while watching the passing vastness and thinking the answer came: an improved frame of mind. The rest would take care of itself, one way or another, and worrying about it all incessantly was a waste of valuable planning time. That said, I made up my mind if the old man started singing, I was ready to block my ears, close my eyes, and bolt.

5

Going down the steps from the plane was much like going up them; canoes were more stable. Once I hit ground level, I stopped and enjoyed the solidity. I was tempted to do a papal act and kneel down to kiss the tarmac. But there was no tarmac, only red dust, and my suit and lips were not designed for immersions in the fine powder covering most of the continent. I settled for looking around. Close to us in one direction, a row of trees spread haphazardly, the other three directions were empty as the sunburnt country the poet loved stretched off into infinity. She may have eulogised its charms, probably from a shady verandah next to a swimming pool, but surrounded by the pitiless empty wasteland, I searched in vain for any feature capable of inspiring the minutest hint of love.

It was warmer than home, about mid-twenties. I took off my jacket and rolled up my shirt sleeves. Considering it was mid-autumn I could only imagine how hot it might get here in summer. Timing, when visiting the far north as with everything in life, is important. I was glad the fact that the Senate didn't sit in high summer meant Fenwick's dramatic exit wouldn't have happened during those months when whatever incinerated all surrounding us was in full blast-furnace mode. I travelled through the Flinders Ranges, north of Adelaide and south of where we now were, twice. Once in winter when the temperatures at nights were low enough to place a layer of rock-solid ice over the car windows, and once in the high heat of summer. Both were experiences I vowed never to repeat. Shirt sleeves up and a mild breeze was comfortable; below-zero nights or forty-plus scorching days were not. The fortunately small number of flies were kept at bay with an occasional Aussie salute; what they might be like in summer was something I avoided thinking about.

The pilot opened a hatch on the side of the plane and pulled out a folding chair and a small cooler box. As he set up in the shade of a wing, I realised the plane's interior, while reasonably comfortable normally, would be less so for a long wait in full sunlight. He'd evidently done this sort of thing before in places like Parnham and was fully prepared. I'd done what I was here to do many times but never in any place resembling where I now was, and I wasn't remotely prepared.

I half-expected Mad Mel to come tearing out of the desert in a testosterone-fuelled muscle car; what arrived was a long white Toyota four-wheel-drive with POLICE written on the bonnet. It turned as it reached us and slid to a dust-raising stop. There were long radio antennae on the bull bar plus a large electric winch with a drum of heavy cable. As well as the blue and red lights, the roof was covered in a complicated array of smaller antennae, spare wheels, spotlights, jerry cans, rolled swags, and short ladders I knew, although with no idea where from, were for getting out of soft sand. It was purpose-designed for survival in the outback. As was the driver.

As he stepped out, his unruly dark hair brushed the door frame; when he stood upright his shoulders were level with the top of the windows. The uniform must have been bespoke; no normal police outfitter would have stocked something his size on the off-chance the force started recruiting from the NBL. The pistol and radio on his belt looked like toys. The stripes and crown said Senior Sergeant, one above the rank I held before I left the force. He took his sunglasses off, put on a wide-brimmed hat the same pale brown as his uniform, and stepped forward, hand outstretched. The smile and greeting coming from behind the dark beard matched the height in scale and reduced the sensation of being charged by a Kodiak bear.

'Senior Sergeant Phil Basham, Marla station. You must be Donovan Miller, gamekeeper turned poacher' — I recognised the use of the name and the gibe as typical Picino game playing and knew my history must have preceded me, which might turn out to be advantageous or, as often happened, not. The smile widened as they tended to when men over ten and under ninety met Maya — 'and you must be Maya Wright. Welcome to Parnham, outer suburb of nowhere much north.'

We both shook his hand and I informed him I was Van. He smiled and I guessed the joke hadn't escaped him. I was surprised his grip, like his voice, was far from the muscle fest his appearance led me to expect. He spoke with a pronounced Aussie accent but quietly; there was none of the cattle-auctioning brashness common to many country cops. And his hand was softer than I expected, not the calloused lump a number of his rural colleagues seemed to have. I shelved my first impressions; there was obviously more to the man than first met the eye. I should have expected that; Picino recommended him and his tolerance for Neanderthals was legendary for its nonexistence. I excused myself and visited the rest room; it's hard to describe because I'm not familiar with the names of native bushes.

Basham gestured towards the vehicle and as we climbed in, me up front riding shotgun — and there was one, held upright in a clamp bolted to the dash — and

Maya in the back, he went and spoke to the pilot. They both laughed and Basham joined us in the car.

'I asked the pilot if he's going with us. He said no because he has a book he wants to read and a plane he wants to have in one piece when you take off later. Apparently, he's used to places like this. Looks like it's only us. It's about a ten-minute drive to where we're going. Before we meet with Henry, I want you to have a chat to Mrs Jessup. She's a friend of his and has information for you. Okay?'

Well, no, if I were being honest. I wasn't there to socialise but to talk to my client. Speaking of whom, I asked, 'Where's Henry Day and who's looking after him?'

'He's at home with a constable armed with a shotgun and my orders to shoot anyone who doesn't have the password.' He chuckled.

'What's the password?'

He chuckled again. 'My face. Don't worry. Constable Ryall knows his job and he's a distant relation of Henry's. He's not happy at what was done, and anyone who arrives with bad intentions will find out what family connections are all about.'

He started the engine and we went back the way he'd arrived. The road differed from the airstrip only in width and the number of potholes. I watched the scenery as we bounced along. There was a lot to see, space-wise. Variety-wise, there was bugger all to see many times. Dust, stunted tree, dust, small bush, dust, fence posts, dust, barbed wire, dust, rocks, repeat in random order. It was a feast for the senses if you'd spent the last decade on the moon. At one point I saw a kangaroo in the distance and my heart leapt. Well, it stirred.

We entered a town. Where I lived was small and semirural; this place could have been dropped into the middle of it and never found again. We turned left into a dirt track lined with houses, all of the same design. Someone with a single architectural blueprint put them together and only varied the colour of the paint, put on in a past distant enough the colours were faded to drab hints of their original existence.

How the hell anyone remembered which was theirs was beyond me to work out. There were no numbers or indeed mailboxes to put them on. All featured satellite dishes on the roof, big ugly birds hunched on the ridgeline, and the corrugated iron showed occasional flashes of shiny metal among the dust and rust. This place must have once been vital and lively; probably in the same decade as the invention of the aeroplane.

Maya's expression was a mixture of wonder and disbelief. I'd seen places similar to this before; she hadn't. No wonder a massive infusion of Chinese money was something the locals were prepared to welcome: the place was post-apocalyptic.

We turned into the second to last driveway on the right and stopped next to a time- and sun-battered Holden station wagon. Unlike the rest of the street, the yard was tidy and the house painted sometime in the last two decades. Standing on the porch was a woman. An old one. Like the yard, she was neat, obviously someone who cared how she looked. Which, unfortunately, was old-fart fussy.

I didn't like listening to the know-it-all didacticism of past generations. I turned to Basham and went to speak. He raised a hand. 'Van, be patient. She's not as olde-worlde as she looks and she has something you might find worth hearing.' He raised his eyebrows. 'Yes?' I nodded, and we all climbed out.

Another surprise. I expected her voice to contain the querulous edginess typifying many of the elderly, especially those living light years from civilisation geographically or intellectually. But she spoke quietly and carefully, with a muted accent. Which meant she was either a native of this state — our neutral accent lacks the immediately-recognisable and cultural-cringe-inducing inflections of the northern and eastern sides of the country — or she was educated. Or both. It was a relief. A vinegary crone with a voice like a chain saw chewing through a railway sleeper and I'd have been out of there in a flash.

'Hello, I'm Marilyn Jessup. Thank you for coming. Please, come inside. Would you like a cup of tea before we get down to business?'

The in-flight facilities were minimal, AKA none, but for bottles of spring water, so I was hanging out for a brew. We followed her in. She pointed towards the rear and we ended up in a kitchen sitting around a solid wooden table big enough for eight. Maya asked for the bathroom and disappeared down the hallway as Mrs Jessup busied herself filling an old tin kettle and lighting a gas ring on top of an oven that looked older than herself. I looked around. It was all quaintly old fashioned and scrupulously clean. Sitting on the table was a hardcover edition of Kidnapped with a bookmark peeking out from between the pages about halfway through. She saw me looking and chuckled.

'Robert Louis Stevenson, yes. One of my favourites. I read a lot. I have an arts degree. Mostly English literature with a bit of history mixed in for variety. I did it online, it took seven years. I wanted to study when I was younger, but I was working to support my family. I was an accountant for several of the local cattle stations. I worked in Adelaide for about five years and gained the experience then I met my husband. We married and moved up here.' She paused a moment.

'After my husband passed on and my children went off to their own lives, I needed something to do and I fancied the idea of studying. It's hard to find someone interesting to talk to around here, I mean, Stevenson, Dickens, Dumas, the Brontës, and so on are hardly on the reading list this far from the world.' She laughed, somewhat bitterly; I could hear and feel the isolation.

Where I lived, the city was close enough to drive to for theatre, movies, or more upmarket dining. Out there was leaving civilisation behind. I said nothing. What there was to say she already knew and it would have sounded condescending.

I sipped my tea and waited for her to begin. More ready now I knew whatever it was might well be worth hearing, more considered than originally expected. I was right; she was educated. It hinted at possibilities. Hinted was the operative word, though. Reading and critiquing Dickens and Dumas et al might stimulate thinking and offer a counter to social seclusion but it was no substitute for practical knowledge. You can receive books in the post; worldly wisdom travels less well: you have to go out and get it!

The other two sat quietly, drinking tea. Basham was allowing Mrs Jessup to take the lead and Maya was doing the same with me. The old lady sat next to me, turned in her chair to look straight into my face, and drew in a deep breath. It was either resignation at what she was about to do or a stimulating blast of oxygen to provide the courage to do it.

'Mr Miller, there are rumours floating around the town Henry Day is going to be accused of killing Alan Fenwick by Aboriginal magic because of their difference of opinion over the sale of Bilden Downs Station and what might happen to the sacred site if the Chinese buy the place. True or false?'

Well, that was certainly laying it on the line. I intended to be equally forthright, as soon as I'd determined whether I was talking to someone with Henry's best interests at heart or the local gossip. I edited the wording when I presented the notion to her and Basham but not by much. This was too important for polite manners to get in the way; I decided to dispense with them. From the look on the three faces, it seemed I succeeded. Bad luck, I thought, if anyone is offended. There was a case to win and an old man to keep out of prison. If I managed to succeed, I'd apologise later. Maybe.

Basham answered, his voice tight with anger. Apparently, he and Mrs Jessup were friends.

'Anything you say here will go no further. You have our word on that. Marilyn is only trying to help and there's no need to be insulting.'

Now it was my voice that was tight, not with anger but frustration. Having to explain the realities of life to old biddies or rural coppers isn't much fun and this wasn't the first time I'd done it.

'If you think I'm being insulting then you're in for a shock once you're questioned in a court room. Whoever the DPP line up to prosecute this case will be the sort of merciless shits who threw their consciences out of their cradles and never went back to find them. They will gouge and tear at any witnesses until their souls bleed and not give a damn if feelings get hurt. They do anything to win and harassing old ladies is something they practise on their favourite granny at weekends. Don't lecture me and get on your high horse, Senior Sergeant, or you either, Mrs Jessup. I'm trying to save Henry Day and I need to know who can assist me and who might turn out to be a liability. I don't have time for politeness or subtlety and frankly neither do you. Are we in this together or not?'

A lot of my anger was put on, courtroom theatrics are excellent practice for knowing how to fool people, and the formality wasn't my usual style either, but some of it was real. As I said, I was determined to find out who to trust; the best way was to make them angry and then watch the reactions. If what I saw was anything to go by; they were genuinely offended; their desire to help had been questioned. I looked at both of them and decided to go with my instinct. Which was they could be trusted. I glanced at Maya and she nodded. Only a small nod: yes, we could rely on these people.

'Right. I'm sorry, but trust for a lawyer isn't a natural first inclination. But I believe you. Yes, Marilyn, Henry is likely to be accused of Fenwick's murder by magic. And I'm going to try and prove he didn't do it. Hopefully with your help. Plus, if possible, yours also, Phil.'

Never trust a lawyer is my motto and no one should. I was lying, and only intended to tell them what they would find out eventually anyway. But I wished to appear to be open and honest. I addressed them by name, smiled, and tried to demonstrate earnest regret for my rudeness and a desire to placate them both. It was total bullshit; I was determined to win and if that meant sacrificing my personal integrity to achieve it, I would.

They were not about to become public enemies, that was Henry's role in the unfolding drama. His interest came first, second, and third. Everybody else waited their turn. I must have convinced them because more tea, the universal pipe of peace, was offered. Fine, we were all best pals again; time to get into the hard stuff.

'One of the sticking points the prosecution face is Henry and Fenwick have never been closer than a straight line between here and Canberra. That's a damn long way to cast a magic spell, especially if Henry doesn't have a phone or use the internet and there's no record of him writing to Fenwick or contacting him any other way. Do you agree?'

The silence worried me and the glances between them made it worse. I was about to get bad news. I knew it, Maya's face said she knew it, and the other faces said they didn't want to give it to me. I waited. Basham broke first.

'I should tell you, I guess. They have been closer than that. About a kilometre apart to be accurate. Right here, in town. A year back there was a meeting, to talk about the Chinese takeover, and the whole town was there. Including Alan Fenwick. He flew in, attended the gathering, downed a couple of drinks and flew out. Apparently, he was due in the Senate the following morning and couldn't hang around. But I asked a few people and Henry Day wasn't at the meeting. He was at home. That's definite. Is someone going to try and convince a jury magic can travel a kilometre and work even if the two people involved never meet? I don't seriously think so. Do you?'

Mrs Jessup chipped in. 'Will anybody take this whole magic spell stuff seriously? A man cursed to death in the twenty-first century. I mean, honestly. Is anybody that stupid?'

I explained that, yes, some people were congenitally stupid, and many of them had influence. Common sense wouldn't be the guiding force in this case. Popular opinion, possibly the least rational collective ever devised, was more likely to rule the day. She mulled it over, shaking her head and muttering about bloody idiots. Tempted as I was to agree discussing the intellectual shortcomings of the common herd was not getting us anywhere. I was trying to decide if the shorter distance was an issue. One kilometre or one thousand, did the distance matter? Face to face would have altered the whole deal but Basham looked into it and they'd never met. I decided to worry about it later; at that moment it was essential to further examine my possible witness.

'Marilyn, tell us what you know. Not what you think, that's obvious and we can take it as a fact that we're all in agreement. But I need to know any definite facts you can contribute.'

'I'm the one who told Henry about Fenwick dying on television. He didn't know until then. He has no TV or radio and doesn't read the papers. I visit him once a week, take him eggs and we have a cuppa and a chat. I mentioned it along with other news items and he looked surprised. Doesn't it prove he couldn't have done it? He didn't know until I told him, long after it happened. And I'll say that in court and clear the whole thing up straight away. Prove him innocent and show this whole magic nonsense is no more than silliness dreamed up by superstitious fools.'

She was beaming, revelling in her tale and convinced she solved the case. It was a shame to burst her bubble but it would be kinder for me to do it than the DPP executioner's heartless swing of the axe in a public courtroom. I looked at Maya, could see she knew what was coming. As did Basham. Maybe not the fine details but he knew I was about to kick the supports out from under Mrs Jessup's theory and her jubilant mood. I took a deep breath. Telling clients and witnesses their pet notions would fail in court isn't much fun; if I enjoyed such things I'd still be working for the firm in Adelaide.

'Marilyn, there are two parts to what you say. One is fine and would be accepted in court. That's the part where you say you told Henry about Fenwick. No one will contest it because it's not overly important and because they wouldn't want to call you a liar, they'll let it stand. But the other part, where you stated Henry knew nothing about Fenwick's death, is the problem. They will argue it's only your opinion that he didn't know and there is no proof.'

'But he was surprised. I could see he was. It was news to him; I could tell by his reaction.'

I softened my voice. I required her to listen carefully. 'Marilyn, I'm doing this quietly and gently, talking you through this. The prosecution won't do it nicely. They will take your testimony to pieces in a way you won't like much and make you appear foolish. It's what they do and how they work. Let me explain. Firstly, if you say Henry looked surprised, they will produce people who will display surprise for the jury and demonstrate how appearing surprised isn't necessarily the same as being surprised. Their aim will be to embarrass you and discount your evidence. Do you follow?'

She did, I could tell. She was not happy, but there was worse to come.

'Even if the court accepts you believed Henry was genuinely surprised and what you say is true, where they'll go next is far more important. Look, if a man rapes a woman and the DNA evidence proves it was him, his guilt is obvious. Yes?' She nodded.

'That half-wit who drove a car through the middle of Melbourne and killed pedestrians, he was seen by scores of witnesses and caught on countless cameras. No argument, he was indisputably guilty. Yes?'

Another nod.

'That sort of evidential confirmation is called proving a positive. It can't be doubted or argued against. The opposite is proving a negative which, in law as in life, is impossible. Proving someone did something beyond doubt is relatively easy, physical evidence, witnesses, visual records and all that. Do you follow?' She did but she was looking less pleased by the second.

'Let me use an example. Did you watch any television last night?' A nod.

'What?'

She paused for a moment. 'That English actress, Joanna something, travelling in South America.'

'So, if I asked you for details, you could prove you watched it?'

'Yes. I remember it clearly so, yes, I certainly could.'

'Great. Now, where were you yesterday between eleven in the morning and two in the afternoon?'

'I was here.'

'Alone?'

'Yes. Why?'

'Did you watch the movie at lunchtime?'

'No. I read my book outside while I ate my lunch.'

'Prove it. Prove to me you didn't watch the movie.'

She looked surprised. 'I can't. How can I prove I didn't...?'

I saw the mists clear from her eyes. Explaining to educated people is much easier; I'd gone through the process before with less worldly others and often ended up conceding failure.

'That's right. You can't. And neither can you, Henry, or anyone else prove he didn't know about Fenwick before you told him. Looking surprised suggests he didn't know and convinced you but in court the prosecution would tear holes in your statement and show your opinion is in no way proof. It is impossible to prove Henry didn't know about Fenwick's death in advance which could conceivably be twisted into showing he knew because he'd caused it. The fact you haven't seen him reading newspapers isn't proof he doesn't either. I believe you and Maya must or she would have said something and I assume Phil, who knows you well, does too. But belief and proof are not the same thing at all. As much as you may be willing to help, Marilyn, your testimony would carry almost no weight and might possibly be harmful. It would be seen as an attempt by me to cloud the issue with irrelevant clutter. That's something the prosecution would demolish in a moment without even breaking into a sweat. Sorry, but that's how it is.'

'How do you know how the prosecution works? How they will do anything, no matter how unscrupulous, to win?'

'What they do isn't unscrupulous, it's the opposite, totally legal as mandated in law. But exploiting weaknesses in the defence's case is their job, what they're paid to do, meaning that moral and ethical considerations are occasionally crushed by the weight of legal argument and precedent. I've seen them at work, and I used to be almost one of them in a previous life.'

That was what Basham meant when he called me gamekeeper turned poacher. My last two years in the police was mostly spent assisting Police Prosecutors and learning their methods, which came in useful when a succession of crises of conscience encouraged my move to the defence table. As a great military strategist once said, first know your enemy. Law and war are supposed to be distinct entities, but in a courtroom, it's often a challenge to discern any differences beyond the available weaponry.

Either Picino told him or he'd spent time online; the Freedom of Information Act can be both blessing and curse. I'd expected someone to raise the topic eventually though. Probably best out of the way early.

We spent another half hour going over details about the public meeting. Henry hadn't been there, that seemed undeniable, and we talked through his life in the town. Finally, all of us, including a frustrated Marylin, accepted that her best-intentioned offer provided no usable evidence. We thanked her for the tea and left, heading for Henry's house. As she waved farewell, she appeared disconsolate. I knew how she felt; I'd been hoping for more from her and all we'd achieved was a couple of hours essentially wasted. Who knows, I figured, maybe Henry might throw light on the case for me. The scenery was no comfort; it would have been depressing to a lottery winner on a hot promise and provided the perfect backdrop to our mood.

6

After a few turns into and out of unpaved streets varying only in compass headings, we ended up at the main highway. Basham waited as a road train rolled past, a behemothic prime mover hauling three protracted double-decker trailers packed with cattle, spectacular in its sheer enormity. My window was down, granting me access to the full range of sensory effects: sight, sound, and smell driven into overload.

We turned onto the bitumen and were soon in the town proper; the motel's garish paintwork a sharp contrast to the decades of red dust covering everything else. We turned off the road and into the forecourt of a roadhouse and service station. I asked Basham why we were stopping.

'Well, Van, I've been on the go since sunup and I'm hungry. Aren't you?'

I was and the noises from the rear indicated Maya's agreement. We went inside. As expected, almost everything on the menu board behind the counter promised saturated fats and fried oils garnished with scraps of unidentified meats to provide a mix of brownish colours and perhaps a small degree of sustenance. Basham ordered a chicken burger and chips and grabbed a bottle of Coke from the drinks fridge, I ordered a bacon and egg sandwich and a white tea — they couldn't get that wrong, could they? — and Maya chose a prewrapped salad sandwich from a shelf and a small carton of plain milk. We moved to one side and watched as the cook incinerated everything on a plate so overheated it radiated fumes and spat oil. I was glad Alex was not there; she'd have a heart attack watching, let alone eating, what passed for edible in

Parnham's single-tenancy café strip.

We were getting strange looks. Basham was obviously well known and rumours of who we were would have been doing the rounds. I was glad to leave, holding onto my brown bag and foam cup as if my life depended on the contents instead of being threatened by them. Once in the car, we unwrapped and ate in place. My sandwich wasn't as bad as I'd expected; the eggs and bacon were overcooked and the thin white bread soggy but the liberal coating of oil smoothed their passage down my throat. As for the tea, it was a cheap bag dunked in hot water and flavoured with milk too long out of whatever animal produced it: a perfect match to the food. I craved nourishment but swore I'd never go there again or complain about my mother's cooking. Maya seemed happier with her choice and Basham looked positively euphoric. He took a final swig of his caffeine, sugar, and artificial black colouring and we were off again.

Within seconds, we left the bitumen for yet another dirt road in need of a grader. At the far end we stopped next to a police-logoed Toyota four-wheel-drive standing in front of a small house. Every window was broken and someone had sprayed BURN THE WHITCH in vivid scarlet letters on a wall accompanied by a huge cross in the same aggressive hue. It appeared the graffitist had been acquiring inspiration in racist terrorism from the Klan. It was obviously Henry Day's place and equally evident whoever came visiting was barely literate. Poorly-educated and socially-handicapped local loser was my guess, in which case the spelling was probably as expected and the destruction and symbolic threat their way of expressing personal dissension.

We climbed out and Basham knocked on the door. A

younger version of him opened it holding a shotgun. I'd assumed he'd been joking about that; apparently, I was wrong. We were introduced to the constable who barely shifted his gaze from the road behind us. He waited until were inside and closed the door after a final glance at the scenery. His attention to detail was admirable, although I was sure anybody who worked for or with Basham for long would be efficient and capable. I remembered my time in uniform and realised I would have lasted about a week up here, most of which would have been spent packing ready to travel back to the city.

An old man waited to greet us. His dark face was a network of intersecting wrinkles below a dense mop of long curly grey hair. The dark eyes looked directly at me and then Maya as we were introduced and Basham received a friendly greeting. Henry, for that's who it must be, spoke quietly and with a slow hesitance. My immediate impression was of an uneducated man of limited vocabulary and communication skills. Instead of speaking further, he made gestures indicating we should follow him into another room; it was the most spartan living space I'd ever seen. A long couch covered in a blanket, three tube and plastic garden chairs, and an ancient record player on a wooden table against a wall. Next to it were untidy piles of seven-inch vinyl singles; the covers I could see included Jimmy Little, no surprises there, plus Beatles, Tom Jones, Dusty Springfield, Easybeats, and many others I didn't recognise or couldn't make out through the patina of dust that probably drifted in through the smashed windows. Scattered around them were LP-sized compilations of old hits with covers featuring girls in tight tops and mini-skirts wearing too much makeup under bouffant hair. It was an impressive collection, possibly worth a small fortune, given the retrospective popularity of vinyl. I looked around more; no books or written materials anywhere. A musical time warp, sixties style.

As we sat, Basham's radio squawked. He stood and went to the other end of the room, talking into it quietly as Henry made signs indicating did we want drinks. We all nodded and Maya asked him if she could help. He said yes and they left, him bent and walking heavily. She allowed him to go first as befitted an older person and, a secondary concern, a potential client. I heard him ask, 'Where you from?' The ungrammatical simplicity reinforced my earlier opinion he was uneducated and possibly even suffering from dementia or other intellectual impairment. It seemed they were going to bond; fine as long as their clans were friendly in the past. Bad joke, I know; I tend to make them, often inaudibly, when I'm stressed, on shaky ground professionally, or suffering from indigestion. Or, as then, all three.

I listened to Basham and couldn't work out what was happening; his end of the conversation was uninformative except at the end when he told the caller to wait and he'd call them right back. Which didn't sound promising. It wasn't.

'A couple of the local dickheads have been out at the strip asking the pilot why he's here. I gave him my frequency in case of, which I guess this is. He wants to know what to do. I told him to hang on while I make a call. One of the boys has long blonde hair and is driving a red Ford pickup. Colin Briggs. I know him well and his father better. Wait here. I need to phone Colin's father, Martin, and tell him to go out there and get his stupid son to pull his head in before I have to pay them a visit which might uncover items they shouldn't have. It's not a conversation I want Henry to hear, he's nervous enough already.'

He wasn't gone long. When he returned, we chatted about life in the outback for a few minutes. Then, as Henry shuffled back into the room followed by Maya holding a tray covered in cups and jugs, the radio made noises. Basham put it to his ear and listened, muttered something about calling back if anything changed, and disconnected.

'That was your pilot. It seems someone drove up and spoke to the boys who disappeared at a great rate. Martin will talk to his son and there'll be no more trouble.'

Maya said, 'Talk to? Will it be enough?'

Basham smiled, not pleasantly. 'After their talk, young Colin may be indisposed for a day or so. Happy families they definitely aren't. Any possibility of ending up behind bars tends to get Martin anxious and he will convey his anxiety to his son. And before anyone gives me grief for not doing something about it, Colin is suspected of two rapes and beating up an old woman who caught him in her house. And compared to his father, he's an angel. Spare me any bleeding-heart sympathies and let's get on with talking to Henry.'

It worked for me. I'd met enough like the Briggs family to have long abandoned any sympathy I might once have felt for their ilk. The fragile-looking old man sitting opposite me was another thing entirely. I'd met old Aboriginal men before; it was part of living and working where and how I did, but none were as definitively ancient as Henry Day. He appeared to have spent most of his life in the open, weathered by sun, drought, and privation to a gnarled petrified-oak finish. His stooped

73

body reminded me of trees I'd seen in the desert, hardened and twisted by the outback's extremes yet still surviving despite the hardships.

When he looked at me, the dark eyes showed a life the body denied. It was a short glance and his gaze soon returned to the floor but I experienced a momentary suspicion that, lack of education and worldly experience aside, the man was not as mentally limited as my first impressions intimated. He might be slow of speech and movement but, as I often found in the past, physical frailty didn't mean that his mind was necessarily as infirm.

As I spoke, I kept watching his eyes. Eyes, I knew, were the one place where concealing subterfuge was most difficult and liars tended to avoid eye contact to avoid giving themselves away. Then he lifted his head to look back at me and all I saw was honesty mixed with confusion. Perhaps, I thought, my first impression was wrong; now he seemed unsure as to why we were here. It was important to ascertain how much he did understand.

'Henry, may I call you Henry? Is that alright?'

'Okay. My name.' It was a short answer but it came out excruciatingly slowly. I knew this was going to be a long and painful process. It would be best if I phrased the questions such that one-word answers would do the trick.

'Henry, do you know who Alan Fenwick is?'

'Yes.' A pause. 'Dead.'

'That's right. Do you know how he died?'

'No. People say I kill him. Magic, yeah?' He laughed, an old man's cackle stopping short of his eyes. He was amused but not necessarily in a nice way; his reaction seemed to possess a malevolent derision. It only lasted seconds then his face went blank again. 'Magic. Bullshit. Ain't no magic kills people.'

I was surprised; I took care to keep it out of my face. I'd had practice telling my expression what to reveal; I was a courtroom lawyer and a married man, outstanding training grounds for effective dissembling.

'Henry, you wanted the sacred site to be protected but you say you don't believe in magic. Is that right?'

He hesitated for several seconds. 'Sacred site good place. People like going there.'

Not what I expected. 'Who told you about Alan Fenwick dying?'

'Marilyn. We drink tea. Have yarn. She tell me he dead.'

Which tallied with Mrs Jessup's story. Which didn't make it true, only a smidge more credible. There were no traces of deceptiveness in his speech or manner and I was inclined to believe him. Conditionally. The condition being more evidence was required and since only he and Mrs Jessup were present at the time, none was available. Meaning there was conditional belief until someone offered confirmation or proved otherwise.

Believing the pair were telling the truth was one thing; verifying it was another and highly unlikely. It was unsupported and no more than a claim based around hearsay a prosecutor could dismantle in a single sentence. I decided to abandon the timing of Henry's knowledge and made the agreed and well-practised hand gesture sign to Maya signalling doubtful and what do you think. The reply showed agreement and she signalled it twice. Meaning either she simply didn't believe it or she might but figured it was too uncertain to be of any use. My view precisely. Onwards and downwards.

'Henry, do you have any idea why someone might think you used magic to harm Alan Fenwick?'

'No.' Short, sharp, definitive, and decisive. The direct gaze he fixed on me as he spoke drove the word home and for the first time, I was thoroughly convinced the idea this man could, or would, intentionally bring harm to someone he didn't know and had no reason to, was ridiculous. I glanced questioningly at Maya; another miniscule nod confirmed her agreement.

We were sure he hadn't done it and he didn't know who had or what the motives of the person accusing him might be; now our main task was to convince the rest of the country's population and a jury if it went that far. Sounded simple. So does water skiing but I once spent an entire day on the river proving it is not.

The lack of any reading matter reminded me. 'Henry, I'm sorry to have to ask this and I mean no offence but can you read and write?'

He looked embarrassed as most illiterates do when their inability is mentioned. 'I write my name. Some words. Nothin' much. Never learned. Don't need it.'

At one point Marilyn Jessup said she was fairly sure Henry couldn't read or write much beyond his name and the complete absence of anything in the house said the same. Literacy was not necessary for Indigenous magic, which I knew passed on orally, but a small amount of reading ability would be necessary for learning who and where Fenwick was. I was talking, I was sure, to an innocent man whose ignorance would be no defence against what appeared to be heading his way. Unless I chose to act in his defence, Henry could be accused, disgraced or possibly imprisoned for a crime he could barely comprehend, let alone carry out sitting alone in his tiny house in the middle of nowhere.

First, though, it was essential to ensure his safety

which, judging by the state of his house meant getting him away from Parnham and to a place where no one could find him. I knew somewhere suitable but before I could take him there, I required him to agree to go and also sign up as my client.

'Henry, somebody smashed your windows and broke into your house. You're not safe here. We would like you to stay with us in Adelaide for a while. Is that alright with you? Senior Sergeant Basham thinks you should.'

He looked at Basham who smiled and nodded. Henry dropped his head and contemplated the floor for a minute then his eyes turned on Maya.

'Hey, girl, you sit with me in plane. I not fly before.'

Maya smiled. 'Sure, I'll sit with you. Today was my first time, we can feel scared together. Okay?'

They both laughed, the musical chuckle contrasting the rough cackle. Henry smiled broadly, the first time I'd seen him do it. 'Hey, you got McDonald's where we goin'? Get Big Mac, yeah? Fries? Been told 'bout it. Never been.'

I interrupted the fine-dining arrangements with a paper for him to sign. In essence, it confirmed my status as his legal representative and provided me with a raft of permissions I was not going to bother explaining in detail because he wouldn't understand them. I restricted it to asking if he required me to act as his lawyer and he said yes. Watching him sign was slow and painful. The hand holding the pen looked arthritic and clumsy; the signature's messy scrawl was barely legible. Basham witnessed the form and I returned it to my briefcase. For better or worse, Henry and I were legally conjoined.

A few moments of uncertainty and foreboding intruded; I'd never done anything with such potential for disaster or on the scale the case seemed to be expanding into. I looked at Maya; she appeared equally apprehensive but managed to flash me a confident smile. It made me feel better; I would have company at my public execution.

If I proved him innocent, those who believed him guilty would line up to flay me alive. If I failed to win and he was convicted, his supporters and my own conscience would probably do far worse. There was no upside to what I'd taken on. I would have sold my soul for a shot of something strong right then but, as a lawyer, I'd given mine away long ago.

Then I remembered my flask and went into the other room to take a quick hit. Maya knew me too well and I was sprung. She gave me an accusing look, grabbed the flask, took a swig and handed it back. We didn't speak, looked at each other, and formed a silent pact. I wasn't sure either of us could speak without exposing our emotions.

As Basham and I prepared to leave, I heard Maya and Henry discussing the possibility of a visit to Macca's. The delights of the big city, which Murray Bridge would seem to someone accustomed to the sparse minimalism of Parnham, awaited him. If he was forced to travel to Adelaide, it would overwhelm him completely. It does me and I spent most of my life there before downscaling and re-acclimatising.

Henry went off to pack for the trip, I used his bathroom, and Basham went outside to talk to his station to give an update and make sure all was well in his absence. The constable, who sat silent in the other room nursing his shotgun and watching out of the smashed windows, went round locking doors and making sure everything turn-offable had been. For reasons only clear to the two police officers, Henry, Maya, and I all rode with Basham. The constable left before us and vanished in a cloud of dust.

Once more I was in the front, the two in the back discussing issues from which I, as a white man, was probably excluded. Maya was working her own traditional magic. Henry might not believe in such things, but she possessed the knack of providing comfort to those of her culture through empathic dialogue and the bond of common experiences and backgrounds. Basham was chuckling to himself and I asked him why. He answered quietly so they couldn't hear. 'Secret business: don't listen.'

Another chuckle. 'She's describing a Happy Meal.'

7

We went back onto the bitumen and sped up for a few minutes then turned off at a battered sign optimistically declaring AIRSTRIP in letters looking as if they were painted by a five-year-old. I hadn't noticed it going out earlier, the rusted rear was blank except for the bullet holes. As soon as we hit the dirt, the vehicle's radio warbled. We stopped under a tree; Basham picked up the microphone and said his name.

A voice, male and young sounding, said, 'Sergeant, we received a call from someone named Martin Briggs. He says his son Colin and his mate were paid to go to the strip and ask questions by a man called Roger Filmer. Does that make sense to you?'

'Yes. Thanks, Mal. Good work.' He replaced the microphone then turned to face me, a serious expression on his face and an equally grave tone in his voice. I assumed I was to receive bad news. Normally I love it when I'm right although there are definitely occasions when the satisfaction is tempered by what it is I'm correct about.

'Roger Filmer is the head priest, or guru, or whatever they call him, of our local loony group, the ACA. They know not to stick their faces into anything public. Many of the locals went round there a while back and threatened to burn their houses down with the occupants still inside. They aren't liked here or anywhere else from what I hear. They pay idiots and losers like Colin to run their errands for them. Being connected to those wankers is a sure way to become even more unpopular than the Briggs family already are. I've been told the ACA has people in all the cities and many larger towns and connections to bikie gangs and others like Colin who will do their dirty work for them. You'll need to watch out.'

Bad news all round. Now we'd come to the serious attention of a right-wing religious collective with ties to organised, or in the case of Colin Briggs disorganised, criminals. Earlier I was sure this could not get any worse but it was heading in that direction at a fast rate. I was in need of assistance. As we started moving again, I looked at Maya and mouthed one word. She nodded. The word was a name: Dean.

Full name Robert Dean but no one ever called him anything but Dean. Ex-army, possibly SAS, but his military days were not a topic he could be drawn into. He owned three martial arts schools in Adelaide, Sydney, and Melbourne and a small security firm staffed with other ex-forces personnel. His wife, Marian, ran the business side of their enterprise, her MBA being more effective training than his MMA for management of anything not suitable for settling with a kick or a punch.

I met him after the coddled son of an indulgent father accused Dean of attacking him outside a nightclub; I was the lawyer the firm chose to represent him against the charge. It was not the stuff of legal legend; a few enquiries unearthed three witnesses who'd seen the arrogant shit call Dean's wife something unacceptable and attempt to follow it up with a punch when Dean objected. Dean claimed self-defence: faced with the evidence, the kid folded and Dean was cleared. Simple, food-on-the-table type work for a lawyer in a big firm. But it initiated a friendship between Dean, his wife, and my family still strong years later. There was an open offer of help if I there were any problems he could assist with. I'd asked, twice, and now felt like the perfect time to take him up on it again.

I saw him fight competitively a couple of times. He gave it up to focus on training younger fighters, partly because he wasn't as young as the sport required and because Marian became tired of sleeping with a man covered in cuts and bruises. They hadn't argued about it, as far as I knew they never disagreed about anything, but she was the only person who ever took him to a TKO without ever raising a fist. I knew the feeling; Alex could do the same to me equally well. I was convinced the two women shared husband-taming tips while Dean and I were sharing whisky.

Maya agreed, and as soon as I could, I intended to ring Dean. He was closer to the airstrip at home than we were; he could be there when we arrived. Then, once Henry was safely stashed, we could decide what to do about the new developments.

We were bouncing along a straight road bordering the strip when the vehicle slowed and stopped. Basham was staring at the rear-view mirror, so I turned to look. About a hundred metres back, a dark-coloured four-wheel drive was rapidly approaching in a cloud of dust. As I watched, a familiar white police Toyota came out of the scrub and jerked to a halt in front of it. The other vehicle was rocking and slewing as the driver tried to come to a stop on the loose surface. He managed to avoid a collision and slid to a halt side on to the police vehicle. Three men climbed out in a hurry and began to walk towards it but stopped as Basham's constable, complete with shotgun, appeared. He must have said something because the three men sat down in the dust.

The constable went to the rear of their vehicle and opened the door. He leaned in then straightened up holding what appeared to be a supermarket bag. He put it down, took a square object out, and showed it to the men. Even at this distance I could recognise it as a brightly coloured vinyl record cover.

We started moving and I lost sight of what was happening but I could guess. I saw the hand of Basham behind the events and when he looked at me and smiled, I returned the grin to confirm I'd seen through his ploy. With stolen goods recovered from their vehicle in the presence of two police officers and two lawyers, the men were done and dusted. I didn't need an explanation but apparently Basham needed to give one for the record.

'Henry's house was broken into and things were stolen. It looks like they included those found in the vehicle my constable searched. It's permitted if there's a reasonable suspicion a vehicle he stops for speeding may contain something obtained illegally. I forget the exact wording, you probably know more of the relevant law than I do, but that's the idea anyway. Later, I'll have a talk to those men — one was Filmer by the way — and we'll come to an agreement. If Henry's house is reglazed by tomorrow night and if I hear no more reports they're making any trouble, then we can all go home and forget about the stolen property recovered from their possession. Otherwise, they get arrested and I'll be forced to search their properties and who knows what I might find? More vinyl records perhaps and the only person round here with ones that old is Henry. Case closed. Yes?'

I must have been looking a touch shocked or something. He chuckled. 'This isn't the big city and we play by different rules. My constable didn't plant those records, they must have been there, but, and this is strictly off the record so to speak, he did bring some of

Henry's property with him and would have used it if it was necessary. Strictly speaking, I'm probably breaking several laws, state, federal, and biblical. But the most they would get for smashing up Henry's place is a fine and that's if I can prove it was them. This way everybody walks away and Henry gets new windows.'

I said, 'There are three men back there and only one constable. What if...'

He laughed. 'Well, when it's that particular constable, the situation is they're well and truly outnumbered. Don't forget the shotgun. Plus, they know if they do manage to get one over him and he gets hurt or they break any laws in the process, then I'll go after them and all bets will be off for a peaceful resolution. Don't worry. He'll send them off home after you're gone and we'll have a chat to them later. I can't prove it but I'm sure the graffiti was theirs as well. Aboriginal culture doesn't use the word witch, they have their own words, and they wouldn't smash up a house owned by one of their own. Him maybe, that's tribal law, but not his property. I reckon either the bad spelling was a white trying to make it look like the work of one of the Aboriginal locals or, more likely, it's the work of a poorly-educated God-drunken white dero, local or imported, who can't spell. We have our share of those up here. Anyway, forget about the ACA. They won't be a problem for you. I figure all they were doing was being nosy and didn't intend to do anything else. But, as I said before, they have friends down in the smoke. You need to be careful.'

I wasn't going to tell him I'd already decided how to deal with that. He might not be a letter of the law cop but telling him my friends knew people capable of making the ACA look like the Salvation Army formed the

84

makings of a bad idea.

I was starting to like Senior Sergeant Basham; he appeared to share my long-held view that sometimes morality was a more suitable option than legality. Furthermore, I could see why he and Picino managed to find common ground. I was convinced my once and long-ago fellow student had no conception of morality as such, but the way he'd dragged me into this case demonstrated he knew when to put the letter of the law back into its envelope and file it in a bottom drawer.

Basham's bush law might have been as out of place in the big city as he would, but up here in the wild northern wastes it was exactly what necessity demanded. If the ACA chose to play rough, then cops who could operate the same way was the answer. Yes, I decided, I did like Basham. But, as with everyone else involved in this case except for Maya, it didn't mean I trusted him.

I'd opted to trust Marilyn Jessup; there was something about her hinting at honest, her straightforwardness raised no alerts in my usually reliable bullshit detector. Plus, I hadn't caught her in even the smallest untruth. Now, if that happened, I would have abandoned my trust on the spot.

Henry Day the same; he came across as genuine although the tiny flash of out-of-place intelligence in his eyes still troubled me. It could have been a spark of anger or other emotion; he could hardly be blamed for getting upset at what was going on even if he didn't fully comprehend it. Perhaps I was chasing shadows, it wouldn't be the first time and a couple of my previous efforts wasted considerable time with one resulting in a severe reprimand from the legal bureaucracy. I decided to place my misgivings in storage and concentrate on the bigger issues. And, on that topic...

Picino? Maybe he was genuine, and maybe he was not. Time would tell and, in the meantime, I'd be careful around him and anyone he recommended. As I knew well, he was a game player and terminally ambitious. But when I first knew him there existed a barely discernible streak of conscience beneath the practised cynicism. Maybe a single positive trait survived years of politics and Eva's controlling neediness. *Right*, I thought, *and maybe taking on this case would net me an Order of Australia come New Year.*

Despite my misgivings, part of me sought to believe there were surviving remnants of those good intentions. I was too old and canny to see much of the positive in people and sceptical pessimism wasn't a comfortable way to view the world; I knew I should be spending my time more efficiently, trying to view it constructively. Then I remembered I was trying to find traces of integrity in someone who'd betrayed our friendship, stolen my girlfriend, and become a high-ranking Liberal politician and an adulterer. By including that last example, I wasn't trying to feel morally superior or judgmental, I was merely rounding out my list of Picino's treacheries.

I wished he hadn't been involved. I wished the same for myself. And, naturally, I saved a last wish for Henry; compared to his storm-tossed troubles, mine were no more than a flurry of wind and wave.

In the back, Maya and Henry finished with fast-food menus and were discussing something of a cultural nature. I tuned out and watched the scenery, a flock of running emus provided a moment of interest, and as we approached the plane, I began sorting the mess in my briefcase. I'd intended to talk to Henry on the flight but since he and Maya were bonding, I decided she'd be likely to get more from him through ancestral kinship than I would using testosteronic links. I'd leave her to it, write up notes, and review progress. Plot our next steps and work out who I needed to speak with.

It was important that I become an instant authority on supernatural magic; the lecturer could fill me in on that. In addition, I sought more information on Fenwick's death; talking to the two pathologists would be the best way to go. If possible, I would like to interview Fenwick's widow and find out why she'd decided to pursue the old man sitting behind me when common sense and medical science dictated otherwise. Plus, a talk with Picino might be beneficial. We could compare notes and plan our ongoing strategy as I sifted out the grains of truth from the harvest of lies he'd been told and was telling.

Then, if there was time, I could possibly consider how I was going to make a living once this case destroyed my career. Alex's surgery was seeking a second receptionist; I knew how to answer phones and I was prepared to sleep my way into the job. Why was I worrying?

8

I soon grew tired of watching the endless desert passing below us. It was time to talk to Henry Day. He and Maya explored their family histories all the way back to when the continent separated from the lands to the north, and I assumed I wouldn't be interrupting anything important to the case or to anybody except one or two obsessive anthropologists. I left my seat and slid into the one opposite Henry who was gazing out of the window as he'd been doing since we took off, even while he was talking to Maya. I was sharing the plane with probably the only man on the planet who would prefer to look at millions of acres of red dirt instead of her. I decided then and there I never wanted to be that old.

I gave a flick of the head as a signal, and Maya told Henry she would see him later and went up front to talk to someone more her age and still manufacturing red corpuscles. Henry probably had them but he sure as hell forgot where they were or what they were for. I felt sorry for him, living alone and in such a dreary place. It was no wonder he was starting to resemble the living dead. And now the combined weights of the legal system and popular ignorance were bearing down on him.

I was determined to help him, out of pure pity, if for no other reason. For the first time since Picino told me about this, I began to be truly angry. And committed to what I had to achieve. I knew this case could easily end my career, but if I didn't try my best to defend the man sitting next to me, I didn't deserve to have a career to lose.

Now I was fired up and raring to go. But where to go was the question with no hint of an answer. While I was waiting for Henry and Maya to finish bonding, I'd worked out what I was going to ask him. The questions weren't tightly focussed but a wiser man than me once said something about longest journeys and first steps so...

'Henry.' He turned to face me. I couldn't read him; the volcanic terrain of his face and the unmoving directness of the dark eyes gave nothing away. But I'd been doing this for a long time and nothing given away tends to surrender willingly. He didn't trust me yet, which I expected, considering my ethnicity and profession. The harsh sounds of colonisation still echo in the ears of the peoples who lost everything, and laws and lawyers fixed their defeats into place. If I were him, I wouldn't have trusted me either. I wondered what his feelings were about Maya working for me; he wouldn't be the first to look askance at the situation, there were those on both sides of the racial divide who disapproved. It didn't bother me, but I knew it troubled Maya. Not what they thought but that there were people foolish enough to think it.

Was Henry weighing his options behind a closed mask? What they might possibly be was beyond me. He radiated honesty and total lack of anything resembling guile which hinted, no more, he might, also no more, be honest and truthful. I too radiated honesty and a lack of guile, I knew I did, because I'd spent years learning how to. In my case though, all it meant was I was doing my job properly as in correctly, if not always properly as in appropriately. Needs must: a proverb not as old as my profession but often indivisible from it.

'Henry, Mrs Jessup, how long have you known her?'

He hesitated and I wasn't sure if he'd understood, then

his eyes opened wider in comprehension.

'Long time.'

I assumed that meant decades and not years. As he said, long time.

'What about Senior Sergeant Basham? Phil. How long have you known him?'

Once more there were squinted eyes and pursed lips. Thought, for him, was not a quick process; it would drive the prosecution mad in court if they weren't accustomed to waiting for answers from old and hesitant people. I was. I'd dealt with too many dithering seniors not to realise patience was the secret. Still, he was slower than most. But he got there in the end.

'Long time.' Not helpful. I was making conversation to relax Henry, not researching his biography. I made a note in my diary to check with Basham later.

'Do you know why those people broke your windows and went into your house?'

Another long pause. 'They think I know magic. No magic nohow. All stupid. Can't spell neither.' He laughed, for the first time a genuine one full of humour. I think I understood what he was laughing at. If an old Indigenous man didn't believe in magic, and they were supposed to be the ones who practised it and passed it onto the younger generations, then he obviously figured, and I agreed, anyone else thinking it was genuine was a fool. Or, to use his word, stupid.

It was a revelation; I always believed the older generations believed all that stuff. Those I met certainly gave the impression they did, and now I'd met one who certainly didn't. Life's surprises are what makes each day different as my granny — who maintained her faith in the power of the supernatural in spite of it never having done anything for her — used to say and for once she was right. It was not an aspect of Henry I wished to become more widely known though. If he said what he'd said in public it could start to sound rehearsed, a hypocritical denial of his cultural heritage revealed to support his innocence. The prosecution would paint it as such; it would need to have a limited readership until I knew how to employ it to best effect.

Before I could do that, though, I sought understanding of why he didn't believe. Getting to the heart of that, I knew, might be difficult and take time. Which we had, at least another hour anyway. I decided to give it a shot.

'Henry, most of your people believe in magic, especially the older ones. But you say you don't. Why is that? Why don't you believe in it?'

He stared intensely out of the small window and I presumed he was watching the ground. Then he turned and I could see his eyes were closed and tears were forcing their way between the lids and flowing down his cheeks. He turned all the way back to face me and his eyes opened, releasing a flood. When he spoke, I barely heard him; his slow mumble and broken words were almost inaudible above the sound of the engines and the rushing in my own head. But I caught it and it hit me like a punch.

'My wife die. I try magic. Friends try magic. Not work. Blackfella magic, whitefella magic, old ways, new ways, all no work. She gone. I not believe. It not help. I not believe.'

He slumped back in his seat, eyes closed, and was immobile. I waited but he was done. I felt awful. This man suffered enough and Fenwick's bloody widow demanded he go through more of it. Well, not if I had anything to say. Cases moved me before but not like this. I was bursting to shout and go mental over the sheer injustice of it all but the cabin of a small plane where the wheels and the ground were a long way apart is definitely the wrong place and time for a tantrum. I raged internally for a couple of minutes then went and touched Maya's shoulder. Time to talk.

We sat at the rear and spoke quietly. I related all his revelations and she teared up as I spoke. He hadn't, she told me, revealed any of that to her, which might be an age or gender taboo, a cultural inhibition, or simply the fact that I'd been at hand when he was ready to let it out. Maybe it was something more basic: a guy thing. It happens!

I told her who I desired to speak to the next day and she agreed to start calling the necessary people as soon as we were on the ground. Neither of us were sure if using a mobile in small planes was permitted and we didn't want Henry to overhear what was said. It looked like I'd be travelling over the next few days and I told her she was coming with me.

'Who's going to look after Henry?'

'Dean or one of his guys will be with him, I'm going to put him out at Ed Foster's place. No one will think of looking for him there.'

The Fosters were friends but not close enough for anyone to spot the connection. I'd defended their son on a drink driving charge a few years back and although I lost the case my efforts impressed them enough for them to offer me any legal business from then on. I knew if I rang and asked for a favour, it would be forthcoming. I'd put Henry and Dean's security people in the worker's huts at the rear of their property. It was isolated enough for Henry to feel at home and for him to be safe.

I had an idea concerning how to organise a meeting with the pathologists who failed to satisfy Veronica Fenwick with their findings. They were highly respected men of science and the odds were high her harsh criticisms rankled, and they were likely to find the idea that death by magic was being considered too ludicrous for their educated minds to accept. My plan was to co-opt their professional opinion to assist my case. The best laid plans, as the man said, though, often go amiss. However, nothing ventured, nothing gained as someone else said. It was worth a try.

Quoting clichés to myself proved I was getting desperate. Or overtired. Perhaps being surrounded by literature at Marilyn Jessup's subliminally influenced me. I was spending too much time thinking about magic and the like. I knew a couple of drinks and a long sleep would fix my problems. The internal ones at least. The others, such as Henry's case, would still be there when I woke up sober.

I also wished to talk to Veronica Fenwick, a goal requiring considerably more finessing; a legal synonym for lying. My idea was to meet her and give the impression I was struggling with the case, not a tough call as it was true. I could try to convince her to open up as to why she was dead set on blaming Henry for her husband's death by intimating I required the information to possibly talk my client into admitting guilt and throwing himself on the court's mercy. Fooling those who are already fooling themselves is easier than it sounds if you have a talent for bluff and are prepared to lie shamelessly. Again, I'd need luck and for her desire to believe anything which might give her what she desired to sway her in the direction I wished her to go.

Lastly, I was anxious to convince Picino I was doing my best for Henry despite the wheeling and dealing going on behind his back. Which meant keeping it secret from him. But if I told him nothing, he'd become suspicious and check up on me and possibly find out things best kept from him for now. I was after a story to keep him happy and in the dark. Any lies would set his alarm bells ringing; I may not like or trust him, but I was not foolish enough to underestimate him. I would be truthful, as far as I went anyway.

The landing was as smooth as the previous one; Maya told me why. The pilot, her new bestie, learnt to fly in the RAAF and they preferred people not to bend aeroplanes during landings. Maya said goodbye to him and tried to pass him a piece of paper unseen. She would have succeeded but I was looking; there was fun for the having and I didn't want to miss the opportunity.

As we descended the stairs, I saw Dean and one of his boys, an ex-soldier named Ronan. He was, according to his boss, one of the few people he was not totally convinced he could beat in a fight, which made Ronan somewhat fearsome. If he was going to mind Henry, there was nothing to worry about. However, if the extremely fit and reasonably young Ronan was going to be hanging around the Foster's place, then their impressionable seventeen-year-old daughter, Claire, would be the cause for concern. But since it was not my problem, or hopefully wouldn't end up as mine, I ignored it.

I gave Dean directions to the Fosters' place and told him by the time he arrived I'd have rung and arranged everything. After he dropped them off, he was going to come back and say hi to Alex before he headed home to Adelaide. I signed a form for the pilot and we watched as he turned the plane around and took off into the twilight. I called the Fosters and, as expected, there were no problems. I did the right thing and offered money; they did what I knew they would and refused it. Maya and I had a short drive, a talk to Dean, and several necessary phone calls by both of us before any possibility of sleep. I was hungry, tired, and in need of a shower and a hot drink. Tomorrow was going to be a long day and if my plans came together, the following ones would be no shorter.

Despite the stress and Henry's emotional tug at my heartstrings, I was feeling upbeat. As was Maya, although in her case, our pilot may have been the cause. For me it was the sensation of being involved in something more worthwhile than most of the cases I took on. Most were everyday lawyering. Me earning a living by helping those who lacked my qualifications and experience. This one was incalculably bigger than that.

Instead of the usual professional objectivity, where wins, losses or draws were equally satisfactory outcomes because that's the inherent nature of my chosen line of work, there was an urgency and drive to succeed kept in abeyance for too long. The somewhat dormant desire to right social and legal wrongs was back in fighting trim, and it felt great. Considering it might be my last battle, I was glad I was doing the right thing for the right reasons.

Then again, so did Thomas Becket and everybody knows what happened to him when he fell afoul of those with power. Somehow, I knew whatever the outcome, no one would be erecting shrines to me; an obituary in the form of a legal-business-for-sale notice seemed far more likely. In my head, an insistent voice silently cursed Picino for dragging me into this conundrum as another, correspondingly forceful, countered I was a volunteer and consequently equally if not more to blame. I knew Alex would go along with both. Only not silently.

9

I slept well, eventually. Dean and Alex and I chatted in for a while but I couldn't keep my eyes open and left them to it. I was woken the next morning by Alex shaking me and holding out a steaming mug. We kissed, I said thanks, and then watched as she prepared to have a shower. I renewed my vow that if I ever tired of that view, I'd have myself euthanised.

We were as close as we'd ever been. I loved her passionate nature and emotional tantrums as I knew she loved my quieter, more analytical calm. If opposites do truly attract, then we were custom built for each other. Apparently, I required constant critiques in the cause of personal improvement and it was comforting to know she cared enough to put the effort in.

Something else about her I admired greatly was her intellect. I reasoned with legal statutes and moral guidelines; she was scientific-logical. The two methodologies bounced off each other effectively and our discussions encouraged me to adopt alternative approaches to my job in the past. It was what I needed again; I was having trouble getting my head around what was happening.

After Rob left for school, I intended to pick her brains by presenting her with the facts and consider her responses. I also required input from someone connected to the case in a more direct way. Meaning Maya. I headed for the bathroom; nature and the shower called. As Alex and I passed each other in the entrance to the shower, the idea almost derailed; there is something about wet female flesh and the scent of soap…

Anyway, we came to her senses and the moment passed without incident. Half an hour later, I'd called

Maya and the three of us were sitting in the kitchen with fresh mugs of tea and hot toast. I figured the best place to start was at the beginning, so I did, taking almost forty minutes to explain it in detail and as requested they asked no questions. When I stopped, they remained silent for a minute. Alex spoke first.

'Van, that's one serious mess you've put yourself in. And before you try to blame Picino, don't bother, I know you too well and this is you jumping, not him pushing. Yes?'

I sensed that one coming from way off, and she was right. I was undecided about whether I'd volunteered or been coerced and it took someone who knew me well to put it into words. Picino may have nudged me, even shoved a little, but I took the first step unaided and then kept moving forwards. Now both women had the satisfaction of being able to blame me for my involvement, it was time for them to stop gloating and start thinking. I said it to them, although not in those words. Mrs Miller didn't raise an idiot — well, yes, she did, my brother, the plumber who made more money in a week than I did in a month. Perhaps, seeing the mess I walked into with eyes wide open, it was necessary for me to conduct a re-count of precisely how many idiots my mother really raised.

'You two think differently to me which,' I added diplomatically, 'is probably not a drawback.'

That earned me two cynical looks. I wasn't renowned for my use of sycophancy; their faces said they knew I was after something. They were right, I was. Challenges to what I was thinking, alternative views, and outright dismissal of anything fermenting that might possibly come across as unreasonable to anyone less familiar with the current events.

I knew it would be Alex taking the bait; she knows me well, and the insight flows both ways. Voluble, temperamental shouters have problems being enigmatic; they show it all and hide nothing. Which is what I was seeking; people who could punch holes in my conclusions, Alex's forte, and offer a more considered view of the minute details, which was Maya's.

The two women in front of me were the right combination. One with no reason to be unnecessarily polite about my misconceptions, if any, who could rip my theories apart, and one who would, more diplomatically, focus on the legal intricacies and any inconsistencies either my cautious legalistic approach or Alex's kick-down-the-door Viking-attack methodology highlighted.

First though, a question troubling me all along. I was sure I knew what they'd say but I longed to hear it said. Who knew what might be revealed? Clearly apart from anything obviously wrong which they would delight in bringing out into the light. This scenario had taken place before, albeit around far less important topics.

Both would be trying to find discrepancies in my reasoning, not because they were nasty or vindictive, but simply with the aim of guiding a lesser mortal, meaning a male, towards a more logical conclusion than he could make a muddle of on his own. If it sounds like something a man might have said sardonically, it wasn't. Alex, with minor variations of wording and politeness, many times.

It was time to get into the question I required their input on. I've always sought the opinions of others and sometimes acted on them. One time when I didn't, I came unstuck and the viewpoint I ignored was Alex's. She never reminds me of it; she doesn't have to — it's burned into my memory. A woman Alex was certain was guilty of murder — Alex knew the doctor who provided the medical evidence confirming the culpability — is currently walking around free because I did my job too effectively. I have mixed and conflicting views on the case; professional pride in my successful and difficult defence of her and shame I should perhaps have allowed my knowledge of her guilt to do what my conscience dictated and not my professional ego. There was no difficulty defending her, but a considerable amount of it defending my defence. Alex worded it more effectively: I was wrong: morally, ethically, professionally, as a member of the human race with more responsibilities than most to ensure justice, and on and on the list went. Pointing out everyone is entitled to a defence under law and is considered innocent until proven guilty beyond reasonable doubt — the quantitative adjective the loophole securing the insufficient-evidence driven acquittal — failed to alter either Alex's opinion or my own. I won; I lost!

It was a contributing factor in my decision to leave the firm and listen to my wife and my conscience more closely. I didn't tell her how I felt, but she knew. She always understood me, something I loved and dreaded to equal degrees. I hid no secrets from her but, then again, neither did I want to. When her face showed she knew I was after something, she was right. And what I sought answers to was...

'Do you two believe someone can will or sing or curse a person to death, especially if the two have never met?'

I was sure what the response would be and I was not disappointed. Who it came from was the surprise: Maya.

'Why is the fact they never met even included in your question? It makes no difference. Killing someone by magic is totally impossible. I know there are many people who believe it because, hey, if you think good magic exists as in religion, then you have to be convinced bad magic also exists, as in demonic possession or supernatural charms and hexes and so on. I have rellies who swear by all of it and are not happy I don't. They claim my lecturers did magic on me to stop me believing what I was taught since I was a kid. I know better, education isn't magic; it's only knowledge replacing the ignorance of not knowing. Listen, Van, forget about whether they met or not, it's unimportant. Can it happen? No, no, and no. You knew already and you didn't need us to tell you. Why ask?'

Alex chimed in. 'He asked because he thinks the same way. He also knows how we think, the reason he asked is to hear us say it. Because a hell of a lot of people are going to hear it's possible, and the gullible fools and the too-lazy-to-thinks will believe what they hear. There's pressure on Van to find Henry innocent and even more from many directions for him to be found guilty. Fenwick's widow is a religious conservative and rich and reasonably attractive to boot' — reasonably? Bitchy-bitchy — 'so her beliefs in the supernatural, both the good and bad varieties, will have convinced her magic spells are possible and her innate racism and social snobbery will add what she needs to accept it without question. To her, it will prove Henry, as an old black man as she would describe him, would consider his opposition to a project she and her husband were supporting as an obvious motive for murder. He knew how to kill Fenwick; he could use the magical skills everyone knows all non-white cultures possess through their worship of the dark side. Everyone who doesn't stop to think and simply accepts what they're told either in the press or bad movies or by gossipy sycophants.'

She paused; I knew her views on the unthinking masses, I'd heard them often enough. Her knowing I required reinforcement was hardly a surprise; she'd seen too many of my moments of insecure self-doubt. Not about her and our relationship but my chosen profession. She believes, and she's probably right, the laws it enforces or, in my previous existence, argues against, are no more than indefinite sciences where the best planned experiments sometimes go wildly astray.

This case was promising to be one of those. Proving Henry couldn't have done it wouldn't simply be a matter of showing I was right; it could potentially involve demonstrating most of the country was wrong. As if reading my mind, any acceptance of which would totally undermine my assertion the supernatural is nothing more than febrile imagination feeding enfeebled gullibility, Alex faced Maya and continued.

'Van doesn't need to show Henry is innocent, he needs to convince a nation populated and led by superstitious fools, informed by a sensationalist press, and infected with endemic ignorance and racism, there can't be a crime for him to be guilty of because no such crime exists. He has to show the public's preconceptions are nonsense, what they're being told is designed to sell papers and airtime, and those politicians who adopt that mad woman's cause are doing it for political reasons and not from any form of actual faith in what is being said.'

She turned from Maya to me. 'Am I right? Are we right? Is that what you were after? Does it help knowing we are with you and support you? Did you think for a second we wouldn't?'

'Yes, yes, yes, yes, and a definite no. I suppose I

needed to hear you say it.'

Two smiles, both warm, and one kiss, even warmer.

My turn. 'Okay. Why are all those people determined to blame Fenwick's death on Henry? There is no evidence, and if it wasn't for the accusing letter, everyone would have accepted Fenwick's death as being a result of natural causes. My question, the one I'll probably be basing my argument around, is why would anyone hope to gain anything from such a move? I can see it undermines any attempts by the local Aboriginal community to argue against the sale of Bilden Downs Station, that I get. But it's fairly weak. Some ill feeling might be stirred up, but it already exists, there's no real need to try and increase it with a spurious claim of death by sorcery. I don't see how anybody benefits from stirring up an accusation based on superstitious nonsense. Even Fenwick's widow will only get added grief from it. Any thoughts?'

Maya looked at me then Alex. 'Van, I know what you mean about the ill feelings between whites and us mob. First hand. No arguments. But there have been crap movies and books using incorrectly applied Kadaicha Man drivel and all they did was cause laughter, not belief. Even most of the people I know believe don't take any of it seriously. When I say believe, they accept it in the same way many Christians believe in God but regard the Bible as nothing more than stories written to either teach moral concepts or provide something that's more aligned to classical myths than actual history. I mean, who can take burning bushes speaking or virgin births or Noah's bloody floating zoo seriously? But a lot of people do. Frightening when you think about it. In the twenty-first century, as well.'

She started looking at everything in the room but us, and I knew she was going to talk about her cultural heritage. From long conversations, I knew her culture and her education were at odds, and it occasionally caused her discomfort, familial and intellectual. She took a deep breath.

'As you know, I'm close to being an atheist, but when I'm with my family on Country then sometimes there's this feeling I get there is something sort of spiritual out there with us. Intellectually I know it's only a sense of our past, culturally-implanted resonances of our ancestry and our connection to the land. But if I can get those feelings, then committed Christians like the Fenwicks and even those ACA fanatics, who accept it all in a literal way, must feel it strongly. I'm no expert, and by the way you have an appointment with the lecturer who is, but I have family and friends who are convinced there's something beyond this life and there are people who can manipulate those supernatural entities to alter our world. Mostly for the better, priests giving blessings, my peoples' ceremonies, even touching crystals or wearing a cross or a rabbit's foot charm. If they think good can be done, then many would also believe bad is equally possible. No bloody joke, Van, if magic was doable, I'd become a believer and have my own law firm. We'd never lose a case.'

She laughed for a quick moment then her serious face returned. She sat up and looked directly at me. I'd seen her in didactic mode before. It showed a confidence she rarely seemed to feel and allowed to show even less often. When she did, I could see the dynamic lawyer she was going to be.

'Van, believers believe. They don't care about logic, or common sense, or science, or rational explanations. They have faith and it beats any worldly interpretation anytime. Alex is a science-based person, you're a logical and educated thinker, and I'm rebellious enough to reject some of my cultural beliefs because I'm educated and don't like being told what to think or do. Especially if I can see the wires operating the tricks. And I can. We all can.'

She took another deep breath and turned to look out of the window. I could see the stress of opening up affected her. Alex leaned over and squeezed her shoulder then turned to face me.

'Van, many people will believe it because they're too lazy or stupid to come up with a viable alternative. A number because they're indoctrinated beyond repair. Others will either pretend to go along for personal gain, such as those pushing for Chinese ownership of Bilden Downs Station, or to profit from the notoriety and scandal. Then there will be those who don't believe it but whose inertia will cause them to sit back and wait to see who wins. For what it's worth, in my opinion whoever started this has a reason and you need to find out what it is then it can be exposed as a hoax. Bottom line, if you can't show why it was done or who did it, then you can't show the reason was malicious, venal, political, or merely someone stirring up trouble. I don't think it's religious, although that's what many will think. The sale of Bilden Downs, since it's not dependent on discrediting Henry or the locals, it seems unlikely to be that, but it will get put up as a cause. Fenwick's widow is looking for an answer and there isn't one, meaning she'll grab at anything even hinting at an explanation.'

She had her game face on, the one indicating someone or something riled her up either morally or through the major human flaw in her opinion, stupidity.

'As a doctor, I know people simply die inexplicably and if two independent post-mortems have found nothing, then his death falls into that category. But I've seen too many grieving relatives who refuse to accept far more straightforward causes of death than this, and she's probably struggling to come to terms with it. According to you, she used to be a doctor and we as a profession don't like the unexplained. It's not surprising she's unsatisfied. That, though, is no reason for her to blame Henry. She might grab at it if someone else does in desperation but sending letters and stirring up trouble, I can't see it. No one has what I'd consider a solid motive. Coincidental and incidental ones, maybe, but all of them seem a tad far-fetched for me. As I said, find out why and you'll know who and have a way to clear Henry of any involvement in whatever nonsense is driving this.'

Like Maya, she finished off by taking a long breath and staring out of the window. I waited a minute until they turned back to face me, smiled at each of them, thanked Maya and told her, truthfully, I was lucky to have her working for me, and made eye contact with Alex. 'How about I go next door and hand out the Panadols and you go to court? You were brilliant.'

She was. A definite improvement on what I expected. The answer I'd imagined but more. I felt relieved, knowing I attracted such a level of support. Unfortunately, I'd have to leave the house sooner or later and then the reality of it was that the three of us versus a much less supportive world would be unavoidable. All of my thoughts had been verbalised by the two of them and any slight lingering doubts were gone.

Not doubts, obviously, concerning whether Henry did

a hoodoo-voodoo number on Fenwick; which was too laughable to even contemplate for a moment. But my latent paranoid fears that I was going about this in the wrong way were completely put to rest. They had, though, turned to tangible fears about what I faced with this case. Win or lose, I was in trouble. It should have bothered me but it didn't. If Alex, backed up by Maya, said I was doing the right thing, then I was.

I felt empowered, my thoughts confirmed, jubilant two of my favourite people in the world were one hundred percent behind me, confident I was looking at this in the right way, and more nervous than I'd been since I was seventeen and found out Carly Belling, wrapped around me in the back seat of my father's car, was wearing no knickers.

Excitement, as then, vied with trepidation as heat and chills fought for supremacy. I was raring to fight and contemplating flight. My mind was racing and my lower intestines were writhing like snakes. It was, paradoxically, what I left the city to avoid and what I studied law to do. Carly and I both accomplished a memorable ending. This case held a possibility of reaching one also; the difference being Henry was likely to be the one being screwed.

10

Countless people are moved by music, with me notably included among the ranks of the hallowed. To the philistines, it's no more than a subliminal soundtrack to a monochromatic half-life, but for those of us blessed with sensitivity it's a major contribution to our lives. When sad music plays, we cry; perhaps not literally but deep within our psyche we shed figurative tears. When the music is joyous and uplifting, the tones and rhythms induce accelerated heartbeats and increased blood flow; we respond as it transports us into a psychosomatic hyperdrive beyond description. The feelings are sublime: entrancing and enveloping the listener. Seemingly demonstrating the effect, as Deep Purple's *Child in Time* moved into the headlong bass-and-drum gallop underpinning the magnificent guitar solo, my entire being sped up to match the furious pace. Regrettably, the same applied to my driving.

I managed to take enough time slowing down and stopping to hear most of the solo but I was in the sort of bad mood only disrupted music or sex can generate. I accepted the ticket politely if not necessarily graciously and proceeded at a reduced pace. To get back on balance, I started the track again. The middle-aged bad news and good news situation came into play: sex requires recovery time, with music, you can hit replay immediately. Listening once more to the ball-tearing vocals and insistent instrumentation I felt restored. Not least because the person I was going to meet first would cancel the speeding ticket; it's often of benefit to have low friends in high places.

The appointment at the university was for midday. As soon as the family plus-one meeting was over, I prepared for work. Since I was going to a place of higher learning, I dressed down to fit in; faded jeans, rumpled dark-red long-sleeved shirt hanging out over an ancient AC/DC T-shirt, and my worn until slipper-comfortable old sneakers. I remarked to Alex I was a fashion statement; her response was that it said, 'I give up'.

After driving Maya to the office, I used the prepaid to call Picino's anonymous number, and we spoke for less than a minute. Then I hit the road, cranked up the volume, and savoured the unbeatable combination of open road and loud music. Until I was stopped. It wasn't an issue, there was plenty of time to do what came first and still be at the university on time.

My memories of uni lecturers were the most serious crime you can commit is tardiness and I intended to be there early. To achieve my goal, I slowed down to arrive at my earlier appointment sooner. It's not as counterintuitive as it sounds; I'd lost nearly five minutes talking to the traffic cop, another one of those and my timetable could be shot to hell. Not to mention my demerit point tally. Thus, slower equals faster. I listened as I agreed with my own reasoning; by the time my head was around it, I was where I was going. Perhaps not mentally; reviewing my last few rationalisations, I certainly hoped not. Fast driving, loud music, and irrational philosophising: the happiness hat-trick.

Any happiness evaporated when I arrived at the most isolated corner of the Mount Lofty lookout car park: Picino was already there. The highest point in the state with an excellent and popular overview of city and suburbs, it was a quiet and secluded place to meet up, especially early before the hordes of tourists arrived. Regretfully silencing *Woman from Tokyo,* I exited my car and entered the only other one in sight. It must have been his own, I didn't think the government provided top-of-the-range BMWs for even the most senior staff. He was desecrating the magnificent German sound system by playing a syrupy-stringed Teutonic dirge probably entitled *Requiem for a Dying Shepherd* or something similar through it. I leaned over and hit the off button; too much Senior Citizens schlock and I'd be tempted to hit my own off button.

We looked at each other for a few seconds while I drew several calming breaths and he glared scornfully at my clothing. Oxygenated and mentally fortified, I made a you-first gesture. He reached into a door pocket and produced what appeared to be a leather-covered diary and opened it to where the ribbon marked a page. He'd always used fancy diaries like it when we first met; that's how I found out about him and Eva.

'Right, Van, there's a few things have happened. My staff are researching everyone connectable to the accusation either directly, indirectly, peripherally, coincidentally, geographically, or biologically. They uncovered some interesting details; I'll give you them first. The letters accusing Henry Day were posted in Parnham, which rules out Ronnie Fenwick or anyone in Canberra. To be certain, we checked travel details for anyone from Canberra who might have flown there to lay a false trail, and as far as we can see, no one did. The only people flying into Parnham since Fenwick's death were you once, the Flying Doctor three times, and a flying vet who goes there every month or so. If they did drive, we wouldn't know but, Jesus, Van, that's a three-or four-day round trip. I can't see it. You reckon someone would?'

'No, not really.' I had a question but he beat me to it.

'We did the same for every other capital city and the larger regional ones. Same result. As I said, no one with any connection to this except you travelled to Parnham recently. My opinion is therefore someone in the town posted them. Yes?'

'Yes. Although it could also suggest someone from there re-posted them after they'd been sent to them from elsewhere. It's unlikely there's a conspiracy but it's possible. But I'm with you, it's a local, with or without outside help.'

He nodded. 'Absolutely. Either way, someone in the town is driving this. Tomorrow, a forensic team is flying up there to check out all the houses for matching paper, pens, envelopes, whatever. They'll have warrants and Basham plus two of my lawyers are going to be there, meaning there won't be any arguments. The first stop will be the ACA, if nothing turns up, they will keep going until they find where the letters originated. And before you ask, they'll be looking at Henry's place as well.'

I burst out laughing. 'Henry? He has trouble signing his name. As for writing those letters by hand, they're individually done. He'd have had to start three months ago to produce them even if he knew enough words to put them together. I know they're short but whoever wrote them is literate and neat, two things Henry's writing is definitely not. I tell you, that's a non-starter, take my word for it.'

He nodded and made assenting noises. 'As it happens, I already know all that. But if we don't treat him as a possible and this all goes public, well, it's not hard to work out what would be said, is it? Anyway, moving on. My people' — God, he loved saying those words as much as I hated hearing them — 'have gone into the cattle station sale from every angle. The thing is, everyone may have an opinion about it and Fenwick's death may have made those against it more confident now his support is gone, but nothing has changed. The sale is going ahead regardless, with the sacred site issue mostly resolved. The single and only change is he is no longer involved. If someone killed him, they wasted their time. It affected nothing.'

He paused: the end of the good news. Sometimes I love it when I'm right; but not always.

'The bad news is the widow Fenwick has increased her pressure on the powers-that-be, federal version, and we, the state version, are being subtly pushed in the direction of forming a case against Henry Day. Details to follow as soon as one of the legal acolytes manages to finalise them. Van, one way or another, Henry will end up in court. I know' — he said with a classic Italian arm wave and twist of the mouth to match — 'it's bullshit, but it doesn't only make veggies grow, it also fuels governments and gets votes. Don't be surprised if the media get hold of this and soon. Either from the widow or a political vote chaser or one of their toadies.'

I laughed again, and he raised his eyebrows in an unspoken query. 'You described yourself and 'your people' as you put it.'

'Van, I know we have history but I was voted in honestly, I achieved this position the same way, and I perform my duties to the letter of the law. Except, obviously, for dragging you into this which was me acting morally and only mildly unethically. I have no more time for the self-servers and power junkies than you do. You can believe it or not but it's true.'

I could see he meant it but displaying genuineness is

part of a politician's trick bag; I would reserve my judgment. For now, I'd listen. Cautiously. To conceal any reservations that might be detectable in my voice, I moved my hand in a carry-on gesture.

'Right. So, we looked at the cast of players closely and applied *cui bono*. The answer is unreservedly no-one. None of them had any reason to wish harm on Fenwick and that applies in spades to Henry. There's no reason to try and put him in the frame for a murder which isn't a murder but a shit-happens piece of bad luck. As I said, the media will be across this soon and then it'll get worse. Sorry I dragged you into this but someone has to be the bleeding-heart liberal defender and you're the most qualified candidate for a number of reasons. I know you're pissed at me but don't waste too much time on that, it's counterproductive. Later, when it's over, you can shout at me. For now, you do the thinking and I'll make sure you know everything I do.'

On that matter I believed him. He would play it straight because it was his game from the start and if it came out right, he'd want to be able to say, if only to himself and possibly me, that he could legitimately take much of the credit. He had a sincere need for me to succeed, even if his motivations were less honourable than his words implied. He'd be forthcoming and I knew in the cause of fairness and equity, I should do the same. We weren't getting anywhere though. There was nothing from the meeting I didn't already possess beyond confirmation, always a welcome boost but virtually worthless as an argument.

But finding out the prevailing opinion was that no one benefited from Fenwick's death changed the ways of looking at it. Henry could now be seen as not only having no motive or opportunity, but the accusations could be relegated to the sidelines. I didn't believe he was murdered, the medical evidence against it was too strong to be denied, but if I could divert the investigation and create serious reservations, I might be able to go further and move the attention away from my client completely. It could go beyond reasonable doubt into the area of fallacious reasoning. After that any allegations would have minimal credibility.

As I pondered the possibilities, I decided not to share them with Picino. That day he and I were sharing an agenda; by the next, the political opportunist might regain ascendancy over the human being. We shook hands, agreed to be in touch soon, and I handed him the speeding ticket. He made a face but nodded. I wasn't worried about the fine, I knew he'd pay it. It was essential for the demerit points to vanish also; many more and I'd need to dust off my bike. I mentioned it to him; he turned the sound system back on and started the engine before I finished. If I sought a reason to dislike Picino, it occurred to me that, Eva aside, his musical taste would be an appropriate place to start. As I walked back to my car, I could hear the orchestra in mourning behind me. Driving off, I opened the windows and offered Picino a triple-forte taste of what real music sounded like.

11

I parked in a multi-storey directly across from the campus, wandered over North Terrace, and crossed the open space in front of the familiar Ligertwood building where future lawyers, including me, began their careers. I watched the passing parade of students, trying to remember when I was as young and eager, and arrived at the lift in the Napier Building with four minutes to spare. Which gave me time for what my mother used to call a rest break, and at ten seconds to twelve, I knocked on Doctor Madison Rundle's door. A voice called, 'Come in.'

Old and arcane history was her specialty. I was anticipating a middle-aged academic cliche with wire-framed glasses, sandals, lip-gloss makeup, and a dress fashioned from flowery curtain material. What I found was a gym-fit thirtyish brunette in trackies and a uni-sport polo shirt. Most of my lecturers reminded me of my mother's older sisters; this one reminded me of my own younger sister. I must have looked surprised, at least I hoped that was what I looked. She didn't remind me of anyone in my family enough for me to not appreciate the view.

'Mr Miller. Hello. Sorry about how I'm dressed. I train at lunchtime and there wasn't time to get changed. As I have no lectures this afternoon, I'll probably wait until I'm home.'

She gestured to a seat in front of her desk and I sat as she did the same behind it. I looked around the room. I used the uni library countless times as a student; for sheer volume and variety her office appeared to be going into competition with some sections of it. I saw a book I recognised; a Bible. Everything else was either written by people I'd never heard of or about historical periods I'd never heard of in places I'd never heard of. Many of the titles were in Latin. Now that, I'd heard of; I learnt Latin legal terminology in the building I could see from her window. Then forgot most of it in the UniBar. *Vinum causa oblivionem*, as someone wise once said: I forget who.

After some introductory small talk, she sat back and looked at me with what I assumed was her lectorial expression. Serious, concentrated, attentive. Considering how young she was, I was intrigued. Which meant as a lawyer seeking experienced advice and a hetero male with a pulse, not asking was out of the question.

'Doctor Rundle, pardon me asking and I don't mean to be rude but when I was a student here most of the lecturers were somewhat older than you seem to be. I know it takes a long time to get cred in History and I was told you are widely published and an expert in historical magic and the supernatural. Again, no offence meant, but you're not what I expected.'

I was hoping she wouldn't be offended. I was in luck.

'Firstly, it's Madison, not Doctor Rundle. Usually Maddie to my students and colleagues. Titled formality is, in my opinion, pretentious and archaic: most of us try to avoid it. A few of the younger ones go with it at first but it soon wears off. Yes, I'm published and although I don't describe myself as an expert, I suppose I do have some experience and knowledge. It's a work in progress, as the study of history usually is. And to put your mind at rest concerning my qualifications and experience, I began studying History and Classics when I was eighteen and I've been at it for twenty-five years here and at a number of other universities in this country and overseas, which I hope satisfies your professional curiosity without me having to say an embarrassing number aloud. I'm not offended, if I were after legal services, I'd definitely ask you for relevant details as well. To not ask would be careless and on the phone your colleague, Maya, gave the impression you are anything but, which, I suppose, is why you're here looking for answers. I hope I can provide some of them. Alright, now we both know who we're talking to, how can I help you?'

I considered asking for health and diet tips but decided against it. Forty-three, Jesus. She looked barely old enough to have completed a doctorate, let alone all she had. Perhaps, I decided, studying History was less stressful than Law. All of the people she related to professionally were dead; many of those I'd related to professionally probably should be.

She obviously possessed a sense of humour. The slight smirk when she acknowledged my professional curiosity showed my less definitively-professional questions were recognised for what they were. I liked her for letting it go; in this day and age, people in her position were more than likely to scream harassment at the merest hint of impropriety.

In truth, it hadn't been anything like that. I like to know I'm dealing with people who are what their qualifications claim them to be and her youthful appearance took me by surprise. It seemed to be something she was used to. As was the appreciation, I suspected. Used to and capable of ignoring in place of complaining about; if not, she'd have been in the flowered dress and flat sandals. Now though, with any doubts about her credentials and worldliness out of the way...

'I don't know what Maya told you but I, we, need

background on the use of magic to influence world events.'

I gave it considerable thought in the car and figured out how to avoid breaching any legal or ethical considerations or hinting too closely about why I was seeking the information. Lawyers who discuss cases with the public usually end up being criticised by the same public and occasionally attract something professionally much worse. I was being circumspect, hopeful I could find what I required without revealing too many details.

'Maya hinted you have a confidential case and you can't be explicit. I understand that; my father's a lawyer and when I mentioned your name to him, he recognised it. He said you're a social crusader and a pain in the arse because of it but he always considered you to be trustworthy and honest.'

I only knew one lawyer named Rundle; he and I faced off in a courtroom several times. I regarded him as an arrogant prick but it didn't seem the right moment to demonstrate my reputation for honesty. I went with the diplomatic option, mentioning only that I recognised the name. She leaned forward, her arms on the desk and apparently about to give what I was there for: I made myself comfortable and prepared to concentrate.

'Magic, or what people think of as magic, has been around for a long time. The Christians, in Constantinian Rome, venerated what they considered good magic and abhorred the evil variety. Obviously, the definitions of good and evil were individual and situational. All who believed, and still do believe, in good magic for the want of a more acceptable term, also equally believe in the evil side. There can be no goodness without wickedness to provide moral contrast and cosmic counterbalance. White witches perform white magic, which has benevolent purposes, and black witches use black magic, where the intent is malevolent, with the colours referring to the morality of the witchcraft, not any cultural or ethnicity-based characteristics of the witches themselves. It all depends on who's using it, what they're using it for, and in many cases, whether the ones using it have the same religious views as you or are what are often labelled as heretics, pagans, or unbelievers. One man's divine truth is another's heretical sacrilege.'

She could sense my scepticism; my impression was that behind the academic objectivity lurked a similar disbelief. I was not after a proselytising sermon on why to believe, I was chasing factual information on what was believed and how it might be relevant to Henry's case. Something only an impartial expert could provide with the clarity of objective distance. Her dispassionate language was of someone on the outside looking in. As I supposed I was. She seemed to want to let me know where it was she stood.

'This is my intellectual passion, not my personal conviction. It's a huge subject and after all these years, I've only scratched the surface. I've written or co-authored books and papers and lectured on it widely and most of what I've taught could be summarised by what I've already told you. Pick any area of the subject and you could study it for years, write a dozen books on it, and barely delve into it at all. Okay, I can generalise for the next week and totally overwhelm you with facts or you can ask specific questions and I'll try and focus on what you're after in a more definitive way.'

She was right but it presented me with a conundrum. Too specific and I was possibly breaking the law; not specific enough and I was probably wasting time. And there was a pressing need to get moving. I was thinking furiously trying to find a way to achieve my aim without scoring an own goal. A glimmer turned to a distant light and gradually brightened somewhere in the back of my mind. What I was working out was more Picino than Miller, and might be seen as treading a fine line between justifiable and unethical. I knew if I tried to fool this woman with any legal flim-flam she would probably see through it and I'd be out of her office empty-handed. I opted for openness.

'Madison, I have a problem. I need advice on something particular but it's an ongoing legal case I'm not permitted to discuss with anyone but my client and fellow lawyers, which in this instance is Maya. If I do, then I, and you, may both find ourselves in trouble. If we were questioned, you could refuse to admit anything but I can't if it's only a private conversation. But, if it's a lawyer-client conference, then neither of us can be forced to reveal what was said. Look, if let's say you were after legal advice about what we've been talking about, I could provide it. Minus names and finer details, but in general terms. If you were to employ me as your lawyer and ask for legal guidance while explaining to me in detail what you required advice on, then it's all above board.'

Not completely, I knew. What I'd said was based in legality, though legal ethicality might be a stretch. But since no one would ever learn about it anyway, all we would be doing was safeguarding ourselves in case she found herself presenting evidence about magic in my courtroom. As an expert witness it was possible, but unlikely. I explained it all more fully and she took only a moment to decide.

'Right, where do I sign?' It was the first time I'd signed a client up on a handwritten document. It felt like I was doing something inherently mischievous. Which isn't altogether a bad feeling. Unless you get caught.

I gave her the facts in a general way. An unexplained death, accusations of magic causing it, a possible public outcry blaming the supposed magician, and so forth. It meant nothing to her then, but I knew in a few days it would. To be completely above board with her, I went through that as well. She shrugged and said she'd go on.

She talked for an hour. The gist of it was every society since humans developed wondered at what they saw as unnatural phenomena and considered them to be controlled by supernatural forces beyond their comprehension. Along the way the control addicts convinced the gullible they were able to utilise those forces to do good or prevent bad. Usually for a price. Sounds like the modern church, I was tempted to say but since I didn't know her views, I kept quiet. Unknowingly echoing Maya, she talked about how believers simply believed without proof or any rational method to their thinking while non-believers tended to the view that what is, is, and what isn't, isn't: end of story.

'If a believer is convinced someone with power has cursed them, they may die because they convince themselves they have no choice in the matter. It only works on the most fanatical believers. Reading astrology charts, Tarot readings, and supernatural concepts in general doesn't affect non-believers or the doubtful because they lack the inner conviction that other-worldly forces can manipulate their lives.'

She moved into specifics about the hypothetical I'd presented her.

'If the man scheduled to die didn't know he was cursed, even if as you say he was a firm believer, then no matter what the witch or sorcerer or whoever did, it would have no effect. The cursed person has to know. The practice of pointing a bone, for example, which is peculiar to Australian Indigenous culture, only works if the one pointed at knows about it. Same with all similar hexing in all cultures. They're all mind control through suggestion, not supernatural forces acting independently. For a charm such as a love amulet to have any effect, all parties involved have to be in the loop and willing. You say the one doing the spell didn't write to the victim or otherwise contact him directly or through an intermediary. The two never met and the closest they ever were was about a kilometre apart. If you proved eye contact, I might be tempted to suspect hypnotism; it has been reputed to occur even with no other interaction taking place. There's no empirical proof but there are too many known instances to totally ignore. It's sometimes called Mesmerism, after Doctor Mesmer, an early nineteenth century German physician who used what became known as the compelling fascination. He verbally influenced his victims, or patients, or whatever you might like to call someone who is dominated in that manner.'

She went silent and I saw her academic objectivity was giving way to personal feelings. A history there, perhaps. I knew the sensation well and also was aware a short break could put it back into its place. And after a quick glance out of the window and an indrawn breath, that was what appeared to happen; she went back into lecture mode.

'The old cliché about a rabbit in headlights is apt. Fixed, helpless, unable to assert their own will. If any spoken communication took place, the connection adds another dimension and I would consider a suggestion could possibly have affected a gullible and impressionable person. Only those preconditioned to respond are inclined to, and in my opinion, the less intelligent are particularly vulnerable to being manipulated. Don't quote me, the less educated or educable are often sensitive about what they, or others, see as their shortfalls.'

She appeared embarrassed; holding that view may have caused her problems in the past. I waited patiently; I shared her opinions and my expression of them socially and professionally caused offence on more than a few occasions. Ironically, not to the less-adepts under discussion but to the supposedly more gifted thinkers; proponents of the charitable and possibly condescending 'all men are created equal' idea being applicable universally to all life skills including the attainment of wisdom. With regard to sentience and reasoning in particular, they believed in a sort of Marxist utopia of intellectual near-parity which I considered to be absolute proof the possession of such sentiments contradicted their own theory.

She obviously felt further exploration of the topic was called for. In my experience lecturers, once on a roll, usually liked to take a discussion through to a natural conclusion.

'But it's true, the higher the innate intelligence or level of formal learning or self-education, the less open to implanted suggestion a person is. Sheep allow themselves to be herded, cats do not. But, considering the distance and lack of opportunity for the magician to affect the victim, I can't see how it could have happened. When it does happen, it's not magic, it's manipulation. Which requires the knowledge and cooperation of the victim, even if given unwillingly or subconsciously as in a hypnotic state. There's a film, 'The Missing'. Cate Blanchett. A Native-American male witch physically harms someone by chanting over then burning the hair of the intended victim without that person having any indication the magic is being done. It makes for great entertainment but in a practical sense it's impossible. Even believers, such as the witched person in the film, cannot be affected unless they're made aware they should be. I know direct influence is possible as in hypnosis, I have seen it done' — the face she made half explaining her earlier reaction — 'but I certainly don't put any stock in ESP and long-distance mind control. The first is the science of influence through suggestion, the rest is the science of fiction.'

She laughed. 'Stephen Hawking as opposed to Stephen King. Anyway, to get more specific, what do you know about witches?'

That was easy to answer: nose-twitching cornball TV comedy, 'Hansel and Gretel', a few Disney movies from my childhood, 'Lord of the Rings', and I'd seen 'The Crucible' and been appalled at how the informed legal process was destabilised by ignorance and mob rule. Also, as it happened, I'd seen and liked the film she'd talked about and I remembered the scene. Intriguing and entertaining as she said but not overly plausible was my take on it at the time. I went through it all for her. Apparently, it was enough to provide an opening for the point she was about to make.

'Almost the perfect example is the one you mentioned. 'The Crucible'. A bunch of immature and overly-imaginative girls invent tales about local women turning into animals and flying around the place. That's the simple version, it's much deeper and we could talk about it for hours. I do, with my classes. I'm glad you've seen it. What stands out in it for you?'

'Superstitious ignorance and how easily it's accepted even when taken to ridiculous extremes.'

'Yes, that's it exactly. How group mentality is easily influenced by a charismatic storyteller. The collective willingness to allow themselves to be pushed in a particular direction they wouldn't normally take. The Crusades were started by a hysterical and fearful Pope pressuring people with rumours of oncoming evils and proclamations of what God demanded. The rallying cry was *Deus Vult*, God Wills It, to conscript the susceptible followers to his cause and reclaim a holy city from the anti-Christs. Half the world went to war because a foolish old man with too much worldly influence and a shortage of worldly intelligence sought to banish his night terrors concerning the possible invasion of his world, literal or spiritual, by the Muslim barbarians. It's a variant of the unfounded overreactions of the Salem story with a different instigator and villain. Same mass hysteria provoked by fear, and the hypnotic effect of verisimilitudinous bullshit. That's what you have here. Someone, unknown at this stage, is stirring up trouble and your client is the nominated witch.'

I was confused. 'Shouldn't it be wizard, or warlock?'

'No, all the fancy terminology came later and is more a western thing. Older cultures, African, Islander, Asian, Middle Eastern, First-Nations American as depicted in the film, even the medieval persecutions, used the word witch, or their version of it, as a coverall term for those who can do magic by supernatural means. Whether good or bad, male or female. Witch is most commonly used as a noun, the person doing the magic, but it's also a verb, to witch someone, the action of doing the magic.'

She paused then laughed, something she did often. Whether at the subject matter or her own reactions to it was uncertain. However, this time it was neither but undeserved self-deprecation.

'Sorry. Professional habits. This is something I lecture on often and it's hard to avoid slipping into — Well, you know what I mean. Where was I going? Oh yes. Even today, witches are not only believed in, but anyone suspect is often killed or driven out of their cultures. Small children, suspected of possessing magical powers, may be rejected and left to starve if they aren't killed outright. There are enough believers everywhere for the witch burnings of medieval Europe to still take place. Perhaps not in a literal sense but persecution and death for being suspected of witchcraft is a horrible ending, whether it be an actual burning, a stoning, drowning as in the old duck pond test, or however. You know what I mean, throw the witch in the water and if she or he drowns they're innocent, if they survive they're guilty and they get murdered another way. Back then it was fire, mostly instigated by misogynistic deviates who revelled in watching women burn to death.'

She grimaced and looked slightly embarrassed. 'Again, sorry about that. It's a part of one of my lectures, hyperbole included, and something I feel strongly about.'

I assured her I understood. I explained I was attempting to defend someone facing a similar fate for no reason other than groundless accusations made by superstitious ignorants. When I finished, she nodded.

'Yes, that sums it up. The same mentality driving the witch burners and drowners is pushing the public here. The media are our version of the village priest and his

God-fearing rants and the stake will be a courtroom but, essentially it's the same play in a different theatre. And let me add this, what happened back then, and still does today, is that perfectly innocent acts by your client will be rewritten in people's minds into magical acts going back months, years, even decades. Suspected witches who argued with neighbours or even simply looked at them sideways were assumed to be responsible if milking cows dried up or died or women became infertile. As I don't believe in it, I tend to avoid prophesying, but since we're considering the topic under discussion, I might as well play the game. Before long, someone, and it probably won't be the original accuser but a person desperate to jump on the bandwagon, will come forward and provide evidence, in their sense of the word and not a legal or even logical one, that your client has done magic before. I'm surprised it hasn't already happened but I guarantee it will. History is a reliable guide to how unremittingly stupid most people can be when there's a chance to join a popular movement. After Henry the Fifth's death, his brother's wife, Eleanor Cobham, was accused of practising necromancy, the sorcery of controlling events by communing with the dead and seeking their help. In her case she was caught using astrology and witchcraft to imagine, meaning induce, the death of Henry the Sixth. Apparently, she'd been involved in the practices for years, reports of the time have her sticking pins in a wax doll of the king and employing a woman called the Witch of Eye to perform magic, but the real motives behind the accusation were political, to remove her husband and herself from their positions of power. The charges were widely believed and their lives were ruined by rumours and superstitious gossip. It sounds like your situation. You need to be aware, as it was with Eleanor, now he's branded as a witch, every move he's made for years will be re-examined and respun to find the smallest hint of any magical intents. If you think it's bad now, wait until the fifteen-minuters get in on the act. Are the press creeping around the town where he lives?'

When I said yes, she nodded. 'It's only a matter of time before those vermin start serving up the rancid remnants the locals dig up and try to present them as edible.'

It was refreshing to find someone who shared my revulsion at the antics of the popular media. Those who fed the intellectually-starved with leftovers and scraps were often not concerned with whether what was being provided contained any calorific substance.

I agreed completely. 'Yes, if it sold papers or airtime, I was sure some in the media would show their own mothers' cancer-induced death spasms.' We shared a laugh mingled with bitterness. In truth, there was nothing amusing in much of what the media did.

In 1972, a university lecturer was viciously bashed then drowned in the River Torrens at a known homosexual beat behind the Adelaide University. After he'd been dragged from the water, the media, displeased with their photos, asked the police to throw him back in so they could get better pictures of his body being recovered. The police, who it turned out committed the murder, cooperated. Miscreations and media, competing that night for the title of worst exemplars of inhumanity.

I mentioned it to Madison and she grimaced. 'Yes, I've seen the memorial and the plaque near the bridge. It's not witch-dunking as such, but the prevailing beliefs at the time, religious and societal, that homosexuality was somehow an evil condition, there's a motivational connection. Punishing what you fear or what offends your faith. In fact, I might use that in one of my lectures, how alternate conducts are often decried as evil. Thanks for that.'

I knew about it as every law student did; the drowned man was a law lecturer. The circumstances of his death often feature in discussions within the university. Unwarranted persecution for inexplicable justifications engendered by irrational beliefs and mass ignorance. Not that Henry would be murdered but, as Napoleon said, death is nothing, but to live defeated and inglorious is to die daily. It was my job to eliminate downfall and ignominy from Henry's future.

My conversion from indifferent defender of those who could afford to purchase their innocence to pain in the arse social crusader, to reference her father's scornful description, was a long story and listening to Madison Rundle, I suspected hers might be something similarly complex. Her emotive descriptions regarding the often-misogynistic awfulness of witch persecutions were way beyond academic involvement. It may have been why she was contributing her time freely. I knew I'd never know why and didn't want to; I was simply grateful she was.

She expounded on all of it for another hour but much of it was spent accentuating the points she'd already made and going into peripheral details involving human hair as in the film, dead roosters, burning leaves, powdered animal innards, snakeskins, homunculi, and a panoply of similar ingredients commonly incorporated into rituals. Leaving those details aside, the end result was if Henry and Fenwick hadn't met, there was no possibility of any psychic transfer and any claims Henry caused Fenwick's death from a distance didn't fit any known and proven cases. She finished by adding, tongue in cheek, STDs don't jump despite what infected people liked to claim, and neither do curses.

She said she'd keep an eye on the media; there were elements to the story that could be used to demonstrate how her historical tales may not be as restricted to the past as many might like to think. I, in turn, promised to keep her updated. She handed me a book with her name on the cover that she said contained much of what we'd discussed. I thanked her, we shook hands, and I left. Outside it was getting dark; she'd been exceedingly generous with her time.

As I drove out of the city, I went back over what she'd told me. Since I'm not overly retentive and she'd spoken for a long time, I was glad she'd made the effort to go back over certain points, and her book would help. I now knew where we stood and we had the basis of a solid argument. If the two men met, there would be a problem. The lack of any indication they were any closer than the length of the town was a bonus, one I intended to utilise. Once I hit the freeway, I put Deep Purple back on. They were once described as the world's loudest band; how else should they be listened to but loud?

My attention was divided between what I'd heard about witches and magic, the music, and the speedometer. I was more positive than I'd been for a while. The case, no matter what was put up by the opposition was, if not winnable, no longer necessarily a lost cause. The indoctrinated villagers may be gathering firewood and building pyres but the evidence — to wholly mislabel it — against the supposed witch was turning to smoke and ash long before the flames could be lit beneath him.

12

Usually, I enjoyed being woken by Alex. The room-service Happy Meal included a kiss, a cuppa, buttered and marmaladed toast, and herself, sitting on the side of the bed talking to me. There was no reason to think, when she shook my arm, that day would be any different. But it was. No kiss, cuppa, toast, warm bum close by; it was her standing over me and demanding I get up, come take a look at the news. I slipped on jocks and trackies and followed her to the lounge. The television was showing the twenty-four-hour ABC news channel, nothing unusual; the large banner across the bottom of the screen was the change from normal.

BREAKING NEWS: SENATOR FENWICK: ABORIGINAL MAGIC BLAMED FOR DEATH

Above the caption a presenter was informing viewers an anonymous source revealed to the ABC that an accusation had been made against an Aboriginal Elder living in a far-north town of causing the death of South Australian Senator Fenwick by the use of magic. 'Viewers will remember the senator died during a parliamentary broadcast and...'

The rest was a rehash of the public demise of the senator and it transitioned into an interview with his widow. She was attractive, as Picino stated less elegantly, and that, combined with the teary face and sobbing grief-stricken verbals, would have everybody in the country feeling sympathy.

Except me: I was furious at her.

Someone, either the widow or someone stimulated to action by her or one of her coterie of social networks, decided to spread the word. I'd known it was likely but figured there might be a warning or that any announcement might be handled with decorum. What I was watching was someone manipulating the media to incite a lynch mob. A someone who knew how to provoke an outcry without providing any sort of legally-opposable details. She, or whoever was acting at her behest or on her behalf, could not be sued for defamation; the insinuations were too unspecified.

In addition, Henry was not an Elder; the honorific denotes leadership, community involvement, teaching and guidance, and is a matter of wisdom, not age. He might be elderly, but not an Elder. The misrepresentation, whether accidental — the media flagrantly displaying its blind eye for detail — or deliberate — an attempt by the unidentified contributor to suggest that the homicidal sorcery, committed by someone esteemed and sagacious, demonstrated a broader cultural approbation — did not, however detract from the underlying message. The meaning and intent were evident; Henry, considering his cultural and demographic characteristics, could do it and therefore almost certainly did. A guilty verdict from an unsworn jury.

I continued listening, simmering, and planning. The accusatory letters were mentioned along with their anonymous sender. Parnham's position was displayed on a map and shaky footage appearing to be at least a decade old showed it from the air. By the afternoon, I knew the Parnham airstrip would look like Sydney Airport at Christmas. Any peace and quiet the locals enjoyed would be a residue of the town's pre-infamy past: the same chaos now applying to Henry Day would spread across the town.

I heard my name and a media photograph of me taken outside one of my last city court trials filled the screen. It seemed my own peace was also hell-bound on a fast train. As if to punctuate the prediction, a phone rang. It was our home line. I muttered several non-magical incantations of my own before glancing at the caller ID, unknown number, and reaching for the phone. Since it wasn't the sly prepaid, and if it was, as I suspected, Picino, our conversation would be official and on the record. Correct on all counts.

'Good morning. This is Attorney-General John Picino. Is that Mr Donovan Miller?'

'Yes, it is,' I replied, working out from his tone that he was in company, either proximal or technological. If we were to be performing for an audience, it was crucial to act according to our arranged script. Paranoia, which someone cynically described as a great cure for loneliness, could also be considered a prime need for caution. Picino, adopting the stiff speech patterns of legal formality, was clearly advising cautiousness. My short sharp opening response made him aware I was there ahead of him and, as a more personal and privately-understood communication, his eavesdroppers were unlikely to recognise, I was displeased with the latest events. He continued in official mode, giving no intimations of his own feelings. Later we could drop the for-public-consumption pretences and argue openly.

'Mr Miller, I assume you've seen the news. A number of issues have been raised. I believe the person mentioned, Mr Henry Day, is with you at this time and we may need to speak to him later. But for now, I was hoping that you and I might meet to discuss the situation. Would my office be suitable? If not, I can come to yours.'

I desired Picino and his political circus and whatever media came along for the ride in my hometown like I was after another few inches of waistline. Eventually they'd arrive, the vultures of mass delusion, pecking holes in lives and vomiting out what they'd torn away. Which left me with only one choice; I told him I'd be bringing an associate and would twelve o'clock be acceptable? He agreed to both and gave me directions to the parking in his building. I thanked him, again in tight-lipped officialese, and we hung up. Alex was quicker. Some words sound even more virulent when spat out by a beautiful woman, especially that one.

I asked her to ring Maya and tell her to be ready in half an hour. Also, the Fosters. Partly to make sure they heard the news and to remind them to not tell Henry plus tell nobody about him and to warn Ronan to be extra watchful. All unnecessary but it was vital for everything to be as required and I was renowned for my pedantic detailing. I intended to be at the Fosters' in about an hour and to expect Alex's car, not mine. Certain I'd covered all the bases for the time being, I went for a shave and shower. If, by chance I did get sprung by the media, I preferred to look like the city lawyer I once was, not the country one I fervently wished I'd remained.

On that topic, I asked Alex to drop my court suits at the dry cleaners and buy new shirts. The levels of sartorial expectations in city courts and rural ones are as vastly different as the geographically relative cuisines. Five stars in smallish country towns meant mainstream beers, crumbed schnitzels, and pasta salads; formal dress meant the same suit you'd wear to funerals. Including your own.

As I dressed, fresh-faced and minus Picino- and media-induced sweat and bile, I reminded Alex to ensure the house was locked. Sometimes, considering our location, ours was a lax attitude to security. No longer. The press wouldn't trespass, it was illegal and they were aware I knew my way around the law. But once our names were public property, somebody less confined by rules might decide to make an unannounced visit. Later, I'd ring Dean and organise a guard.

Rob asked if he could stay home from school; something he tried on every time I took on a case with potential for social criticism; usually moneyed divorces or influential public figures accused of drink-driving or domestic violence. For once he was told yes. Not only off school but he'd be going to stay at the Fosters' with Henry and Ronan for the short term and maybe to Adelaide with relatives if it became a necessity. There were no arguments; he and Clair Foster were friends and maybe more: he was happy. How her parents felt might be something different. Especially if they took my advice and kept her home for a few days as well. I trusted her to keep quiet but we all slip up occasionally and I preferred to avoid crises whenever possible.

Maya and I delivered Rob, spoke to the Fosters, and broke the news to Henry. I wasn't completely sure he understood, Parnham life was hardly a preparation for national infamy; but he seemed to receive it all philosophically.

'Mister Miller, people talk, yeah? Worryin' bout it don't help.'

He was right; worrying doesn't help. Neither does ignoring problems in the hope they'll simply vanish, although what happened to Fenwick seemed to fit the bill perfectly. The idea caused me to smile, which caused Maya to ask me about what, which caused me to avoid answering. Lots of causes with few effects beyond my slight embarrassment at my skewed sense of humour asserting itself at an inappropriate moment. Nothing new there, and her knowing I was hiding something almost certainly in bad taste was also nothing new. I changed the subject and confirmed her suspicions. She was perceptive and would become an excellent lawyer; I hoped we wouldn't end up on opposite sides in a courtroom. I knew what I was doing; the problem was, after working with me closely, so did she.

We chatted quickly to Ronan away from anyone else then left for Adelaide with plenty of time to spare. In the car we discussed our mutual puzzlement concerning Henry's calm outlook. We moved on to considering the probable cause, which was that he simply failed to comprehend what was happening. That highly likely scenario, in the long run, boded worse than a philosophical acceptance. I'd never been inclined towards the passive surrender to fate but if it could allow me to remain as calm as Henry in such circumstances, I figured it might be worth trying, since the ignorance is bliss thing wasn't in the offing.

For now, there was a meeting with Picino about a case he'd pushed me into which was going downhill like an Olympic bobsled. I wasn't feeling passive, silently swearing at the providence which put him and me together in the first place and then, worse, the second place. And, to further confound the situation, after seeing Henry and remembering what was at stake, I was forced to accept capitulation was definitely not on the list of viable options. Neither, with Maya in the car, was the much-longed-for panacea of brain-crushing heavy rock.

She mentioned the news was all over social media, which she knew I had absolutely no interest in, and was giving me the details when I noticed a police car following us. As I checked my speed, a phone rang; the dodgy one, an appellation applying to the technology and the caller. I hit the hands-free button to include Maya in whatever new disaster might be appearing.

'Hi Van. Have you seen your escort? They're people I trust and I don't want you followed or hassled by those I don't. Any problems, the boys behind you will deal with them. See you soon.'

Short, not sweet, and welcome. I saw Maya staring at a phone she didn't recognise. I told her I'd explain later. It was true, though when later would be was a question I'm glad she didn't ask. What she did enquire, though, was, 'Okay, Van, what exactly is going on?'

I didn't recall teaching her to question people, especially me, in that way, so I knew she was worried. Or pissed. I decided to be truthful, which for me usually meant revealing carefully-selected portions of the truth and telling no actual lies. That time, though, I intended to be totally honest.

I started with, 'This whole thing is going to pieces...' and went on to explain why. By the time I'd finished, we were in the city and I let the GPS guide me through the twists and turns. I used to know the streets and buildings well; in my absence they'd changed many of them. It annoyed me, or perhaps I was making an attempt to occupy my thoughts with something, anything, other than my rapidly disintegrating case.

A flunky met us in the lobby, signed us in, and escorted us up to Picino's office. It was grand and spacious; well worth the effort he'd made to get there. Almost worth being stuck with the ambitious Eva.

Like hell! For that I'd want Hampton Court complete with staff plus access to Henry Tudor's cutting-edge innovations in marital counselling.

I introduced Picino to Maya and vice versa. Politely, officially, and for the record. They shook hands and I was sure I saw her following my advice and counting her fingers afterwards. Perhaps not. He took us further into his citadel and introduced a man I recognised instantly. Most people are aware what the Premier of their state looks like. The remaining fortunates are to be envied their ignorance.

I don't like politicians. I've met far too many of the breed and in my opinion they're all overpaid, underqualified, ego-tripping, self-serving power addicts who are more harm than benefit. I could remove one of those from Picino's list: when it came to law, he was certainly qualified. But what he made up for in one regard, he more than compensated for in his ownership of the other flaws. As to the Premier, I'd never met him, I hadn't voted for his party and, since I tended to either ignore press reports or disbelieve those I couldn't avoid, I knew next to nothing about him beyond that he and Picino were political soul mates and, according to rumour, friends. Neither of which worked in his favour as far as I was concerned. And there he was, with a single question outstanding: why?

I also don't like surprises and the look I threw Picino as his boss was shaking hands with Maya would have broadcast my displeasure loudly and clearly. He gave a quick apologetic shrug and silently mouthed NMC. It was a joke from our days of university and catholicity; Latin as in *Non Mea Culpa*, which means not my fault. I'd assumed that; I wasn't annoyed about the Premier being there, I was angry at Picino for giving me no warning. Then again, perhaps Picino had also been surprised;

along with everything else, we'd discuss it later. I perceived there were no note-takers or other support people present. The Premier noticed me noticing.

'We felt this discussion might be more effective if we kept it between ourselves. As far as the staff in this building and anyone else who asks is concerned, this is an informal chat about this morning's press release and I'm getting an update in the presence of my senior legal advisor. The reality is, and here I'm being absolutely frank, I, and others, are concerned. It seems this whole issue may end up clouded by fanatical obsessions and Indigenous politics instead of simply focussing on the fact someone is attempting to convince the people of this country that we're in a Harry Potter film where witches fly, shapeshift, and conjure up infernal death and destruction. I mean, this is Adelaide in the twenty-first century, not darkest Scotland in the twelfth. Therefore, Mr Miller, what now?'

Ignoring his adventurous potpourri of popular culture, historical periods, and geographical locations and feeling confused, I was under the impression he favoured Henry burning on a pyre, to persist with the current theme, I explained the morning's surprises were exactly that; we'd expected them but later, not sooner. As to where they originated, only God knew, and since we weren't talking at the moment, I wasn't convinced he'd agree to cooperate.

The Premier didn't smile and I recalled hearing he was Catholic, which partly explained why he and Picino were close, apart from their shared political ideology. Rome's spiritual version of the Freemasonry boy's club, gender ins-and-outs intact, was a global uniting force. Or should it, I thought, be farce?

Picino's devout family, especially the joyless women, made the Inquisition look like an atheist support group. He'd always talked the talk, English, Italian, and Latin versions, convincingly, while behind the pious exterior beat the sceptical heart of a born-again pagan. I'd found it funny in the old days — the pragmatic heretic, desk drawers packed with rosary beads and a crucifix necklace keeping company with the expensive whisky and Swedish porn — making pretences at piety to keep his mother and aunties happy. Now it was integral to his public persona the fact he was overtly saving a soul covertly up for sale aroused more pity in me than the humour of times past.

He'd often laughed at me for my attempt to maintain my integrity and many of the comments he made recently showed he still was. But I was sure the mirth was covering a degree of envy regarding my convictions; I'd chosen a path and travelled it whereas he wandered in whichever direction the capricious winds of opportunity blew him.

I abandoned my cognitive historicising and returned to the present, explaining to the Premier that Fenwick's widow was a devout believer, and magic, whether initiated by godly priests or devil worshippers, would definitely be embedded within her faith. I went on to add that I suspected her of the letters and leaks but there was no proof. The Premier said he agreed with my suspicions and would be taking steps to see what could be found. I formed the impression he was not enamoured of the Fenwicks' project, which may have accounted for his involvement; I made a mental note to ask Maya to conduct more research.

I went through what we had, taking care I gave no hints that anything I knew could have originated with Picino. The two seemed to be allied in this, and they did belong to the same political party, but Julius Caesar was stabbed to death by those he regarded as friends and many an Australian Prime Minister has been escorted to the scaffold by past colleagues. I trod carefully, trying to ignore Maya's eyes as she heard about a collection of anonymous sources she didn't know we possessed.

'I'm working on the concept that the accusations thrown at Henry Day are worth nothing without evidence. The two never met and according to my information, influence by magic, for lack of a more accurate term, has been recorded but in every case there was need for personal contact or the victim having knowledge of the curse. It doesn't matter if they label Henry a magician or Kadaicha or whatever, or they point out Fenwick was a believer, a committed one, and was vulnerable to suggestions. No contact means no transmission of a curse means no case. For them to formulate an accusation would be like trying to accuse someone of violent murder if the evidence proved those accused were in another country at the time. Beliefs are not proofs and supernatural imaginings have no place in law as accusations of wrongdoing. As you said, this is here and now. The post-enlightenment world where secular law is the rule, not religious bigotry and ignorant superstition.'

I liked the last bit. I didn't intend to admit to anyone I was quoting Madison Rundle with a level of plagiarism I never employed as a student. I supposed it was in the nature of professional development, which all legal practitioners are mandated to continue throughout their careers. It proved I'd been listening though. More than could be said for the long lectures on business law I'd mentally zoned out of in the neighbouring building.

We talked for another half hour but there was nothing

else to say, so no one said it. I told the Premier I'd inform him and Picino of any developments immediately and he didn't believe me, while he told me he was one hundred percent behind me and Henry and I didn't believe him. To sum up, two politicians, one a lawyer, and two lawyers, one me, in a room; the odds in favour of truth and honesty were in the vicinity of sub-zero. Those two sought to clear Henry's name but without sacrificing any votes. I longed to have Henry found innocent but without losing my business. And Fenwick's widow was desperate for someone to blame and might of public ignorance was in her corner or soon would be, if past demonstrations of the reactions of the thoughtless masses were anything to go by. Not to mention her collective of conservative God-fearing politicians who'd rally to any cause that might display their moral righteousness and, as a side benefit only, needless to say, influence the ballot count their way. Politicians do serve the people; most of all the ones living in their own houses. As we left, I felt as if we were breaking out of the asylum.

As we entered the freeway, a phone rang. My business one. Maya took the call and listened then told me to pull over. I stopped in the emergency lane and behind us our escort did the same. She put the call on hold and looked straight at me: eyes wide and excited.

'It's the ABC. They want to interview you. On air. TV type air. In the morning. The breakfast program, you know, the one with the pushy woman journo and the guy in the blue suit. They want you to present your point of view because the public… you know… all that crap. Well, yes or no?'

What else could I say? There was an urgent need for

me to get what I wanted to say out there and what was on offer would be my best chance to present our side of the story to a broad audience. As I heard Maya telling them she'd call to work out the details as soon as we were back in the office, I drove off with a smile. The morning's shocks may have seemed a bad start to the day and the meeting with the eternally-vacillating Premier and his personal Renfield hadn't improved matters but a nationally-transmitted ABC interview was definitely a move forwards and in the right direction.

I'd have settled for a sound bite outside my office from a sympathetic journo; an interview on the most-watched breakfast television in the country surpassed any of my expectations. I knew the programme was based in Melbourne and I'd be interviewed via a video link but I often watched it and half the time the interrogators and interrogatees appeared to be tête-à-tête. It didn't matter; I was getting the opportunity, which was the important issue. It called for a celebration.

I stopped at Crafers — ironically in keeping with my elevated mood, the highest point on the freeway — for petrol and we both had an ice cream. I was in generous mode, buying two extras for the cops. They seemed pleased; trailing round after us can't have been a career highlight, although doing favours for Picino might be a career booster. And a free ice cream bought by a defence lawyer was not something they'd get every day. The story would do the rounds.

Once we were in the office, I told Maya to get Basham on the phone. Then, while I was talking to him, to try and contact Mrs Jessup. It was essential to determine if they'd told the press and ask them independently before they could discuss it. I was almost certain they hadn't; I trusted them and was convinced they wouldn't lie about it.

Half an hour later I knew for sure. It wasn't them: neither said anything to anyone. My money was still on the grieving widow or someone close. If I could only talk to her. Yeah, right, I figured: two chances!

Maya informed me I'd be on air at seven thirty-ish, which meant I was required at the Adelaide studio early. I decided to spend the night in the city; there were friends who'd happily put me up. One call and I was set. I needed to go home to pack a change of clothes and my notes before repeating the trip to the city. I'd done it more times in the last few days than the previous six months.

I love freeways; the chance to listen to loud music and drive fast — although not too fast was the new norm — is terrific but even those delights could get old if this went on much longer. I didn't think it would; news stories based on smoke and mirrors tended to vanish through a quickly-recognised lack of anything substantial and the human race's predisposition to minute attention spans. Once this was all shown to be no more than a nine-day wonder, I'd be back to wills and divorces, hopefully not my own, while Henry and the Fenwickian psychodramas would have been erased from the public consciousness.

I asked Maya to call the Fosters: make sure Henry was okay and ensure he was kept away from the television. I remembered I was going to call Dean to get security on the house; I asked her to do it and he promised there would be someone in place as soon as. Picino, in the end, would be paying the bills and I could afford to splurge. A sort of unofficial tax rebate without the hassle of trying to communicate with the Tax Office electronically or intellectually. I was convinced my phone connection from last year was still listening to hold music.

I couldn't think of anything else and headed for home. I knew the interview would be confronting; The ABC's political ferals didn't achieve their fame for their insightful interviews by exhibiting reverential politeness. It would be a challenge. But if I could discount, as per Madison Rundle's material, any claims regarding the potency of magic, augmented by Henry's lack of involvement, the mutually-supportive medical reports, and the video evidence, as shown on and owned by the ABC, that Fenwick had, to put it accurately if a tad callously, simply switched off at the moment in every politician's wettest dreams when the cameras were pointed in his direction, I could present a viable defence. Henry had no motive, no opportunity and, most significantly, no means.

Whereas those seeking to promote the accusations had nothing beyond a distraught woman's hysterical allegations and a risible contention that weaponised magic was feasible. The might of right and the lure of logic were on my side: what could go wrong?

13

The problem with rhetorical questions is that people line up to answer them. The morning began well. I drove the short distance from my friends' inner-suburban house well before the rush-hour reached its full fury. I arrived at the ABC building at two minutes after six, parked the car, and was met at the door by a young lady who looked like she was on high school work experience. It transpired that she was filling in time as a minor functionary while striving to reach the exalted heights of weather presentation. I'm paraphrasing but somewhere on the journey from entrance to make-up room it's what I heard. Twice.

I'd been on television before, although the experience hadn't prepared me for what awaited that morning. Standing on the court building's steps being screamed at by a ravenous horde of scandal-hungry ghouls seeking the sustenance of a titillative sound bite was a far cry from being ushered into a small room with three chairs positioned in front of large mirrors where a woman who looked like my auntie invited me nicely to take a seat then started to decorate my face. A dab here, a touch there, a step back and a critical appraisal then more squodges of goo and tissue wiping. Half afraid to speak I told her not to get carried away; I didn't want to make my first appearance looking like Dame Edna. She laughed and continued sloshing and brushing.

Then it was off to a waiting room near the studio where I was to hang around until air time. Obviously, I knew nothing about any of it until next year's meteorological icon told me. I was sure she was new; she was gazing at me and chatting, clearly attempting to ascertain if I was like, you know, like famous or like important or like something like, you know, like worth mentioning to her like, you know, friends. I like, you know, tuned out, settled in, and like, you know, waited.

There was a copy of the day's paper, I took one glance and threw it back onto the table. I was disgusted with what I saw; if they asked, I'd happily have given them a more flattering picture to use. It had been a long hot day in court and I'd changed my clothing and lost weight since then. It didn't matter; in a few minutes I'd be seen as the new me. Nice suit, unwrinkled shirt, conservative tie, trimmer physique, neat hair, composed manner. The image the public would remember, the one they saw that morning over breakfast.

Before long I was in a studio. In a comfortable chair, facing a huge monitor showing empty seats in a studio in Melbourne according to a graphic in the top corner. The soon-to-be climatological celebrity brought me a glass of water and fussed around me, made sure I was settled in alright, stuck an earpiece in my left ear, clipped a microphone to my lapel, ran a wire inside my jacket, and fastened a small box to my belt, all while telling me repeatedly there were only like you know, a couple of minutes to go. If she was to be the future of weather forecasting, I would hang up a length of string and rely on the old if it ain't wet it ain't raining style of meteorological divination.

Suddenly, a woman's face appeared on the monitor, almost life-size. It looked as if the person about to interview me was Katia Pavelli, a political journalist normally referred to by her initials. She waved cheerily and, assuming she could also see me, I waved back. She mouthed Hello but I heard nothing before someone nearby obviously realised from my non-response I lacked volume and provided it. I asked the someone why the morning programme's usual presenter was not interviewing me as Maya was told. In a tone suggesting I was out of touch and irredeemably ignorant, the someone informed me she'd left the program a while back, her replacement was unwell, and KP, the ABC's premiere political reporter was filling in. She added that the story I was involved in was one of the top issues of the day, meaning whoever held the controls decided to award my interview the best journalist in the business.

As I digested those facts and my ignorance regarding breakfast television staffing, I remembered that KP, whose usual role was hosting a night-time panel-based brainstorm session renowned for its hostile audiences, was famous for her astute political disembowelments on camera. If I'd known I was to be interviewed by her, I wouldn't have accepted the invitation. Then the opportunity to back out was gone; the familiar voice was speaking to me and I was talking back.

It was slightly surreal, like something out of Star Trek, the disembodied long-distance chat and the face on the screen, but Katia, after asking pleasantly if we could be on first name terms to which I agreed, attempted to put me at ease with a discussion about how it would all happen and what sort of questions would be asked. Also, not to be offended if she seemed to cut me off; time was in short supply and she wanted me to be as informative as possible considering the limitations. I said it was fine. It sounded easy; she asked, I answered, repeat as necessary.

Off to my left I could see another monitor with the main programme showing. The other presenter, the one Maya called the guy in the blue suit, and he was, could be seen in front of flashes of sports footage talking earnestly to a muscular and immaculately-groomed female journo I

knew from seeing her before to be an ex-Olympian —
although in which sport was a mystery — in a short skirt
and long heels. Even without audio, the interview
scenario conveyed hardly anything about sport and a
great deal about encouraging male viewers to pay serious
attention to her segment. It featured the subtlety of and
possibly the same costume director as a Beyonce music
clip and was a far cry from the old days when sports
journos wore check jackets and beer guts.

It was time. ON AIR signs lit up, as did Katia. She
faced her camera and began talking confidently; I faced
mine and listened nervously. She smiled at the audience,
I didn't. One of the first lessons I learnt as a practising
lawyer: if you smile too much, you appear to be mentally
trivial while offering the impression you are not taking
the legal process seriously. Consequently, I reminded
myself, no smile, listen to Katia, speak clearly and
confidently. And adhere to the wisdom of the Bible:
refrain from anger and turn from wrath; do not fret, it
leads only to evil. Or, as Alex put it: keep your cool, no
matter what. That's the post-gentrification version of her
precise phraseology anyway.

Katia looked me straight in the eye. At least, that was
how it appeared when I watched the playback later. In
reality the ocular connection travelled through the eight
hundred kilometres of air space and incalculable lengths
of wiring separating us. It was unnerving having her
electronic image staring at me and knowing mine was
returning the gaze. I've used Skype and Teams many
times with relatives and colleagues interstate and
overseas and I don't find it natural or comfortable. I tried
to relax and her first words helped. Mainly because they

were aimed not at me but at the viewing audience.

'Recently a member of the senate, Alan Fenwick, passed away during a televised sitting. Subsequent tests have failed to determine a cause of death and the conclusion reached was that it was simply a matter of natural causes. It remains unexplained. This isn't a unique phenomenon and in fact, there are a considerable number of equally inexplicable deaths each year. Most are accepted, and in those cases, the grieving relatives, with no viable alternative available, surrender to the inevitable and accept that they will never know what caused their loss. However, in the case of Senator Fenwick, there has been a development, a claim all isn't as it first appeared and there may possibly be a cause of death to be considered. An accusation has been made that the senator was murdered and the method used was a hypnotic or other suggestion implanted by an Aboriginal man who lives in Parnham, a town in South Australia's north.'

She rolled on, covering in detail the various issues prevalent in the town and, following the draconian rules of social inclusivity, described how they affected the local population in general, the Indigenous community, the Chinese buyers, the religious groups, and Veronica Fenwick who, in reality, this was all about. Henry, at the centre of the whole affair and the alleged villain, didn't get a mention. None of what she said was fabricated, but the truth was given enough of a racking to gladden the most demanding Spanish inquisitor.

In other words, she did what reporters always did and put a misleading spin on it to guide listeners towards the subliminal message: the tacit lie. Prevarication is an effective technique, one I've used in court and television advertisers exploit every day. KP is skilled at it and I'd admired her expertise many times: this wasn't shaping up to be the latest addition to the tally. Once the viewers were mesmerised into accepting her revisionist equivocations, it was time to hear my version. She explained who I was and began attempting to guide me in the direction she required the interview to go.

'Mr Miller, you're Mr Day's lawyer, is that correct?

'Yes.' The one-word answer took her by surprise; she expected me to fill in the silence. Only guilty people do that. First year legal studies, Common Law 101, first year of marriage, Common Sense 101, the legally-mandated right to non-committal silence in action. She recovered quickly.

'How did that happen? He doesn't live near you and you've been involved in no legal work in his area. How did you meet?'

Predictable; I was prepared. The law-lecture staple, the five Ps, in action. Prior planning prevents poor performance.

'A friend recommended me to him and, for legal reasons, I'm not able to provide any further details.'

Somewhere I sensed Picino fondling his rosary beads and gasping a sigh of relief. The breathing space was short-lived though.

'We were informed you were asked to act for Mr Day by someone in government. Is that correct?'

Hells Bells! Picino would want to know where that came from. Me too. In spades. A miniscule number of people knew he and I spoke: either there was a leak or they were guessing. If the latter, they were doing a bloody efficient job of it. Too well for comfort.

'No. I don't know who told you that but it's simply untrue.'

If the true story came out now, I was royally screwed. A clear breach of legal ethics, known as a perjurious falsification, enacted on national television and as preserved for eternity as Fenwick's passage through the veil. Picino and I could share a cell. She went on, clearly not prepared to accept no or my denial as an answer.

'Would you be prepared to reveal who your connection is?'

'No. Would you? Tell me who told you? Of course not, journalists don't have to reveal sources as outlined in section 72B of the Evidence Act of 1929, as you and your employers know. Well, neither do lawyers as outlined in section 119 of the Evidence Act of 1995, relating to private communications between lawyers, their clients, or third parties. In other words, our confidentiality, like your own, is mandated and protected by law. And, for the record, my answer to your earlier question is still no. I can't give an answer if I don't have one to give. I'm a defence lawyer, the government and I barely communicate, the only thing we collude in is avoiding each other.'

Gotcha, I thought. I was practised at reading faces. I knew from a side glance my image was going to air as she spoke but the monitor in front of me still had her face on it. It's usually subtle to the point of invisible through long practice but even lawyers and journos have tells. There was a flicker of her eyes, possibly at the teleprompter or maybe she was listening to a producer's voice in her headset. Whatever, she'd blinked when she should have blanked.

If I hadn't been paying close attention, I wouldn't have caught it, and if I didn't do what I did, I might not either. But I used to be a cop, then a lawyer, I'd had Eva for a girlfriend, Picino for a friend, and lived with a teenage son and a sneaky dog. I could pick a lie blindfolded at midnight in a dark room; with her features magnified on a big screen right in front of me, it was not even a clever trick. It's a matter of knowing what to look for. I knew she'd try a lie, or perhaps misdirection is more accurate, eventually. And it didn't work. I wasn't nervous anymore; this was like being in court and I was in my comfort zone. Thus armed, I readied for her next predictable move.

'Our research shows you and the Attorney General, John Picino, were at university together.'

Maya said someone would find out and run with it and we prepared my answers. All convincing, all shot the connection to bits, and all were true. It's not a combination that turns up in court often: this would be easy.

'That's right, we were.' No point denying what would be bound to come out. Her next question was equally predictable.

'It's been suggested his involvement in this case, and maybe others as well, could be seen as beneficial to your legal practice.'

We saw that one coming but not in such strong language. Picino would be pissed and the ABC would need to be careful to avoid a defamation suit. She realised her blunder and sidestepped.

'Obviously, no one's suggesting any impropriety on his part, but friendship does have its perks. Nothing illegal, more a quiet word now and then.'

Nice try but not a full recovery; my response was ready. But I was seeking to let her dig herself in deeper. This wasn't why I'd come on the show but apparently it was why I'd been invited. Oh well, tease the dog, you get bitten. I'd let her have one more poke with the stick she'd chosen and then it was my turn. I shouldn't have been enjoying myself, as far as the case went, it was a waste of time. But she started it.

'No. Nothing at all. Someone has misled you.'

'Not only did you study together but we're told you were close. His wife used to be your girlfriend.'

Bingo! 'Well, that's true. I have no intention of going into details, this isn't Dr Phil, but we had a fallout while we were at uni and haven't spoken since. I have been to his office where we exchanged information only once, and that was yesterday. It was our first meeting in years, and there were two witnesses present who will support my claim that we didn't conspire in any way.'

I'd have loved to be a fly on the wall if she challenged the Premier on the content of our meeting. Even she-who-scares-PMs would have trouble with that particular assertion. I was in safe territory as far as our meeting was concerned which is why I mentioned it. It knocked a hole in any assertions about Picino and me and the way I'd worded my answer meant I wasn't telling a lie. Misdirect, okay; lie, not. It's a fine line but one I wasn't keen to cross. I went on.

'Also, three of the people I knew at university are serving long prison sentences, one other is an executive in your organisation, and yet another sits on the bench. As is the case with me and John Picino, I have not talked to any of them recently either, except for the judge who I acted in front of five years ago. I won the case; are you going to claim there was conspiracy due to our historical connection? How about your executive who I distinctly remember having drinks with in the UniBar, is he also suspect?'

Maya's suggestion, and a genuine zinger. There was no way Katia would put someone senior at the ABC in the firing line, therefore my use of him as a subtle threat ensured my other former uni associates were equally protected. Including Picino. Especially Picino, who by then was probably strangling his rosary beads and churning out Hail Marys on an industrial scale.

'To sum up, no one in the government contacted me to suggest taking Henry Day's case. A friend put us together, I took the case, and that's all there is to it. Now unless you have any more non-existent scandals to bring up, please may we return to the reason I was asked to be here?'

As I was doing my outraged-innocent act, I saw her listening carefully but not, I was sure, to me; it looked like her producer was using her earpiece to offer behind-the-scenes prompting. She gave a small smirk, it quickly vanished. Something in my head said oh-shit but I couldn't do anything about it. She spoke and something in her tone was different. A touch of confident assertion not there previously. I'd seen her acting similarly in other interviews; it was reminiscent of a hungry lioness catching a scent of fresh blood.

'Certainly, Mr Miller, I'm sorry, there was no offence meant. Perhaps I phrased it badly.'

Which was true but her intimation of badly as in inaccurately, which signifies error, didn't gel with the reality of badly as in improperly, which signifies malign intent. I couldn't guess which was in play; perhaps a blend of the two. There were reasons she was one of the best interviewers in the business and it wasn't because she was necessarily nasty per se; she was merely mercilessly insightful. Ask many of our retired Prime Ministers. She won't be getting honourable mentions in their memoirs; she's part of why the adjective former features prominently in their political biographies.

I ignored the issue and moved on. 'The accusation made was Mr Day somehow caused the death of Senator Fenwick, and how he might have achieved it has me and my staff, not to mention Mr Day himself, totally mystified. Apart from that no viable evidence proves such things possible, even if it did then anything described as such would require contact between the two men for a suggestion to be implanted in Senator Fenwick's psyche or for another, perhaps psychological, transfer to take place.'

I went on, shamelessly quoting Madison Rundle and supplementing her academic language with legalisms supporting her points. Katia sat there watching, made the odd interruption for clarity and to remind the viewers and her bosses she was still in there and punching. I shared my new-found knowledge about how curses were impossible because magic is all manipulation and trickery with no place in this enlightened day and age. Simply because someone decided to make an accusation didn't mean there was any offence committed under laws which, as it happened, didn't include it as either a proof of causation or, in fact, mention it at all. I wound it all up by reiterating the lack of contact hypothesis almost word for word as I'd been given it by Madison Rundle.

I expected them to cut me off; I went on for several minutes. But for some unknown reason I was allowed to continue. I assumed I'd been convincing and entertaining not to mention newsworthy. When I finished, she smiled at me and thanked me in a way I took to mean it went well. I was feeling pleased. All I wished to say I'd said. The earlier misgivings seemed foolish as I waited for her to do the wind up.

'Thank you. I wonder if you would mind if I asked one

more question before we run out of time?'

'No, of course I don't mind.' When you're on a roll, keep on rolling.

'While you were speaking, our producer relayed something to me we'd appreciate your feedback on. Our Sydney office received some information yesterday and one of our people, in the company of a member of the Parnham town council, looked into what it said. What they found was this.'

A school exercise book with writing on the cover appeared on the screen. Another shot, what looked like the same book but open at a double page replaced the first. On it was list of names.

'It was stored at the rear of a filing cabinet along with other records of similar meetings and community business. Naturally, we handed it to the relevant authorities. This is the attendance record of a meeting taking place in Parnham six months back. The list includes all who attended. It comprises the guest speaker, Senator Fenwick, plus almost everyone in the town and surrounding areas. The subject under discussion was the sale of a local property to a Chinese consortium which was causing dissension and anger in the community. Senator Fenwick was in favour of the sale and the meeting was an attempt by him to increase support by pointing out the advantages to the community. Have you heard of that meeting, Mr Miller?'

I agreed I had. Since the meeting was reported in the media, it was hardly new information. Which I also said.

'Yes, but this might be.' As the screen changed to a close up of the names, I stared in shock. One name was there that shouldn't be. It was at the bottom of the page and appeared to have been put there by the same writer as the other names and with the same pen. Basham told me it wasn't there because the named person didn't attend the meeting. As I was assured. But it was there. My brain rained expletives as my mouth said nothing despite being open in disbelief.

'One of the main arguments you put forward against any possible accusation of Henry Day is that he and Senator Fenwick have never met. Well, according to this attendance record that's not true. As we can all see, Mr Day was at the meeting. Taking it into account, Mr Miller, were you misled or are you misleading everybody else?'

I was too stunned to speak. Knowing how it would look to the whole world but I stood up and walked out of the studio. I stopped at the dressing room to retrieve my belongings and paused as I realised I was still wearing the earpiece and other equipment. I hauled the wire out from inside my clothes, rolled it all around the box complete with earpiece and microphone and threw the whole thing at the wall. Fast moving electronics and solid concrete are incompatible and the sound of it shattering was unbelievably satisfying.

Having imagined doing such a thing was almost as fulfilling as doing it for real. If I'd been stupid enough to do it, with my luck, it would still have been turned on and the whole country would have witnessed the final act of my meltdown. It would probably have been a close imitation of my reputation disintegrating, with the wrecking noises lasting less than a second while the ones from the damage to my life went on considerably longer. More calmly than I felt, I placed the equipment carefully onto a desk and left.

Answers to rhetorical questions are rarely given and equally rarely welcome. The one following my what-could-go-wrong musing of the previous day fell perfectly into that category. I received it at precisely seven forty-two, Adelaide time. I know because I've seen the playback. Alex recorded my interview for posterity but what it more resembles is me exposing my posterior.

Fenwick died on public television and my career, while not following him into the afterlife, wasn't in the bloom of health. I used to enjoy blind-siding the prosecution in court with unheralded surprises; Katia Pavelli, ABC political assassin extraordinaire, did the same to me. Ambushing me using those tactics might possibly count as a breach of journalistic ethics but were more likely to be seen as a victory for media-instituted transparency. In front of a jury of tens, if not hundreds, maybe even thousands of thousands; the court of public opinion. The one I'd hoped to seduce with my televised appearance.

My reputation was not the important issue. An important one for sure but not *the* important one. In only seconds, Henry's chances took a dive from reasonable to seriously endangered. Some shadowy bastard falsified evidence to engineer the demise of our case, and I had no idea how to resurrect it. Sitting outside the building afterwards, I felt only anger at whoever was trying to, and clearly succeeding in, ruining Henry's life for no purpose I could think of.

If no one ever heard of him or of me, then everything taking place in Parnham would have gone on to widely-welcomed obscurity. Fenwick's widow should have been focussing on grieving more than aggrieving. The countless gullibles who were convinced that the supernatural imaginings portrayed in schlock horror movies and low-budget low-brow TV shows could occur in life needed to get one. Politicians should concentrate on the bigger picture and stick to ruining the country in toto, not one citizen at a time. And country lawyers should not accept phone calls from treacherous ex friends.

Persecuting the old man was unnecessary and unpleasant; there was no gain to be had. With the riddle in mind, I kept wondering why. Soon, if not sooner, the phones would start ringing and many others would be asking me the same question. They, like me, would be angry. And, like me, the person they'd be angry at was me. I'd fallen into a trap through impatient carelessness and there was no one to blame but me for what happened. I fought off the anxiety gaining momentum in my thoughts and started the car. There was no music to suit my mood and I drove in silence but for the accusations filling my head. They were deafening, and in my own voice.

14

I made it home without a speeding ticket although I'd been well over the limit several times. Perhaps my guardian dark angel, Picino, watching over me. Or maybe it was luck. I went fast and didn't get stopped, a small win, but they're usually the ones you value the most. I tried to use it to improve my mood.

I stopped at the office and told Maya we'd be leaving in five, ducked in next door for a moment, said hi to Alex, got a hug and a sympathetic condolence in front of a mystified patient, and headed off to talk to my client. Somebody was lying not only to me but to the entire nation. I couldn't recall asking Henry if he'd met Fenwick, it simply hadn't occurred to me he might have. But now it was time to determine what the truth was, what the lies were, and to reinforce the one and refute the other.

Maya stayed silent but her face spoke for her. I'd made a serious error and I could see she knew it and wasn't going to say anything. We trailed a cloud of dust along the Fosters' driveway and pulled up next to their workers' hut now repurposed as a hideout for those accused of committing murder using thought waves. I turned to Maya.

'Obviously, you saw it. Honestly, who didn't? Despite me proving to the entire country I'm an incompetent who does poor research and the fact our client is considered to be more guilty than before because the well-presented argument I presented on television has been shot down in flames, I'm still convinced the whole thing is complete crap made up by someone with a grudge.'

I took a breath, necessary because I spoke loudly and

quickly, and to stave off the rising panic. My racing heartbeat was pounding in my head and causing my chest to ache, and for a few frantic seconds I suspected I was having a heart attack. Alex once told me lawyers don't have heart attacks for the same reason snakes don't have knee replacements. Remembering the terrible joke and seeing the concern on Maya's face plus a couple of deep breaths and my pulse slowed from a full gallop to an unsteady canter. When I could continue, my speech was also slower and quieter.

'What that grudge is and why it exists is beyond me but starting with Henry, I intend to talk to everyone involved to find out. Are you with me on this?'

I knew she was supportive: I deserved the caustic response. 'Van, get bloody real. That's not fair, you know I'm with you. You were set up. Well, perhaps not set up as such, it looked to me like the info about the meeting attendance was a late arrival. But she could have stopped the interview and warned you. Instead, she cheated and stabbed you from behind, and you bombed out. And as for the comment about being incompetent and a poor researcher, being honest, as a researcher you are a bit slow. And inaccurate. And unimaginative. And uber-dependent on me. And–'

I stopped her by joining in her laughter. It felt wonderful despite its bitter taste. Plus there was the boost of confirming she was with me. And also right, I'd not been ambushed as much as not given the respect of a warning. The two things were different. If KP started the interview knowing she was going to come at me from left field, I'd be far more angry. But to introduce a late-breaking flash was effective journalism. A mite disrespectful and recognisably unethical, which is an accurate description of most journalists: the reputable ones. The rest defy description, or anything you'd verbalise on prime-time television anyway.

Maya went to get out and said, 'Okay, it's time for the team of Wright and Wrong to go to work,' leaving too quickly for me to formulate a response. I exited and we climbed the steps side by side. I still felt a need to rip someone's head off, figuratively if not literally, but I wasn't sure whose. I was relieved I'd calmed down. It wasn't the first time Maya's sardonic humour withdrew me from fury to a more considered and controllable anger. I sometimes wondered if Alex, who was an expert at it, taught her the trick or if it's a chick thing. One day I'll ask, carefully omitting the word chick from the question. Women may be nurturers but they can easily turn into neuterers if proper care isn't taken. KP was a definitive archetype of the breed.

Ronan opened the door wearing only a pair of running shorts and a sheen of sweat. Judging by the indrawn breath to my left Maya noticed. We followed him inside, me first for his own protection and to frustrate his new admirer, and found Henry slouching in a big chair. He stood up, shook Maya's hand at length and mine almost unnoticeably. I thought for a moment he might have seen the news and that was why I was getting the miniscule attention, but I remembered their cultural links and our lack of them and told myself to stop being foolish. I repeated the auto-didacticism when she was offered the best chair and a drink.

It was not until I, too, was handed a drink that I relaxed. Henry lost his wife many years back and was enjoying the company of a woman and the opportunity to be nice to one. He also lived in a country where affluent white men once and still served his people badly and he was possibly enjoying the opportunity to be dismissive to one. I wasn't sure what was behind the favouritism until I saw the unmistakeable gleam in his eyes as he passed a drink to Maya. He might be elderly and frail but something in there was still alive and kicking. Which explained why I'd been relegated to second place in the greeting roster. I knew how he felt; when I'm up close with Alex, every hormone I possess starts reliving the last five minutes of Riverdance. If Henry could still feel some hints of the vibe, then perhaps I had a few years yet to go.

Social conventions over, his attention changed direction. With regard to the case, I was the focus of his interest. I saw Maya lose his attention and felt his eyes boring into me. Pre-game warm up over, it was time to kick off. I liked sporting metaphors; most of my clients could follow them with almost no mental effort involved. About the same miniscule amount they put into obeying the law, which is how I wound up with them as clients.

Clever criminals went to big law firms where equally clever and, in my opinion, often equally criminal, lawyers misrepresented them to juries. There I was, a simple country lawyer defending a simple country gentleman in what might easily turn into the least simple case of the century. If it was on television, I'd have enjoyed watching it. Then again, after my disastrous collision with the medium that morning, I doubted I'd ever turn the damn thing on again.

In the car I'd chosen to let Maya start the questioning, but Henry's obvious respect for the older male in the partnership changed my mind. Men's business only. Maya worked out what was happening and remained silent. I assumed it was a cultural thing; males in certain societies have more regard for other males than they do for females. It wasn't, considering many of the women I knew, remotely defensible. But the chances of early twenty-first or even early twentieth century gender equality finding a home in Parnham or even mainstream Australia in anything like the near future were marginally south of non-existent.

In the town where I lived, less than an hour from a capital city and populated by many educated women, the old paradigms were dug in like cattle ticks. At social gatherings men strutted, hogged the grill, guzzled beer, grunted obscenities, farted, and kicked footballs and each other while women cut up salads, sipped wine, and discussed children and gardening. When Alex was present, her frustration became palpable, and by the time we arrived home, there was a stockpile of outrage bursting from her in waves.

Years ago, we worked out how to fix it. We left Rob there with his friends and went home alone. She ended up calm, as did I, if being unable to walk, speak, or breathe normally counts as calm. I was sure I was atoning for the sins of my gender when I was being assaulted, but if hell contained similar punishments, I'd buy a lifetime ticket. I realised I'd been lost in thought and Henry was staring at me puzzled. I refocussed. No offence to Henry but going mentally from Alex in Victoria's Secret to him in an old blue singlet was less fun than it sounds.

'Henry, as you know someone has said you caused Senator Fenwick's death by magic. Do you understand?'

His face screwed up and I wasn't sure he'd understood but then he cackled loudly and I realised he was laughing. When he spoke, his poor articulation was hard to follow but, as he squeezed each syllable out inchmeal, I caught the drift if not all of the words.

'Yeah, right. I do magic. Get rich, yeah? Get car. New clothes.'

He offered a valid point and showed an unexpected grasp of irony, although I knew from Basham and Mrs Jessup plus our short time together, what he said could not be taken entirely literally. He wasn't as poor as he made out, owned no car because he had no driver's licence and nowhere he wanted to go, and as for the worn clothes, I'd seen worse threads on lawyers on weekends. What he was saying didn't totally add up but if he chose to go with the poor old Aboriginal man schtick I wasn't about to argue with him over it.

It answered my question, though. He understood the accusation. I wondered if anyone spoke to him about it but rejected the idea. The Fosters wouldn't and neither would Ronan; Dean's people knew getting involved wasn't part of their duties. The opposite, in fact. Finally, I decided it was a simple concept and he'd spent time thinking on it and gotten his head around the idea. Which was helpful. What came next might not be so straightforward.

'Henry, I've been told magic, you know, putting a curse on someone, can't be done unless the two people meet and it only works if the person who's been cursed knows about it. It only happens if someone believes they can be cursed. Is that right?'

He looked totally confused. I went through it again, step by step and pausing if a word or phrase seemed to lose him. It took a while but eventually his face cleared.

'Yeah, s'right. Fella don't know, he don't get magicked.'

'Right.' Long journey, first hesitant step taken. It was hard work. I'd talked to slow clients in the past but this set new records. I'd keep going, syllable by syllable, until we got there, though; if we were forced to progress at a tentative crawl for me to glean enough out of it to formulate a decent defence strategy, then crawl we would. Mind you, I was thinking by then I could be well past retirement age or dead of mental exhaustion.

Maya told me to take a break and give her time to talk to Henry. I went outside, sat on a chair under the verandah, and watched the sheep eating and shitting. They weren't putting on any false fronts, which was a relief, and knowing they hadn't seen the morning news allowed me to relax in their company. I was fast asleep about an hour later when Maya came out. She woke me with a nudge and sat down smiling.

'Okay, Van, got there. Henry understands what he's accused of and that we don't know who's doing it. He says he wasn't involved in the dispute over the Bilden Downs sale even though he was concerned about the sacred site issue but as far as he knew it was close to resolved and he decided to keep out of it. He isn't an activist for Aboriginal issues, doesn't make trouble, keeps to himself, and barely remembers Fenwick's visit. Someone mentioned it to him, he thinks it was Mrs Jessup, but he's not sure. He knew about Fenwick's death, thinks he heard it from her as well but he can't remember when. Much later is his best guess. He wasn't interested; according to him, one dead white politician is a step in the right direction, laugh, laugh. When I asked if he was at the community meeting, he says he hasn't been in the place for years and if his name is on the list, then someone put it there to, and I quote, make bloody mischief. Why, he has no idea. Probably the same person who is, also in his words, stirring the shit about him in town. Basically, he denies being there, which means he denies meeting

Fenwick, which means he could not have cursed him, which means someone forged his name in the book to mislead us all. He has no idea why anyone would do it but he did add if long distance cursing was possible, whoever it is would be the one he'd do it to first. He found the idea amusing, and seems to be finding the whole thing ridiculous. He's kept to himself for years, minded his own business, offended no one, and yet he's been blamed for a death he believes no one's responsible for. Sometimes people, he says, just die. No reason, no part in it by anyone else, and it's simply how life is. End of. He wishes this would all stop although he likes being here. The people are nice and the hills and greenery are more appealing than the flat browns of Parnham. He has a point; how can anyone live out there?'

I was gobsmacked. 'You got all that? In such detail?'

She smiled. 'Obviously, I'm paraphrasing and translating Henry-speak into Maya-speak and filling in the gaps. But, yes, in essence, it's what I got from him. Van, he was never there. I believe him and you should as well.'

I told her I did and it was true. Which put us back dealing with the nonsensical idea that magic, even if doable through some form of suggestive or chemical transfer, demanded personal interaction. There'd been none: Henry's involvement was a non-starter. The problem was we were convinced but everyone else was equally persuaded he'd been there and cast an evil eye on Fenwick. My original thinking concentrated on the premise, as Madison Rundle put it, that curses don't jump. However, disproving the theory about magic doing long-jumps was no longer necessary; that the two men seemed to have been proximal changed everything. Maya agreed.

We said goodbye to Henry and Ronan, who'd disappeared during the talking and disappointed Maya by putting on a T-shirt. I blew the horn as we passed the Fosters' house. When it was over I'd offer to pay them, they'd refuse, and then a big bank transfer from the government would turn up recompensing them for unspecified clerical errors. Picino would play the game; I may not have trusted him with some things but he always paid his debts, as did I. Ronan, too, was spending time away from the city; I'd make sure he was looked after. Right then it was time to visit the office, say a longer hello to Alex, and do serious strategic planning. Otherwise known as lunch.

15

Alex joined us at the café and we brought her up to date. We walked back together and Maya and I settled into my office. I suggested tea and she went to stand but I told her to wait. Through the gaps in the vertical blinds, I saw two men walking towards our front door and knew immediately who they were. Maybe not who, but definitely what.

Put a mixed bunch of state and federal cops in a room together and every one of them will know immediately who works for whom. Out of uniform cops from different states possessed minimal signifying differences, but they're all vastly dissimilar to the feds; the AFP and other federal bodies stand out. These two, with their tidy haircuts and dark suits, might as well have been wearing AFP vests and holding up their IDs. In Adelaide, they would have been instantly recognisable to an ex-cop like me; in the Bridge they stood out like two Great Danes at a cat show. I scribbled something on a piece of paper and told Maya to make the tea as I handed it to her. As she went into the rear, they came in the front, closing the door behind them and locking it. One of them pulled on the chains closing the street-facing vertical blinds as the other stood in guard position behind him, glaring at me.

The blind-closer was tall and well-muscled, the other shorter and running to fat. Both were armed — if you know where to look and what for, it's unmistakeable — and neither was smiling.

I stood up, stuck out my hand, and said, 'Hello. I'm Van Miller. Can I help you?'

Not surprisingly, neither of them picked on my poor grammar or responded to the outstretched welcome. They moved nearer to my desk and stopped. The taller one, who on closer inspection appeared to be the older, though both were still some time short of thirty, did the talking. I expected a deep voice, perhaps with rough edges. What I heard was a well-modulated baritone and an eastern states accent; Sydney would have been my guess if I cared enough to make one. His professional base was more important. My estimate was Canberra; ACT feds have an air about them. I'd been on a course once with three of them and by week's end, the rest of the participants were desperate to shoot them. Some, over drinks, worked out how they could get away with it. They were not generally liked or likeable. That's how these two looked.

'Mister Miller, agents Doherty and Barron, Federal Police. We have questions we need to ask you.'

Quiet yet commanding but with a hint of uncertainty. I understood uncertainty, but years of court appearances and angry meetings taught me how to cover it up. Either they hadn't yet learnt the trick or they were not confident about what they were there for. Why was the riddle; why were they there and why were they short of confidence? It was not a normal characteristic of the feds, whose self-confident stances usually reek of arrogance. With those two it was absent. The best way to exploit their lack of assurance was to assert my own. I delivered my next demand straight to their faces in a strong voice, a courtroom tactic proven effective when questioning police witnesses or anyone overly assured of their own assailable position due to position, connections, or birthright. I didn't play poker but someone who did taught me the art of bluff; act as if you have a winning hand at all times and never flinch.

'Show me your credentials.'

I was annoyed they hadn't followed proper protocol

and showed their identification before speaking but that wasn't important. What mattered was I was trapped in the office with two armed men who may or may not have been what they claimed. If they were, the issue was probably containable; they had rules to follow; I knew what they were and we could sort this out. Whatever this was.

But if they weren't who they said they were, the situation was different. They could, I knew, be from the ACA, the neatly-styled hair and suits hinted at conservative religiosity, from another group connected to the case, or were here for unspecified reasons I wouldn't like either. Whatever, I was a tad nervous. Not scared yet, but definitely edging in that direction.

They whipped out wallets and flashed them past my face too quickly for me to read anything. I insisted on another look and they ignored me.

Maya came back and put a tea mug and a stack of files on my desk. The two men ignored her completely and kept their gaze on me. She asked if they would like a cup. The shorter one answered.

'No. Sit down. Who are you?' Maya told them and they seemed satisfied, as if they expected someone of that name and description. I tried again.

'What can I do for you?' No response. There are people who believe ominous silence and a fixed gaze is an effective way to put people off balance. I'm one of them; I'd used it as a cop and in court. Now I was on the receiving end. Not for the first time, but judges, intimidating as they may be, are not armed and court rooms are public places. In the office, with only the four of us, I was feeling the strain. So...

'Unless you have a legal reason for being here, I'd like

you to leave. I used to be a police officer, I'm now a lawyer, and I know the regulations. You need to identify yourselves and state the purpose of your visit or leave.'

If my words influenced them, the effect was too subliminal for me to pick up on it. A moment's silence then the tall one put his hands on my desk and leaned towards me, his forehead furrowed into a scowl and his mouth turned down in disapproval. Before I'd been worried; the amateur theatricals stopped my fear dead, and I was more curious than worried. What next, I thought. Threats? Well… yes.

'If you don't tell us what we need to know you'll find yourselves in a lot of trouble.'

Now, as well as being intrigued, I was amused. Not that I'd show it. There are people you can laugh at; those who steal their dialogue from bad movies and worse TV shows are not the ones. They tend to take themselves too seriously to appreciate the humour and react with anger and violence.

Knowing what feds looked like, I was half-convinced they were the real deal, but the other thing I knew for certain was that if that was the case they were not destined for success in their chosen field. Those ranks are filled with people who can apply subtlety and carefully worded questions, not hack lines and body-language clichés.

'You're the lawyer representing Henry Day, right?'

I confirmed I was and they looked at each other and nodded. Considering I'd been on national television and the front pages of most newspapers their deduction and self-congratulation were hardly a major achievement but from the way they smirked you might think they'd solved the crime of the century. I was still amused, although the aura of threat and that they were armed took some of the shine off the amusement.

'We want to know where he is. Where you're keeping him. We need to question him. He's a suspect in a murder case.'

'Seriously. Feds are now investigating murder. That's new. Demanding access to someone from his lawyer, with no warrant, also new. All before any serious legal accusation has been made, this is getting worse by the minute. Threatening a lawyer and his assistant in their own office and seeking to take their client away for questioning. I don't know whether to laugh or get angry.'

I was saved from having to choose. A new voice entered the room. It was emanating from the mobile phone poking out from under the files Maya placed on my desk. I recognised the speaker.

'I think some of both is called for, Van. Hello to the two men in Van Miller's office. Do you know who this is?'

The two men looked at each other with puzzled expressions, clearly wondering how someone else had managed to enter the conversation. I knew, my note contained an instruction to Maya to go into the kitchen, get Picino on the phone, and tell him to listen without speaking. The tall one took the bait.

'No, I don't. And I don't care who it is. This is federal police business and it's private. Go away before you get yourself into trouble.'

Oops, I thought, *bad move*. I didn't say anything. Just waited and watched. This was going to be interesting. And fun!

'This is John Picino.' Short pause, with no response to the name. Which, by Picino, would have been considered an insult. Better and better. Or, for the visitors, worse and worse.

'Sir, as I said we are federal officers and we are here on a matter of official business. Again, please hang up and allow us to do our job.'

'I don't doubt you are who you say you are. But I happen to be the Attorney-General for South Australia and I'm wondering what you two are doing in my state, harassing respected lawyers, and attempting to interview a man who hasn't yet been charged with any crime and even if he was, murder is a state issue, not a federal one. Do you know how many local and federal laws you are breaking? Van, how many do you reckon?'

'I count five but I'm out of date. What do you think, Maya?'

'I make it eight but there may be more federal ones. Let's make it eight minimum with an option of a few extras.'

The two men looked as if they'd been hit by a bus. What should have been an easy ride had turned into a train wreck in a matter of seconds. The one leaning on my desk straightened up.

'We're leaving but we'll be back. At that time, you'll need to tell us where Henry Day is.'

They both turned to leave. I grudgingly gave them credit for trying to brave it out and extra kudos for their escape attempt but their suits and official arrogance were not going to be the get-out-of-gaol-free card they expected. I watched as Picino's voice stopped them dead.

'There's an Alan Whiting on my other line. Know the name?'

I did. The senior AFP officer in the state and not a patient man. I'd met him once; it was enough. I could see the name was familiar to my intruders. Picino wasn't finished. I knew the tone in his voice. He was pissed off and about to go seriously ballistic on these guys.

'Alan says, and I quote, if you're not in his office in Adelaide two hours from now he'll be taking your IDs and weapons and travel documents and you can hitchhike back to Canberra. Personally, I think he's joking but, then again, you never know. Even considering the traffic two hours is possible. However, before you go could everyone look out of the window, please?'

This was where it would get somewhere beyond interesting. When we were at university, a leafy-suburbs doctor's son named Patrick called Picino a wop and seriously insulted his girlfriend of the moment. Picino didn't respond and walked away. A week later Patrick was hauled into the security office after an unignorable quantity of drugs was discovered in his backpack. Who put them there and told security was a mystery. Picino swore it wasn't him and I believed him because he produced a verifiable alibi; what high-achieving law student wouldn't? But I knew he knew who did and was behind it. The doctor complained to the university that Picino framed his son, they all attended a meeting, and the top-of-his-class law student showed why he held the position and how he'd later become a successful lawyer and politician. Legally outgunned, the doctor apologised, his son followed his example, and then, the master stroke, the university accepted Picino's convincing arguments that Patrick was not the type and someone must have put the drugs in the pack, and that Patrick was undoubtedly innocent. The moral of the story was, try not to antagonise high-achieving Italian law students who not only know the meaning of vendetta but could summon up cultural atavisms of how to employ it effectively. Picino rubbed the jerk's nose in it in front of his father and two faculty bureaucrats then shown how easy it was to make him feel worse, putting him in Picino's debt by proving his innocence. Unmistakeably Italo-traditional old-style payback: Picino channelling Machiavelli, who we'd both read and one of us hero-worshipped. Now he was about to do something similar to the two inept clowns who threatened someone he knew and invaded his legal, political, and personal sovereign territory. If the two were convinced it was already bad, they had no idea how much worse it might get. Neither did I but, unlike them, I was enjoying the waiting to see.

I liked the please, Picino was always polite when he was on the threshold of taking someone apart. Playing chess or tennis, practising law, running for politics, stealing girlfriends, humiliating out-of-bounds cops, it didn't matter. When he became polite, somebody got shafted. The two peered through the blinds. I didn't, I knew what might be coming. Not in detail, but the Picino of old would milk this until dry, and he'd do it legally yet mercilessly. The lawyer, the politician, and the total shit all acting in concert. Machiavelli's Prince, on whom Picino, when we first met and probably still, modelled himself, would have been ecstatic with pride. I confess to similar feelings; it was masterful.

'There are three police cars out there and five officers. They've been instructed that two armed men, as yet unidentified, have invaded that office and wish to surrender themselves. I need you to place your weapons on the floor and go out with your hands in the air.

Quickly, please. If you don't and you're still in possession of your weapons as you exit the building my officers will assume you have hostile intentions and open fire. As they should do, in defence of the public. There are dash cameras in their vehicles and I can see the entrance on my computer. If something like that happens, I'll be a witness to their actions and they'll all receive commendations at about the same time as you receive indigent funerals. Your choice.'

Their bluster gone, faces downcast, they did as directed. I watched from the door as they were locked into the rear of the paddy wagon. I knew the cops by sight, especially the sergeant who gave me a cheery wave as she climbed into her vehicle. One of the officers said hi to us then retrieved the weapons from the floor. He went to one side and cleared them, placed them in an evidence bag, and took it with him into the passenger side of the wagon. It took off in the wrong direction to be heading to the local station. I'd suspected it was Picino playing games and now I was certain. He confirmed it by laughing.

'Did you like that, Van? The five outside were in on the joke, they know it's feds acting up unofficially and they'll deliver them to the AFP office in a while. After a short stop outside the remand centre in the city to put the wind up them for a bit longer. Anyway, now I have to talk with Alan Whiting who'll speak to their supervisor and maybe by late tomorrow we'll know the story. Somebody made an error, and whoever it was will regret it. Talk soon. Ciao to you both.' As he hung up, I heard another chuckle. He'd had his fun and I knew he'd have more before it was finished.

We locked up and drove home. There may have been a humorous element to what happened but there was a serious one also. Somebody, somewhere, was taking this to another level.

As we pulled into the driveway, I saw a four-wheel-drive and a caravan parked off to one side. I stopped the car as the caravan door opened and two people stepped out. I recognised both. One was Colin, another of Dean's employees; the other was Cheryl, Colin's girlfriend.

Their first meeting was the stuff of legends and the story, as recounted by Dean, was funny even in the repeats. Colin, working security at a nightclub, found himself set upon by four drunken dickheads. By sheer weight of numbers, he was losing until a girl stepped out of the crowd of onlookers and booted the biggest of the four between the legs from behind. After the setback, the other three were easy for Colin to handle.

Cheryl told Dean later Colin was getting his arse kicked and it was much too nice an arse for that to happen. She was also famous for her comment that stationary testicles and fast-moving Doc Martens shouldn't socialise. It was, Dean reported, love at first fight. After mastering less genitally-destructive techniques and qualifying for a security licence, Cheryl joined Dean's firm. She and Colin preferred working together and apparently looking after my house, complete with mobile accommodation, was their current joint project. Assuming half of what Dean told me about them was accurate, if they made love, I assumed the caravan would be unlikely to survive the night.

After the introductions, Maya disappeared in the direction of her place as I went inside and poured a long drink. I decided to tell Alex the afternoon's events then sleep. Or not. I was wound up. The case was getting to me. I had to talk to someone about how I was feeling. I was hoping Alex was up for a chat. She was. I told myself for the millionth time being married to a doctor was the best thing to have happened to me. I knew it was; I've been told the same thing countless times by a doctor and everybody knows you can trust them.

We talked for a while but I was too tired to stay awake. We went to bed. As a couple of long drinks and Alex settled into place within and without, I was drifting into sleep when the phone rang. I turned the bedside light on and answered it.

'Van, it's John. Picino.'

'Yes, John, what can I do for you?'

Behind me I heard Alex mutter something her mother would have disapproved of. Picino must have caught a hint of it as well.

'Oh, is that Alex? Tell her I said hi.'

Considering they never met and if they did, the most likely outcome would be her going to town on him verbally, it wasn't a greeting she'd welcome. I was right; Alex's reply was muffled and fluent Athenian dockland. I translated. 'John, Alex says hi back.'

A punch in the shoulder. I must have grunted or something because Picino asked if I was alright. I said I was and moved out of range.

'Van, what happened today has people stirred up. Those two morons are on their way home, probably in the baggage hold, if Alan Whiting has anything to do with it. The phones have been ringing hot in Canberra. They were, it seems, told to go there and try and bluff you into revealing his whereabouts, have a chat to him, and report back. It's the story I'm getting and I think it's only part of it. Some clown way up the food chain leaned on someone lower who talked someone else into despatching them here. No names given or admitted, and I suspect they never will be. Much loss of face and what's left is seriously red. Meaning it's federal denial and cover up time. Which is fine by me, since there's no real harm done. They were concerned I threatened to have their officers shot which is when I followed their example and did the denial routine in return. Neither side believed the other but for the sake of pragmatism — well, you know how it works.'

I did, and I didn't like those types of political machinations. Since, for once, they were working in my favour, I said nothing. Picino knew me as well as I knew him and he heard the distinct and strident disapproval contained within my silence. He allowed me a moment to grieve for the death of my soul, as he used to describe my crises of conscience, then proceeded to make it worse.

'However, what's concerning the collective gods at Mount Olympus is what you'll do. If you go public, you gain back much of what you lost this morning but at the same time you'll probably alienate many who are prepared to support you. Not to mention giving the federal government bad publicity which they don't need or want. Agreed?'

'Agreed. Is that what you called for? To update me on the management failures of our federal bureaucracies and try and talk me into taking pity on them and not profiting from their ineptitude?'

'Were you thinking of doing that?' Questioning and challenging: an unpleasant combination and a familiar Picino approach.

'I hadn't been, but since the idea has come up...'

He interrupted. 'I have a more helpful idea. In truth, I didn't have it, they did, but it's a more productive way to go all round. They avoid public ridicule and you end up with part of what you desire. Van, which people would you like to talk to if you were given a free choice? About the case, obviously, Kylie isn't part of the deal: don't even ask.'

'I don't need to think about it. Veronica Fenwick and at least one of the pathologists. But there's no way... Hang on, are you telling me if I don't make a public issue or legal points out of today's circus you can fix for me to have meets with those people?'

'No, I can't. But I know someone who can. He has been on the phone refusing to take no for an answer from anyone. Tomorrow, no, hang on, it's after twelve, which means today, and the real tomorrow, you have meetings with the widow Fenwick, who is cooperating under protest, one of the pathologists, a Professor Hamley, who is agreeing on the promise of a free dinner, the Indigenous member of the House of Reps, Linley Manning, who is already poking her nose into it and is probably the only genuine one out of the whole bunch, she's likely to be doing it to make Black Lives Matter bonus points, and the PM, who is making it all possible because... Well, God knows why he's doing it. Oh yeah, in the interests of natural justice for all. Avoiding a political and judicial scandal is the last thing on his mind, as I'm sure you realise.'

He laughed and after a second I did too. Hearing such an amoral apparatchik openly chiacking the profession he cherished membership in was a rare delicacy to be savoured.

Picino was back in professional mode. 'Anyway, I'll make sure the flights are booked, courtesy of the Government's tax-funded tourist centre, no strings attached. I'll get you on something early, probably about eight or nine. Okay?'

'No. Too early. I need sleep and there's the drive down. We'll be there at twelve, lift off whenever. And Maya is coming with me as my independent witness, make it two tickets. I don't trust you much and them not at all.'

'Van, you can't tell important people what time to expect you or add people in. You have to go along with their plans. You only, there by late morning Canberra time, as arranged.'

'Fine with me. How about you go and explain while I ring the ABC and organise another appearance? KP and I are best friends now and we have an unfinished interview to resume. With recent additions she's sure to love.'

Two minutes later, barely on speaking terms, we hung up. I rang Maya, apologised for waking her, and gave her the updated itinerary. I settled back onto my pillow, leaving the light on, waiting for what was coming.

Alex stuck her head out from the covers. Her words and voice showed how annoyed she was; her dark eyes went even further. 'So you're off to Canberra? You and Maya? To talk to the angry widow, an incompetent who was unable to determine a cause of death, and vote-hungry parasites. This isn't getting better; it's going under. I'll drive you to the airport in case it goes totally off the rails and you end up in an offshore detention centre.'

'Not funny. No, we'll be fine. I'll drive and leave the car in long-term.'

'Van, do you need a hearing test? I'm driving you. Okay?'

She stared straight at me as her mouth asked the question her eyes were answering. The Greeks invented the rhetorical question and she was an expert in using it to make her point. Sometimes, to annoy her, I'd answer them, but discretion, also known as cowardice, seemed to be the better part of valour, also known as foolhardiness.

'Thank you, love. That would be nice.' Not a hint of sarcasm entered my voice but I did intend, for a change, to have the last word. 'By the way, one of those parasites we're meeting is the PM.'

I knew PM was not a word but an acronym. Close enough.

16

The three of us, showered, dressed, and in my case freshly shaved, breakfasted together at eight the next morning. Alex was mostly silent, mood painted visibly on her face. When her eyes were aimed at me, I could see anger, sadness, concern, doubts, and love. Actors spend years trying to learn to convey each of those emotions individually. Only when the emotions are heartfelt and inescapable can they be seen together in a single look. I smiled at her, suspecting what she saw was as transparently false to her as it felt to me. Before Maya arrived, we talked. I was worried, she was worried, and, seeing us, Maya was starting to look worried. Hat trick!

One of Picino's elves rang to inform us we were due to fly out a few minutes after midday. The e-tickets would be at the counter; we would be going via Melbourne and returning via Sydney late the following day. Alex made a suggestion Maya and I both agreed with and I asked for alterations to the return itinerary to include twenty-four hours in Sydney. Also, could someone please speak to the most senior person in the Chinese group purchasing Bilden Downs and request a meeting. If I was going to be armed with information, it was prudent to ensure I was fully equipped.

What I'd been told about the impending deal was probably only one side of the story, and a biased one at that. All it would cost me was an overnight stay in Sydney, and eventually Picino and the taxpayers would settle the account. The caller agreed to organise the requisite flight changes and forward the request then hung up abruptly.

Alex finally smiled, whether due to my following up

her suggestion or because remaining morose was too difficult to maintain. Her hesitant smile lifted my spirits and induced a similar effect in Maya. For better or worse I was, and they by connectivity were, trapped in what was happening. I felt both up and down simultaneously. I was compelled to back out but, conversely, was raring to go. The contradiction felt bizarre but somehow not unpleasant. Later I'd be treated to the unpleasant details of an autopsy by one of those experts who, professionally hardened concerning dismemberments of the dead, was likely to fill my thoughts with Shelley-esque gothic imaginings destined to haunt my thoughts for days. And nights! Also bizarre and everyhow not pleasant.

I'd been there before; on a scale of one to ten, my dislike of medical horror stories was a fifteen and rising. On one of our early dates, Alex described a particularly gruesome corpse she dealt with, an old woman finally found after two weeks sitting on the banks of the Styx waiting for the ferryman — or in her sad case a less-than-proficient social worker — to finally turn up. It took a large amount of alcohol to calm my stomach afterwards. She apologised profusely, distracted my mind nicely in recompense, and never described her work in graphic detail again.

Of all the arranged meetings, the one with the man who made his living exploring the makings of dying was the one I anticipated least keenly. Ronnie Fenwick, in the flesh, was something to look forward to for obvious reasons, a notion I failed to mention to Alex for equally understandable ones.

The rest fell somewhere between the two. Racially-motivated activists made me nervous, as did all dedicated cause-driven fanatics, whatever their culture or fixations.

Maya could be one under certain circumstances but most of the time she kept her ethnically-based passions in check. The person I was due to meet was, I knew, a professional campaigner for Indigenous rights. In my view, the country, and especially those she agitated for, required such people, and I had no adverse ideas about them and what they did. Only occasionally about how they did it; the democratic process should never deteriorate into a battleground.

I was still at home and there was a growing sense of occupying a besieged city as the invading armies gathered outside the walls. I'd been feeling that way since initially hearing Picino's name on the phone the first day; by now it was a familiar sensation. Familiarity, though, was not creating comfort but unease.

As I mulled over my misgivings concerning self-inflicted punishments, I finished packing. What was one night turned into two and wearing the same wrinkled garments to meetings with those with immediate access to unlimited supplies of fresh threads would be a poorly considered move. I packed a small case containing shoes, shirts, and what my gran used to call sundries plus my flask full of a twelve-year old Scottish highland distillation included for medicinal purposes only, a suit carrier with three suits, and a carry-on bag filled with papers to discuss on the flights.

To travel, I was attired for comfort: jeans, a soft cotton shirt, my old hiking boots. A thick woollen coat with every step of its many voyages visible was tucked between the handles of my carry-on; we were going to Canberra and I'd learnt the lesson of the occasional arctic conditions of the nation's poorly-situated capital long ago. I survived the near zero temperatures by purchasing suitable clothing during my first visit, including the boots, coat, and thermal underwear. Alex laughed at the thermals initially but when we travelled there together, I arm-wrestled her to get them back.

I neither have like nor dislike of Canberra, but I actively hate the frigid winters they experience that someone long ago described to me as a perfect fit for the emotional mindsets of those ruling the country from there. I considered it a harsh judgment at the time; since then, I have met many political types, including a Deputy PM, and changed my views to a full agreement. Public service and genuine emotion seem to be mutually exclusive. Many of the elected make the news regarding their negative activities; few get the same attention with respect to any positives. Maybe it's because lust sells more papers than love; I'm certain the media's cognitive processes originate somewhere marginally south of their navels.

Alex and Maya waited impatiently as I vagued out on irrelevancies, fussed over my packing, and generally dawdled in a doomed attempt at postponing the inevitable. Mutterings of complaint and impatience were delivered in stage whispers. The luggage was carefully organised in the rear of Alex's Toyota and we were on the road by nine-thirty. Alex, who never speeds, always seems to arrive much earlier than I would. She doesn't listen to music in the car which, she claims, means she can concentrate on the job in hand more effectively. Also, unlike me, she seems to arrive at every set of lights on the green.

Whatever her secret, we parked at the airport at a few minutes to eleven and by ten past, retrieved our boarding passes, ambled leisurely through the security checks, and were seated in a café with hot drinks and a sense of having achieved something. I was glad Alex drove us; the city traffic and parking hassles would have me on edge and seeking alcoholic sustenance. Being chauffeured negated such issues and we made idle chat as we waited for the flight to be called.

Maya appeared calm and was not. I, according to Alex, looked stressed and was. Alex was worried but hiding it well and I knew she would have preferred to be going with us or talking me out of going at all. The customary positive vibes were conspicuous by their absence and the boarding call was a relief. Alex and I hugged, kissed, touched hands goodbye. The women hugged, Alex wished us both good luck, and we proceeded through the check-in and followed the other passengers along the jetway.

We were in cattle-class which, on the deliberately no-frills airline, named after one of the more inconceivable biblical mistranslations, meant occupying a space with dimensions last considered suitable for human travel in the era of wooden slave ships. It was possible we were back there because business class was full which, I'd noticed in passing, it was. I, though, suspected the hand of Picino, exercising his warped humour at our expense. Speaking of expense, I made a mental note to jack his account up by another ten percent. Those cheap seats were going to cost him more than the upgrade.

Maya and I waited for an overweight guy in a death-metal T-shirt, whose deodorant and mouthwash were on strike to stand up and allow us to squeeze past him and into our seats. I sat by the window while Maya ended up in the middle: rank has its privileges. The arm-crushing closeness caused him to give her an admiring look and a friendly grin. Her stony expression sent him facing front and probably induced his hyperactive sweat glands and stale saliva, not to mention other less immediately displayed bodily fluids, to all go into drought mode. Normally she was more sociable; the day, and the case, were getting to her. I knew the sensation but I could handle it better. Age, experience, a window seat, and a state of Zen-like tranquillity achieved by taking two hefty belts from my flask before placing it back into the case to be surrendered at the check-in counter.

The stop in Melbourne was too short to grab a drink but long enough to visit the facilities without enduring the cramped conditions the same activity on the next flight would entail. The plane was half empty and we left the middle seat vacant. We talked in general terms about the case but with the seats behind and in front occupied, there was no real opportunity to get into it in depth. The first meeting was for seven; time enough at the hotel to discuss strategy far from prying ears.

The flight was short and we were reclaiming our baggage when a middle-aged man in a suit walked up and asked if we were who we were. Since we were he smiled, grabbed a bag with each hand, and asked us to follow him. What awaited was the expected government car, mid-sized and lacking frills, but after the plane, the rear seat of a VW Beetle would have seemed a luxury.

Our driver handed me an envelope containing a short note. Apparently, the PM was unable to meet with us due to the pressures of his position. Translated, he was staying away from any personal involvement while permitting his wife's proxy use of his power to support her friend. It's called politics: whether national, state, local, or familial. I looked on the upside; there was no necessity to be polite to him. Which was the one part of the day I dreaded most, even taking my upcoming meeting with the pathologist into account. Now I could spend the day acting like a defence lawyer. Defensive. Aggressive. Offensive. Regressive. Sometimes I like the freedoms inherent in my profession and self-employed status.

We sat in the back and gazed out of the windows as the scenery floated past. Maya had never been there; she was looking at everything. I had, and while I may have been facing the window, what I was seeing was the possibly bleak futures of my client and my business as a series of discomforting images. Later on, I'd be talking to Doctor Hamley; his expected Boschian word paintings would soon drive my own imaginings into a well-deserved oblivion. I both dreaded what was coming and eagerly awaited the distraction.

The hotel was a considerable improvement on the flight, mainly because I'd picked it. I'd stayed there twice before and while it wasn't five-star fussiness, it was comfortable and the restaurant served great food. Maya's room was next door but one to mine on the fourth floor and both were a short walk from the lifts. The plan was I'd meet Hamley and she was off to see the sights. My appointment was for seven at a city restaurant I hadn't heard of but was one the doctor apparently liked. Which no doubt meant it was expensive and upscale. I made a mental note to collect receipts.

As I sorted out a tie and shirt to match, Maya arrived in jeans and a bright coloured windcheater. I told her the expected after-dark temperature and she vanished, returning a minute later with a heavy coat, gloves, and a woollen beanie. We moved to the ground floor bar, me with my paperwork, she with her tourist guide. Her party-bus night tour was due in an hour; plenty of time to go through the plans for the meeting.

Maya said, 'As I see it, there's three things you need to ask him. One, how common are unexplained deaths. If it's not overly unusual, why is Veronica Fenwick, who used to be a doctor, making such a fuss over something she almost certainly understands and should not be trying to blame somebody for? Yes?'

'Yes. But as far as I can tell it's been a long time since she practised medicine and the gap between a long-retired GP and someone of the pathologist's experience and knowledge is similar to a first-year law clerk versus an experienced QC. Let's not make stereotypical assumptions about medical professionals, just because she was a doctor doesn't mean she's necessarily highly intelligent or up to date. In truth, what we've seen of her lifestyle shows negligible evidence of high intelligence or current thinking. Snobbish socialite trophy wives like her tend to be insular and disengaged from the real world. If it isn't footwear, fashionable clothes, the Melbourne Cup, or anything else guaranteed to get her on the fashion pages, then it's outside her range of interests or experiences. You agree?'

Maya nodded. Her low opinion of women who spent their lives being pampered and indulging in vacuous see-and-be-seen games was well known. She'd be going to meet Ronnie Fenwick tomorrow with me; it promised to be interesting. The upwardly-mobile professional who rode a mountain bike face-to-face with the spoiled dilettante social ornament who rode on a cloud of entitlement. I couldn't wait. Alex commented on it before

Maya arrived; she expected raised fur, bared claws and teeth, and nail-spitting, even if it was all purely figurative, and requested a full report.

Maya went on. 'Secondly, how do he and his colleague feel about the accusation of magic causing Fenwick's death? I read up on both of them. One is religious although possibly only the familial Easter and Christmas obligation type of worshipper. The other has a nodding acquaintance with Richard Dawkins and shares his views, he's the one you're meeting. I think the answer will be obvious but the question is will he state it publicly and risk making political enemies or would he prefer to disbelieve in private. He's stated several times he couldn't find a cause of death as with his colleague, yet isn't prepared to commit himself to categorically claiming to know the answer as to why. Which neatly avoids being contentious while leaving the possibility open something hitherto unknown did the dirty deed. He's being a coward to my thinking, although perhaps he sees it as a diplomatic non-committal resolution. Yes?'

I agreed. The doctor was refusing to commit himself outright and at the same time attempting to avoid any intimation he might be supporting the pro-magic lobby. He was exercising tact and diplomacy. The first was often an avoidance of responsibility and the second commonly a lie disguised as pragmatic indecision. Cowardice was laying it on strong, but I was basing any judgments, as was Maya, on media reports and a couple of documents Picino hadn't officially given me because it would have been illegal and unethical.

Over dinner, and a few drinks, I was going to try to find out where the man stood as regards unexplained passings and magical murders. Then we might be in a more advantageous position to decide whether he'd make a credible witness for or against us.

'I reckon he's playing both ends, waiting to see what ends up as the middle then he can sit firmly on it.' My jumbled metaphor out of the way, I raised my eyebrows at her. 'You're up to number three I think.'

'Yup, terrific counting. Nice to know you're paying attention. Third guess, he's been got at. Someone in his position must know a bunch of the Canberra highflyers and surely many of them must associate with Ronnie Fenwick or one of her coven. Maybe he's been asked to refrain from ruling magic out at the same time as he avoids the ridicule he'd get from ruling it in. If he hedges his bets and stays quiet and uninvolved, no one can blame him either way. A hint of pressure and what he genuinely thinks is never heard. Same with his offsider. They're friends as well as colleagues, according to the press reports, which means they're unlikely to give contradicting results and will support each other with a mutual display of indeterminacy. Maybe they considered it's more suitable to imitate their patients and avoid upsetting the apple cart than to make waves and rock the boat delivering the supplies to their island.'

And I'd been convinced I could jumble metaphors.

'I agree. To sum up, why is a trained doctor not accepting the verdicts of two far more highly experienced ones? What are their views on the press reports about the use of magic? And have they been pressured to keep out of the discussions beyond simply stating collegially no cause of death could be determined? It must be hard for them, both doctors admitting, or pretending to admit, they're professionally confounded, which must be galling. Mind you, to a lot of people that sort of embarrassment is preferable to a social one. Can't find an answer we can live with beats can't go to the tennis club because we found one nobody there will let us live with.'

Having relived for a brief moment the liberalistic obsessions of my youth, I returned to the nominally-democratic present, finished my drink, the price of which was anything but egalitarian, and stood up, which was free and therefore a manifest representation of pure classlessness. I agreed with everything Marx said — Groucho, not the Teutonic killjoy with the Santa Claus topiary.

I said to Maya, 'I need to look like someone he might want to confide in. That will involve dressing to impress, eating overpriced food, and listening to his lecturing. Next time you do the talking and I'll hit the singles scene. Enjoy your sightseeing. Canberra at night, eh? Don't talk to any strange men.'

As I left, she murmured something quietly. It sounded suspiciously like too bloody late.

17

The restaurant was in the centre of the city, a white double-storey oblong block with unrealised Italianate aspirations and a black-suited oblong block guarding the door. In spite of my love of Italian food, the illusory character of the place was a turn-off. It may have looked, smelled, and served Italian, perhaps been run and staffed by Italians, but it and similar places are constructs, existing only to charge high prices to people who think paying more means receiving more. The best Italian eateries I'd been in looked like the run-down cafés I saw in the poorer parts of the Sicilian countryside, not a third-generation Australian's idea of a Venetian palazzo. If Picino's restaurateur cousin in Adelaide saw it, he'd either have laughed or taken out a contract on the architect. Behind the faux-Italianate gloss and glitz it was a social climbers' club, which told me a great deal about the man I was here to meet.

A fawning maître-d' informed me in accented English that my host, Dottore Hamley, called to say he'd be late, then took my overcoat and escorted me to a table in a secluded corner, as the doctor's assistant had been asked to arrange. Money and power talk, and every wish is granted. In places like that, mention the right name and you could order the manager's wife stuffed into a calzone and get insalata and vino thrown in.

The music was suitable, if purely predictable. Usually, I favour anything in preference to what Italian places often consider appropriate. I'm sure both Dino Martin and *That's Amore* were great in their time, but *when the moon hits your eye like a big pizza pie* on fifteen-minute replay doesn't work for me as accompaniment to food and wine.

The night's more sophisticated alternative, Verdi's *Il Trovatore*, while also Italian and operatic, meaning frantic and noisy, was thankfully muted to the point of ignorable. It wasn't to my usual taste, and I only knew what it was because a tortured electropop version of it was the hold music at the firm I'd worked for and out of a long day's bored curiosity I asked somebody with a fine arts background what it was the modern arranger decomposed. His expression as he answered announced his own aural sufferings.

I took advantage of the wait to look around. I saw several well-known politicians, small-screen actors, and a couple of famous journos I quickly turned away from, although they were totally engrossed in each other and I could have walked right up to their table and sat down without being recognised. The rest of the place was filled with those trying to look and feel successful in the surroundings and the company.

Many of them were working hard at not being seen staring at the famous seated amongst them. The few glances coming my way rolled straight on past. Obviously, there were no regular ABC viewers in the place, although my appearance, while noteworthy for its finale, would have been equally forgettable due to its brevity and, out of context, mine was simply not a famous or memorable face. I'd never sought fame and did my best to avoid cameras outside the courts. Most of my current crop of clients appreciated reticence and the few who expected me to pose for the press because I was their lawyer soon received an invitation to take their expectations elsewhere.

I experienced something resembling a Warholian quarter-hour as a cop when I arrested a dealer in a crowded pub and there happened to be a media photographer drinking nearby. My picture ended up between two advertisements on page nineteen or something equally unread; far enough from the front page for my needs.

I saw the maître-d' heading in my direction accompanied by an older man, mid-sixties, in a suit worth as much as my entire wardrobe and a tie looking suspiciously like the badge of membership of an exclusive club. His full head of hair was snow white and well styled and his scarlet-tinged cheeks stood out against the paleness of the surrounding skin. In summary, not sufficiently vain to dye but enough to favour careful grooming and power-dressing, and liked a drink but not the sun. I wasn't surprised he drank: I definitely would if my days were spent in an artificially-lit cellar communing with the decaying organs of cadavers.

He arrived and thanked his escort who turned and left: both moves looked like an audition for *Disney on Ice*. The doctor looked down at me, probably doing the same tallying up I'd done on him. Hopefully with different results.

'Good evening. I'm Richard Hamley and you must be Donovan Miller.'

I forgave him the long use of my name because he hadn't used his title. It's often only done by those who seek to impress but possess next to nothing to offer. From Maya's research, I knew the man had nothing to prove to me or himself; he'd earned his reputation many times over and could comfortably rest on his imposing laurels.

I stood and we shook hands. 'Richard, it's Van. Donovan was my mother's idea.'

He laughed as we both sat. 'I had a mother also. I understand. I don't like shortening mine, I've inspected too many dicks to feel at home with the result.'

He laughed again, I was certain the joke was well worn and might be something he used with young medical students to show them white hair and wrinkles don't necessarily signify dullness or conservativism. His voice was Australian yet cultured, no Strine in there at all, and behind the bright blue eyes I saw intelligence and awareness.

I'd been concerned I might be trying to communicate with an overarticulated, overdressed, overeducated, and overbearing version of Henry. The differences between the two men, who were only a year apart in age, may have begun with the obvious cultural variance but seemed to include every aspect of their existence. Good, now I could enjoy the meal I'd be paying too much for and perhaps gain knowledge at the same time.

'Van, do you drink wine?'

Avoiding the usual scatological responses featuring bears and woods I went with, 'I've been known to.' He put up his hand and a waiter materialised instantly. I was impressed; I've tried that with absolutely no success many times. Then the waiter called him by name and I realised it's not how you do it, it's who's doing it. Not exactly breaking news, more a reminder I hadn't made it and he had. Yet I was paying. There was something not fully kosher there. At least it explained the obsequiousness when I arrived. I may not have been one of the chosen but I was going to be dining with someone who was, hence, I was deserving of a higher degree of deference. The only bonus to his sort of affectedness was we'd receive a higher level of service than if the unidentified peasant was here by myself.

He and the waiter discussed the selection and he chose

a South Australian red from the Barossa Valley I'd drunk many times. Whether he picked it for my benefit was unclear, but at least I could relax. It was exceptionally drinkable, and I was relieved I wouldn't be sipping an overpriced snob-attracting vinegar designed to impress the social set while scarifying the taste buds. I'd been there many times also. Many of the self-appointed wine connoisseurs would drink mouthwash with a fancy label and an astronomical price tag.

I hadn't yet worked out if the dick joke had been a true sign of who he was or a test. I decided to remain cautious until I took his measure or he'd drunk enough for it not to matter. The red lines on his cheeks asserted it was a likely outcome that might assist me to pick his brains. At the prices on the wine list, it would also leave me bankrupt if Picino wasn't funding my night out.

We ordered entrées; I went with the stuffed mushrooms and he chose oysters: natural, not adulterated. I was starting to like him for his good taste and bad jokes. Whether I'd feel the same about his medical and magical opinions remained to be seen. I was trying to think of a diplomatic way to start the conversation when he spoke. His first words, low voiced even though nobody was close enough to eavesdrop, knocked any thoughts of diplomacy right out of the park.

'So, Van, unless I'm mistaken, you believe I and my colleague are either giving in to pressure to not commit to an opinion concerning Alan Fenwick's cause of death, we are cautious about offending the pro-magic or anti-magic supporters, or we are, so to speak, covering our glutei maximi to disguise the fact that two of the leading men in our profession are unable to determine what sent him gentle into that good night with no forewarning. Added to which you, and everyone else, cannot fathom why Ronnie Fenwick is obsessively determined to find someone to blame for her husband's death and since we failed to provide one, she's lashing out in all directions, one of which is occupied by your client. Which means I am, or we are, indirectly to blame for the situation you find yourself in. Am I anywhere in the vicinity of correct?'

He'd repeated everything Maya said. A different order of delivery and a more pedantic diction, plus a soupcon of Dylan Thomas and Latin medical jargon demonstrating his education included more than the dissection of cadavers and expensive dinners, but effectively the same points. She'd been right as to what I should be asking him, but the canny old bastard beat me to it. I'd been seeking to phrase the questions using subtlety and politeness and he'd asked them himself. Using neither.

All I could do was look at him; if I'd spoken, I'd have shown my surprise. For a lawyer that's akin to whipping out your dick, to use his medical term, and we, as a rule, prefer to keep our actual feelings, like our genitalia, to use my courtroom-appropriate medical term, unexposed. The expression on his face showed he knew the effect his words produced, including the use of the diminutive form when referring to Veronica Fenwick. It was not a huge surprise they knew each other and I wondered what his inability to give her an acceptable answer did to their relationship.

It occurred to me if I waited, I might find the answers to that and other questions. There was an agreeable twinkle in his eyes and I realised I was dealing with a man who'd been questioned by countless lawyers, sometimes not favourably. He asked if he could continue;

I said the cleverest thing I could think of: I nodded.

'Firstly, Van, I'd like your assurance anything I tell you is strictly between us and not for repeating in a courtroom. I agreed to this meeting because I believe your client is innocent and a victim of stupidity and ignorance. Which is why I am prepared to offer any assistance I can. Up to and including testifying in court, which, considering my profession and that I performed one of the autopsies, I will no doubt have to do anyway. I have no issues with that but what I would find objectionable is if anything you and I discussed was treated by you as evidence in support of your cause. If you wish me to present my professional opinion in court, I will. Happily. If you intend to parade my private opinions, then please let me know now and we can enjoy our meal and discuss the weather or the cricket. It's your choice.'

He took a long drink from his glass and leaned forward in a confidential and encouraging manner.

'If you give me your word, I'll happily accept it. I was informed you're too honest for your own benefit, a notable recommendation coming from where it did. I won't mention the name but you know of whom I'm speaking and while I respect his position, my overall view is he's not to be trusted. He and I have eaten here, he's the one who introduced me to it.'

It had to be Picino he was talking about; the description was too close to my own take on him to have meant anyone else. The restaurant suited him; an apparent genuineness disguising a social climbing falseness accompanied by syrupy aural wallpaper and reverential servility with enough Italian influence to satisfy if not convince. Picino, maestro of the false-front, would feel right at home. And too honest for my own good was a description he'd used about me many times before he moved on to something more vitriolic, in both the verbal and romantic senses. Definitely him: the man with no name, to continue the Italian theme à-la-Leone.

Still, a recommendation inducing others to cooperate with me was not something to let go to waste. I sought to honour the compliment, if that's what it truly was and not, as countless times before, pure mockery.

'Richard, you have my word anything you tell me is strictly between us. I may need to mention it to my colleague but nothing will be repeated further without your permission. Is that what you were after?'

'It is. I might sound as if I am being somewhat precious, nitpicking over probably irrelevant details, but my professional and private views are often at odds with each other. Not as regards the technical aspects of what I and my colleague were asked to do, but with how we feel about the way others are handling this incident. Politically, personally, and publicly. I will tell you what my feelings are before I discuss my medical findings, which will offer you a more beneficial opportunity to see where I am coming from, as they say, and an understanding of why I'm being cautious. I apologise if how I go about this might sound didactic but as well as carrying out pathological work, I also lecture at several universities. Which means didacticism is an occupational hazard. It also prevents misunderstandings, there is no such thing as too much detail when explaining a complex subject to those who have no knowledge of it. Do you agree?'

I said I did. 'I've tried explaining the law to many of my clients. Most of them know enough to effectively break it but not sufficient to comprehend why they shouldn't. My wife is a doctor who tells me constantly I know absolutely nothing of what she does. She's right, although I don't like admitting it nor do I have a burning desire to correct my lack of knowledge. I don't need the intricate medical details' — or want to hear them, to be brutally direct — 'what I'm after is more an overview I'd be able to explain with enough clarity for a jury to follow.'

'Yes, I see,' he replied. 'I'll attempt to curb my usual flair for pedantry and keep what I say relatively simple.'

I could not decide if it was an agreement or a slight and decided not to care either way. I was after information, and he possessed it. Whether it was delivered in a cooperative and friendly manner through a desire to help or a supercilious one based on a free dinner was not relevant; obtaining the information to win my case was. Still, paying for the dinner if I ended up not liking who was eating it would be hard to accept. It wouldn't be the first time, though the prices were undeniably setting the bar at a new high for humble pie washed down with bile.

It was time to put my personal feelings to one side and focus on the task in hand, which was consuming my entrée. The mushrooms were fantastic, the red wine a perfect match. I've always attempted to adopt a philosophical view of professional meetings: enjoy the benefits and ignore the negatives. I munched, drank, and tried to avoid thinking about how I might feel about my dining companion. Entrées done with, we sipped wine and prepared to pursue the reason we were there. We kept our voices low.

'Van, let's deal with the obvious first up. My colleague and I have known each other for thirty years. We disagree on many issues. Politics, music, theatre, sometimes even medical matters. Our disagreements are well known and cause others as much humour as they do us. Friends may argue without endangering their friendship, and thus it is with us. We believe the apparent disparity encouraged Ronnie Fenwick, who is incapable of discerning the difference between harmless banter and harmful rancour, to seek a second opinion when she was disappointed with the first. She asked me to re-examine the evidence because, putting it as accurately as I can recall, she was somewhat distraught at the time, there was according to her no possibility Alan could have died without external cause and that was not altered because Matthew Gedding couldn't find whatever it was. I might add, her dismissal of his professional ability caused Matthew considerable annoyance and her overt dismissal of his findings became embarrassing. She, and he, approached me, and I agreed to a second autopsy. I knew I would find nothing more but it seemed an effective way to calm her down and bring an end to the debate. Unfortunately, it was not. She still refuses to believe he died of an unknown but natural cause and the refusal is as embarrassing for both of us as it should be for her. She is a doctor, even if it was years ago and she was no more than a rural GP, and she should accept the medical evidence and grieve peacefully instead of looking for someone or something to blame. Matthew and I have a theory, Alan took a long look at the shallow non-entity he was married to and willed himself to death. Ha, ha, ha.'

He took a huge gulp of wine; I could tell the poor-taste humour was a cover up for anger. Anger could work in my favour. The professional insults she'd thrown were not acceptable at the level of proficiency the offended experts both attained. I didn't want to but couldn't avoid asking.

'Was there any pressure on either of you to produce a different result? From her or... anyone else?' I was not going to mention any names or even categories, either of which would be likely to include serving politicians. I'd be surprised if he supported Helen Ranley or any others of the lunatic fringe, but I was taking no chances.

'Not as such. There were attempts to encourage us to admit we might be wrong or we may have made a mistake: that sort of nonsense. But not pressure in the sense you mean, no one would dare. Not to us.' The 'us' was packed with self-assurance. Probably because he was becoming packed with wine. We'd nearly finished our second bottle and I only drank two half glasses. Obviously, he'd not been reading his AMA journals. Or his own blood pressure: the red glow in his face was beginning to resemble an outback sunset.

Anyway, the question was asked and well and truly answered. He was understandably upset by whatever had been said to himself and his colleague. Said, or suggested. Different procedure, same results.

The main courses arrived, both fish, and we ate as he calmed down and I mulled over what he'd said. He, they, might not have been able to pinpoint the reason Alan Fenwick made such a spectacular exit, but lack of evidence could be in our favour or act against us. It was time. I posed the next question, abandoning all pretence of diplomacy.

'Doctor Hamley, either you believe in the possibility that magic caused your failure to find something or you don't. Which is it?'

'Van, this is the twenty-first century and we live in a secular country where religious beliefs and all the other supernatural ignorances have no place. I, we, may not be able to put a name to whatever killed Alan but we can certainly attach one to what did not: magic. I know what is being said, I saw your ABC interview. You were making some excellent legal points and then you were hijacked. It was disgraceful journalism at best and at worst was ratings-seeking sensationalism. Walking out was the right way to go. If you tried to argue the point, it would have made you appear ineffectual and given them an edge. By leaving, you made a declaration of disgust at their actions and demonstrated disdain for the nonsensical notion they were trying to present to a gullible public. The unthinking multitude believe anything said by television personalities, if that's the proper description, and nothing they hear from actual experts or professionals. Then they wonder why their beliefs turn out to be wrong. I'm not a proponent of eugenics but judicious regulation in the form of a mass neutering of those proven intellectually vacant would improve the next generations of the species.'

He laughed, took a long drink, and refilled his glass before going on. 'It doesn't matter if your client and Fenwick were in separate hemispheres, different states, non-contiguous postcodes, on opposite sides of a room, vis à vis, drinking from the same glass, or making the beast with two backs together, magic can't kill because it doesn't exist. And that's that. I have heard the theories about hypnotic suggestion, and we have all seen *The Manchurian Candidate* film. The truth of it is although stage hypnotists can convince weak-minded fools to behave like demented chickens, that's no indicator they could convince a non-murderer to act against their natural instincts. Total fabrication. That, by the way, you can quote both of us on. There may be issues Matt and I fail to view the same way but when it comes to anything to do with the supernatural, whether connected to this case or not, we are in complete agreement. Singing a man to death, in this day and age? Honestly!'

That determinate speech and the unexpected final exclamation ruled out the necessity for my next question dealing with any possible hesitancy on their parts to commit an opinion possibly offensive to either side of the debate concerning magic. I was glad, considering which way his opinions were going, fuelled by the red, and after his mention of eugenics, a definitely socially-unacceptable political non-starter, who knew where we might end up?

My next one was delicate and I wasn't sure how to put it without risking offence. I didn't have to; he beat me to the punch again. I'd noticed a lot of people were doing it lately. Were my thoughts written on my face or was I only coming up with questions that were obvious and therefore easily predictable? Or, alternatively, was my approach to all of these topics in alignment with the views of others, with those similar mindsets driving us along the same paths of thought? I'd talk to Alex about it later, if she didn't arrive there first and open the discussion for me.

'I notice,' he said in a voice slurred by wine and emotion, 'you have yet to enquire as to how my colleague and I were unable to determine a cause of death. The answer's simple. Thirty years of experience, having seen every possible factor bringing about death more times than either of us care to remember, and knowing exactly what to look for and being honest enough to admit when we are unable to find anything at all. Alan Fenwick was in excellent health at the moment he died. As strange as it sounds, no element of his body displayed any symptom that could cause him to feel unwell, let alone pass away. But he did. It isn't an unknown phenomenon, and Matt and I have both spoken to people we knew, and some we did not, here and in other countries, who have been faced with the same problem. They too, have been criticised for their supposed failure, and their response has been the same as ours. If you seek an alternative result, then find someone who is prepared to deliver one, and if you want the truth, we both provided it.'

He drained his glass, the man could certainly drink, and when he ended up on his own examination table, they could enter his blood in a wine show and in all probability end up with a Gold Medal for Best Red Blend. I asked if we required another bottle and thankfully, he said no. He said it was time for him to leave, there was an early start in the morning and his customers tended to be impatient, laugh, laugh.

The man imbibed enough to put me on the floor and he spent his daylight hours delving into the innards of corpses but he could still make jokes about those he ritually disembowelled. How he remained cheery in the constant presence of death defeated my understanding; how he remained vertical and made his way unerringly between the tables was a similar mystery. Long practice at both aspects of his life was my best guess although my own currently-strained tolerance for alcohol, while far inferior in degree to his, was inhibiting my ability to formulate best or even second-best guesses or any thoughts beyond not bumping into anything or anyone during my exit.

Somehow, we arrived at the front counter at the same time. He turned and pulled me away into a corner. There appeared to be more to say and I gained the impression that without the vinic lessening of his professional inhibitions, he would have been less forthcoming. Bitterness resulting from insult or injury and fuelled by alcohol has driven many to act out of character; what he said next was something I knew he might regret later. He spoke quietly.

'My opinion is what's occurring is Ronnie's doing. She can be considerably vicious if she fails to achieve her desires. I know, all women can act in that manner, but when Ronnie is upset with anyone, whether with cause or as in this instance not, she tends to go over the top. If you're pursuing the instigator of your client's troubles, you probably need look no further.'

He appeared embarrassed at being overt and also relieved he had. 'Please don't tell anyone I said anything but at the same time don't ignore the possibility. Only someone with her money and connections could have organised it, the letters and so forth. She knows people in the area and not all of them are as trustworthy as you and I.' He paused, trying to decide in his befuddled state if he'd committed an irreversible gaffe.

I leaned closer, 'Richard, I'll keep it to myself. You have my word.'

It seemed to be what he sought to hear. 'Van, I sincerely hope for your sake and your client's I was able to provide some of the answers you were seeking.' He had, more than expected — probably more than intended — and I told him the first and skipped over the second. And he'd done it minus the gothic hyper-descriptiveness I'd expected and dreaded. As well as his admirable capacity for alcohol, he could certainly talk. I'd known many who became garrulous after a few drinks but with this guy, adding alcohol was like putting coins in a jukebox and pressing play. I assumed it must be a side effect of his profession; those he spent his days with were unlikely to be reactive listeners. Although from my days at uni, I did remember students in lectures whose detectable responses were barely indistinguishable from the ones I'd seen inside open caskets.

I thanked him as I shook his hand with barely a thought for where he'd been putting it for the last three decades. Then again, I slept with a doctor and never worried about where her hands had been: only where they were going.

I'd told him the truth, he'd helped. If he, or his colleague ended up in court, preferably several days removed from any alcohol, their contribution would assist us, their seeming lack of evidence counting as its own form of evidence. But Veronica Fenwick wouldn't be able to harness their support and, if she and the two doctors were friends or even only social acquaintances before all this, I was sure those relationships travelled the same road as her husband. Only with a cause even she'd be unable to refute.

As Hamley made his surprisingly steady progress toward the door, I paid the bill, which was painful, told the maître-d' everything had been excellent, which was true, and I knew I'd made a mistake in assuming Hamley chose this place for reasons connected to social status. The heavy-drinking idealist, character traits often seen together, was also a foodie, and the faux-Italianate atmospherics notwithstanding, the food there was fantastic. The dinner was worth the expense for a number of reasons; I was sated for all of them.

While I was paying, I asked if someone could arrange

a taxi. I retrieved my coat and headed for the door: time for bed. Tomorrow, I had more meetings and suspected they might not be as profitable or satisfying. I didn't recall having too many glasses of red but the freezing Canberra air hit my system like an electric shock. Getting into the taxi took concentration. And two undignified attempts.

I decided to ring Alex when I reached the hotel and try to convince her I was working hard. *Perhaps*, I thought, *a coffee or two first*. I asked the driver to find somewhere serving what I craved at that time of night and in a hurry. I find life-firsts enjoyable, especially when I'm several glasses gone, and going from 5-star haute cuisine to drive-through McCafé was not only funny, it was possibly all I could still afford.

18

Over breakfast I filled Maya in on my night's events while she refused to give a hint concerning her own. Which I was convinced meant it was either enjoyable and she was not going to tell or it hadn't and she was not going to admit it. She wasn't looking tired or hungover; I assumed it was a bust and said so, gaining me a look encouraging dropping the subject and moving on to my conclusions about my obviously more rewarding outing. I was wondering what was wrong with the current generation. When I was a young man the presence of someone like Maya in a crowd of guys full of Dutch courage would have her trampled in the rush. Apparently, it wasn't only music lacking balls in the newest iteration of the human race. Which, if women like Maya went ignored by the men, might well be the last. I left my musings about the parlous state of modern romance to concentrate on the two important matters in hand: unfinished breakfast and unexplained demise.

'Hamley and his colleague are pissed about the fuss being made over their lack of findings. They're putting Fenwick's death into the "shit happens" basket but there's pressure to submit closure in place of indeterminacy. To them, it's not vacillation but simply no cause found or findable. He says if the two of them can't find anything, there's nothing to be found. It may not be the answer people are after but it's all there is. Accept it and move on. The short version, it took him considerably longer.'

She was not impressed. 'It's what the press are bitching about, there must be something to be found, no one dies of nothing. But he didn't die of nothing, but of an undefined cause. Certainly not by magic, although the media are milking that explanation for all it's worth. They're catering to the stupids who will only buy papers or watch TV programs confirming what they think they already know. What was the doctor's opinion on Henry's supposed use of the supernatural to kill a man he had no reason to wish harm on?'

'Totally dismissive of any of the arguments pro-magic and he discounted the use of hypnotic suggestion, whether through immediate contact or long-distance ESP style thought transmission. In other words, whatever killed Fenwick may be inexplicable scientifically but there's no way it's supernatural, mind control, or anything related to either. He's prepared to state that off the record although he doesn't seem keen on involving himself or his colleague in publicly-discussed contentious issues. I don't blame him: I wish I'd made the same decision.'

She looked at me directly. 'No, you don't. You may have at the start but now you've met Henry and seen what's happening to him, you're enjoying the fight. You're on your white horse, Saint Van, with sword in hand and flag flying, you're ready to do battle with the legions of hell. Speaking of which, what were Hamley's thoughts on the demon Ronnie?'

I wasn't sure I agreed with or even liked her description of me as the valiant knight-errant tilting at windbags, but she was right about one aspect of it all; what began as a reluctance turned into a quest, to continue her metaphor, for justice for Henry. Hamley may have displayed reticence to commit himself openly as I was doing but his views and mine concerning the situation were identical. To answer Maya's query...

'His view, unattributable, is if someone is behind all this, making it happen, and you and I are in agreement there must be a hand guiding it, then it's probably Australia's answer to Catherine de Medici.' The questioning look demanded explanation.

'She was a sixteenth century queen of France whose use of political power and position made Lady Macbeth look like Mary McKillop.' Another facially-transmitted query.

'Obviously, you know who Lady Macbeth was, but if you weren't a heathen, you'd recognise the name of Australia's only saint. She lived in Penola, in the south-east' — the superfluity sparked a glare — 'and Mother Mary, as she's known, is extremely famous for miracles and turning a nice country town into a charm-and-relic tourism-based junkshop. Perhaps you should look them all up later. You might learn something.'

Sensing another glare in the offing I decided moving on appeared safer. 'Hamley says Ronnie, as he calls her, is nasty, vindictive, and manipulative, plus she has contacts all over South Australia, including in the north where Parnham is, meaning she'd be capable of stirring up this trouble. You know, getting the letters written and inserting Henry's name in those meeting records wouldn't be difficult to organise. But my issue isn't whether she could do it, it's whether she would. There's no motive beyond, as Hamley put it, lashing out in all directions and hoping to find someone to blame. She's after an acceptable solution to give her peace and he feels she doesn't care what it is, as long as there is one. The current lack of anything explicable, he says, is her problem. I admit she has the opportunity and the means, but any motive to aim the blame at Henry in particular escapes me completely. It's possible, but unlikely. Still, after I meet with her, I might change my mind. Or rule her out altogether.'

She nodded and went to leave; there wasn't much to say and there was somewhere to be. At eleven, we were due at Parliament House for a meeting with Linley Manning. I knew her activism might present us with yet another viewpoint on the issues or totally exacerbate the situation, but I was not optimistic about her being able or willing to contribute anything overly useful.

To assist in connecting to her both culturally and genderly, Maya was going to be leading the discussion. I wasn't in the best position to gain the confidences of a committed Indigenous woman activist whose outlook was, while not necessarily hostile, inclined to the negative regarding the opinions of someone of my age, ethnicity, and gender. Hamley would have responded less to Maya than to my membership of his Euro-originated patriarchal demographic; today we would be attempting to minimise the issue by having someone not qualified for membership of that grouping making the running. It would be the same game, with the rules and roles reconceptualised.

I'd seen Maya interacting with her cultural kin and marvelled as the educated progressive influences forming much of her character vanished behind a screen of speech and behaviour patterns denying her achievements and masking her private feelings. I often did something similar when talking to clients with minimal learning and life knowledge; complex rationalisations and well-formed diction reduced, by necessity, into something close to lower-working-class speech patterns and conceptual simplifications. It's termed code-shifting, and all professionals need to do it when they're a guest in someone else's comfort zone.

Needless to say, the politician on our agenda would

know it also, and be on the lookout for any attempts by us to manipulate her. But we wouldn't be going in with the intention of presenting a false front to inspire connection; Maya would be her own self. In her hopefully more acceptable role, she'd present the truth and nothing but the truth.

If not necessarily the whole truth. It's a legal indeterminate: some saw it as lying, others a selective variant on the no-comment option. I had no ethical dispute with using it, unless we were forced to choose between sticking to it in the face of a specific question, which would constitute a lie, and coming clean, which might derail the conversation. I decided to wait and see what developed and go with the most suitable option, reconsidered with any extra information added to the mix. In other words, we would proceed extempore. Or, as my younger self used to say, we'd wing it.

The taxi dropped us off and we made our way to the entrance of Parliament House. We were expected, our names on a list held by the uniformed security officer. My respectful professional persona completed the formalities as an impious alter ego covertly disputed a conundrum: was he employed to guard the gates or prevent the inmates from leaving?

A young woman, her dress severe and vaguely officious, was there to escort us. I'd done the tour. Less fussy than Buckingham Palace but recognisably its spiritual kin; displays of monarchal pomp, whether the inhabitants are gifted occupancy by lineage or election. It was, though, Maya's first visit to the Hall of the Mountain King, and she stared around as we followed our guide through the taxpayer-funded polished stateliness. We stopped in front of a solid and expensive-looking wooden door and the woman, whose name badge said Karen, knocked quietly but firmly. A voice, barely audible, said something I didn't catch, Karen turned the handle, and we went in.

Karen announced who we were, which seemed to me taking formality to a wasteful extreme. I mean, how many visitors was the occupant expecting at eleven o'clock? Having done her shepherding and presenting duties, Karen turned smartly and left, closing the door softly behind her. I fancied her job; minimal training involved, no conversational skills required, lots of free time, and nice surroundings.

We moved further into the room as the sole occupant came forward to greet us. She introduced herself by name, Linley Manning, no titles and please call me Linley. As with Hamley, I was impressed by the lack of formality, but she'd worked for a long time to be where she was and I felt the need to demonstrate my respect for her remarkable achievements. It would be Minister unless she further insisted otherwise. She shook Maya's hand then mine and I realised our ploy to relegate me to second chair had already occurred.

We were invited to sit at a small coffee table and as we sat Karen came back into the room and asked if we would like anything to drink. Assuming anything strong was off the menu I asked for tea, Maya coffee, and Linley nodded. I suspected it meant my usual; if the usual turned out to be a glass of red, I was going to be annoyed for not choosing the same.

We made how-was-your-trip small talk until a tray covered in silver pots, milk jugs, sugar bowls, and decorated china cups and saucers was brought in and set down and Karen departed. Appropriately, the Minister, paid by our taxes and employed to look after our welfare, poured from the pots and dispensed the appropriate cups then, abandoning her chosen profession as servant of the people, told us to help ourselves to the additives. As we milked and stirred, she leaned back and took a sip of her own unidentified beverage, which she drank minus augmentation. I sensed a herbal aroma and thanked whatever deity haunted the constitutional temple I hadn't been offered the same. Politeness and suffering, at those times, run conjointly.

The Minister appeared self-possessed; it was understandable, the odds against someone of her cultural background and with the added complication of her gender penetrating the Anglo-Australian old-boy's club were considerable. For her tenacity she earned my admiration; for some of her other efforts she gained my respect. The two are not always the same.

I'd seen her on television: the Parliament-in-concert-mode, the media, plus various talking-heads waffles. For our meeting, she was less formally dressed, and I remembered it was a non-sitting period. Cotton pants the colour of beach sand under a dark green blouse, minimal jewellery and makeup, and a dot-painted scarf tied loosely around her neck. In my suit and tie, I felt overdressed and a bit pretentious, although it was more appropriate than her in Prada and me advertising my downbeat rusticity. Maya fitted right in, down to the colour scheme: Simpson Desert tones and a brooch with an Indigenous design on it. Nice touch. Perhaps, I figured, I should have worn an appropriate culturally-motifed tie; I own one, a gift from a grateful client. But those gestures can be received either way; it was more diplomatic to stick with the non-partisan dark grey, as I had. Blue, red, or incorrectly logoed; the potential perils for the universally worn declaration of membership, the tie, were, in a political setting, beyond calculation.

As I sipped my tea, I looked around the room. There were, no surprise, Indigenous artefacts, a couple of framed parchments, random brics and bracs that looked like souvenirs, and two framed and signed photos of well-known Indigenous actors. I'd seen one in many films, including an early example where his burgeoning talent was overshadowed by the bounteous au-naturel nubility of the imported Anglo actress. The other I'd seen in a memorable Bell Shakespeare production of Othello, groundbreaking for the use of an Aboriginal actor in the title role, and some films and television productions. Both displayed a dignified gravitas in their work and were living examples of how success and acclaim are possible for all, regardless of race or origin. It was the same quality seen in the woman who occupied, and in my opinion thoroughly deserved, the office we were in.

Her opening words demonstrated intelligence and awareness while containing elements of caution. She must have known who I was and what I was seeking but, until she was able to ascertain my motivations and clarify the details to her own satisfaction, I was certain she'd tread carefully. I knew how she felt; I was proceeding in the same way. The conversation may have been a meeting of possibly-conflicting politico-legal viewpoints but the unpredictable countless shadings between the two extremes were where the dangers lay. For both of us.

'Mister Miller, Van, may I call you Van? I don't like too much formality.' I nodded agreement and she went on. 'You are in a difficult situation. As is your client. I feel sorry for him but I'm uncertain as to how I may be able to assist you or him. I have to be careful about involvement in legal issues unless they directly affect my own constituents. Since this case is in a different state than my electorate and is, unless I am mistaken, a local and not federal issue, I may be unable to provide support. However, we'll see if we can work something out together.'

She paused for effect, allowing her last words to hang in the air with their intimation of possible mutual benefit through cooperation. It's a clever trick. I used it many times in meetings, in court, and in arguments with Alex or Rob. Politicians employ it regularly in press conferences and occasionally in Parliament and now one tried it on me. It is designed to encourage: it didn't. She seemed to be expecting me to look encouraged: I didn't. What I was expecting, as a reaction to my lack of one, was for her to press the point: she did. Although not directly.

'My sources inform me he's in poor health, with limited education, and seems to have barely any conception of what's happening to him. Is that right?'

I let Maya answer. We were talking about an Aboriginal man and any comments I offered might be seen to have negative connotations containing possibilities for offence. Maya had no such restrictions: she belonged.

'Minister, it is. You're also right when you say this is a state issue but it appears to be turning into a national one, since the man who died is a member of the Senate. Someone, at this point unknown, seems to be doing their best to put the blame for the death onto Henry Day. Their motive is unknown as well. There's unhappiness at the results of the autopsies which were indeterminate. The evidence against Henry is mostly falsified and it appears the only people on his side are Van and me.'

I was glad she left out Picino and the Premier; Linley Manning may have been everything her supporters said she was and thus trustworthy, but secrets only stay secrets if you keep them to yourself. Claiming we stood alone in the fight was not a lie, it was a tactical omission. But in the building we were in, something was considered to be a truth until it was shown to be a lie, at which point it became a denial. Which is an anagram for And Lie.

So, when in Rome, as it is said. The same destructive elements bringing about the downfall of the Roman Empire existed in the building we were in. Missing were the vomitoriums and communal toilets, and here the Caesars were stabbed to death with knives made from folded ballot papers.

'The problem we have,' Maya continued, 'is the accusation of magic. Or hypnotic suggestion or mind control or whatever today's terminology is. We can't present a flat-out denial of the existence of Indigenous magic without offending those who believe in it and we can't acknowledge it exists without undermining our case. What we need to do is demonstrate it was not used. The men never met, despite the introduction of what looks like evidence they did. We know they didn't but can't prove it. We also know Henry has never involved himself in anything spiritually or supernaturally based, but again we can't prove it. Those accusing him have no proof he did anything but they've thrown enough mud for much of it to stick. If this goes to court, which would be damaging enough to Henry regardless of the verdict, then the weight of public opinion alone might be influential enough to carry the case against us. Judges know who pays their salaries and jurors tend to think what the television tells them they should.'

The last part was pure Van-think and I was unsure if it should have been included, but too late, it was out there, come hell or high water. Maya, as if regretting the unprofessional vituperation, was looking stressed. The case was emotive and she was talking to a woman she admired greatly for her achievements and high position. The combination of those factors and her outburst was making her nervous; I could see the repeated clasping and unclasping of her hands. But her voice remained steady and she'd summed up our dilemma in a few succinct and comprehensive sentences.

One day I knew she'd be a formidable lawyer, possibly reaching similar heights to the person she was addressing and the two in the photos. A credit to herself and her culture as they were, and someone I'd be sure to avoid opposing in a court room. Although at least if I lost, I could tell everyone I taught her all she knew which is why she was so effective and successful. As Shakespeare put it in Hamlet, I'd be hoist with my own petard. Or, as a less-poetical client once put it, strangled with my own guts.

The Minister listened closely to Maya; now it was her turn. 'Maya, Van, you're in a tight spot for certain. But you're not alone. Knowing you were coming, I spoke to a number of my friends and colleagues who work with me in the programs I'm involved in. Many of them believe in what you are calling magic, although they have many different words for it, both in their own languages and in English. What they say agrees with your approach. If you try and prove magic does not exist, you will fail. Too many have faith in it and won't be persuaded otherwise. Not all of them are Indigenous; Christians and Muslims and many other faiths are convinced magic is real. Good and bad. Your only possible way to go is to show your client, Henry, could not have done what they say. You need to prove he and Senator Fenwick never met, which considering the evidence, whether real or planted, will be difficult. At the same time, you need to demonstrate he had no motive, therefore why do it, even if he could?'

Well, all she said made sense but there was nothing new in her words. She was restating what we'd come up with ourselves and heard from others. We were no further on than when we walked in, apart from having a nice cup of tea and Maya getting to hero worship at close quarters. My turn.

'Minister, knowing we have your support helps us greatly.' Not at all except as a placebo, unless you're going to go public with it, which seems unlikely.

'I know Henry admires you greatly for your hard work.' Now I'm talking crap, he told me he'd never heard of you when I mentioned we'd be speaking.

'Would you be prepared to give him your public support? Speak to the media, show Henry isn't alone.' Putting your money where your mouth is, in effect.

'It might convince people to rethink their attitude and possibly influence the federal and state governments to reconsider whether or not to push this forward.' Two chances, Buckley's and none.

'If we can stop this now, the damage can be minimalised.' If and can-be, a conditional pairing indicative of reluctant acceptance of a doomed quest. Any elected legislature in the known world would be as likely to make a rational decision on a vote-damaging issue as I would to achieve levitation, but I was talking to one of the political in-crowd and therefore professionally obliged to make the appropriate affirming noises. I decided that spreading the bullshit was in a virtuous cause, which was true, and I'd be more sanguine about it later, which was not.

The Minister thought for a minute or so. She sipped at her tea, which must have been cold, made a face, and put the cup down.

'Yes, I'll show support and ask my parliamentary colleagues to do the same. But to be honest, I'm not confident it will achieve much publicly. An Aboriginal politician — there are two marks against me instantly — defending one of my culture who is accused of murdering a popular politician will be viewed as cultural favouritism. Even more when my defence is restricted to simple denials of what many are viewing as evidence, even though it isn't anything close to the legal meaning of the word. Anything I do will be purely moral support, which might be uplifting for your client but is essentially useless in a court of law and not much more use in the court of public opinion. There will be enough people denouncing magic which is likely to anger some of my support base. For practical reasons, I can't be an active part of that.'

She looked thoughtful and worried and I knew I was about to get more bad news. Not that she chose to give it to me, it was more she had to and didn't like doing it.

'Firstly, it would alienate many of my constituents needlessly and secondly because I embrace cultural beliefs upholding its existence. As concerned as I am about your client's predicament, I won't commit professional suicide which would achieve next to nothing anyway, and I'll not deny my own beliefs and tell an outright lie. I'm prepared to say what I can but I'm afraid that's all I can do.'

Another pause, she was trying hard, I could tell, and it was causing her stress not being able to come up with anything solid. Her own sense of ethics was holding her back, a concept I could easily relate to. As for the professional suicide, how could I consider encouraging someone else to follow my example and throw their hard-earned gains away in a hopeless cause?

Doing the right thing would be, however it was contemplated, doing the wrong thing. One such idiot connected to the case was enough. I decided if she offered, I'd have talked her out of it. I wished someone had done the same for me.

She wasn't finished airing her Cassandran thinking. 'I could even use my privilege to ask questions in the House but I believe what it would do is attract more adverse attention in the media, which may not be helpful to you.'

It was obvious she'd worked out in advance nothing she could do was going to achieve much at all. She was nice enough to explain in person; a lesser being would have sent us an email or told their version of Karen to pass on the message at the door. For her concern, politeness, and honesty I was grateful. I knew she'd speak of her concerns and allow herself to be seen as supporting Henry in principle. I also knew it was all she could do. I'd known it before we came, as she had. That limitation was demonstrated in her words, compassionate ones for certain but lacking any viable effect. In any real sense, we were still on our own.

I did, however, have one final question. 'Minister, do you think Henry could have done it?'

She paused for a moment and I was convinced her expression hinted she was considering the legal duck-and-dive of 'no comment', but she appeared to make a decision, one she wasn't pleased with but felt compelled to follow.

'According to my own beliefs, I think it's possible.

Alan Fenwick's death is a question, and maybe the answer lies in something inexplicable in this-world terms. It may be part of the other-world, what we call The Dreaming. Do I believe in magic? Unconditionally, yes. Do I believe your client used it to commit murder? Unconditionally, no. One belief is spiritual, the other intellectual, neither has any tangible evidence beyond my own convictions. For me, those two elements are in a constant state of conflict, it's all part of belonging to an ancient culture but at the same time living in the modern world. I know it doesn't help you at all but hopefully it does answer the question you asked.'

She shook her head and looked sad. 'I'm sorry.' I thanked her for her honesty and stood to leave. She and Maya exchanged quiet words; from where I was, Linley's contributions sounded encouraging and the look on Maya's face could easily have been described as ecstatic. After handshakes and further apologies for what we all knew rationally was an impossible situation despite best wishes and intentions, we left. Someone, probably Karen, arranged a taxi. As we drove away, I took one last look back at the Canberra Camelot.

We'd spent time with one of the few sincere people working there and she could do nothing; there were too many of the other types in the same building working against us. Plus, the malign anonymity with a hidden purpose who seemed to have it all worked out long before I, or anyone else, even suspected there was an it.

What was it I'd thought? Any help she offered would be nothing more than a minimally efficacious placebo? I was wrong. The blend of tea and sympathy may have been a placebo, but it lifted my spirits. Knowing someone was behind us was encouraging, even if the vagaries of circumstance and political realities meant there was almost nothing she could do. I told Maya how I felt and she agreed; she'd been lifted by the affirmations both of us were convinced were genuine. I asked the driver if he could recommend a decent pub. Naturally, he could. Enough tea and bloody placebos, it was time for the proven efficacy of brews, fermentations, and distillations to take over the healing process.

19

'Tea and sympathy. It's all we have.' Several salutary drinks later, Maya and I were back in our hotel, sitting in my room, now switched to coffee and tea respectively and getting ready to confront Veronica Fenwick. She was, I was all too aware, meeting with us under protest and after considerable pressure. I didn't know how it was achieved, and didn't give a damn. But it had, she'd agreed, and we were due there at five, which was in slightly over an hour.

I intended to shower and change the more intimate items of my clothing, and probably my shirt and tie. I was not out to impress Lady Fenwick, but I'd been in the current set of clothes since early in the day and I'd drunk tea, talked at length, and sat in a pub knocking back a few stimulating bevvies. I could smell the alcohol leaking out of me and if she did, it would place me at a greater disadvantage than her social pretentious sense of entitlement would naturally create in her mind.

Maya showered and changed for similar reasons and because women tend to be competitive around other women who are archetypes of glamour and elegance. Personally, I knew there was nothing to worry about. All Ronnie possessed was money and social prestige. Compared to Maya's brains and talent, those supposed attributes equated to a plastic letter opener employed against a razor-sharp scalpel.

While in servitude to the city firm, I met many of the society pages set, and a few were clients. Most of them floated ethereally in a fog of self-obsessed vacuity, their lives devoted to the inane and meaningless. They existed for the grand social events where vapidity and pursuit of worthless mutual acclamation were considered de rigueur. Annual gatherings of the cloddish clan such as Adelaide's own Oakbank Easter Racing Carnival were their opportunities to convince themselves their hollow hedonism possessed substance. Like a flock of screeching parrots, they landed, disrupting the tranquillity and lowering the average IQ of the Hills region over the four-day weekend, posturing for each other and the cameras as the rest of the country sniggered at their preposterous plumage and frivolous festivities. Champagne drinking; alcopop thinking.

All of our research, most of which came from magazines whose sole purpose was to incite envy in women forced by circumstance to suffer the realities of the world beyond the colour supplements, indicated Veronica Fenwick was one of those dilettante socialites, possessed of nothing beyond a commendable degree of vacant self-acclamation. I was unable to imagine what, if anything, the meeting might gain us, apart from a recharge of my disdain for those afflicted with a self-induced shortage of functional cognition. She wouldn't come up to my way of thinking and, unless she hit me over the head several times with something heavy, I wouldn't drop down to hers.

Still, we were there and with time to spare, and a pre-game discussion seemed appropriate. Which is why I'd made the tea and sympathy comment. It was all we had, a notion I decided to run past Maya and see if she concurred. I tried to speak objectively. Professionally. But by then I wasn't sure I was capable of either state of being. I began with a summation.

'Both Hamley and Manning are full of support but are unwilling to display it if it might incur negative responses from the people who pay their wages. In his case, the government, and in hers the voting taxpayers. They're the same thing, in the end, the taxpayers fund the government. For either of them to martyr themselves for Henry's sake would be as professionally damaging to them with the powers that be and the voting masses as this whole thing is for us with damn near everyone. The difference is we're committed, or probably should be' — she laughed, but not humorously — 'whereas they aren't stupid enough to follow us into the arena and run towards the hungry lions. Any support they might give would be well meant but lacking in punch, meaning they may as well not bother.'

Maya had been nodding but at my last words the steady head movement turned into a vehement shake.

'Van, any support, no matter how half-arsed, can only be beneficial. Even Picino's hidden help is working in our favour. Without him feeding us info and secretly donating funds, we'd be restricted to our own money and guesswork. You need to stop being so resolutely negative and start appreciating what we're getting, instead of obsessing on what we're not.'

She was right, I did need to do that. But when you have rising water lapping at your chin, noticing it's refreshing doesn't quell the panic induced by the certainty of drowning. But I needed to look at what was working for us, and Picino's clandestine assistance and the previous night's plus the morning's affirmations concerning our moral righteousness were positives to be taken on board and comforted by.

As the leonine teeth tore at my flesh, I knew I should bear in mind eating and being eaten were elements necessary to the ongoing circle of life. Somehow, though, the whole David Attenborough acceptance of nature's cruel inevitability was not doing it for me. I decided to do three of the four things considered among the best cognitive non-chemical pick-me-ups known to the betesticled half of the human race. It was shit, shower, and shave time.

Then, reinvigorated mentally and cleansed physically, I could face with fortitude whatever the grieving widow might throw at me. Or perhaps adopt a more philosophical acceptance of my impending destruction.

I always spent an inordinate amount of time on trial preparation. Disputing a speeding offence, something I did far too often for myself but which when done for others comprised a profitable portion of my professional life, would hold my attention for half a day. The five Ps were the primary rule of my professional life. A traffic fine appearance may have been only a minor entry in the legal canon, but acquiring small victories was a satisfying advance on losing. Careful success brought more work, whereas careless failure sent future Senna wannabes elsewhere. Unfortunately, now there were six Ps. Picino was invading every aspect of my existence.

I was psyching up for the approaching confrontation. Thinking, planning, deciding, strategising. I'd done it before meeting Hamley and Manning, endeavoured to visualise their points of view and thereby work out how to either get in lockstep or combat them effectively. In both cases it proved unnecessary; neither were opposing me: the opposite was true. But I suspected Ronnie Fenwick would be a different case altogether.

I needed to get into a head space of readiness for whatever came along. To be prepared to counter her claims without becoming too confrontational or argumentative. I was after information, not open dispute. Extracting opinions and determining biases requires subtlety and care. I was well aware of that; I thought it through at length under the shower. Plus, Maya told me the same thing in the taxi. Twice.

The Fenwicks' Canberra residence was where Veronica Fenwick moved after her husband's death; apparently, she preferred it to Adelaide and once the political ties to South Australia were gone, so was she. Where we were headed was an apartment high up in a building with intercom access. I pressed the buttons, spoke my name, and the door clicked open. We sped upwards in an elevator big enough for four if they were all extremely good friends complete with benefits. From the hallway window opposite the Fenwicks' front door, there were unlimited views of lake, trees, and hills. I wasn't a fan of communal living but for that panorama I might have been persuadable. Maya pressed the button and in the distance, I heard Big-Ben chimes announce our arrival. The door opened and I caught my first sight of the woman Picino waxed lyrically over.

He'd been right. Ageing agreed with her, a few fine lines which may have been grief added distinction to a beautiful face above a flawless figure. It all appeared natural; no after-market alterations by a medical sculptor, as many of her set indulged in, seeking eternal youth through surgical defiance of nature's heartlessness. For a brief moment I imagined, considering the supernatural aspects of this case, there might be a painting of an elderly crone in one of the spare rooms. I resisted the urge to laugh at my imaginings. Or to ask if I could take a peek.

However, it was no female Dorian I was talking to, but someone with natural genetic advantages enhanced by cossetted living. Even without considering her impressive physical attributes, everything augmenting her striking beauty was equally flawless. The outfit was expensive and new, along with the freshly-styled hair and too perfect to be DIY makeup. Unlike Linley Manning, who dressed down to suit the occasion, Veronica Fenwick dressed up to control it.

She sought to impress, and failed. I expected something similar due to my personal experiences of her social grouping and what we'd read of her public persona, and I wasn't disappointed. I let none of my true feelings show. Hypocritically, pragmatically, and perhaps a tiny soupçon hormonally, I put admiration into my expression as we shook hands and I inhaled her expensive French perfume.

I'm no expert on such things but I'd known clients, and female colleagues, who not only used similar smells but liked everyone to be aware they did. The eau-de-toilette had to be borderline unaffordable for those poseurs to consider it borderline acceptable. Alex used Opium, the Yves Saint Laurent scent, not the also-inhalable Chinese brain basher, and I considered that fairly costly. Compared to whatever was assaulting my senses at that moment, it was likely to be, price-wise, akin to two-dollar-shop aromatic water.

Veronica — somehow Hamley's familiarised Ronnie didn't suit the fabricated image — made it obvious by her efforts that realism wasn't on the agenda. Forewarned, I was forearmed, and ready for whatever followed. I glanced at Maya as the two women did the handshake routine, Maya's professionally firm, Veronica's perfunctorily flaccid. Maya's face showed nothing, which for someone who knew her well displayed everything.

Veronica's power play may have worked on the less wary and more testicularly-motivated of her usual associates, but Maya and I were both cynics and lawyers. We believe nothing without evidence and accept nothing at face value. Especially tarted-up neurotic narcissists. It was a stylish performance, but the wrong audience.

Her voice, as she introduced herself and welcomed us, was soft, husky, breath in the ear sexy, and I formed an uncharitable thought it was something put on with the makeup each morning. Then again, the throatiness may possibly have been grief induced. The protective male instinctively said yes, that was it; the aggressive cynic and lawyer intuitively argued against it. And won. One against two, an unfair contest. The chivalrous one fought fair, while the other two tended to be backstreet brawlers.

Reality television, one of the least truthfully-descriptive oxy-morons, with emphasis on the M word, was full of Veronicas. An American family, famous only for fame and a widely-publicised sex change, stood out among the multitude, but I remembered a pair of baroque English scatterbrains whose specialised redecorations of women cursed with outdated or non-existent fashion sense resulted in much more refined and contemporary versions of tastelessness. There was always a market for programmes like those. They were first cousins to most second-hand shops: throwaway junk relabelled as collectibles.

I was up close and personal with the nation's fantasy: the subject of male wet dreams, à la Picino, and female envy, as evinced by the numerous and voracious inhalers of the glam mags. And all I longed to do was leave. Perhaps, I figured, I should announce it on the ABC. Talk about publicity, I'd probably get asked to headline the next Sydney Mardi Gras. Or, in our more backward states, forced into gay-conversion therapy.

I sneaked another peek at Maya, whose non-committal non-expression was non-committing and non-expressing at full power. Veronica Fenwick appeared to be impervious to what either of us were thinking and was gazing around vacantly. Probably, I assumed, searching for a mirror containing the image of someone worthy of her serious attention.

I knew my onslaught of negativity was not going to help the meeting go well; I coveted feeling the indifference Maya was displaying. The problem was, her not showing was all show. Anyone knowing her as I did would have no trouble discerning her silent disdain for the shallow non-entities, exemplified here to great effect by Ronnie's unconfined display of conceited affectation, as time wasting and ludicrous.

I did a mental head shake and tried to adopt a courtroom frame of mind. Serious, focussed, on task. Ronnie's neckline was not helping and the fact Maya saw me eyeing it was even worse. I put in the effort and moved my gaze upwards. An improvement: the red-rimmed eyes and sad mouth set the mood perfectly, considering the topic that would form our conversation. I realised the vacant look could also possibly be alcohol or tranquilisers, perhaps in combination, and my initial impressions might be mistaken. She had, after all been a doctor, something I knew from Alex's many lectures took years of hard work and superior intelligence to achieve. The realisation put me in a more sympathetic frame of mind.

We moved into the room and she gestured towards a table set with six chairs. We all sat. She spoke first. 'Can we do this quickly? It was not my idea and I have things to do that are more important than talking to you. I'm only doing it as a favour.' And fare thee well to my sympathetic mood.

Or empathy. Or anything other than working out her hostility was something I chose to take into account and try to avoid any exacerbation of. I looked at Maya and signalled she should begin. The glance I received in return failed to convey her appreciation for the opportunity. I didn't blame her; I was sitting back, the male animal at rest while telling her to go and catch dinner. I'd pay for it later, her eyes declared.

When she turned back to the other woman, her face and voice were saying something totally different. It's easy to sound sincere when you're with people who have no idea what the concept is. All lawyers need to learn the trick, as I had. I once offered unlimited sympathy to a man who battered his wife to death with a wine bottle and he was seeking for someone to understand how she'd pushed him until he had no choice. To this day, he probably believes he'd managed to convince me it was all her fault.

The secret was to maintain eye contact, speak in an even voice, and never use any words or phrases hinting at criticism or judgment. As I sat watching Maya playing the game I described to her many times, I was amazed how effective she was. And she was going to be even more successful in the future, I'd most likely end up working for her. I enjoyed watching her draw Veronica Fenwick in. None of it was lies and none was truth. All of it was relying on the fact people like Ronnie simply want to be told what they want to be told. After that illumination, all you need is to work out what it is and you're home and hosed.

'Mrs Fenwick, thank you for agreeing to meet with us. Please, may we offer our condolences on your loss. It was a shock for us all. What we want to do is find a way to find the truth. If our client is innocent, then we, and naturally you, would want him to be cleared of any involvement and allowed to go back to his life. But obviously, if he is guilty, then as those who are employed to uphold the law, we want to see justice done. The truth is our goal and anything anyone can provide would assist us in ensuring the right result is found.'

She paused for a silent moment. I was not surprised, any bull churning out that much shit would have been on the floor and gasping. The other woman showed no reaction, staring at Maya, which was good and ignoring me completely, which was better: my face must have been a picture. I don't dissemble well unless I'm the one spreading the manure, then I'm in the groove and rolling. But hearing Maya doing a Van move that effectively was a knockout moment. Mary Shelley's reconstructive medical student would have been proud of me for the creation I'd stitched together and enlivened, who was moving in for the kill.

'We do understand how difficult this must be for you. I've lost relatives, close ones, and it's almost impossible to come to terms with their leaving. It's easy to see why you're searching for an answer. As are we. Although our job is to defend Henry Day, we want to do it honestly, which means we have to try and understand why people are convinced he's innocent and some, such as yourself, are adamant he's responsible.'

She stopped and waited, watching the other woman's face for any hint she'd followed Maya's reasoning. I'd be surprised. I'd helped her write the script and I was hardly keeping up; the chemically or emotionally detached woman sitting opposite her must have been wondering what on earth Maya was going on about. Her head straightened up and she produced a half smile for a second before lapsing back into her grim stoniness.

'Do you believe in God?' Quiet, controlled, but underneath a subtle hint of frenzy. Fanaticism held in check by grief? Something prescribed or from the bottle shop? Something neither prescribed nor listed by the Therapeutic Drugs people? Whatever, it was a start.

I was still being blanked: I knew if I used the same words as Maya, we'd be outside on the landing. I could successfully schmooze small children, dogs, and homicidal career criminals; women I didn't do as well with. Alex says I came across as patriarchal; my answer was nothing could be father from the truth. Having to spell the joke ruined the effect.

Maya answered. I'd have given a flat out no! Which she did, but in a way where the denial was almost undetectable, hidden in clever wordplay and outright deception.

'Well, you see, Mrs Fenwick, in my culture we don't have a God as such. Our spirituality is deep and personally important but unlikc many religions or belief systems, it's not based around the concept of a single God.' I was holding my breath, waiting to see how a devout Catholic would respond to the admission of what must have sounded like pure paganism. I half expected an attempt at proselytising or a quick anti-hexing sign of the cross to ward off the heresy. What we got was…

'Yes, I understand. It is important to have something to believe in even if it's not the same as knowing the true God. Anything, I suppose, is an advancement on nothing.'

Oh, yeah? Maya's face was a tight mask of anger and injury. Veronica didn't notice the effect her words had; a state of affairs I suspected had been the case for decades. I needed to speak to allow Maya a moment to recover.

'I was brought up a Catholic.' It made her smile, which I suspected wouldn't have been the case if I added I hadn't dipped my fingers in holy water, spoken of my hand-held shame to a priest in the show-and-tell cupboard, or gone up to the altar rail for a cannibal-cracker since I was curiously examining my single digit pubic hair collection. I felt a vestige of guilt at deceiving her, although I'd told the truth. What she took from my words, rightly or wrongly, was her problem. I felt Maya's eyes on me for a short moment then she returned her attention to Veronica.

'Mrs Fenwick, may I ask why you're convinced your husband's demise was caused by something connected to Henry or a form of supernatural influence?'

As with Hamley, it was all a matter of finding the right button to press. The woman straightened up and her expression cleared. She'd been asked for her opinion, something she was all too practised at sharing. Many times uninvited was my guess. Also, she was talking to a primitive soul in need of conversion, Maya, and someone whose proclamation of Catholicism lacked credibility. Mea culpa.

I'd mixed with religious types before and short undefined answers aren't what they give. What would result in a simple yes to most questions goes much further if the topic under discussion is spiritual. My concision and reticence induced suspicions of recantation and heresy and Maya's confession of the sin of never having found the one true God was the signal for Ronnie's missionary zeal to go viral.

'My husband, Alan, and I, were devout believers. We attended mass three times a week and socialised with others of our faith wherever possible. We both read the

Bible from cover to cover and studied the history of the Christian faith in depth. We knew of the goodness resulting from asking God, or his servants, to provide assistance in times of need. The opposite is also true. Those who seek to distort the truth and ask the inhabitants of the darkness to give them what they should not have are equally capable of changing the world. As a doctor, I know death without physical explanation can only mean one thing: the reason is interference caused by interaction with the supernatural world. Someone appealed to the evil one or his minions and asked for my husband to be taken. I had no idea who it was until your client's name was mentioned. Then I knew who used heretical evil to cause Alan's death. It had to be someone with a reason and our support of the sale of Bilden Downs Station and the closing of the so-called sacred site is the most obvious one there is. No one else has cause to wish him harm, therefore your client's guilt was not a difficult conclusion to reach. In Leviticus it says a man or a woman who is a medium or a spiritist shall surely be put to death. They shall be stoned with stones, their bloodguiltiness is upon them. That is your client, God will punish him as should the law. It includes you and any others who give him succour. The person who turns to mediums and to spiritists, to play the harlot after them, will be cut off from among his people. That's also in Leviticus; it's one of my favourite books and from whence I have gained much spiritual comfort at this time.'

Bloodguiltiness? Succour? Whence? Harlot? Spiritists? I couldn't speak and apparently neither could Maya. What possible response was there to what we'd heard? Holy shit? Perhaps not!

As she was sermonising, I imagined the phantoms of

those holy pesterers whose callous interventionism ruined or ended the lives of millions choralising joyful hallelujahs as they capered around us. Though what those blinkered impotents would have made of her Parisian come-and-get-it-while-it's-hot incense and saint-seducing decolletage was beyond imagining.

Veronica clasped her hands together, whether in prayer or passion I wasn't sure, and gazed fixedly at the floor for a few seconds. Then her head rose and she appeared to be looking at something situated midway between us. It was the same expression I noticed when we first arrived; the sensation that while we were there, we somehow weren't. Her disconnection was disconcerting.

Alex occasionally did it to me during arguments but that was deliberate and forced. This appeared to be genuine. It reminded me of old horror movies where the person in the room doesn't register the presence of the ghosts. I felt I should touch Maya to check we were truly there and not apparitions. Before I could move, Veronica turned to Maya.

'Did I answer your questions?'

Well, it certainly answered most of them. Were Veronica Fenwick's ducks all flying in the same direction? No! Had her grief driven her into her current state of unreality? Probably! Was her exaggerated religious fervour to blame? Her religious fanaticism, with three masses a week, reading the entire Bible and then quoting the outdated and unlearned teachings of the developmental Christian religion as relevant arguments in the modern age would count, I decided, as precisely that. She and her husband had been, and clearly, she still was, far removed from contemporary or even enlightenment thinking. Not to mention overly reliant on medieval and possibly pre-medieval superstitious hysteria and uninformed ravings.

Grief, anger, and fervent piety form a disturbed and dangerous combination. Add in a cocktail of prescribed, and possibly proscribed, medicinals, and the chances of a smooth passage through the travails are slight at best. In short, she was mentally unstable, perhaps initialised by the shock of seeing her husband's on-screen appointment with the grim reaper then intensified by the unhealthy ways she tried to deal with it. Her off-balanced state led her to grab at any half-baked reason for his death. Considering her biblical leanings and Henry's membership of what she considered a pagan culture, the letter denouncing him must have seemed like Moses hearing a choir of deifically-voiced burning bushes delivering the ten commandments in four-part harmony.

I'd been hoping for more, but whatever was coursing through her psyche, and likely her blood, not only neutralised her social filters but also put the brakes on her system big time. Her declarations of religious indoctrination and intolerance appeared to have exhausted her energy and she was sitting still and almost unmoving. I had the unkind thought she resembled her husband when he simultaneously achieved everlasting glory in this world and the next. I didn't let it show on my face, although Maya was giving me a strange look; my clenched jaw muscles may have surrendered an involuntary twitch or two.

Our main questions were answered anyway. Hoping for a result based in at least half rational explanation what we ended up with was something the Inquisition would have been proud to claim. No evidence, an accusation made for no reason beyond putting someone in the frame for a personal gain as yet undetermined, and a total unwillingness to look beyond that accusation for anything more in touch with secular reality or scientific fact.

I was uncertain as to why someone imagined talking to her might assist us or provide explanation for her campaign against Henry. It had, but not anything we could use. One mention of the beautiful and popular widow's chemically-enhanced mental whirligigging and we'd be in the firing line from all directions. She had too many followers who believed the same, and many others may not have shared her views but even the most fervent unbeliever thinks twice before openly describing faith as a form of insanity. A colleague once described religious faith as the only mental illness that comes with guidebooks. Funny, but not a suitable comment for me to repeat under the circumstances.

It hadn't been a completely wasted afternoon. Negative results could be viewed positively if you viewed what they showed in the correct manner. What the meeting demonstrated was that Veronica Fenwick was one hundred percent convinced Henry summoned up the devil and persuaded him to stop her husband's clock. Speaking of which, it was time we were going. Our hostess, without moving, had already departed: our cue to leave.

Maya politely, and calmly, assured Veronica that, yes, she'd answered our questions and thanked her for her time. She remained seated and offered no response to Maya's words. We made our own way to the exit and as the door closed behind us, we stopped and looked at each other. Maya mouthed 'Jesus Christ' and I grinned. Then she got it and we shared a moment of silent laughter.

The old European monarchies and affluent industrialist families produced excuses for their often inexplicable behavioural and intellectual failings. A notable inclusion was consanguinity resulting from marital snobbery and a limited market, bringing about increasingly contaminated bloodlines. Also, many of them may be the descendants of clever people but raw intelligence isn't always inherited. Being born in a fifty-room mansion doesn't necessarily indicate you possess more mental furniture than someone born in a two-room shack; it simply permits you to conceal your limitations more successfully. Aussie royalty, more dollar than dynasty, couldn't use the same excuses; some, like Veronica, simply chose to act irrationally and then life imitated art.

I craved a drink and I was positive Maya did too. In the pub we could tot up our score thus far. Two in Henry's favour but neither in a position to go overboard with their support, and one anti-Henry borderline psychotic whose views we couldn't quote without sounding anti-religious or as if we were levelling accusations of uncontrolled mania. We were not even close to notching up a high run rate.

Tomorrow, we had an appointment in Sydney with the head of the Chinese consortium purchasing Bilden Downs Station. I was cautiously confident it might be more in our favour, with no reason for them to want Fenwick dead and no desire for any negative publicity connected to their outback plans. The diametric opposite was the case. Then again, the thousands of years of superstition Confucianism, communism, and capitalism failed to wipe out might incline them towards believing Henry was acting in the interests of his cultural heritage and protecting the sacred site from the foreign invaders. How it might go was anyone's guess; perhaps, I mused, I should try Leviticus from whence I might gain succour and cure my bloodguiltiness.

By my count, there was a grand total of about ten

actively, albeit clandestinely, dismissing claims of Henry's guilt while twenty million Australians were going willingly, and witlessly, along with the anonymously-origined and media-exacerbated campaign against him. Those odds I was convinced we could manage. If more than a billion Chinese joined in though, we were in real trouble.

20

When I began my breakfast in the hotel restaurant the next morning, I was feeling up. I shouldn't have been; the trip, while educational, provided marginal assistance. But after getting back the previous night, I'd rung Alex. I told her of the three disappointing meetings and my hopes for the last one, she'd given encouragement, verbal and intimated, and I'd hung up feeling refreshed and slept deeply. The fifteen-minute call took my post-Veronica downbeat mood and put me back into the positive. Which continued until I'd slept, showered, shaved, dressed, and met Maya downstairs for breakfast and the realities of the case soon returned. A few minutes and the negatives were eating at me almost as hungrily as I was tucking into the bacon, eggs, and toast.

I didn't like being separated from Alex. Since we started living together then married, we'd spent maybe fifty nights apart. Knowing I would be back home that evening improved my day by itself. She provided my lifeline, in spite of her occasional desires to strangle me with it.

My mother was Olympic standard passive-aggressive. She could have lectured to Irish-Catholic clergy on functioning as a travel agent for guilt trips. She delighted in engendering feelings in me that I was responsible for every bad thing since the day of my birth and perhaps even my conception and definitely including the much-agonised-over discomforts of both. She was my mother and there were obligatory residues of filial love, but the word orphan resonated comfortingly in my head every time we were in contact.

I hadn't married a mother substitute: there were no

Oedipal or Freudian bats in my belfry. Alex exhibited no passive element to her aggression. If she wished for me to feel guilty, she said so. No subtle hints or sneaking in from the blind side with sucker punches designed to get her own way by battering my conscience. It was all uncomplicated and unambiguous. We argued, often heatedly, but both of us would choose to be in conflict with each other than in a state of loving peace with anyone else. We'd gone to bed together not talking; the important bit was the together, the closeness was in the silent communication. Half the time we were around the house together we didn't speak. Not in words.

I'm always amused when I watch films or television where loving couples, or parents with children, feel the need to constantly verbalise their love. Such sentiments may be in place on a Hallmark card or in a rom-com but there are many ways to say "I Love You" without expressing it aloud. A touch, a glance, handing someone a drink or something to eat, being in the same room, joined by a bond transcending the spoken affirmations which tended to sound trite, rehearsed, and obligatory.

The hotel provided an excellent breakfast, and the tea, unusually and agreeably, was brewed and not dunked. The day started well, and since I was going home, it would end the same way. All I required was for the middle section to not be as downbeat as its predecessors and the lurking sense of moody unease refusing to go away might reduce to the level of ignorable. As I shared my rack of toast with Maya, I did the same with what was triggering the dark musings.

'We're not doing too well. Support, yes, but none of it's strong or overt enough to be useful. And as for bloody Veronica, her mental furniture isn't in storage, it's been used for wood chips. She's popular, beautiful, politically connected, and determined to get what she wants with no regard for anyone else's wellbeing but her own. She decided Henry caused her husband's death and is after justice. Or is revenge a more apt word?'

I went on in a like manner as I ate, and Maya listened silently. There was nothing to say, and I was insisting on saying it at length, repeating what I'd already said too many times in a number of ways over the last few days. We could offer no defence because there wasn't one since there was no crime to defend against. With no accusation worth a damn legally, how could we come up with a counter argument worth one?

Garlic and crosses might effectively ward off the attentions of vampires, if they existed. Since they didn't, knowing where to buy the best bulbs and crucifixes was redundant. Yet the law, encouraged by social networking, religious mania, and collective stupidity, was hellbent on finding legally-anachronous justifications permitting the scapegoating of the sacrifice the public appeared to want. It was all ancient civilisations based; the gods are displeased, find an innocent or two to offer up. The Aztecs spilled blood like rainwater, thousands dying to appease the Sun Gods. Veronica only worshipped the one God, but her obsessions and methods were as egregious as those designed to placate the sanguinary hungers of the multiplicity of pagan deities.

We were in trouble. Why did I get involved? Bloody John Picino, why could the mad bitch not grieve and move on? I couldn't wait to be out of bloody Canberra and back home, and so on, ad repetitio. My insistence on going over the same ground continually showed I was unravelling. I knew it, Maya could see it, and even Alex picked up on it through our long-distance connection. It worried me; I longed to hold it together but wasn't sure if I could. I'd been there before, and remembered many of the times well, and others fortunately vaguely. The embers of the unholy fires burning my inner being in the past were heating up again. I had to find something to douse the sparks before they burst into flames and consumed my sanity.

If Henry Day was going to be put on trial for committing a crime which lost any credibility several centuries earlier, then the inmates were definitely in charge of what Einstein described as the lunatic asylum of the universe. And, despite my opposition to the general consensus, I was heading towards a madness of my own. Different symptoms, same affliction. Depression wasn't physically communicable but it was psychically infectious. Mine was like malaria; it came home regularly for a visit.

Being in Canberra was not helping. There's nothing wrong with the place but it's often been described as soulless and clinical. To me, the other capitals were like progressively developed fine buildings, gaining National Trust status through the gradual achievement of grandeur; Canberra is like a kit home, thrown together from a basic design and lacking either gravitas or personality. I knew I was being unfair and judging harshly. But the world was demonstrating an inordinate degree of unfairness and all I was doing was returning the disfavour. And Canberra, Veronica, and Maya were convenient targets. The first two received my angst, Maya my toast and the unceasing verbals. She digested both in silence.

The flight to Sydney was short, bumpy, uncomfortable, and too crowded for conversation. Which prevented me from giving Maya yet another version of my expanding collection of complaints. I gazed out the window and she read our notes as two young guys in suits tried in vain to impress her with loudly pretentious conversation pieces and smiles. Behind us a baby rehearsed for the leads in Don Giovanni: the tenor and soprano parts, as the mother, headphones in place, ignored the hate-filled glances sent in her direction and continued nodding vacantly to music I confidently assumed was not Mozart.

The wind was intense and we landed roughly. After wending our way to the baggage reclaim, I saw a young Chinese man in a tailored suit and silk tie holding up a sign reading MILLER. He introduced himself as Peter Kwan and we all shook hands, Maya receiving the same firm grasp and eye contact I did. I was impressed. Either he was truly one of the new generation of Chinese men or he was well trained in western business etiquette. Probably both. They expect their representatives to impress and those who are stuck in the old mindsets are not offered the jobs which feature foreign travel. I knew all that, but I'd always wondered if what I'd learnt would eventually produce any practical application. Now it had.

Bags in hand, we followed him out to the car park. I expected a limo but he stopped at a four-wheel drive. Great Wall brand: undeniably nationalistic and loyal. Maya climbed in the front, I'd been to Sydney many times, the back seat was fine. He drove as he dressed: carefully, precisely, professionally. It seemed unlikely he was only a chauffeur and I asked what his function was. Nicely, politely, but firmly, as lawyers learn to do. We're socially house-trained, but it's similar to an out of sight litter-tray indoctrination than a wait until you can do the nasty stuff outside gentility. Manners, they say, cost nothing. In my experience freebies usually produce results equating to the level of payment. Besides, the mood I was getting into, I was rapidly nearing the onset of total indifference.

'I'm Mister Lao's personal assistant. I handle much of his business affairs and am involved in the matter you are meeting to discuss. Will my presence be acceptable to you?'

'I have no objections. Does Mister Lao speak English?'

'Yes. He studied at Harvard university and has lived here for five years. His accent and vocabulary are, as he himself describes it, a mixture of American and Australian. I was educated in London and can recognise the difference between either of those and proper English.'

He laughed at what was probably a well-practised ice-breaker. But he was right. His pedantic speech was colloquial business class English, not the language-classes instruction-pamphlet version. And it was as different from American or Australian English as his features, dress, and bearing were from the entrepreneurial archetypes of either of those countries or those I'd seen of his own. Not to mention his diplomacy in the face of what could easily be construed as an offensive query. Which all sorted one concern out though; I'd been worried about linguistic misunderstandings, and I still was, but the communication failures, considering the educational and professional backgrounds of the man I was meeting, would most likely be on my part.

We stayed under the speed limit; we were passed more than passing. Fine, we were in no hurry and it was a nice day. Sydney looked magnificent in the sunshine and Maya tried to stare in six directions at once while I spent the time gazing inwards. A bad sign, I knew. But Peter informed us we were having lunch at Doyle's, which lifted my mood slightly. Eating at what was probably the country's most famous fish restaurant would lift anyone's spirits. I was surprised though; I suppose I'd expected a Chinatown five-star establishment or a quiet business club.

When we followed Peter in, he was welcomed effusively by the duty greeter and I assumed he and his boss must be regulars. I hadn't assumed the choice of eatery was designed to impress me or to make points socially, and I'd been right. It appeared to be somewhere our host liked and frequented, and the fact he'd chosen to go there impressed me. My early judgment of Hamley's meeting place was wrong and I was trying to reserve my opinions until the evidence was in. It's not easy, especially without regular practice. Pre-trial guesses are not my style usually and after the total miss of two nights back I was being more careful.

Then again, I wasn't giving Lao bonus points yet. Someone like him, and in his position, was capable of analysing how I might think and act to counter it. Or was I being carried away by the smoke-filled pavilion of mirrors the complex case was turning out to be? I decided to wait and see. I suspended judgment and focussed on what I might have for lunch.

Lao beat us there although we were still ten minutes ahead of the arranged time. My opinion of him went up several more points, making a late entrance was a management trick he clearly found unnecessary. Or too obvious to employ. Realising I was back to overthinking the under-important I shook hands and looked around. We were at a window table with Sydney Harbour as our backdrop, and we were noticeably distanced from other tables. I assumed Lao orchestrated the setup; we wouldn't be overheard.

Nearby I saw TV soapie stars talking naturally, which must have taken serious rehearsal time, two politicians together, one from each major party, which should have resulted in a press orgy, although probably not in Doyle's, where taste was not only reserved for the menu, and a world-famous tennis player renowned for his infantile on-court dummy-spits, who gave the lie to the adage that sport builds character. He was with a woman; I hoped she was his shrink or someone trained to operate a stun gun if he didn't like how his fish was cooked. Everybody sneaked a quick look at our table, decided we were of no interest and went back to their self-absorption. I felt like shouting out that I'd been on the ABC then realised that particular accolade applied to more than half the room. Feeling ignored and glad of it, I turned my attention to our host.

Mid-fifties, well-dressed but tastefully, carefully and expensively groomed, and clearly comfortable in the surroundings. It was hardly a typical communist hangout, and he was definitely not a typical communist. I met a number from his country who spent their time casting angry looks at anything smacking of capitalist excess. Successful entrepreneurs can do what they like; even communist dictatorships can appreciate the value of imported money. Cuba made the mistake of distancing itself from useful capital, and others who nominally trod the same ideological path learned from Castro's insular fumblings. The Chinese didn't drive recycled American fifties gas gobblers kept running by band-aid mechanical make-do; they manufactured their own cars using technology bought, borrowed, or stolen from the west and other Asian countries. Communism and capitalism may have been ideologically antithetical, but when they did cooperate, great things happened. One of which was rich socialists took poor capitalists for a meal at expensive restaurants. It worked for me, and, it seemed, for Lao. Perhaps also for our two countries. Make lunch, not war!

'Mister Miller, and Miss Wright, have you been here before?' I had, she hadn't. I complemented him on his choice and Maya stared at the array of media-anointed personalities.

'You may be wondering why I chose this place. As it happens, I like seafood, sea views, and excellent service. Here we find all three.'

The first two were there for sure, and at the prices I almost went into cardiac arrest over on my previous visit, the service was certain to be outstanding. This time, though, either he or Picino would be picking up the bill. The basic fish and chips I paid imported lobster charges for last time was going to be replaced with something considerably more upmarket. I ordered Morton Bay Bugs, Maya went for a dish containing octopus, and Lao decided on a fish I'd never heard of that I suspected may have been a corner fish shop staple relabelled to suit the place's reputation and exclusivity. I found the pretentiousness amusing; flake, even if served in the more upmarket seafood establishments, is still only shark. Jaws but with more sophisticated cello music.

Peter Kwan disappeared and I didn't ask why. Hired help in similar meetings, even at his level, aren't usually invited to the high table. I doubted he was sitting on the beach chomping on a burger and fries from Maccas, but whatever he was having, he was having it somewhere else. Lao may have wished Maya gone also, but it was not going to happen. She was there as my witness and to provide any details I couldn't. I was sure he knew that and was displeased with the arrangement. My sense of it though, was that he sought to clear the air about Chinese involvement in matters of Australian business ownership, specifically regarding himself and the cattle station about to be recycled as a rest clinic, and he chose to achieve that by speaking to a lawyer who was unsophisticated enough to allow his assistant to attend the discussions. Whatever the tone of his thinking about my business acumen might be, he realised her presence was not open for discussion. Maya stayed. But not Peter, and when Lao spoke, I found out why. He faced me and ignored Maya. She, seemingly indifferent to the snub, sipped her drink, ate her food, and watched the passing boats and our fellow diners. All of it a front; the preoccupied-assistant stereotype Lao identified and disregarded was listening intently.

'Mister Miller, may I call you Van?' I nodded and he smiled. 'This meeting must remain totally private. Whatever we say must stay between us. I have political masters and business superiors, and neither group would be impressed if I become involved in the politics of your country. They all know we're meeting but I informed them this was a courtesy and not an intention to make any statement able to be interpreted as anything other than a polite personal comment. If it is a problem for you, I suggest we spend our time here discussing the weather, perhaps the tennis, or have a conversation about movies and literature. However, if I have your word what we say will go no further, I will trust you, then we may wander into areas where we possibly should not. Do we have agreement? Naturally, I assume any agreement would also apply to your assistant.'

We did, and it did, but I was disappointed. Four meetings, and no result worth anything. I was gaining a great deal of valuable information and being asked, no, told, to keep it to myself. For a lawyer, that's frustrating. I was trying to defend an innocent man and everyone remotely connected to the case was doing their best to tie my legal hands behind my back. Still, there was no harm listening. As he spoke, I started on the Bugs. I soon lost any hope he might be able to help although, alert for any hint if useful information, I was still paying close attention. The combination of seafood and whatever astronomically-priced wine he'd chosen was compensating for my half-expected and fully-delivered disappointment, and it was evident Lao could sense my dismay. However, he was apparently keen to explain why he couldn't help.

Peter Kwan was right; Lao's accent was a curious blend of Australian and American with no hint of the grammatical and pronunciation mistakes which usually indicate a second language is being used. The impression brought on by his fluency and general demeanour was that the speaker's years away from his homeland caused him to become more western than Chinese in his approach. Once again, my penchant for hasty and erroneous predictions let me down as his next words proved my assumption to be way off target.

'I, and my country, don't like it when foreigners, Americans, the English, Europeans, and you Australians, choose to inform us publicly that some of our decisions fail to meet your standards of moral and ethical behaviour. It is insulting and often induces us to anger and frustration. You are entitled to your opinions, but we would prefer you keep them to yourselves. We rarely criticise your social or political decisions or standards, and this must also be one of those occasions when we decide to refrain from becoming involved. My personal view is your client is being ill-treated and accused senselessly of a crime that's not only impossible to prove but equally impossible to carry out. Death induced by a vindictive thought involves sheer lunacy to imagine it, far worse to make moves to go ahead with a legal case against him on such a foolish notion. Which is my own private opinion. My public one is if your country wishes to go ahead with this case, then we will make no comment in the same manner we would prefer your representatives do the same the next time we do something you disapprove of. Do you understand?'

I did. If I was to be scolded like a naughty child as a representative of my country, then there were many worse places it could happen. But I wasn't in step with my country on this issue and I was aggrieved at being seen as a part of the whole ludicrous farce. Obviously, Lao knew that.

'Van, I'm aware you are not who I should be giving this lecture to. I am, as the saying goes, preaching to the choir. And the only reason I insist on being frank is that I know you and Miss Wright are almost alone in this fight. You have my sympathy but I am afraid it is all I have to offer. There is a bigger picture, and my sense of remorse at what is happening and my inability to do anything to assist you in this is genuine. I am a representative of my country, which in this instance you two are not, and I have no choice in my actions, as you, it seems, also do not. However, my pressures are practical and political, whereas yours, I suspect, are more morally based. I do not have those options available to me. I took payment for my soul long ago and the devil, or in this case my chosen ideology, gives no refunds and allows no change of heart unless previously approved by the highest level of my government and gainful politically, financially, or ideologically. I'm sorry but my hands are tied in this matter, much as I wish they were not.'

I believed him, and now I knew why Peter Kwan was not part of our discussions. There were no witnesses and Lao knew his unsubtle comments about our moral stance applied to any revelations about our talk. We couldn't speak of it, neither would he, and the secret would remain unshared.

Which brought the count of silent supporters up by one. It was encouraging but legally unusable. I once lined up a witness who could have cleared my client with one short statement and she refused; he ended up in prison. That situation was of the hell hath no fury variety but in the end, the silence was much the same. Whether it was because of anger at betrayal or impotence through pragmatic self-interest, the end result was what demanded to be heard remained unsaid, as it was turning out to do in this case.

I thanked Lao and told him I understood, which was true. To put him at ease and negate whatever the Chinese do in lieu of Catholic guilt, I changed the topic to his plans for Bilden Downs Station. They were, apparently, going ahead at a fast gallop. I found out that Alan Fenwick, as a firm supporter but not politically tied directly to the area or the project, contributed less to it than anyone addicted to only praising the dead was admitting, something else I couldn't use. Speaking disparagingly about the dear-departed is considered as seriously disrespectful. Even if what's said is true.

So, Saints Alan and Veronica would have their names somewhere on the property and in the public consciousness despite one being merely a figurehead whose contributions to the matter were close to irrelevant and the other an intellectual lightweight whose entire existence was a carnival of irrelevancies. Canonisation and deification by social media. It worked for Jesus: what were the gospels if not the world's most widely disseminated blogs?

I congratulated Lao and wished his endeavours well, and meant it. I knew what it felt like to be stressed and in need of recuperation, and I was only a country lawyer. If I were making the sorts of international decisions and risking the money Lao and his ilk were working with, I'd need a permanent booking at the re-imaged station.

The next hour was more genial. Lao asked about where we lived and seemed interested; we asked about his background and found it fascinating. At one point he was inebriated enough, drunk would be too vulgar a term for how well he managed his considerable intake, to ask where I stood on capital punishment. 'Well back from the trapdoor,' was my reply, and he burst into laughter. Which showed a western sense of irony and proved he assumed I was joking.

In a way I was, chemical executions were more humane and less messy than hanging. But the concept was one I could, and sometimes did, make a viable argument in favour of. I didn't tell him though; having those who held power in the PRC knowing my attitude to something contentious would be a bad move indeed. And I knew my concept of secrecy and Lao's were not the same. As a businessman representing a country where verisimilitude had long been the prevailing governmental policy, I trusted him to pour the wine and no further.

We left feeling unfulfilled case-wise but extremely replete gastronomically and socially enriched. Also, he offered to pay to compensate for his inability to provide the assistance he knew we 'd been hoping for. I felt like telling him people with far less to lose did the same but didn't. The meeting's agreed confidentiality meant breaking any confidences of others would be hypocritical and unprincipled. And, in addition, contrary to my personal code of ethical behaviour.

Maybe he was right and I was morally driven. The French philosopher Voltaire, in declaring he had no morals but he was a moral man, nailed the dichotomy of publicly-observable versus privately-observed morality. I attempted to be moral but rarely felt I achieved it. At that moment and after several large glasses of magnificent wine, the best Bugs I'd ever had, and a tiramisu dessert richer than the prices, I was feeling close to sated, but far from sainted.

Our flight was at six; time to change and down something to keep the contents of my bloated stomach under control in the air. I drifted, half asleep, as soon as the car took off, Peter Kwan was driving as cautiously as before and the traffic was barely noticeable. Maya said nothing. Later, we could discuss Lao's words but if he didn't want his PA to hear at the time, then we'd respect his decision. We could talk on the plane, on the drive back home, or in the morning. Maya woke me at the hotel with a dig in the ribs. As we waited for the lift, she looked at me and shrugged.

'Well, it was a nice holiday. Pity we didn't get any work done.'

'Not totally true. After these four meetings we know

with pinpoint accuracy where we stand — on the edge of a high precipice and tipping forwards.' She laughed but I could tell it was more obligation than amusement.

21

The flight was smooth, which suited my overindulgence, and the landing was barely noticeable. When I headed up the ramp at Adelaide and found Picino waiting instead of Alex, I was surprised, not pleasantly. But I wasn't going to ask questions in a crowded airport, and Picino's ultra-casual clothing, including baseball cap, sunnies, jeans, and dark five o'clock shadow indicated that while I might be recognised by someone in the crowd, he wasn't intending to be. He caught my eye, made a hand sign indicating follow me, and headed off in the direction of the reclaim area. The message was clear; meet outside. Why the charade was in place wasn't part of the deal, not yet.

I was mystified. Partly his decision to make the appearance himself when he hired anonymous elves to do his meets and greets, and where was Alex and how did he convince her to allow him to welcome me home? We trailed behind with our luggage as he walked to the short-term parking and climbed into an old white SUV in need of a wash. No Beemer and fancy dress; this operation was definitely flying under the radar. The last time he and I did something similar, the girl we were meeting had a protective father who hated uni students in general and lawyers in particular. We were sprung and fortunate to escape with minor bruising.

Picino told us to look at the floor as we drove out. I risked a quick sideways glance as we passed two media vans and a small crowd holding mobiles and microphones.

'The media knew you were coming. Someone told them, probably spotted you at the far end and made calls. But I have contacts at the airline and somehow the media here were given the wrong flight information. I suspect the next flight from Sydney will be met by a crowd of ill-wishers and journos. I don't mind if they talk to you but not until after we have a chance to update each other, as the saying goes.'

Maya's face showed her disapproval; accustomed of old to Picino's often homophobic bad-taste humour, I did what I used to do and ignored it. We exited the airport and turned left away from the city; apparently, we were not going to his office. I said nothing and watched the suburbs drift past. Fifteen minutes and we turned into a driveway, passing a small red car I didn't recognise, through the open doors of a garage, and stopped next to a Toyota I knew well.

Behind us, the sunlight turned to ill-lit gloom as the roller door closed. As I climbed out of the car, a young woman introduced herself as Emily Parsons. I knew the name; Picino's PA. A number of inappropriate, or perhaps perfectly appropriate, comments came to mind, but Picino's stern expression at my smirk showed that type of banter was not the way to go. I settled for dirty thoughts, encouraged by Emily's short skirt and tight T-shirt. We followed her through a door, up some steps, and into a large open room containing leather lounge furniture, a huge television, high shelves packed with books and DVDs, and Alex.

She stepped towards me, I did the same and, after enacting our Cathy and Heathcliff routine for a few moments, we split and turned to face Picino. He asked if anyone fancied a drink and the three yeses and choices caused Emily to vanish through a doorway. Picino made sit-down motions. We did; Alex and I together on a long lounge, Maya in a huge recliner, and Picino on the coffee table. He looked at home and I figured we'd be talking about it later. Apparently not!

'Welcome back. FYI, Emily's not only my PA but my wife's niece. Before Van's dirty mind goes somewhere it shouldn't, I'll clear up any misunderstandings. I've known her since she was born and this place belongs to my wife and me but Emily rents it. Families, what can I say? She's on a short list of people I trust completely. Van, and Maya, you're probably wondering why the cloak and dagger routine. Well, your faces are known to the press, as is Alex's. Mine is also but not dressed like this' — he took off the cap and threw it across the room — 'and lacking my normal fashion sense and in need of a shave, the risk of being recognised was minimal. If the press spotted Alex, they'd have simply hung around her until she met you. I called her, explained the problem, and here we all are. No press, no hecklers, and no one outside the family knows about this place. We can relax. I shouldn't say it's a bonus the media will be pissed off at your no-show, but I don't need to, it's obvious. Well, they don't play fair, as you saw with the ABC, who like to promote themselves as the best-behaved of the collection. Yeah, right.'

Emily arrived with drinks, tea for the Millers, coffee for Maya, and something dark and oily in a glass for Picino. Undoubtedly, a Sicilian mountain remedy brewed in the back shed of a Barossa winery from the detritus the health department wouldn't allow to be included in retail consumables.

At uni, I'd tried one of his mystery concoctions once, and once only. Somewhere between diesel fuel and goat's piss and with elements of each plus several other unnameable toxins were my best guess. He'd laughed and said close enough. He was still drinking it, and I was tempted to ask if staying married to Eva was the reason. It was the only thing I could come up with that would have induced me to go back for more of that diabolical brew.

As three of us sipped our hot and non-toxic drinks, Picino looked at each of us in turn before speaking. I knew bad news was coming, and he was not keen to share it. He proved me right by starting with, 'So, how was the trip? Get plenty of support, did you? Make serious progress?'

The answers to all of the questions were negative, I explained, sticking to short, sharp versions and finishing with the conclusion Maya and I agreed upon. Many supported our effort, unfortunately not openly. If Henry went down for his supposed crime, then sympathy would abound, but it would be like the pragmatically cautious millions who opposed Stalin in the secrecy of their own thoughts and publicly lit candles before his picture every day. Knowing there were many behind us was gratifying; knowing how far behind us they were, out of sight to be accurate, was the kicker. Picino listened carefully and without interrupting, not a bad effort for a lawyer, a politician, a narcissist, and a showboat, and kept his eyes on my face as I spoke. When I finished, he looked at Maya.

'Do you agree with what Van says?' She matched him stare for stare and nodded. I was impressed with her courage, he was one of the highest-ranking politicians in the state, after all. I was equally impressed with his inclusion of someone as low on the pecking order in the discussion; apparently, he'd achieved personal growth recently. In both egalitarian and gender matters. About time!

'Effectively then, Van and Maya, you're no further forward after talking to those people? Yes?'

Me again. 'We are. Sort of. Three of the four are in our

corner even if covertly. That means while they won't be speaking out for us, neither will they be active against us. The only one who openly declared war on Henry was Veronica Fenwick.'

At the mention of her name his eyes lit up. I wished he'd been there; talking to the decorative vacuity in person was a mental cold shower. I explained how she was but I wasn't sure he understood. For a legal highflyer, a successful politician, and after all his years in the public arena, Picino was still, it appeared, as unbelievably shallow as he'd been years ago. I tried for a couple of minutes and Maya backed me up but his views on such beautiful women had always been through the one blind eye and not the two in front of his brain. In the end I simply gave up.

'Hamley won't give us his blessing but neither will he tell lies for political benefit. The same with the minister and Lao refuses to be involved in another country's business. Considering his interests here, I can't blame him. There's already enough anti-Chinese sentiment in the air; it's to his advantage to remain non-committal. To answer your question, then, we didn't achieve much but we learnt a lot. There are few actively pushing for Henry to be blamed legally or even verbally, perhaps public interest, or non-interest in any meaningful way, might cause the whole thing to blow over.'

The look on his face was one I knew well. My optimism, already faded almost to the point of vanishing, was about to be quashed. Hard. And he didn't want to do it but he would anyway because he couldn't avoid it. If he didn't, someone would; he probably figured it might as well be him. Maya, Alex, and I were all staring at him. We sensed what was coming was not pleasant. He took a breath as he stared at the floor then his head came up and his gaze fixed on a point midway between me and Maya. He wasn't ignoring Alex, he was focussing on the two most involved in the growing mess.

'In the last couple of days, there've been developments. Those two who came to your office. There are serious persuasions to forget it ever happened. They've been taken to task for their overzealous behaviour and whoever was responsible for sending them has also been given the message such ideas are to be discouraged in future. In other words, no one's talking, accepting the blame, or is prepared to take the matter further. I've asked, they've answered, and what I learned about it was something a long way short of nothing.'

He took out a handkerchief and wiped his face then rubbed it under his nose. A cold or signs of nerves? Most likely it was him pissed off because the big fish in the local pond had been threatened by the sharks in the ocean of federal politics. Picino in full retreat: something to savour. And to be concerned about. If he was intimidated and worried, I should be both and considerably more. But I had less to lose: my everything was minimal compared to his. For inexplicable reason that struck me as funny. And logical. *Jesus, Van,* I thought, *you are definitely losing it.* All the Its, intellectual and material.

Picino went on. 'It was, I'm told, a matter of poor judgment, and as such should be relegated to the rubbish bin of history. That, by the way, is a quote from someone who apparently favours academic phraseology and is probably educated beyond his ability to think. However, he obviously was not speaking on his own behalf. And whoever put the words into his mouth got them from way, way up the federal food chain. No idea who: I tried and failed. But the one profit to us is now they, whoever they are, know I'm keeping an eye on the case, purely from an objective and legal viewpoint' — he laughed, the sound bursting with bitter cynicism — 'and I've kept the Premier up to date and he's made calls. There will be no more attempts to pressure you from that direction. He and I managed to let them know our feelings on their actions without hinting in any way of our true involvement. If there's a lining with even a glint of silver to it, then that's it.'

He stopped and I knew what was coming was worse news. Picino in hesitant mode was similar to a cautious Siamese fighting fish: there ain't no such thing. It was a side of him I'd never seen, and much as I detested him, it wasn't pleasant to see. I preferred him displaying confidence bordering on arrogance, something I understood and could work around. Picino nervous and fumbling for words was likely to throw me far off balance. My nerves twitched as my inner black dog stirred, turned over, and went back to the stillness of half sleep. I diverted my thoughts to avoid further disturbing its restive state.

Was it possible, I wondered, *the case was affecting him personally? Had the once-dynamic proponent of the writings of John Stuart Mill and other liberal-minded thinkers rediscovered his humanity?* Picino capitalised the L in his political stance and, between ambition and Eva — the proof positive of the behind every successful man was a woman schtick — achieved, through elitism and self-centred disdain, high office and status where lower-case liberal views were forbidden entry. Power, politics, promotion, position, popularity, privilege, prominence, palaces, possessiveness, perdition, parasitic, Picino. All same-same.

But was it possible the egalitarian activist survived, albeit in a minimalised and damaged form? Was the current Picino a palimpsest, the original concealed beneath an overlay of imperial hauteur? And could that reinvigorated conscience be raising insecurities about where this was all going and how he might feel if what he'd covertly set in motion met the death it seemed destined for? He and I might find ourselves simpatico for the first time in years, fighting a combined rear-guard action on the losing side of an unwinnable war.

Legally, it was possible we were headed for a stalemate, but whichever side won or even if that prediction came to pass with both sides the losers, Henry's fate would be the ultimate failure. He was already in trouble: his public condemnation, based on nothing more than unfounded accusations, was a harm he could never totally recover from.

Alex warned me of something similar; for the first time her concerns appeared inevitable. I looked at her and her eyes showed only support. Not a hint of I told you so. It's impossible to not love someone like that. I glanced at Maya, who appeared worried but determined. Right then, I could have stood up and walked out, leaving Henry to his fate. I longed to, but Alex's look said hang in and it will all work out and Maya's expression was more of the bring-it-on variety than any indication she was ready to give up. Plus, awarding the other side victory by default would oppose every legal and moral principle I'd ever held close.

As Springsteen sang, *No Retreat, No Surrender*; a code I'd been ruled by since my only two schoolyard punch ups. I lost the first one: the rematch, later the same day, with me fired up with planning and determination, went my way. To the extent my pugilistic career — my later interaction with Picino and some conflicts innate to policing aside — came to an end, and my time at that school along with it. What I learned though, was win or lose, survive or perish, you have to commit to the fight. Or raise a white flag and submit.

Thus it was once again. Someone was required to stand firm: for Henry's sake. And it seemed fate, Picino, Maya, even Alex, and maybe a God who was punishing me for not believing in him, were united in their choice of champion. Or was that sacrifice? But the pessimistic thoughts were growing in number and clamouring for release. I closed my eyes tightly for a few seconds and forced myself to ignore the sensations coursing around my mind, switch to impersonal professional, and focus on what Picino was saying.

His tentative pause turned into, 'However, to be honest, Van, your case is in deep trouble.' Normally I like, even prefer, total honesty. But right then, a serve of comforting lies would have been a blessing. And since when was the case a matter of your and not our? I knew he hadn't meant it that way but the unintentional intimation of desertion in the face of the enemy initiated a flicker of alarm anyway. It was not yet the camel-crippling straw, but my reaction to his use of the singular pronoun in lieu of the inclusive indicated I was nearing that point.

'Many people have been talking to the media and they've been talking to everyone who has anything to say. My spies tell me tomorrow it's going to kick off big time. Locals in Parnham have come forward, or have probably been dragged forward with promises of airtime and perhaps financial rewards, with tales of magical doings by Henry dating back years.'

It was spot on, as Madison Rundle predicted. I hadn't necessarily been convinced her words would come true: my bad indeed. Experts exist to be listened to, as I bloody well knew!

'I've talked to Basham, he's talked to Mrs Jessup and others, and they all say it's bullshit. But the press doesn't care. They're sucking it up and spitting it out all over the country as soon as they can get it to their organisations. Most of it is incomprehensibly stupid and no one will believe it; apparently Henry turned into an eagle and flew over the town. Whatever that clown was on when he told that story is anyone's guess. As I said, most of it's beyond laughable, and while we can't stop it going out, we sure as shit can shoot it down in flames shortly afterwards. Make them look ridiculous.'

I could tell the idea appealed to him. As with the guy he'd legally and psychologically eviscerated at uni, beating someone unseen wasn't as much fun as waiting until they painted a target on themselves then hitting it dead centre with a full broadside. I may not have liked his vindictive methods but, as they were about to be put into play in my favour, I'd live with them. Anyway, I figured, it might be entertaining watching from the excellent vantage point of my moral high ground. Sort of like football, the modern version of the gladiatorial gorefests, was my view. Blood, violence, scraps, splashing mud: all with me too far back to get splattered.

'But a couple are less crazy and are likely to become problematic. One woman whose husband is in Yatala doing eight years for assault and robbery claims Henry made her husband do it and wants her old man out because Henry, and not he, is guilty. She says Henry's magic worked on her husband because he has an Aboriginal grandfather. It's all total crap but she's extremely insistent and articulate, with nice-ish looks, at least by Parnham standards, and therefore the press are going with it. Basham knows her husband, says he'll go troppo when he finds out his missus is making a fool of herself. He suggests you talk to the husband and get him to talk to her. Perhaps a warning about jail terms for perjury might get her to pull her head in. What do you think?'

I agreed, and at a look from Picino, Emily disappeared, phone in hand. I craved sleep but it seemed I was making a prison visit. Never a highlight of any day, especially one where I was overtired and people-fatigued.

'What's the other? You said there were two.'

'Yes. Basham's looking into that one. A few years back Henry and a neighbour got into a blue over the neighbour's barking dog. Henry apparently stared at the dog and it died. Do you reckon the media loved it? Another resident said the dog died of old age five years after the argument but others say it was the same day. Once Basham starts asking questions. we should sort it out and then the press will get told either they only print the provable truth or I'll go to town on them. I don't mind a bit of poetic licence but publishing and broadcasting hysterical nonsense can be seen as incitement to violence or hate speech or simply trouble-making. Whatever, if they don't stop. I have two clever and aggressive young lawyers poring over books trying to find ways to kick the offending journalists where their keyboards plug into their arseholes. Normally I prefer to play fair' — I laughed at that while Maya merely smirked and Picino winced at his own gaffe' — but if they break the rules then I might have to bend a few as well.'

Emily came back in and gave him a nod. He said, 'Now?' Another nod. We were, it seemed, off to prison. Alex decided to miss the golden opportunity to see humanity at its worst, and Emily invited her to stay. That interaction would be something I'd pay money to hear. Alex would tell me, but only after considerable rewrites and redactions took place. Picino went off to turn himself into himself as the rest of us made small talk and finished our drinks.

Yatala Labour Prison, a twenty-minute drive north of the city looked, the original mid-nineteenth century section anyway, like something out of Dickens or our colonial convict past. Modernisation and advances in incarcerative practices brought it into the twenty-first century, although for a mild claustrophobic like me. it wasn't somewhere I'd choose to be voluntarily. Which I had, and regretted as the first barrier closed behind us.

The room chosen for our visit was more cheerful than most, which isn't saying much. But, as prison visiting areas go, it wasn't excessively depressing. Then again, I owned a get out of jail free card and, despite his wife's absurd efforts, the man shown in after us didn't. Nor would he, as I was about to tell him. And, in case he didn't believe me, Picino was there to reinforce my words. And threats. Or whatever it took to get Jack Milton to tell his better half to pull her bloody head in, to quote the only politician in the car during our drive there. He apologised to Maya for his sexism, which was a mistake. There are few things Maya hates more than a man treating her, to use her expression, like a "blushing Victorian maiden with the vapours". One of them is men who think women should be told what to do and not asked. Both at once. She said nothing but her face was a picture: all one thousand words. Most expletives.

Milton was tall, slim, grey haired, and shook hands with all of us. Maya got a longer shake. I was sure considering his imprisonment-surviving skin tone. her welcome was more cultural than sexual, although after five years alone in there. I'd have snuggled up with Typhoid Mary. Something inexplicable passed between them and both gave a small nod as their hands met. All I, as a lawyer, received was a fleeting smile, more grimace than grin. Picino, the inmates' Angel of Darkness, was ignored. It didn't seem to bother him and, as agreed, he left the room and took the prison officer with him. It was to be our show and legally at least. he sought to demonstrate non-intervention. Which left the three of us.

Minus the impressive assortment of facial scars. Milton might have been considered handsome, and if not in prison clothes. would have seemed like an ordinary bloke, albeit one with a penchant for violence. His eyes were wary, as if the reason for the meeting was unknown. Which proved to be the case. as I asked the obvious opening question.

'Mr Milton, are you aware your wife is trying to get you released by blaming Henry Day for using magic to make you commit your crimes?'

He stared at me; I was worried he hadn't understood. Then he laughed — exposing a noteworthy collection of dental destruction that was probably, like his scars, the result of constant fighting — and stared at the two of us in turn as we nodded confirmation, then laughed again.

'Joke, right? Hey, I know she wants me out but shit, guys, even the mad bitch wouldn't try something that stupid? Doesn't she know how much trouble she could get into, and everyone will be laughing at her, and me, for being bloody crazy. Jesus Christ, how could she…?'

Well, at least I didn't need to explain the legalities of the situation to him. just convince him to write a letter telling her to see it the same way. I was about to ask. when he offered to talk to her on the phone. I was certain it would achieve what we were after in quick time, but in the car. Picino vetoed the idea.

'Phones,' he argued, 'can be bugged. Or she could say we pressured her husband into saying what we required. And recording the conversation would be legally and ethically marginal. You need to go to Parnham and talk to her. Take a letter, maybe a recording, and give her the hard facts about possible consequences of her foray into fame. Get her to retract her claims and get her on the record doing it. Something to bash the press with if they don't retract when you ask them nicely. Ideally, I'd say take her husband with you but I doubt even I could make that happen. Plus, if I let him go and he did a runner. my next position would be cleaning the courthouse toilets. If I was lucky enough to avoid ending up in his empty cell.'

It turned out Milton could write, and the recording, his tone mildly pressuring but, at Maya's insistence, stopping short of threatening, also went without a hitch. We thanked Milton for his assistance and watched as he was escorted back down the hallway, still chuckling over the stupid bitch's bullshit. I was sure I heard Maya grinding her teeth.

Picino asked if we had changes of clothing, which we did, left over from the trip, Then he rang Emily, telling her to book a plane for early, seriously early, first hint of sunlight early, Adelaide to Parnham, return later the same day to Murray Bridge. He dropped Maya and I at a hotel near the airport where Alex was waiting. Maya was in the next room. We dropped our bags, booked immediate laundry service and ignored the promise of extra charges; we weren't paying them, we weren't even booked in under our own names. Then we went to the in-house restaurant.

Two hours later, feeling satisfied gastronomically and in other ways, Alex and I were asleep. Maya expressed hopes over dinner that we'd have the same pilot as last time then refused to explain why to Alex. I relayed the news then fell asleep while Alex was offering to see us off the next morning before driving home.

22

It was the same pilot as last time. Maya, not surprisingly, sat up the front and talked to him; I sat at the rear and went over my notes. Then I dozed. Alex had showed me how much she'd missed me and I was a tad sleep deprived. Afterwards I watched the scenery and planned the day. I was going with Basham to talk to Milton's wife, show her the letter, play the recording, and try and talk sense into her. If that didn't work. I was going to threaten. It isn't my initial choice of actions; I favour attempting the make-haste-slowly notion first. For a short time. Things were moving fast and getting away from me and a long version of slow and easy was not an option. Five minutes of Mister Nice Guy then...

We landed smoothly, probably Maya's presence encouraging serious showing off and, as the engines wound down, I looked out of the window and saw Basham. He seemed to be alone; then again, he didn't need anybody else unless he was outnumbered in double figures. When I was young, I longed to be big, figuring it must make you feel invincible. Then a client of mine who barely made it up to my shoulders killed a guy taller than me using a tiny knife and I realised size didn't matter: it was innate meanness providing the strength. The problem was, I didn't have that either. Until the day I knocked seven bells out of Picino in front of half the student body. I'm not sure if it made me feel mean. Definitely better, though.

The reality was that going into the coming meetings wound up and angry wasn't sensible; I took two deep breaths and a double belt from the flask helped. We climbed down the stairs, still far too unstable for my liking, and walked over to Basham. After the handshake protocols, we moved towards Basham's four-wheel-drive. Elevated on the side-step as I climbed in, I took a look around; there was nothing new since last time or probably from before I was born. Maya waved to the pilot, saw me watching and blushed; now that was new. Basham started the engine and we took off along the fence line.

I explained my strategy. Maya to talk to Mrs Jessup, Basham and I to visit the wife with the husband problem and the dog owner with the chronological issues, meet back there as soon as we were finished, and fly home for dinner. I commented to Basham the ACA were noticeable by their absence and he told me to look off to the left. Half hidden behind a tree, I saw a red pickup with two men in it.

I asked about the pilot's safety and he told me to look past the plane. Standing under a tree I could make out a man in the same-coloured clothing as Basham who seemed to be holding something long. I asked, and it was a shotgun. It was also the same officer who'd stopped the other vehicle last time. I relaxed. If Basham was sure he could handle it, who was I to question his judgment? Obviously, the Senior Sergeant was a careful man. And, I was sure, Picino would have told him we were valuable and were to be looked after. Between that thought, the two slugs from the flask, and the all-important deep breaths, I was starting to chill.

Mrs Jessup was outside waiting. I wasn't surprised: the sound of the plane could probably be heard for a long distance, and I doubted whether the airstrip was busy. Maya climbed out, Basham gave the old lady a wave, and we headed off. It was a short trip, three minutes tops, and we turned into a driveway differing from all the others I'd seen only in the fact it was extremely tidy and the sparse garden was well tended. There was no rubbish or wheel-less cars, only kids' toys with matching kids. As we got out, the two, one of each, rushed up to Basham and clasped his legs. Clearly, they knew and liked him. Great, I figured, that should make life easier. They ignored me which made walking easier.

A woman came out of the door. Like the house, she was neat and tidy, wearing a cotton shirt over jeans and riding boots. RM Williams; archetypal bush fashion. I also saw the clothes were well worn and carefully looked after. Part of me, considering her husband's current status, expected someone less together. I'd met many prisoners' wives, and considering some of them, being inside must have seemed like a holiday for their men. Not this one. Not only was she working hard to get her husband released, she seemed at first sight to be worth coming home to. She also looked bright eyed and intelligent, which made threats a poor second option. When she spoke, her voice and manner confirmed my first impression. Better educated and socially a cut above many of the women with menfolk inside.

'Hello. I'm Carol Milton. These are our children, Joe and Chloe, and I believe you've met my husband, Jack.' Basham got a smile as I was becoming sure was normal for him in the town, ACA excepted.

'Please, come inside. Would you like a drink? Tea, coffee, or...?'

I accepted tea, Basham coffee, and she disappeared for a few minutes. As I heard rattling sounds at the far end of the house, I looked around. The place was spotless and tidy; it put my own house to shame. I looked at Basham and raised my eyebrows. He leaned in and whispered.

'She's the positive influence in this family. Jack needs to be controlled and most of the time he can be. But he got drunk with his mates. It's not a mistake he'll make again. Carol has told him if he does, she'll leave and take the kids, after which her two brothers will come around and break his legs.'

I must have smiled. 'She means it. Don't be fooled, she's one tough lady. She does bookkeeping for many of the locals, which is how she keeps it together with Jack away. But she misses him, I know she does. She told me. Her talking to the press was unusual, she doesn't normally show her vulnerable side, but it's her only chance of getting him out early. I spoke to John Picino, and it's a total no go on early release. It's up to you. You've got nothing to offer her except getting her dignity back. Knowing her it might work.'

He stopped as Carol came back in carrying a crowded tray. Two pots, three mugs, and a plate of what looked like home-baked biscuits. I admired her for the way she was acting. If it was me in her place, we'd have been given a glass of warm water on the verandah, if we were allowed through the gate and hadn't been given directions to commit a physical violation on ourselves. Basham said she was alright and I'd seen nothing to contradict his opinion. She poured and added, we all took a sip and put the cups down, and I was on.

'This must be difficult for you. I understand, and I'd like to help you if I can.'

She looked surprised, probably expecting something more legalese and threatening. When she spoke, it seemed like my plan to go in gently was the right choice.

'Thank you. I've given this a lot of thought. I suppose you want to convince me to retract what I said to the press. You probably have a letter or something from Jack saying the same thing.'

I didn't speak: just handed her the letter. She took it out of the envelope and read it, then tears welled and rolled down her cheeks. She wiped them away with a tissue then looked straight at me.

'Yes, well, he's right. You're right, I know what you're thinking. It was stupid. I don't know why I said it. The silly girl from the TV was bloody convincing. And persuasive. I said yes. I didn't even get to say much. She hinted and put words in my mouth and before I knew it, she was telling the world poor old Henry Day hypnotised Jack into breaking the law. At the time it seemed harmless, but now it all seems damn foolish. Especially after reading that letter.'

I knew what it said. It was full of understanding and love, plus a plea for her to withdraw her claims and get her pride back. In those words. No hints of how he'd spoken at the prison. Inmate talk tends to be hyper-masculine; it's a survival mechanism. Writing his letter to her was a long-term version of the same impulse, boding well for their future together, which I knew from experience was far from the norm for inmates and their relationships.

'It won't help Jack, what I did. Will it?' I shook my head and felt relief as I realised her husband made my case for me and there was no need to turn nasty. 'It probably embarrassed him. It certainly has me. If I give you a letter, could you get it to him?'

I said yes. She half smiled, stood up, and went to the other side of the room where an old grey landline phone stood on a small table. She pressed buttons. Someone answered and she asked to be connected to the newsroom.

'This is Carol Milton. Yes, that one. If you put out any more of what your smooth reporter talked me into saying I'll consult a lawyer.' A short pause.' Well, I didn't sign anything and don't want your money, and if she ever comes here again, I'll kick her halfway across the town. Same for you if my name goes public again. I want you to show a retraction of what I said earlier. If you don't, how does sole parent with husband in jail raising two kids pressured by media into making false claims sound? You'll look stupid and intimidating, I'll get money from your channel, and public sympathy will move from you to me. If you want to see a great performance of a struggling woman trying to survive in a desert town and hassled by big city reporters, then ignore me. I hope you're recording this because I'm only saying it once.'

She hung up, not softly, turned to me, and smiled. 'There. Sure felt good. They caught me at a weak moment and I hate it when people do that. Do you think they listened?'

I wasn't sure about that and even less hopeful what it might achieve, but I intended to call Picino later and he could get one of his many contacts to reinforce her message. Carol's days on television would be over or, knowing Picino, the reporter's would. I drank my tea and ate three biscuits. I don't know what was in them and out there I was afraid to ask. But they were terrific and the boost seemed more sucrose-related than what similar looking cookies in my student days often contained.

Carol started getting teary again. She went out and we waited until she returned and handed me an envelope. It seemed a perfect time to leave. As she and I shook hands, she kept hold of mine.

'Please tell Henry I'm sorry. And then get them to find

him innocent. I don't know him well, but he says hello in the street or if I see him at the shop. Good luck to both of you.'

We went to go and I had an idea. 'Carol, were you at the meeting? The one about the sale of Bilden Downs?'

She thought. 'The one at the community centre. The big one?'

'Yes. Did you see Henry there? Was he present?'

She thought again. 'No, I don't think so. I didn't see him anyway. The Fenwicks were there and I didn't like her. All overdressed snootiness, teeth, tits, hair, and no brains. I stayed outside and listened through the door. I can't be sure, but I don't remember seeing him.'

Another flash. 'Was Jack there?'

'No, he was away working.'

It didn't prove anything one way or the other. But I was fairly sure if Henry was there, he too would have remained outside, and Carol would have seen him. But it wasn't evidence, and while I could theorise for ever, I wouldn't get any further with my desire to prove he hadn't attended. Still, it was worth asking.

It exceeded my expectations though, and as we left, I made a note in my diary to talk to Picino, both about the reporter and to see if he could find any way to help the Miltons. Especially Jack.

The kids ignored me and gave Basham a hug goodbye. I was bemused. The guy looked like a yeti and was welcomed like Father Christmas. Kids can see past looks, though. Which was why, despite my mild manner, conventional clothing, and lack of lethal weaponry, they sensed I was a lawyer and therefore untrustworthy. To be avoided. Clever kids.

Following another short drive, we pulled up in front of a house I realised was next door to Henry's, which appeared newly glazed, freshly painted, and with a spotless garden. Making it the total opposite of the feral tip we were going into. There wasn't a sign saying Keep Out, and there didn't need to be. Basham went to open the gate and two huge dogs came from behind the house and stood facing us through the wire mesh, growling. Menacingly. Basham took his pistol out and pointed it at them, also menacingly. I couldn't work out what breed they were, my best guess was Siberian wolf crossed with American grizzly bear. I like dogs that like me: the mutual dislike was tangible. I was hoping Basham could shoot faster than they jumped gates.

A voice from the house called out loudly and the dogs ran quickly towards the rear of the house. That title was misleading; it resembled a depression-era ruin after an earthquake. We went through the gate and walked towards the front entrance. Behind a torn filthy fly screen, I saw a man watching us. Next to me, Basham, pistol still in hand, watched both the man and the corner around which the dogs vanished. I saw the man look at the pistol, then at Basham, and come to a decision. He called backwards to someone to lock the damn dogs up. If this was the man who claimed Henry killed his dog with illegal magic, then he certainly wouldn't have chosen to lose two more to legal bullets.

He swung the screen door open and came out. The torn, stained blue singlet, ragged track pants, worn thongs, and baseball cap ragged and filthy to the extent I couldn't make out the logo, told me this meeting might not be as pleasant as the last one. I certainly wouldn't be accepting a cup of tea from him: I was uncomfortable breathing the same air.

He was long overdue for a shave and a haircut, but those were the least of his hygiene requirements. I could tell he'd once been white, but years of ingrained dirt, sunburn, and what looked like used oil had tinted him to a mottled shit-brown hue. As he came nearer, his stench preceded him and I tried not to inhale. He looked and smelled like the central character in an exhumation I was obliged to witness and the eau-de-dogshit from the mounds strewn across the yard wasn't helping. There were blowflies everywhere, buzzing black clouds dining alfresco at the faecal banquet and beginning to notice our presence. How the press went the distance was beyond me. Perhaps they felt a kinship with him: his body and their souls. When he spoke, it turned from worse to worst.

'Wadda yous want?' Great start. After that greeting, I wondered, where do you go from there? I had no idea. Basham did.

'Mister Peel? Clarrie Peel?'

The man stared at him and said nothing. I was beginning to think he was several latitudes south of compos, which was in our favour, because the evidence of someone with his limitations would carry no noticeable legal weight. Accompanying the body odours, I detected something highly familiar. Along with his natural disadvantages, Peel was stoned and judging by how the second-hand aroma coming off him was holding its own against strong competition, he'd been that way for a considerable time. The vacuity was a blend of intrinsicality and induction.

The trip was mostly an unnecessary waste of time. Carol Milton was in need of someone to convince her to retract her claim and had, and any testimony of the socially-inept loner would be legally discounted on grounds of mental incompetence. The media, as always, blew the two stories up without doing any serious research into validity and probably applied financial or other pressure to convince vulnerable people to say something convertible into headlines. I was beginning to think attempting to get this man to change his tune was not worth the effort, and I was mentally preparing to leave when he spoke.

'Old Enry, he dint like me dogs. Said they bark all the time and the shit smelled bad. One day he stared at one of 'em, Jessie, me heeler. Coupla hours later she died. All okay till he make evil eye on her, then she gone. It was him done it. Abo magic.'

Oh, shit. He clearly wasn't as mentally impaired as I'd thought, and could even string enough of a sentence together for me to recognise what he was saying was almost word for word how the media reported his claims. After running it through spell check several times. Apparently, they'd been telling the truth, at least as far as reporting what he'd said anyway. Which is what the press should do. With the accent on should.

I couldn't take it seriously, and they had. Probably more out of sensation-seeking self-interest than true belief. But I couldn't, and shouldn't, have been feeling angry or critical of their actions. They were only doing their jobs. Then again, many concentration camp guards tried to use the same excuse at Nuremberg. It didn't work then, and still doesn't, to my mind.

I wanted to ask him questions, but had no idea which ones to ask or if it was worth the effort. I felt a wave of negative emotions flooding in. Considering everything about the man, no one who met him would take what he said seriously. However, those who were taking the media versions of his tale on board would never meet him, and the media crews were too canny to let him talk on screen. Well-edited and probably well-distanced shots only. Which meant his carefully reconstructed statements would be taken as gospel, and Henry would be seen not only as a murderer but something far worse: a dog killer. Not only in the media; with Peel cleaned up and his testimony orchestrated by a sharp lawyer, what he had to say was bound to carry some weight in a courtroom. Not a great deal, but those who wished to believe wouldn't require much convincing. He was starting to represent a problem.

Basham's voice broke into my self-pitying reverie. 'Mister Peel. Sorry about your dog.' Even in my state I could hear the cynicism and lack of empathy, and I tuned back in. Perhaps he had questions, mine seemed to be hiding from me, and maybe, a tiny maybe, this could be sorted out. I felt a straw to be grasped at and listened.

'You say your dog died a couple of hours after Henry looked at it. Over the fence. Is that right.' The blank look didn't change but Peel nodded. A small movement only but definitely, and more important legally, recognisable as a nod if witnessed by a lawyer and a police officer. I didn't know where Basham was going but since I was lost and mapless, I figured I might as well follow him.

'Some of your neighbours tell us a couple of hours was more like five years. What do you reckon? Bit longer than you thought, maybe?'

Not a nod but a mumble. 'No, they lyin'.'

Basham stared at him for a few seconds then showed why Picino's opinion of him was high. On the last trip, I'd seen him dispense bush justice. Not according to the letter of any official law but conforming to something more primally necessary. Harsh land, tough people, needing harsh measures and tough actions.

'Mister Peel,' somehow the scrupulously polite formality highlighted what followed, 'here's the thing. If you insist on sticking with your story, then Mister Miller here will call you as a witness. You'll have no choice because he can get the court to order you to turn up and give evidence. Which means if you refuse, I'll come and arrest you and drag you off to Adelaide. After you lie in court, and we both know you are now and probably will again, don't even think about telling me you're not, he'll put your neighbours on the stand and prove you're lying. Doesn't matter why you are, money, publicity, or plain everyday shit on the liver. Why isn't relevant. What is though, is if you lie to the court, it's called perjury, and it's worth time in prison. A small cell, shower every day, eat crap food, your dogs will have to be put down, and I'll get a warrant to search your property and who knows what might turn up. Bad for you all round. It's either that or you sign a declaration you lied to the press, we get them to acknowledge it tomorrow in the paper and on the TV, you look a bit foolish, or we could make it look as if they pressured a doddery old man and he became confused or whatever. In the end, Henry isn't accused of killing your dog, which we all know he didn't, and you're left alone with your dogs. Okay, Clarrie, what's it to be? Say you made a mistake or risk jail time and losing your dogs?'

Five minutes later, signed retraction in hand and windows fully open to fumigate our lungs and evict a few persistent blowflies, we were on our way. Before we did, Basham told Peel if there were any complaints about his dogs menacing people, then he, Basham, would personally come back and give them a humane termination. His words. It wasn't necessary, I think he was trying to strengthen the sense of fear he'd aroused in the man. It seemed to work. The cowed and hunched man who went back into the house was not the same angry and confrontational one who'd come out. As I said, bush justice. Normally I preferred the strictly legal, although the effectiveness was undeniable and we saved a fortune in court fees and other costs. I did have one question.

'Did you know most of what you said about the court ordering him to appear and the possibility of jail for perjury was all seriously bullshit? He's mentally impaired, by birth and bong. Nothing he said would have any meaning in law.'

Basham smiled. 'Yeah, I know. I was making it up as I went. But listen, Van, I'm the senior police officer up here, I'm big and authoritative, I have a gun, which I was holding when he first came out, and I threatened to shoot his dogs if he didn't cooperate. In a roundabout way, not directly, but he got the general idea. Plus, he's an ignorant, anti-social old prick who only uses newspapers to wipe his arse and has never read one, let alone a book, and he knows less than nothing about anything. Don't you reckon I was on safe ground bullshitting someone like him? He was lying, and in my opinion, doing it simply out of pure meanness pepped up with racism. I played it the same way. Worked, didn't it?'

I'd spent years learning the law and it didn't apply a great deal out there. Something more primitive and simpler was the norm, and it worked well. It was not, strictly speaking, an eye for an eye. Or maybe it was. A confused woman I was prepared to bully responded to kindness with kindness, and a nasty old social misfit reacted to a dose of his own medicine by admitting defeat the instant he was put under pressure. I couldn't apply those methods back in civilisation, but out there, they seemed to suit the circumstances.

Maya was ready when we arrived at Marilyn Jessup's house. We refused the offer of refreshments, and after thanking her for her time and assistance, we headed to the airstrip. On the way, I thanked Basham at length. He seemed embarrassed, and I assumed that what I'd found unusual was merely a part of policing in the remote bush. Or perhaps letting me see how he did his job bothered him a bit. I told him I found it interesting and educational. Which was true.

As we pulled up near the plane, I noticed the red pickup was gone, and the pilot, whose name I decided to learn if only to keep Maya happy, was chatting to Basham's offsider. We made our farewells and minutes later were airborne. I sat on the left side, the afternoon sun was glaring in through the right side windows, and watched in amusement and a small degree of envy as Maya and the pilot made animated conversation and swapped looks. *Had I*, I wondered, *ever been as happy and carefree?* The answer was yes, and once this case was over, regardless of the result, I intended to work hard to reconnect with those aspects of my life.

I knew Maya was affected by it too, but she seemed able to compartmentalise more successfully than I could. Talking to someone she liked, even fancied, was an advancement on sitting in despondent silence, dwelling on the seemingly insurmountable difficulties facing us. I got on with doing that and she worked on her plans for something more positive as we flew south. Although we left from Adelaide, we were to be dropped back at Murray Bridge where Alex would be waiting, accompanied by Colin who was watching out for her. The day surpassed my expectations, considering the case overall; the two letters signed, witnessed, and outright denials of what was now legally unignorable hearsay. It was a small win, and I couldn't think of any way the situation could possibly get worse. It wasn't complacency as such; more an unwillingness to indulge in any more melancholy predictions.

One of my old aunties claimed she could see into the future. She was long dead, which was a pity, mostly because I liked her but also for her supposed gift. I didn't believe in any of it, but I was ready to welcome any assistance I could get.

23

Later that night, Picino called. He sounded jubilant. Or drunk. It was hard to tell, so probably both. 'I made enquiring calls and the stories of your client hypnotically causing a crime spree and killing dogs won't only not be repeated but most of the networks intend to provide retractions. They'll probably be about five seconds long and placed immediately before an ad break when everyone's off for a piss or a cuppa. Still, anything's an advancement on nothing. Alright, Van, how'd you do it?'

'Charm, persuasion, legal knowhow, all the things I have and you lack.'

'Yeah, right. The unhappy single mum would have been a walkover, she only said what she did because the media grubs harassed her until she spouted something remotely-quotable and then distorted it beyond recognition. But did you and Basham lean on the dog man a bit? I saw him on TV and if he stunk half as bad as he looked, I'm glad it was you there and not me. He also looked bloody determined. Tell all.'

'No. If you want to learn legal tricks, Adelaide Uni have an outstanding law program. Only this time, listen instead of spending your time in the UniBar or in bed with other people's girlfriends.'

He wouldn't have liked that, which is why I said it. He'd been a far better student than me and we both knew it, but I was angry, only partly at him, and seeking to lash out at someone. We were no longer bitter enemies but our relationship was a long way from friendship. He chose not to retort and changed the subject. A Picino speciality.

'Anyway, with those two out of the way, the only other ones from Parnham are of the too-silly-to-go-with type.

You know, turning into a flying eagle, summoning animals to him and talking with them, and all the other bullshit.'

I hadn't heard about the conversing with animals claim. 'Apparently there are people going off the rails with this.'

'No kidding. Since there was only one witness, the same person who sees Jesus on a donkey in the main street regularly, it didn't get mileage. Also, Basham's been doing the rounds and he says nobody in town will confirm whether Henry Day was at the meeting. He hinted that lying in court could lead to charges of perjury and if Henry's attendance was proven either way, those who said the opposite might be in deep shit. Therefore, it's more appropriate to go with no comment. Sounds like something you might have put him up to. Yes?'

'No comment.' In truth it was yes, but not directly. After seeing what Basham did with the dog man, I intimated it might not be a bad idea to continue the idea around the town. If he'd spoken to the right few people and they'd followed the rural laws of gossip it would have spread like a plague. But if anyone found out Basham did it, he'd be in trouble, as would I and maybe even Picino if he admitted he knew about it and did nothing.

'It sounds feasible but legally and ethically it would nudge the line too closely for comfort. Perhaps Henry burnt a few gum leaves and sang them all into a more supportive frame of mind.'

He laughed, more courtesy than appreciation. I knew he knew I was lying. I also knew Basham wouldn't contradict me or indict himself; our short private conversation covered all eventualities. Now Picino did know, but did not know. Too much like the back alley manipulations of politics for me, especially late at night. I ended the call and went to bed, where Alex, who heard about the day as soon as I arrived home, called for details. Then she demanded something else. I was too tired and said no. She insisted; I surrendered. By the time I finally got to sleep, it was more than late, it was early the next day. I slept deeply though. Love beats chamomile tea every time.

The next morning, I watched the ABC news and glanced at the Advertiser and the Australian. All three plus two of the commercial stations issued retractions. The TV our-bads sped by faster than a boob shot in an old BBC costume drama and the newspaper ones weren't as far back as the classifieds but were a long way from where they might attract any serious attention. Still, they'd done it. A win. I once won five dollars on a scratchy after spending ten on buying them. A pyrrhic victory only but it still felt good. And their back-downs showed they were listening. Maya had scanned the two letters, then emailed them widely as soon as we'd hit town the previous day. I knew they'd cave, although I didn't expect it to be as quickly. Although, after a number of serious chastisements concerning political reporting recently, perhaps the Fourth Estate were being twice shy.

I munched on bacon, eggs, and toast and sipped tea as repetitious stories about Fenwick's death studiously avoided contention. There was a mention of a Northern Territory paper, a target of regular mockery by other states' media, running an article about Henry's avian transmutations and Dolittleian chat-fests. The ABC hosts, as always, seemed to find the Territorian reportage humorous. Me too, although I knew that some in the gullible population would believe it. Hopefully, they wouldn't go public about it, though. Not a problem for us but the inevitable post-retraction ridicule might be for them.

Alex finally appeared, ready for work, and Maya wandered in to hitch a ride. Rain was forecast and even the most expensive bikes are not waterproof. I finished my tea and stood up to get ready but stopped when I heard a thump at the back door. Dogs and cats scratch, God's messengers tap, salespeople and friends knock, and ill-wishers thump. Rule of nature.

Alex was at the door before I could say don't. She opened it slightly then stepped back as whoever battered on it pushed it open wide and stepped in. He shoved Alex, who retreated towards me, followed by two men. I knew instantly they were trouble. On the cupboard was a panic button for signalling the two in the caravan. I pressed it three times before facing the intruders. Which was what they were. Whatever they were selling, it wasn't going to dust, wash, vacuum, or perform anything equally beneficial. It was going to hurt, and there was nothing I could do about it. There were only two of them but I was outnumbered by more than the simple maths.

The one who pushed Alex was over two metres tall and heavily built. What was filling out his T-shirt was serious muscle or solid fat. Either way, it looked powerful. His close-cut hair was dirty blond, both in colour and condition. From across the room, I could smell sweat and musk. Primal, feral, bestial, suggesting unrestrained physicality paired with the promise of uncaring violence. I realised I was being dramatic, but when I looked at the two women, I could tell they felt the same way. We were all afraid, we couldn't hide it, and the leering grin on the man's face showed he enjoyed arousing the sensation. This, I knew, was about to get nasty.

I looked at his companion. My height, a slim build with ropy muscle. Longish greasy hair, and an expression as vacant as the one my grandfather displayed in his coffin. He might not be as violent as the big man, but he'd be equally unsympathetic to any pain caused. I'd met the type before, even defended a few. Then, I'd been on edge sitting in a police station with uniforms at the ready. In my own home and with Alex and Maya also in danger, I was more than on edge, I was feeling angry and helpless.

The younger one I was sure I could deal with if he was alone, the bigger one I wasn't sure about but I might have been tempted to give it a try if only for my own peace of mind as I spent time recovering. The two together, no chance. Part of police training was knowing when to retreat and regroup. I stood still and waited.

The bigger one spoke first. The voice didn't match the appearance, he was far more articulate than I expected. But an excess of something, most likely raw spirits and tobacco, roughened the edges, and gave the words an extra rasp they didn't need.

'Henry Day. Is he here? If he is, show me where. Or someone'll get hurt. Probably her.' He pointed at Maya who fell into a chair shaking. I was desperate to do the same but I was trying to salvage pride and stand up to them at least a little.

He shouted. 'Where is Henry Day? We wanna talk to him. I know you're his lawyer and you know where he is. We don't wanna hurt him or anyone else, just talk to him, but if you don't tell me then we'll hurt someone till you do.'

I didn't believe they weren't about to hurt Henry but I did believe they'd hurt us if we didn't cooperate. I didn't get a chance to answer. The door behind me opened and Cheryl walked past me and stood between us facing the bigger one. She only came up to his shoulders and looked like a child fronting a gorilla. A slight amazed smile appeared on his face.

'What you want, girlie?'

Behind the pair I heard another door open and saw Colin come in. He placed himself behind the smaller man who turned to look. His mouth literally dropped open. It was obvious he knew Colin, who smiled at him. Not warmly. 'Hello, Ade.'

The friendliness of the greeting was lost on Ade, who turned to look at his hulking companion in panic. The bigger man didn't notice. He was too busy running his eyes over Cheryl and licking his lips. I mean, it was eighties tough-guy action-movie cliché time. Perhaps he reckoned that was how he should act, or maybe the movies imitated creatures like him in their depictions of the villains Stallone, Van Damme and company smacked into the pavement in every scene of every movie.

Cheryl looked him straight in the face. The overt challenge she was making was unmistakeable. In her bright green running shoes, Lycra shorts, and vivid orange T-shirt, she looked harmless and I was hoping Dean's reports of her were true, otherwise she was about to get hurt. For a few moments no one moved or spoke, then the hulk started to raise his right arm towards Cheryl. His hand was open ready to touch, the intent clear.

What wasn't clear was what happened next. I saw it but then again, I didn't. What I can recall was a flash of orange, a dull thud, a sharp cry, and the hulk standing motionless, right arm hanging like a wet sock and face the colour of old concrete. He seemed to be whining softly, although I thought perhaps mewling might be more accurate. He was plainly in intense agony and shock, from whatever was done to him and because a tiny girl did it. Who was standing looking at him as calmly as before she did it.

His companion went to move towards him but a sharp word from Colin stopped him dead. Again, nobody moved, and if it wasn't for the big man's pathetic sounds of distress the room would have been silent. *Well*, I thought, *Dean was right about Cheryl. Hellfire, had he ever been right*.

Alex moved to Maya and put her arms around her. I decided to make drinks. I filled the kettle and got five clean mugs. I knew how Cheryl and Colin took their coffees. I started spooning granules and digging milk out of the fridge. Behind me the two intruders stood motionless as their guardians watched them carefully.

Colin spoke first. 'I called Dean. He's on his way.'

The smaller man's entire body twitched. 'Dean? He's coming here? Shit. No. Oh no.'

From which I gathered he knew Dean. Probably the same way he recognised Colin, a martial arts connection. The fright in his voice was tangible and for the first time his face showed something other than blankness. Fear. Brilliant, I decided. Bloody brilliant!

Cheryl told the two men to sit against the wall, adding a warning I couldn't catch but didn't need to. The smaller one helped his companion sit down, the move clearly causing the bigger man pain, which I confess I enjoyed hearing. Colin moved a chair close to them and sat down,

Ade looking at him like a dog expecting a beating. Which answered the question of whether Colin was also considered good at what he did.

I handed Maya and Alex their drinks and, not wanting to go near the two men, told Cheryl hers and Colin's were also ready. She took his over and positioned herself on a chair close to the men, neither of whom showed any visible inclination to movement beyond the bigger one's occasional squeezing of his dangling right arm with his left hand. I didn't know what she'd done but I wanted to learn how to do it. I mean, I hadn't even seen her move and she'd disabled a muscle-bound giant without even breathing heavily afterwards. Jesus!

Alex and Maya vanished into the other end of the house. I came to the realisation my presence was irrelevant. After one last look at Ade, staring morosely at his friend who appeared to be sleeping, I made signs at Colin who nodded, and I left.

Maya was crying softly, something I felt like joining in with, and Alex was sitting in her chair with the sort of expression that meant someone was in for a serve. When I sat next to her, she smiled, and I knew it wasn't me, but who? I didn't get to wonder for long.

'Goddamn bloody Picino. Getting us all into this mess. Federal cops getting heavy in the office and now gangster thugs in our house. Nobody signed up for this. Van, we moved here to be away from all that shit. What now?'

'We're waiting for Dean to turn up. He'll sort this and if he can't then Picino will. Maybe both together, I don't know, to be honest. But you're right, this has gone out of control.'

I sat quietly staring at the carpet. She put her arms around me and I let myself relax. It wasn't my fault and it was. It wasn't Picino's fault and it was. It wasn't Veronica Fenwick's fault and it was. And the list went on. In reality, this time it was the fault of whoever sent those two bastards to my house and I needed to know who they were. I stood up, went back out into the other room.

'Right, you two, who sent you here?' That was as far as I got before Colin assisted me back through the door.

'Van, Dean said not to speak to them. He'll deal with it. We need to wait. Please.'

So, I went and sat with Alex and Maya, who were looking better but nowhere close to best, and, as instructed, we waited.

The thing about Harley-Davidsons is you can hear them coming a long way off, especially if they're being ridden hard. Nearly half a minute before Dean came roaring up our driveway like the vanguard of Armageddon, I knew he was in the town. My neighbours would be unhappy and I tried to pretend I was capable of caring.

Dean strode in looking worried, angry, and flushed from an obviously fast trip up from the city. He took a quick glance into the other room and I assumed Cheryl or Colin let him know it was in hand because he came straight back. He said hello to Alex and Maya, asked how they were then turned to me. 'Can you fix speeding fines? I'm certain I copped two on the way here.' I told him yes, then I told him what happened.

I'd never seen him so pissed off and I was glad it wasn't aimed at me. He asked Alex for a glass of water and drank it all. He took several deep breaths, beckoned to me, and we went into the other room. Cheryl and Colin appeared more relaxed now the boss was there and Ade looked terrified while his mate appeared to be unconscious. Dean took Cheryl to one side and she explained what she'd done and why. I heard him chuckle. Which meant he approved of her actions. It boded well for her future and ill for the one who raised a hand to her.

Who was Dean's next stop. He leaned over and squeezed the big man's upper right arm which produced a loud moan and wide-open eyes.

'Good, you're awake. Means we can have a chat.'

Dean sounded pleased at the idea; the object of his attentions appearing to be considerably less impressed. He was not looking particularly worried, though, while Ade was shaking and trying to curl into a ball and hide in the corner. Which meant, I assumed, Ade knew who Dean was, and the other man didn't. Dean worked that out as well and moved to improve his knowledge.

'I'm Dean. I teach martial arts and Ade is one of my students. Which is why he's hoping I'll focus on you and not him. Tell him, Ade.'

Ade was having trouble speaking but a glare from Dean and a step forward by Colin assisted him to find his voice.

'Yeah, Glen, tell 'em what they wanna know. That's Dean and he's like real dangerous and the other guy is Colin and... well, he's totally mental, man. I don't know who the bitch is but the shit she pulled on you... I mean, shit, man. Heavy shit.'

Despite the grammatical problems, it seemed Glen, now with a name which was socially a step forward, got the message. His face took on a wary sly look. Not yet scared, but the day was young and I had a feeling Dean was only getting started.

So did Ade. 'At least that Ronan isn't here. I tell you, Glen, that guy is seriously lethal.'

Dean leaned forward. 'Ade, now we've all been introduced, I should tell you Ronan is on his way here and the bitch, as you called her, is a close friend of his. It would be helpful if we can sort this out before I get him to ask you what I need to know.'

I was certain Ade was going to pass out; he was definitely regretting calling Cheryl a bitch. He looked at her and mouthed sorry. All he got back was a glare which made him shrivel up again.

I know I shouldn't but I was starting to have fun. Those two scared me and more importantly Alex and Maya. Seeing them feeling fear was, if not pleasurable, then at the least was giving me a surge of vindictive satisfaction. Dean continued.

'Glen, I'm not going to ask who sent you because if you tell me we might have to reveal it in a courtroom and none of us want to involve the law in this. Do we?'

Glen mumbled something that sounded like agreement. Dean let it go.

'What we do want to know is what you came here to do. But first you owe the ladies an apology. Cheryl' — he gestured and she went out — 'will fetch them and you'll tell them you're sorry. Do I need to mention what will happen if you don't convince them you mean it?'

Apparently not, and once Alex and Maya came in, both men managed to put an apology together. It was less than completely convincing but not too shabby, considering one was having trouble remaining conscious and the other looked like he was about to wet himself. Dean asked the two women to leave, saying he wanted to have a talk to the men, promising it would be conversation only and unless absolutely necessary, he wouldn't make a mess of the carpet. As he spoke, his back was to the men and I saw him give Alex and Maya a wink. It seemed to comfort them and they left. I remembered seeing the same wink seconds before he unloaded on an opponent in a tournament. Basically, it signified Dean cool and in control while manufacturing adrenaline and angst before combat.

He asked me if I needed to leave but I could tell he wished me to stay. It didn't matter; I was going nowhere. Whatever happened, violent or no, my damaged self ached to witness it. Almost certainly a bad idea legally; psychologically was an entirely different situation. Behind me a door opened and I turned as Maya came back in. I went to tell her to leave but she spoke first. 'I'm staying, Van. Alex is in the lounge watching television. Don't worry, she's okay now.' She sat in a chair and stared at the two men like a microbiologist studying plant specimens.

Dean turned to Glen. 'Okay, why are you here and what were you after?'

It took a while. Glen's shoulder was obviously hurting and he kept twitching intermittently. Dean explained to us that what Cheryl used was a Krav Maga technique called a Brachial Stun, a blow delivered to the neck causing muscle spasms and pain in the nerves of the Brachial Plexus which control the shoulder and arm. I made a mental note to ask Alex about it later. It would, Dean said, wear off after a few hours but might hurt for longer. Sincere sympathy was noticeably absent from Dean's voice, even more noticeable when he explained to Glen that a repeat, and harder, dose could easily result in permanent damage. He rubbed it in by asking which hand Glen used to wipe his arse and laughed when he got an answer. On the surface, it sounded almost like friendly banter; underneath the affability were serious threats and, as dull-witted and pain-distracted as Glen was, he got the message.

They'd been sent by someone they knew who was acting for someone they didn't know. They were told to find out where Henry was and it was all they knew. Dean asked them why someone might want to know and Glen said he didn't know but Ade, who was the more scared of the two, joined in by saying once they found where Henry was, someone else was going to go there and take care of him. Dean asked what he meant and Ade said, 'You know. Talk to him, tell him to stay quiet. We don't do that shit but plenty of others do. We scare people, which is small shit, not worth the cop's time, then someone else does the serious stuff.'

I was in shock. Pressuring Henry and us was one thing but these clowns were talking about extended violence, or maybe even murder. I was starting to feel awful; my guts were churning and I was getting a headache. Dean turned and gestured for me to follow him out of the room. Maya followed and Dean wisely decided against trying to leave her out of the discussion.

'Van, these idiots are nothing but hired muscle. Sent to find out where Henry is. We could push them to say who sent them but in truth I'd prefer not to know. If this all goes arse up, what we don't know can't drag us into court. Besides, it's all someone who knows someone and so on, along the line. I reckon I can deal with these two but taking it further could get heavy. But it's your call.'

I looked at Maya and we agreed without speaking. 'No, it's your call.' He nodded and we went back to the other room.

'Now, guys, we need to have a talk. I could threaten

you but even though Ade knows not to come back for afters, I'm not sure, Glen, you do. Let's look at this a different way. Do you know who Jimmy Wilson is?'

Ade looked blank but the name got Glen's attention. 'Yeah, mad abo, runs a bike shop down by the port. Used to ride with the Angels but they chucked him out for being too crazy.'

'Yes, sounds like him. I'll pass your charming description on next time I'm in there having my bike serviced.'

Which not only increased Glen's attention but turned what colour had returned to his face back to mottled grey.

'Yes, guys, I know Jimmy well. Do you know the two he hangs with?'

'You mean the Dougals?'

'I do. The Dougal brothers. Couple of nature's mistakes, almost as mad as Jimmy. Have you heard the story about the bloke who insulted Jimmy's sister in a pub? About a year back? No? Well, I'll tell you. It was her birthday and Jimmy was on his best behaviour for the family, which is something I'd have liked to see. Anyway, this pissed up dickhead makes a pass at her, and she was only fifteen at the time. He gets knocked back, calls her a dyke, several times and loudly, and is taken out by his mates who, being less drunk, understand the situation and vanish. Sister tells Jimmy who does nothing. Unusual but hey, it's a family dinner and he acts all family. However, about a week later, the police come to see Jimmy. Apparently, the guy disappeared. They've narrowed the time down to a few hours and where were Jimmy and his friends between those times and all that cop stuff. Rock solid alibis all round, which was the end of it. But a rumour went round the mouthy drunk was last seen going into the gulf with a V-eight engine block chained to his legs. Alive. Now, I think it's possible Jimmy started the rumour to entertain his mates but then again, it might be true. What do you think?'

Whatever they were thinking remained unsaid. Verbally anyway. Their faces related the story effectively, though.

'Now, all that guy did was get drunk and make a stupid comment to Jimmy's sister. What do you think might happen if someone seriously threatened one of Jimmy's family? Take a look at the young lady here' — he pointed at Maya — 'and you might notice a cultural resemblance to Jimmy. There's a reason. They're cousins. Not she's my cuz type of friend, but real shared DNA blood relatives. Maya's mum's sister is one of Jimmy's… shit, something or other, I can't remember. Close enough to make them family anyway, and you threatened her and her colleague and a close friend. I'm curious, how long can you hold your breath under water? Assuming there's enough of you still alive to be breathing after Jimmy and the Dougals finish giving you a lesson in manners. Still with me?'

They were. Me too. Those two might not be totally scared of the police or even Dean and his staff, but what Dean presented them with was a whole new ball game. And judging by their expressions, they didn't have the balls to want to play.

'So, here's the deal. You go back to whoever sent you and tell them to pass on the message if anything happens to these people, Henry Day, or anyone connected to this whole case, even if it's only a dirty look or a chipped nail or a paper cut, then I'll talk to Jimmy Wilson and if I do, then he, the Dougals, and whoever else he can drag along will come and find you to collect names, after which they'll go see them and there will most likely be few survivors and those who do will wish they hadn't. Is there anything you didn't understand?'

It seemed not. Dean reiterated the important points

adding in if he or any of his people saw either of the men again, they'd consider it as a threat and act accordingly. To prevent that happening, and since Adelaide is small, they might consider an interstate move in the near future. Which isn't precisely how he worded it but that's what he meant. I was certain, even in their current state, they received his message clearly.

Maya and I went into the lounge to set Alex's mind at rest as Dean, Cheryl, and Colin helped the men to their car and saw them on their way. When they returned, I served drinks and we all sat in the kitchen around the dining table trying to wind down. Dean congratulated Cheryl on her victory and she in turn praised his bluffing. I had to ask what bluffing; I'd totally believed him. Cheryl laughed.

'Dean only met Jimmy Wilson once. When he bought his bike. He swore he'd never go near him again without rabies shots.' We all laughed, although there was still strain in the joviality.

Maya chipped in. 'That's not all. Jimmy and I aren't cousins. I've seen my family tree and there's a few poisonous berries there but no bloody root rot in it at all.' More laughs, getting slowly less hard to produce. I made another mental note to tell her not to mention today's events to the poisonous fruits or even her more normal rellies. There were enough problems without her mob declaring war. Or worse, word getting to Jimmy Wilson through pub gossip and him going ballistic.

And I couldn't tell Picino without risking it coming back to haunt Dean and his people. Whoever sent the two men would get the message. Plus, they hadn't found out where Henry was and in a few days he wouldn't be. More satisfying all round if the day's events, along with Glen and Ade, simply went away.

Dean promised Cheryl and Colin bonuses, which produced smiles as they went off holding hands to the caravan. Cheryl looked like a schoolgirl in love and not a barely-contained nuclear strike. Before Dean left, I had two more questions.

'Was it true about the guy being drowned in the gulf?'

He smiled. 'Not sure. I wouldn't put it past Jimmy and his boys but maybe the bloke got some sense and shot through and it would have been a shame to waste a great story.' I wasn't convinced. Too many who fell foul of bikies vanished inexplicably and it's a big gulf.

'How will you know how to find those two again? If you need to.'

'Well, we have Ade's details and I'm sure if we asked him nicely, he'd give us Glen's address. But to be certain, two of my boys are waiting by the freeway to follow them home. They'll also put a tracker on their car once it gets dark. Then, in a couple of days, I'll pay them a visit and reinforce what I said today. If he's free, I might take Ronan, he should convince them to stay in line. Now, Van, don't forget, speeding fines. Please.'

I promised I'd see to it and watched as the huge bike went considerably more sedately and quietly down the drive. As he passed the caravan, he blipped the horn twice then rapped the engine wide open for the last stretch to the gate. I didn't blame him; victories need trumpeting to the world. Maya and I headed towards the lounge and Alex. I asked her if she was alright and she came up to me and we hugged.

'Yes, I am. But I have a favour to ask. Can we go back to the fun and laughs of speeding fines, assaults, wills, divorces, and domestic violence after this is over?'

24

The next morning Alex brought my morning tea. She stood by the bed and stared at me; the wife was concerned and the doctor even more so. I could tell but couldn't respond; I felt like death reheated. As a policeman, I'd seen many awful things and experienced a few down times because of them. As a lawyer, a few cases caused me off moments; defending a rich wife-beating thug and seeing him walk free due to his social connections was one of the more highlit lowlights.

Having the occasional connection to the lives of society's dregs was something I could handle. But as those cases became more common, I went home each night nursing a desire to scrub my skin with steel wool. It was as if the moral corruption was seeping clear through to my soul. In the end, to save from drowning in what seemed to be an endless flood of the waste products of the human race, I moved to the country and refused to act on behalf of such people.

Those times past, the pre-dropout ones, spread over several professionally unhappy years, saw my thoughts of quitting the law expand from intermittent musings to an almost omnipresent obsession. The effects of daily surrendering my ideals, defending the indefensible, exacerbated an innate tendency to mild anxiety and overthinking into a serious medical problem. But all the days, weeks, months, years of soul destruction and sleepless nights filled with moral panic and self-loathing didn't remotely resemble the stress I felt about Henry's case.

A poor, uneducated, widowed, lonely, marginalised, and unworldly old man being persecuted by the rich, the powerful, the ignorant, and the plain mean-spirited, was beyond any reasonable level of comprehension. It was certainly outside mine. I could have handled all of that but having an entitled harpy induce her political allies to send police officers to threaten and harass me in the interests of placing extra pressure on my client, plus the hired bully-boys intimidating me, Alex, and Maya, in my own house, brought back the anxieties and feelings of helplessness in the face of unopposable forces driven by unfathomable motivations.

I felt unsafe, frightened for others around me, especially Henry, and had minimal confidence in my own ability to put up a convincing enough argument to even achieve a hung jury, let alone a favourable verdict. I lost cases before, but none this far-reaching and important for all concerned, including me, and where the massed guardians of the law were confederated in their attempt to convict an innocent man on the basis of judgments proven to be farcical centuries earlier in Salem and other hotbeds of ignorance and blind stupidity.

Even the event starting this all, Senator Fenwick's highly public demise, was bothering me. A poet once proclaimed how any man's death diminished him; that particular death was diminishing everyone. The tragic and unfortunately-timed passing was seized upon as a cause célèbre. I'd never known anything in my life where tragedies seemed to collect and multiply endlessly and countless parasites seemed utterly determined to feed their own self-interest from them.

Death, grief, religious mania, vengeance, power plays, even a hapless victim; it was like a work of Shakespeare. Missing were the sexual double-entendres and comedic absurdities, although that many people seemed convinced instigating death by supernatural means was feasible certainly conformed to the latter. That concept may have been considered borderline acceptable in the Bard's sixteenth century, but it was nothing short of ludicrous in the twenty-first. Not for the first time, but far more intensively than ever before, I desired to give it all up and retire from the world.

I pulled the covers up to my chin, ignored the offered cup, and closed my eyes. Images flashed across my mind in a random sequence. Henry, the ABC studio, KP's vulpine smile, the smashed windows and graffiti of hate and ignorance seen in Parnham, the parliamentary broadcast of Fenwick's death that was a viral hit on YouTube, the AFP, the ACA rent-a-thugs, and all the other egregious bottom-feeders of a human race bent on inflicting damage on itself thoughtlessly and callously.

Confronted by the horrors, my intention was to stay there indefinitely and hide from them. I felt for Henry, I truly did, and possessed a modicum of sympathy for the vengeful widow, only kept in check by the fact that because of her social connections, his less-popular cause appeared to be a lost one with my life and career as doomed as he was. I decided to remain where I was until it was all over, then retire and spend the rest of my life reading books, listening to music, and pretending the world didn't exist. It was a well-reasoned and feasible plan with only one flaw: Alex.

The loving wife sat back as the cruel-to-be-kind doctor took charge of the situation. 'Van, get out of bed. You have too much to do to get into one of your sulks. You know it's the wrong thing and I won't let you do it. So, up. Now.'

I didn't move. There was no way I was doing anything

except what I was doing, no matter what she said. For once, she was not changing my mind as she had every other time. No way. I pulled the covers over my head and tried to ignore her. From outside my protective cocoon, I heard swearing; a concoction of English, Greek, even a couple of swear words I was sure were Latin, something both our professions have a working knowledge of.

There was a moment's silence and a loud indrawn breath then my protective shield simply disappeared. The covers were ripped off and as my eyes opened in shock, I saw them vanishing through the door into the hallway. What I saw next was one pissed-off woman glaring at me from a short distance. I knew the scowl; I tried to brace mentally but I may as well not have bothered. There are things in life too overwhelming to protect yourself against. It would have been like trying to stop an onrushing train by holding up my hands.

I was glad Rob wasn't at home and hoped Maya couldn't hear. Alex, in full flight, was an awesome sight and sound spectacular. From past experience, I knew she wouldn't stop until I did what she required but I was deep enough into my self-pity to give refusal a shot. She demonstrated no intention of stopping. It was a terrifying blend of temperament and volume.

'Van, get out of that bloody bed. Right now.'

I knew she was seriously angry. She only resorts to shouting when she's beyond reasoning and it rarely happens. I knew I was going to do what she demanded but I turned over and made one more attempt at disappearing into the pillow and my head.

'Van.' Quieter but no less forceful.

She got my attention. She knew I understood she was upset both with my inability to cope and the deteriorating situation, and her usual approach was to manipulate the situation, in the nicest possible way and for the best of reasons, by persuasion, not further bullying. She'd done it that way before and I preferred it. And hated it when she was stirred up enough to shout and harangue. As, I knew, did she. But we'd been here several times before, although to much lesser degrees, and her first attack was intended to shock me out of my funk. And it worked. After a fashion.

I wasn't ready to cooperate, but I was at the point where I conceded that I was going to. Not willingly, or even remotely happily, and certainly not for my own sake, but for hers. Seeing Alex upset tortured me worse than what caused me to put her through it. Therefore, reluctantly, I would do as she said. Get up, probably shower, dress, then sit somewhere quiet and try hard not to think.

That worked, except it was Alex I was dealing with. The best laid schemes of this particular mouse were, as per Robert Burns's hapless victim, definitely about to go astray. I always felt sympathy for his unfortunate rodent; now I knew how it felt as its nest was destroyed. My bed and the contents of my head now strongly resembled similar wreckage, and my poetic musings, an attempt to embrace indecision and ignore the oncoming force in the person of Alex, vanished as she verbalised her less poetic and more decisive plans. I listened as she outlined the day's plans; I was not invited to contribute.

'We're going to get ready then we'll go and see Henry and say hello to Rob. Then we'll come back here so you can talk to Maya about the case. I say we because I'm taking the day off to make sure you do what's important and don't disappear inside your own head again. You have a duty to your client, your career, and your family to get on with this. Once it's over, you can spend a whole month in bed and I'll make you tea, tuck you in, and leave you alone. Until then, there's no time for you to chuck a wobbly. Get up. Now.'

Normally, I was amused by her attempts to sound colloquial. Like most who have English as a second language, her speech was calculated and precise, many times a cause for laughter for her husband and son, both of whom were reasonably articulate but far from her level of correctness. But at that moment, being amused was not a possibility so, surrendering to the unarguable and to avoid inflicting pain and worry on the woman I loved beyond measure, I did as she asked.

I often wondered if she spoke to her patients in the same way or if I was the only one lucky enough to be bullied in such a fashion. Bullied is a deliberate choice because that's what it is. Same with lucky, because that's what I am. To make it up to her, I showered quickly, no shave though, and put on a shirt she liked. It earned me a kiss and a hug and I guessed we were friends once more. It didn't help much, I was too far gone, but the tiny amount it did help, helped.

Maya came in and accepted a tea then sipped it and looked at me, her expression a combination of tremulous smile and worried eyes. She'd heard about my moodies, as Alex called them, when they were well and truly absent but not witnessed one. Small examples, flying files and once a broken telephone, but they were all of short duration and momentary flickers of a soon extinguished bright flame. This time was different. Distant flashes of thunder turning into a hurricane. She seemed to be wondering if we were in the calm respite of the central eye awaiting the second instalment or if the storm had abated into a tropical depression. I concluded that was an apt description of the situation.

In the car, with Alex driving, she kept talking. 'It's called, ennui, Van. It's an illness, partly psychological and partly physiological. You simply run out of steam and feel unable to carry on. Everyone gets doses of it, usually small and cured by a nap. Sometimes, as today, it hits worse and renders the person almost helpless. The best cure is to do something to replace it. In your case I recommend doing your job. Sooner or later, your involvement in your work will kick you back into gear. We've been there before and we may go there again, but together we can get through it. Yes?'

I said yes, not meaning she was right but yes, we'd been there before. But one of the symptoms is a focussed forgetfulness where a panicky mood supersedes the memories. She was correct and we both knew it. It would pass and I'd be alright. Unfortunately, during an attack, alright seems like a foreign and unachievable concept. It's bad enough for those, like me, blessed with a great support system. For anyone attempting to survive it alone, it must be hell on steroids.

I was aware Alex was explaining for Maya's sake as well; her shock at finding me disabled obvious enough for me to notice through my self-absorption. She was sitting in the back seat, still looking worried as she listened to Alex's words. Normally I'd have been embarrassed. At that moment I was too busy concentrating on the sound of Alex's voice. As we turned onto the dirt road leading to the Fosters' farm, Alex went silent, replaced by a voice inside my head telling me to turn around and go home; it was all too hard: why bother? Alex put her hand on my arm and squeezed: the voice stopped. Seconds later, the car did the same. *Now*, I thought, *for the hard part*.

Seeing Henry made it worse. All I could do was think about how the odds were aligned against him and his only hope was someone who craved crawling back into bed and giving up. As we shook hands, I longed to burst into tears and apologise for failing him. I couldn't speak; I sat in a chair and listened as Maya and he discussed the case. His poor English wasn't helping either. The whole country seemed to be determined to persecute an old man who couldn't formulate a sentence and appeared to have almost no grasp of the dire situation he was in. What I felt was a crushing, powerless anger.

Anger at Henry for his inability to comprehend what was going on, which I knew was illogical but couldn't ignore; lucidity wasn't available to me at that point. Anger at me for being unable to rectify his situation; equally unreasonable and seemingly unshakeable. Anger at Picino for getting me into this mess, which was manifestly illogical since he'd been trying, for once, to do the right thing. Besides, as Alex commented when this began, I'd jumped and not been pushed, if I were being rational. Which, at that moment, I knew I was anything but.

Anger at all those who, for political, personal, or other less specified aims were allying against Henry and, it seemed, me. I had a list of people I included in that category: Veronica Fenwick, her supporters, the ABC, the ACA and all the god-drunken fools who believed in the supernatural, and everyone who wasn't speaking out in support of Henry and in rage at the illogical stupidity of the campaign against him. Basically, then, I was angry at the entire world including myself. In my haze of self-castigation and crushing paranoia, I was aware there are names for what I was feeling. Alex used one earlier. I knew several others, none of them remotely medical or polite.

The overwhelming helplessness made it worse. Everything I'd done seemed to be working and then something new would come along and shoot us down in flames. I don't believe in curses but a niggling voice somewhere in the back of my mind was telling me we'd been the target of one. For a moment I considered that the Indigenous community employed a Kadaicha man to witch Henry and his supporters. The idea vanished as quickly as it came; the realisation that in entertaining those notions I was probably losing my sanity, though, wouldn't disappear along with it.

Watching Maya and Henry talking, I heard nothing except the roaring in my head, and I couldn't take any more. I stood up and went outside. By the time Alex followed, I was in the car, seatbelt on, and tears rolling down my face. She went back and I saw her talking to Maya, then she drove us home and put me to bed.

I couldn't relax. She came and sat with me and I felt her hold my arm gently. I sensed there were other people in the room, then sleep took over.

Like the parade of technicolour thoughts earlier, the dreams marched rampantly around and around in my subconscious. Everybody involved in the case formed a procession, much like the Sorcerer's Apprentice scene from Fantasia, except the benign, two-dimensional, smiling and dancing Disney characters had taken on the malignant distorted corporealities and scowling faces of medieval demons and gothic gargoyles. They all writhed and capered, leering with bulbous eyes, displaying broken sharpened teeth and protruding tongues that licked obscenely at blood-stained glistening lips. Mickey, the pointed hat now a crown formed from a smashed nest and the magic wand a satanic trident, became Burns' pitiful mouse, augmented with the features of a starving plague rat, open slavering mouth not singing the familiar joyous tune but emitting a continuous high-pitched screech. I was trapped in an animated Hieronymus Bosch painting and the horrendous tortures and torments of his maniacal visions of hellishness were all being enacted on Henry. Somewhere, distantly, I heard Alex's voice calling to me and I tried to go to her but was unable to break through the masses of the damned. I was screaming I didn't believe in hell and everyone, including Henry, began to laugh. Then it all vanished and I was enveloped in blackness and silence. The peace was sublime and I surrendered and sank into its soft embrace.

25

When I woke up it was dark outside. It wasn't how I normally woke, a rapid transition from sleep into wakefulness. It was gradual; the feeling I was being held down then progressively released. It was like trying to swim upwards through treacle. After what seemed like a short time, although it could have been a week, I couldn't judge it properly, I became aware I was truly awake. I lay still and gazed at the ceiling, coming to grips with the realisation I felt better.

The panic was gone, my heart rate felt normal, my thoughts were more akin to my usual state of benign haphazardness, not battling opposites tripping over each other in a mental kaleidoscope of violent colours and patterns. There were vague memories of nightmarish scenarios involving demonic figures. *Perhaps*, I thought, *my in-laws made a sick call*.

A look at the clock told me I'd been out for nearly fourteen hours. The sleep, if something that long and overwhelming could be accurately described with such a simple word, slowed me down and banished the fiends. I was hungry and thirsty, I remembered I hadn't eaten since the previous day. I desired food and drink; calories and caffeine. I went to get out of the bed and stopped as Alex came in and told me stay where I was. Apparently, I was either on the mend or beyond help; I did as she said. She sat next to me.

'So, love. How do you feel?'

I said great, thanks, and received a hug and kiss. They were both dismissively short and I realised I smelled awful; I must have sweated a lot. Both my body and the bed required attention in the hygiene department and I again made moves to make a move. I was halted by her doctorly voice which told me to wait a while and her wifely hand which pushed me back to the horizontal. I asked what happened. I knew I'd slept, but that length of time was a new record for me and the extent of my recovery was astounding.

'Well, Van, it was all Henry's doing. Maya brought him here; they were both worried. I was wondering whether to take you to hospital and he asked if he could try traditional healing on you. He collected leaves and bark and burned them in a metal bucket then we all waved the smoke over you as he muttered incantations in his own language. Maya joined in and you went off into a peaceful sleep after a couple of hours. Maya took Henry home; I looked in on you every few minutes. Looking at you now, I guess it worked. However, it sort of screws up your legal defence and we should keep it to ourselves but I'm glad to see it made you better.'

I closed my eyes and mulled that over. It was counter to all of my core beliefs but the way I felt compared to earlier was nothing short of magic. I sought to get my head around it. She was right; if Henry could do healing, then it undermined all of the defence I'd prepared. I wasn't a practised enough liar to convince anyone of something I knew to be untrue. All my negative feelings started to return and the realisation made me determined to fight them off. Fix me first; the case could be dealt with afterwards...

I opened my eyes and looked at Alex and saw I'd been had. Well and truly. She's a terrible liar: her eyes crinkle up because when she lies, she wants to laugh. Which is what she was doing. I was annoyed for falling for it. And I loved her for doing it. It meant more than I could put into words. I showed my feelings in the way we always did: with the banter that forms the true language of a comfortable relationship.

'Burning leaves and healing smoke my arse. Come on, tell. What did happen? And stop laughing, it's not funny.'

'Yes, it is, Now. It wasn't funny earlier and I was being truthful when I said I was considering hospital. But I managed to send you off to sleep and after an hour of restless movement you lay still and your face unwound. I knew you were past the worst of it.'

'Okay, I get it. But what took me past it? Not Henry's magic, that's for sure. I should tell Maya what you said, see if she finds it funny.'

She laughed again and I found it as wonderful as I always had. 'Telling you was her idea. She and Henry cooked it up. They decided it was funny, although Maya was convinced I wasn't enough of a liar to get you to believe me. In the long term she was right but for a couple of minutes there, I had you. Go on, admit it.'

I did but I was still intrigued. If Henry hadn't used magic smoke to restore me to mental health and I knew from past experiences, all of which were minimal compared to this attack, I couldn't do it alone, then what was the secret? She smiled a half-smile telling me something a bit left-of-centre occurred and confessing it might cause her embarrassment. Not with me, more professionally or with others. Like the one time we'd smoked pot together, or our early morning skinny dip where we were almost sprung by a picnicking church group, or the time she admitted, in Rob's hearing, she found his sports teacher sexy. That sort of embarrassing.

'I gave you a shot of something. A bit more really, a couple of shots of several somethings. Each might have done the trick alone, together they have a kick, it seems to have been the one you needed. I don't suggest you get up too quickly, the effects might make you a bit unsteady. Something to eat and a cuppa and in a few hours, you'll be fine, but for now slow is the go.'

Right, I thought. *That's all fine. But…*

'Is what you gave me legal?'

She looked away for a moment, considering her answer. Which wasn't necessarily no; I knew of old it meant the answer fell into the grey area called maybe.

'Legal, yes. I'm a doctor and I knew what I was doing and I wasn't breaking any laws or using anything smuggled in a tube rammed up someone's rear end. Ethically, that's a bit less easy to define. Normally such combinations are given under hospital conditions but since a hospital wouldn't have let me give it to you, the point is a bit contentious. Not to mention irrelevant. There was no danger, it's the strictly medico-ethical position that's a mite questionable. I was worried about you, Van, and nothing else mattered except making you well.'

'What was it?'

'None of your business, and you wouldn't recognise the names if I told you. Let's say vitamins and a booster and leave it there, although booster is a slight a misnomer since it tends to slow the system down. If you ever get asked under oath, you have an answer that won't get either of us into trouble. Okay?'

'Okay. But what about you?'

'Medical ethics. Patient confidentiality. Similar to lawyer-client don't ask, don't tell. I'm unable to reveal such information. Plus, women know how to keep secrets. You know that.'

I was tempted to respond 'not about Picino and Sophia Natuzzi' plus three or four other confidences that came to mind, but my instinct for self-preservation far outweighed my desire to score points and I resisted the urge. The ethereal floating sensation in my head reminded me...

'Will there be any lasting effects beyond this feeling of slight euphoria?'

'That's partly due to the long sleep and one of the drugs tends to lift the spirits. It will wear off and you'll be back to your old grumpy self in no time. Oh, yes, and please don't die for at least thirty-six hours. What I gave you would show up in an autopsy and I don't want to go to jail.' She laughed.

To recap, I'd been given borderline ethically-acceptable drugs clandestinely by a respected doctor who was making jokes about her husband having an autopsy. That, I supposed, was what passed for humour in the medical profession. Speaking of her profession...

'Do you realise you've never treated me before? It's a first.'

It was; I'd always seen other doctors. When I'd required a prostate exam for a small infection, she spent days getting the giggles afterwards at the thought of her giving it to me instead of the male doctor at the hospital who had. Jokes about how the examination could have added spice to our sex life abounded and when I, in a mentally absent moment, told her she was being a pain in the arse, she nearly collapsed from laughter.

We always studiously avoided using each other's professional services. But since she'd initiated the exchange and gotten amusement from it, I figured I should take my turn.

'Well, if you get caught injecting people with illegal

substances, you can engage me as your lawyer. Considering how I'm doing with Henry's case, I can't guarantee keeping you out of jail, but perhaps I'm due for a change of fortune.'

She didn't laugh, perhaps the drugs had been more outside the acceptable limits than she was admitting. But I did; that's definitely what passes for humour in the legal profession.

There were memories of others in the room but I wasn't sure if they were real or a pipe dream. I asked.

'Yes, Maya was here and Rob came for a look. They were worried about you, we all were. By then you were starting to relax, I asked them not to speak to you and I told them I'd let them know how you were later. Which I did. They said to say hi. Henry was not here, that wasn't true. No burning leaves, either.' We both laughed. I was relieved to find out we were able to, even if her joie-de-vivre was at my expense and mine was almost definitely chemically augmented.

We looked at each other and more was said in the glance than any words could convey. I realised the irony; I was defending a man accused of passing a harmful message of hate through eye contact because I didn't believe it was possible, yet Alex and I were sending healing messages of love using only the same medium. *If*, I thought, *the one was possible, why was the other not?*

I decided to think about it later, when I was drug-free and clear of thinking. For now, I was going to relax and enjoy the magic privately which I had to convince the world publicly was nothing more than an illusion. I'd never questioned the power of a look before; this case intruded on my life in ways no other ever had. Those two realisations induced a frisson of unease I was incapable of ignoring. It, and the residual chemical buzz, were a discomforting combination.

Alex said, 'Henry was worried about you. So was Maya.'

I was tempted to think both were only worried because of the case and I instantly felt ashamed. Maya was too genuine to be callous and Henry, I was sure, was feeling lost and mostly unaware of where he was in the big picture or what he, we, faced in the coming days. The fact someone in his position spared me a thought was both comfort and concern.

I stood, sat down again, and decided to wait a few seconds and try once more. Considerably more slowly. Alex witnessed the attempt.

'I told you to take it slowly. I may have improved your mood, now I need to find something to help with your attention span. Food?'

'Yes, please. And more of… you know.' I ducked; the flying pillow missed. The kiss didn't.

Who needs drugs?

26

For the next few days nothing of major import happened. I recovered from my mental sabbatical and spent time closeted in the office with Maya. We went to the city for three meetings with Picino, two at his cousin's eatery, and one at Emily's house.

Press hysteria slowed, although the case managed several mentions a day. Someone, or more likely a collective of someones, was fuelling the flames. Possibly Veronica Fenwick or one of her political or social acolytes, maybe the ACA and their right-wing contacts that seemed to include low-rent thugs and high-rent businessmen, possibly Parnhamites worried their town-saving financial deal with the Chinese was in danger of disappearing and taking their hopes for new and richer lives with it, at a stretch even the Chinese themselves. Perhaps somebody else, hidden on the sidelines with an inexplicable need to have Henry found guilty of a non-existent murder. God only knew, and he wasn't talking to me ever since I unfriended him; the Old Testament highlights how vindictive he could be when he was in a moody with someone.

Nobody in the nation's capital was talking to Picino or his boss which, according to Picino's sporting metaphor of the moment, meant they had something on the boil and were uncertain as to whether or not the local players were truly a part of the national team. He said he could think of no reason why they should think that and I pointed out political betrayal and paranoia weren't concepts invented by Shakespeare, they were innate to politics worldwide. I used Stalin as an outstanding example; trust no one and get them before they get you, even if they weren't out to get you except in your own imagination. Authoritarian Politics 101: first kill trust then kill everyone you ever trusted.

Trust was the issue; the Canberra-based sceptics doubting Picino and the Premier had none, and the fact that in this case their distrust was justified changed nothing. They knew nothing for certain, and Picino would, I knew, have been scrupulously careful. I couldn't be a party to it; the deceptions, back-stabbing, and mistrust. There was enough of it in this case to put me off politics for life, whether it be national, state, town council, or a high-school parents group. I'd represented murderers, rapists, paedophiles, wife beaters, and a man who'd embezzled from post-bushfire fundraisers, and I was convinced my involvement with the current collective of miscreants was hitting an all-time moral low point.

Since they were being secretive, it was obvious they had a plan. The problem was, we didn't. I'd learnt law and practised it for years and given any normal accusation, I could, with enough time, come up with a viable counter to almost any legal scenario. But declaring someone was willed to die, even allowing for an eyeball-to-eyeball meeting, was hard to refute. Simply hearing it made it hard to keep a straight face. It resembled the hyperbolic satire of Monty Python or The Simpsons. I'd spoken again to Madison Rundle who reiterated the only way to counter accusations of magic was to prove it didn't exist and since countless people attempted that for centuries without success, then best of luck. Fairly bloody unhelpful, I told her. She laughed, and asked if I managed it, could she have the book rights?

All of which meant waiting until the prosecution revealed their strategy and fighting each of their assertions in turn. Most of which wouldn't come up until the trial, if there was one. That decision, to trial or not, was to be considered at a Committal Hearing in five days. The DPP, exercising its independence from the political machine, was opposing the Attorney General's advice and demanding Henry be remanded from as soon as until then. Which included a weekend; there went the days of rest, one Judaic, one Christian, and both for atheists and lawyers who were under-the-gun. Great song by The Killers, not a good place to be for those defending one.

The DPP phrased it in more formal terms but essentially it meant Henry was to be incarcerated for both his own and the public's safety. In reality it was to quell any public criticisms and to placate those higher up the societal and political hierarchies who were applying pressure. In other words, it was all lip service carried out with those same lips firmly, and pragmatically, smooching the appropriate rear ends.

An unhappy Picino informed me, unofficially then officially and almost certainly in the presence of the usual eavesdroppers, that Henry was required to be at the Adelaide Remand Centre as of ten o'clock the following morning. Did we require transport? No, thank you. Security? Also, no, thank you. And onwards through the legal hymn book, singing our contrapuntal duets to the in-the-room or online audience. By the way, our less-widely-attended discussion revealed there were likely to be protestors waiting our arrival. Pros and cons. Hopefully, Picino added, they would be too busy beating each other up to notice our arrival. We both laughed, neither of us amused. At least we were talking politely. Were we, I wondered, refinding our former friendship? Maybe. It was too early to tell, and I was too busy to be distracted by it.

Picino added that the media knew of Henry's enforced appointment and would be there en masse, with my office and house plus everywhere between them and the city likely to be under siege from the small hours. It was neither unexpected nor particularly troubling news. Since Henry was at neither, any media watchers would be unrewarded, but I still had to get Henry to the city and into the Remand Centre without attracting a following. I called Dean, who came for lunch, bringing wine and suggestions.

The day before Henry was due at his new lodgings, he, Maya, and I spent several hours sitting outside at his temporary residence going over everything, watched only by the sheep and, from a position where he could keep an eye on the road, Colin. We hadn't been followed there, meaning the media hadn't hit town yet but I knew from friends that motels and caravan parks received heavy bookings from the coming night: they were on their way. Good for them, bad for us.

Nothing new came up but we confirmed that what I was going to say in the hearing was the truth according to Henry. He'd not attended the meeting and had no idea how his signature ended up in the book. He didn't use magic on Fenwick and wished me to stress that, unlike the stereotypes accepted by most whites, old Aboriginal men like him didn't all practise magic. Some, he added, might, but he personally had never seen it or heard of any believable instances of it happening. As for the flying eagle story, it was the first and only time I ever saw him laugh out loud. I wish, he said; walking wears my old legs out. I asked about the dog man and his response was substantially less cheerful.

I talked to him about the Remand Centre. Picino

assured me people he knew would oversee Henry's treatment at all times. I didn't tell Henry that, Picino wasn't a secret I was prepared to share. Only five people knew of our dealings. Two senior politicians whose careers would vanish if they were seen consorting with the enemy, and the enemy itself, which was Maya and I plus Alex, whose enmity with Picino was for life, regardless of what transpired.

There were ongoing suspicions about our connections, especially from Canberra. But speculation isn't proof, in either politics or adultery. It would take a fearless person, federal politician or no, to level such an accusation at a Premier or an Attorney General, who ironically was guilty on both counts. Even the media, if they had any inklings, shied away from that one; career suicide would be a likely result. Even if, by a miracle, someone managed to provide proof, their own reputations would vanish much more rapidly than any implications could affect the ones they were attacking. Even the ABC was being reticent. Or awaiting their chance to attack again from the rear: I wasn't sure which.

Our secret remained that way, and another one, the route we would take from home to the city, wasn't revealed even to Picino via the clandestine phone. I trusted him, now, but if anything went wrong, the less who could be pressed to admit what they knew, the better. Besides, if I told him, he wouldn't like it and I didn't feel like an argument. What I'd tell him and what we were going to do varied. In three things. When, which way, and what vehicle. I was truthful in one aspect; I told him we'd be there as requested, and experienced a small moral glow.

I told him, for public dissemination, that Henry, his

two lawyers, a driver, and three security people in another vehicle, would proceed, at eight o'clock in the morning, down the freeway, enter the city through the parklands and go directly to the Remand Centre. The logical and most direct route. And therefore, the obvious one for any media, protestors, or other interested parties to follow or intercept our progress. Since it made sense, why would anyone doubt it for a moment?

However, it was all smoke and mirrors. At five in the afternoon a four-wheel-drive with Dean at the wheel left the Fosters'. I was in the front left, behind me in the middle seat, Henry, wearing a dark-coloured baseball cap and sunglasses, flanked by Maya and Cheryl. Further back, sitting sideways on a rolled-up swag with legs across the cramped rear compartment, was Colin. As we pulled onto the road, two cars followed us. In one was Ronan and two of Dean's martial ruffians, and in the other four more of them. Any unwanted company would be in for a rude shock. We meandered around the town for a few minutes, the other cars splitting off and checking for tails. There were none; we headed out of town.

We went the long way. Before the freeway existed, visitors to Murray Bridge and beyond enjoyed a pleasant country drive from Adelaide. I'd always liked going that way if I had the time, and even in the coming twilight, it was a more scenic journey than the featureless sterility of the freeway. We twisted and turned, taking time, there was no hurry. We even stopped for snacks at a small-town general store. A pimped lollipop green muscle-car containing three guys pulled up near us and they all stared as they went into and out of the store. I was worried they recognised us until I realised they were eyeballing Maya and Cheryl. Both women waved at them using the energy-efficient single-digit salute, and the jilted lovers returned the gesture before piling into their car and compensating for their damaged male egos by burning rubber in three gears. Maya shook her head and muttered, 'Well, I suppose that's a wonderful chance at romance ruined for both of us.' Cheryl and Colin laughed and Dean smiled as he started the car and we moved out. I tried to summon a smile but that part of me wasn't working; it was in seclusion and nursing its wounds.

Eventually, we came down out of the hills, bypassed the city and surrounds, and headed north towards Dean's place. We drove straight into the open garage while the other cars went off to park where they could keep an eye on the house and streets. We made it. No media, no hostiles, no equally unwelcome attention-drawing friendlies. Only us.

Inside, there were introductions and Marian served dinner from take-away cartons and drinks from the fridge. Then there were conversations and allocation of sleeping places and bedding. By eleven, everyone was tucked in and probably sleeping. I know I was.

Next morning, I was showered and resplendent in my traditional lawyerly public appearance suit and tie. Dean, for the first time in my memory, was also in a suit and tie I had no idea he even owned. I was going to tacitly attempt to pass him off as part of my legal team and only admit if challenged that he was my enquiry agent and security consultant which, after a quick signing of a hastily-written contract, he now was. His troops left thirty minutes before us to blend with the crowd and hopefully provide security when we arrived. We travelled in a smaller four-wheel drive with tinted windows, one of

Dean's staff behind the wheel with his boss riding shotgun and Henry in the back sandwiched between me and Maya. We took a circuitous route into the city and at two minutes to ten we turned from West Terrace into Currie Street.

The crowd outside the Remand Centre, a blend of recycled old hippies, right-wing dullards, the occasional suits, a few earnest youngies, and a large group of Indigenous supporters, held banners displaying emotive and unimaginative slogans ranging from FREE HENRY DAY to SATANIC KILLER and other protest cliches. All to be expected. with the less supportive sign carriers battering the sides of the van as we stopped at the gate. One bearded lumpen with a swastika neck tattoo and wielding a bottle raised it to hit a window then collapsed as Colin, in a beanie and shades, melted back into the crowd who stepped over the falling body. One or two others who were hitting and kicking the vehicle seemed to suddenly lose their aggression and I suspected Dean's people were doing their jobs. I hoped they remained unseen; as we passed through the open gate, I didn't see any of them being challenged. The Remand Centre staff and the police seemed content to leave the crowd to sort out its own differences as long as they didn't attempt to follow us into the compound. Finally, we were inside.

The excitement was over. We spent nearly an hour filling in paperwork and watching Henry being processed, then, with a final farewell and supportive words from us where I reassured him he'd be in safe hands and we'd see him soon, he and two Correctional Officers vanished into the depths of the building. He hadn't shown any signs of worry; then again during the whole time I'd known him, he rarely had. I wished I could be as sanguine and self-contained. Not stressing nor needing the support of others.

Perhaps it was innate, although he'd once been married which, even in the worst cases, required some form of personal interconnection. More likely was it developed since he'd been alone; the years of solitude breeding a determined independence. If that was what it took to be strongly self-sufficient, I'd stick with my accompanied dependence, thank you. The important thing right then, though, was a few nights in a solitary cell were not likely to faze him. According to Ronan, Henry was politely distant with him and their hosts out at the farm, preferring to sit alone outside watching the animals and scenery. Time alone might suit his hermitical nature. It would drive me insane, although in my present condition, that trip was in its final stages.

We went out and climbed into the vehicle unchallenged, which was satisfying if unexpected. The media seemed to have lost interest in the supporting cast, now the leading man left the stage. I rang Alex to tell her it went as expected. She told me there were cars outside my office and at the end of our drive, full of people who took off at high speed when they realised what they were after seemed to have departed without them. She found it funny. I'd laugh later.

As we drove out, I noticed most of the protestors were gone; shouting at an unresponsive gate and even less reactive staff can't have been particularly gratifying and I wasn't surprised they'd gone. Undoubtedly, they'd surface at the Committal Hearing. They were unimportant; I put them from my thoughts. I had four days to get ready. Henry was safe and secure, one less thing to worry about, I could concentrate on my legal strategy. Which, right then, meant adopting the words of the old song and flying on a wing and a prayer.

27

Committal Proceedings exist for one reason only. To allow a magistrate to rule on whether a case requires an expensive and time-consuming trial or if there is insufficient cause to proceed further. They save time, expense, and effort; many accusations are dealt with quickly and efficiently. There are no juries to convince; seasoned magistrates are more able than press-ganged citizens fulfilling their unwelcome civic duty to grasp the complexities of a case and form decisions with alacrity, guided by extensive legal knowledge and experience. It's outlined in many of the legal tomes occupying the Adelaide University Law Library. Various magistrates mentioned it to me over the years as well.

The evidence is in the form of witness statements and arguments from the police prosecutor and defence lawyer. The prosecution needs to provide sufficient credible evidence of motive, means, and opportunity to convince a magistrate to commit public resources to a trial. In our case, I knew how they planned to do it.

Witness statements would attempt to assert Henry's vocal opposition to the sale of the cattle station to a Chinese business group and demonstrated active involvement in the Indigenous community's concerns about the sacred site issue. I wasn't convinced the short discussion Henry and Mrs Jessup conducted in the local shop, which was now a matter of record, counted as vocal opposition in the manner the prosecution seemed likely to assert. The truth according to Mrs Jessup when Maya rang her was Henry had been somewhere between non-committal and totally disinterested and, as far as the old lady knew, and she was certain no one knew Henry better, his community involvement, notably on the issue of sacred sites he'd never been known to visit, was virtually non-existent. I could come up with no viable ripostes to the prosecution's claims, and the problem with assertions offered by a capable lawyer is that they're often mistaken for facts when manipulatively presented as such. They, it would be claimed, demonstrated motive.

Some experts on what was often labelled as magic, specifically the use of influence and suggestion, would testify as to its effectiveness, and proclaim there were recorded instances of it causing illness or death. By showing it was known to have been done, the prosecution's claim would be Henry, as an older Aboriginal man, might reasonably be expected to have knowledge of how to do it. Reasonably is a loose term and they intended to take full advantage of that looseness in proposing the racist and unfounded assumption of knowledge as a signifier of means.

Finally, the letter claiming Henry and Fenwick's proximity at the community meeting would be read out with Henry's name in the attendance book used to verify its authenticity. The document and damning entry were a masterstroke on the anonymous someone's part. Number three: opportunity.

They scored the hat-trick: motive, means, opportunity. Even if it didn't proceed beyond the committal stage, the damage to Henry's reputation would be absolute and whoever was gunning for him would have achieved their aims. It was a meticulously-orchestrated stitch up. I possessed no answers to any of it.

Consequently, my intention was to listen to the prosecution's case and formulate my responses on the run, refuting the various accusations with either appeals to common sense or outright denials. It was a viable working plan. As, in theory, was the mid nineteenth-century Burke and Wills expedition to cross the continent from south to north. Three of the four men, though, ended up dead. Their problem was never poor preparation; their inability to improvise when the planning failed brought about their ruin. I had no plan per se but considerable practice at improvisation at a moment's notice. Which was, I supposed, a plan of sorts; spontaneous reactive offence in lieu of coordinated proactive defence. The concept is outlined in legal textbooks; usually listed under Don't.

Picino heard from an unnamed source that Division 7A of the Act, specifically the part focussing on mental harms, was being torn apart in search of concealed meanings or subtle nuances susceptible to revisionist manipulation, but he went over the wording and doubted there was anything that could be rephrased to surpass the original dry legalistic prescriptiveness. However, he added, presentation was the key — I thanked him less than politely for the advice — and what was inscribed in statute could sound vastly different if spun by verbally-mesmeric experts, something the DPP possessed in bulk. So, he added with yet more of his habitual needless condescension, don't be complacent just because there is no law covering the accusations directly: this was all about orchestrating the phrasing to suit the situation without turning it into anything provable as falsity. He'd done it, he said, I'd done it, and the DPP built a corporation around it.

I gave the legislation a lookover and saw nothing of concern; then again, I wasn't seeking to subvert its intent. Well, in truth, I was, but if there was a pitfall, it was too well buried for me to unearth. I agreed with Picino; if that was their best game plan, then active diversion would have to be their primary fallback. Meaning I needed, with each fallacious inference in turn, to establish their misdirections as such to reveal the weaknesses in the case and exploit them. Sounded simple: yes. Would be: no!

What was not going to be said was that Henry used magic to kill Fenwick or even such a thing existed. As Madison Rundle predicted, there were claims Henry cured or cursed others over the years. None of them were verifiable and many were purely risible, but mixed in with everything else, they would provide something resembling proof for the more devout and loopy supernaturalists. As to prosecution under law for usage of magic, especially to bring about a death, I knew from Picino the concerted attempts to find viable precedents were not going well. The work in progress was lagging behind the legal timelines.

It was a pity it would be off the table: there was unlimited ammunition to shoot that one down. Madison Rundle sent me enough information by highly respected experts from several cultures worldwide including the homegrown ones to argue it right out of court. It was my main defence, and it wasn't going to be heard. Not without a miracle, and my prime argument was such things weren't real. Which meant if one did happen, it would be self-defeating. It's a strange feeling, realising you're the only committed atheist who truly believes he's cursed by God. Difficult to find exactly the right prayer to cover that.

At ten minutes before the Committal Proceeding was committed to proceed, everyone who was directly involved, the huge media contingent plus anyone able to obtain a seat through personal, political, or any other form of influence, was in place. Getting in was a challenge; I'd never seen as many police and Sheriff's Officers around the building or outside the courtroom.

Room 12 of the Magistrates Court was where the committal hearing was to be held, and it was packed. The area immediately in front of the outer doors was full to bursting; King William and Angas Streets and Victoria Square looked like the scene of a riot. Judging by the noise as we came in and the emotive nature of the case, it possibly was. Hence the extraordinary presence of those whose job it was to prevent the untoward from disrupting the legal process.

If I could make a solid case in this room, this entire farce would vanish, and the obsessed delusionists would be left to gnash their teeth, don the sackcloth and ashes, and cry foul to their chosen Gods. If I didn't, those who demanded Henry be set free might decide to break a few things. Starting with me.

I'd appeared in that courtroom many times in my previous life as a defender of the terminally-indefensible and twice since my rural rejuvenation. It's divided into two halves: the front where the magistrate, court officials, and lawyers all sit, with the Sheriff's Officers at a desk and near the doors, and the accused and those minding them in a fenced area to one side. The rear section is for the press and public who get to watch the antics but not join in.

I was dressed as I hadn't been since taking a vow of rusticity. My best suit received a going over, under it a pale blue shirt, best for the TV cameras, fronted by a subdued dark blue tie. The shoes were new and shiny and

I was wearing brand-new cotton jocks. The total effect, visible and hidden, was one of professional competence and understated authority. I felt like an overdressed imposter.

Maya was in a dark pants suit with low heeled boots and a light green blouse. I had no idea about her underwear and wasn't brave enough to ask or mention my own. Her makeup was minimal yet more than I ever saw her wear previously. We told each other how great we looked then laughed. It wasn't our scene but it was necessary. Everyone else did the best-party-clothes dress up routine and we didn't want to feel left out. It was not important simply to be professional and capable, in places like that it was compulsory for you to look the part. It provided a strong reminder of why I left it all behind.

I turned from my front row seat and looked around. There were five large Sheriff's Officers scattered around the court. All of the uniforms looked freshly laundered, as did those wearing them. The court worker bees may have been equally washed, polished, and decorated but since they couldn't be seen from the neck down and their heads were permanently bent over piles of documents, it was hard to tell and it didn't matter: none of their primping and preening did. Without their efforts none of this was possible but to all present, the functionaries would be as if invisible. At this performance all eyes would be on the stars, not the rude mechanicals.

Five uniforms, all male, in the room verged on overkill. Someone demonstrated foresight, and there were many more outside ready to pitch in if the court went out of control. I doubted it would, those allowed in were not the type to go ballistic, but no chances were being taken.

I knew the police prosecutor, Peter Ford, and he and his apparel also appeared washed, dried, and ironed to a standard not often seen. Slovenliness was never his norm but the recently barbered and impeccably attired man sitting in the prosecution chair was an archetype of whatever the antonym of unkempt might be.

So not only the security had been considered and well planned; any possible reportage by GQ or Marie Claire was also covered.

I scanned the media area. The ABC reporter, no doubt an acolyte of Katia Pavelli, ready to report back on my impending disgrace in which they played a pivotal role, was obvious. The commercial channels were out in force, hoping for someone decorative and famous or a cute fluffy dog to appear, and to one side were others I assumed were imported; today's events garnered international interest. The print press were all sitting together, huddled and whispering.

At the rear, I saw a local radio reporter I loathed; his determination to arrogantly assert in each broadcast that his half-baked fully-biased reasonings exhibited validity formed the core of his crimes against common sense and acceptable diction. According to rumour, many followed him regularly; his detractors retorted that seagulls do the same to a rubbish truck.

Around the media space, I saw writing pads and poised pens, mobile phones beneath hovering fingers, an air of expectation I figured was akin to ancient Romans staring at lions and crosses about to hasten the gruesome endings of hapless Christians.

I swung further and surveyed the public gallery. Picino was there, front row. I felt sorry for him; I knew his professional and personal interests were in opposition. The practised calmness on his face gave nothing away; he could have been waiting for a play or film to begin. He caught my eye and minimally raised an eyebrow. It was a gesture I knew from the less-engaging lectures of old. Basically, it meant to hell with this, let's go and get a drink. Sounded like a fantastic idea but when I considered all the people we'd disappoint, I abandoned it reluctantly and moved on.

Then he flashed me a confident knowing smile and a foolish hope flashed that he'd somehow managed to convince the DPP to drop the whole thing and we could all go home. Then I saw the reason he was feeling cocky: double entendre doubly intended. He was sitting next to Ronnie Fenwick.

The prosecutor had been given a full detailing and tune-up, compared to her he'd run a rag over his shoes and finger-combed his hair. I was convinced she'd gone the whole way for our private meeting: not even close. I know enough about women's clothing to recognise several thousands, if not tens of thousands, worth of fancy threads and footwear. And the hair and makeup must have taken more than a few hours and, as before and probably never in recent history, she hadn't done it herself. The grieving widow was here to see her god-drunken vindictive wet dream come to life and then gloat. Madame Defarge, sans knitting needles, front row seat at the execution.

Picino was right, she was stunning. But, notwithstanding her spectacular physical attributes, vacuous Barbies are not to my taste. I reserve my admiration for women of substance, possessing wit in all connotations of the term, not plumy birds of paradise arrayed in Prada, Jimmy Choos, and gaudy baubles, harbouring grandiose delusions about their own importance in relation to the inferior beings surrounding their fairy-tale existence. The glitterati widow of an innocuous politician whose single claim to prominence was breathing his last on national television, her demeanour of sombre grief was attracting pitying glances. For a member of the social butterfly brigade where one of the premiere skillsets was effusive smiling, it must have cost her significant effort to sustain the solemnity.

My projection of Veronica Fenwick into Madame Defarge, the vengeful, bitter, sanguinary harridan of revolutionary death, induced further resonances of the film *A Tale of Two Cities*. Sitting there, looking around, it was the execution scenes in rerun. The blood lust of the snarling mob waiting expectantly for the condemned man's tumbril to roll into view, the Damoclean guillotine blade poised to deliver its version of justice, the heartless Revolutionary Tribunal controlling the Reign of Terror, Les Tricoteuses with Defarge at the forefront all knitting shrouds and savouring the parade of violent death, even the uninvolved and merely curious: they were all represented there in court. The air was redolent with anticipation, the imminence of unnecessary and unavoidable tragedy palpable. I was unable to shake off my dread that the conclusion would be as heart-rending as the one Dickens gave to his ill-fated character. He too was a lawyer; it was fortunate I didn't believe in portents; the parallels were disturbing.

Next in line was the Premier, making valiant attempts to gain the media's attention and ignore his neighbour's neckline and failing at both. I hadn't expected his presence. I should have; like Picino, his interests were divided. Attendance at such events was vote-grabbing, and I'd long held the opinion politicians only existed for that single purpose. I suspected they must have other uses, but on their wages, I was sure they pay someone else to mow the lawn, wash the car and, through the availability of private boarding schools, parent their children. Time was moving on, so I did the same with a quick scan of the rest of the lynching party.

There were many others I recognised and several gave me encouraging glances. One who didn't was my old boss. We parted badly, for him anyway. I was delighted to be leaving and unconcerned about the case load dumped in his lap before departure. He spent a lot of time telling anyone who'd listen I was an ineffectual lawyer and more trouble than I was worth. If I were inclined to pettiness, I'd consider a win today would be a smack in the face for him and his vituperation. Fortunately, I'm above such things, contenting myself with one short glare announcing, watch this space, you prick.

With a minute to go, I faced front and inhaled deeply. Maya, seated next to me, appeared calm and composed. Under the circumstances, it had to be a front. No one inside or outside that room, standing in the street, or watching news services nationwide, was remotely calm or composed about this proceeding. How could she be? My verdict then: she wasn't. How could she put up such a front? I was about to ask her when the command 'All rise' was given and the magistrate entered.

His name was Clive Redding, and I knew him in passing. On my single appearance before him, he passed a sentence of eight years onto my client which was harsh, considering the crime under discussion. But I knew the person I represented was guilty of far worse and not been punished for it. I advised him to forget about an appeal because it would have a negligible chance of succeeding. Take the time given, behave and try and shorten it, and get a new life after being released. That's not how I worded it, but it was the gist. I was sure Redding also knew about my client's other crimes and factored them into his sentencing. It's illegal, immoral, and unethical but I said nothing to anyone. Those same adjectives applied in triplicate to the sentenced man, and everyone's lives were improved with him locked away.

What it meant was we were in front of a man who liked to exercise the law for the greater good; a factor in our favour. His harsh and punitive side was another thing completely. What I did know about him was I'd never heard the slightest hint he allowed personal considerations of religion, race, or gender to influence his decisions. It was a positive and I was desperate for some of those.

A slight negative: I'd heard he nurtured political ambitions, like many in the legal profession. Would he seek to impress Picino and the Premier by supporting the public, and inaccurate, assumptions concerning their personal aims? If that happened, the irony would be overwhelming. Unfortunately, so would the result.

He sat, we sat, he scrutinised documents, we scrutinised the top of his head. He looked up and nodded at someone seated close to him, I saw her lift a phone and dial. As she hung up, a door opened and Henry came in. Four Sheriff's Officers, two in front, two behind, accompanied him into the dock.

Four? Was Henry mistaken for a member of The Black Liberation Army? The man didn't require containment, he was in need of a cuppa and a biscuit. All five sat, Henry in his habitual slouch, hands on knees, head down, hair over eyes, the others stiff-backed and guardsmen square on their chairs. Normally, I knew from past experience, they relaxed into a more informal manner. Not bevvies at the beach casual, more a tea break between court cases when their supervisor was nearby lack of ceremony. Today, under massive scrutiny, their posture, like their dress, was polished to a military standard. The scene in the dock looked like the US President's Honour Guard minding their boss's dog.

Grandstanding bullshit, I thought. Television cameras are not allowed in the courtroom, although several networks tried hard to get it to happen, the media's mobiles were for sending texts only with dire consequences for any of them foolish enough to snap a career-ending photograph, and the recordings from the security cameras, while possibly worth a small fortune to some, were guarded by people who were steadfastly incorruptible.

In my previous incarnation, I knew lawyers who tried to breach those defences; one of them worked as a bank teller, another drove a taxi, and the third was four years into a six-year sentence while the court officer they'd tried to suborn received promotion. Every day I give thanks to whichever deity convinced me to refuse to join the attempt to purchase the video footage. My refusal was moralistic integrity intensified by fears it might go disastrously wrong. When it did — anyway, I mentally light candles and offer fervent thanks and hardly ever feel foolish as I do it. Certainly, nowhere as stupid as if I said yes.

I looked at Henry and he raised his head returning my gaze evenly. Like Maya, he seemed unnaturally calm. Was it, I wondered, a cultural thing? A philosophical acceptance of merely going along with what can't be avoided? A form of Zen meditation technique? Perhaps it was far more simply that the few days in the remand centre had given him time to come to terms with his situation? I'd seen him many times since the beginning and we'd talked at length — with his hesitant diction, longevity was unavoidable — but I couldn't begin to grasp where he was placed emotionally. It bothered me but the right time to ask eluded me, along with the appropriate words. Perhaps I'd ask later, either at the celebration or the wake, whichever came to be.

I took one last look at the assembled crowd. People aren't soundless, even when they're not speaking and buildings and large rooms have a subliminal noise of their own making. There wasn't a silence as such, more an ethereal thrumming pulsing the air. When the serenity was broken, the disruption arrived like a clap of thunder from a clear sky and in a way no one expected.

Henry stood, ignoring the attempts to restrain him. I say stood; towered would be more accurate. This was not the Henry I knew. The one standing in the dock was taller, straighter, and with broader shoulders, a transfixing gaze, and a right arm raised with index finger outstretched like Light's Statue showing tourists the way to the Adelaide cricket ground. I, along with everyone else, looked where he pointed. In a straight line from his extended finger was Veronica Fenwick, eyes wide and mouth half open in shock.

She wasn't the only one; I was fairly certain if anyone looked at me and not him, they'd have seen the same expression. But nobody was. All in the room were staring at Henry or her and apart from the Sheriff's Officers who were attempting in vain to get Henry back into his seat, there was no movement or sound anywhere. Easily, almost indifferently, shaking off the attempts by his four totally bewildered attendants, who escorted a mangy old house cat into the dock and found themselves trapped in there with a full-grown tiger, Henry stepped forwards, took a deep breath, and let rip, his voice no longer the hesitant barely-articulate growling mumble I knew well but a thunderous baritone onslaught.

'That bitch there killed my wife. Doctor Veronica Haddon was drunk and in the Parnham clinic on the sixteenth of August two thousand and two she injected Amy Day with an overdose of penicillin. My wife died and it was all covered up but it's a matter of record. She's a murderer.'

The words, commanding, compelling, delivered in tones suffused with emotion, filled the big room. They were inescapable. Unignorable. Dominating. There was no trace of the Henry I knew; the one who now controlled the proceedings was a stranger. One whose awesome presence held everyone in thrall. At that precise instant, I saw it all or enough to see how I'd been duped. That one extraordinary moment was the sole reason why we were all there.

The frustrated quartet were attempting to get a grasp on his arms while demonstrating the same mouths-open eyes-wide pose as the rest of us. When he finished speaking, the room was silent. I heard nothing but pens scratching on press pads, the frantic clicking of texting mobiles and, something I was sure was mine alone, the thudding of a heart going through the gears into overdrive. Three seconds and the stillness erupted again as Henry repeated his message. Word for word, decibel for decibel. Despite the absence of the initial shock value, it conveyed all the invective potency powering the first delivery.

He probably didn't need to say it all again; the original, I felt certain, was seared into every brain present, most especially Ronnie Fenwick. The cool regal haughtiness gone as if never existing; what remained was a hunched and sobbing wreck trying to hide behind a mass of exquisitely coiffed blonde hair and Picino's shoulder. Madame Defarge strangled with her own knitting.

Henry was done. Majestically impressive and appearing dismissive of his surroundings, he turned and led his shaken escort from the room. As he left, Picino murmured something to Veronica Fenwick, freed his arm reluctantly from her clutches, stood up, and approached me. It was a clear breach of court protocol but I didn't think anyone gave a damn.

'Van, get the hell out of here before you get mobbed by the media. I'll look after Henry. Don't worry and I'll call you when it all calms down. But for now, go. Quickly. I know you had nothing to do with this, I saw how you reacted. Knocked sideways like the rest of us.' He turned to Maya. 'You, I'm not as sure about. We'll talk later.' And he was gone.

Maya was tugging at my arm. 'Van, we need to go. Picino's right. We'll sort it later. Van, come on.'

I couldn't move. I was barely able to think. What had happened? I mean, I knew the immediate what; but not the bigger picture what.

Maya was still hauling on my arm saying, 'Come on,' over and over. Finally, she leaned in close and shouted, 'Will you bloody come on!' Shocked, I'd never heard her raise her voice to me before and she used profanity about as often as I attend Mass, I started to stand up. Still not sure what was happening and with a peripheral sense of the advancing media who were ignoring the Sheriff's Officers' demands to leave, I surrendered to the only choice I had. I came on.

28

I craved a drink with the ability to numb what I was feeling but the odds in favour of being cornered by the leeches of the Fourth Estate in a pub were too high to ignore. We settled for caffeine, milk, and sugar. There was hardly anyone in the café; we ordered and squeezed into a corner booth where we'd be unseen unless someone was seriously looking. No one would be; those who might were all occupied after what occurred and no one else knew who the generic business type caffeine-chugging duo was. Maya sipped her coffee and stared at the table; I nursed mine and stared at the wall.

The silence lasted several minutes while I loosened my tie and collar, used a couple of paper napkins to wipe the tension-induced sweat from my face and neck, and thought deeply. I was feeling deeply; thinking that way seemed suitable. During the short silent walk, I worked most of it out; I have an incredible clarity of hindsight, pity it hadn't been foresight. I knew what guilt looked like; I'm a lawyer. And I knew what Maya feeling uneasy looked like; I was her landlord, her boss, her friend, her confidant. I knew something was wrong. But not what. I wasn't angry, though I suspected it might happen later. I was curious and disappointed. There were few enough people I trusted, one of them the young woman in front of me. It seemed I'd been wrong. Time to find out.

'You knew. Didn't you? What he was going to do in there?' No answer. No visible response.

'Maya. Talk to me. Please.'

She raised her head and looked at me as tears slid down her cheeks. 'No, I didn't know. Not in detail. I suspected there might be something. But no, I didn't know he was going to do that. I wasn't sure what.'

I had to ignore the tears to keep going. Not easy but necessary. I cleared my throat before I spoke.

'He fooled us all. Me, mostly. All that's happened, it was planned and put in place by an old man who wasn't anything he pretended to be. He isn't senile, ignorant, or unable to speak or write properly or... well, any of it. He fooled us all. Except you. Yes?'

'Yes.' She didn't look away but nor was she making eye contact. Her face was pointed at me, but her attention was somewhere else. Somewhere past me. She grabbed a napkin and wiped her face. When she sat up straighter, I could tell she'd made a decision; it was time for me to listen. I didn't want to break her train of thought and lessen her determination. I stayed silent.

'Van, promise me something please. That what I'm about to tell you is between us. Or I'll say nothing. I'm asking you to do this. For me.' I contemplated saying no and couldn't. I didn't for a moment consider saying yes and going back on my word because I wouldn't, couldn't, and she knew it. There was a decision to make and I made it. I reached out and grabbed her hand and nodded. She pressed my fingers for a second then let go. There were a few more tears which she wiped away and then for the first time she looked into my eyes. Properly. Directly. With friendship. And trust. Now, whatever happened, I was trapped. Pierced by her gaze, Madison Rundle's rabbit in headlights analogy popped into my mind. Fitting really, since I'd been Henry's bloody bunny!

'I worked it out. In theory anyway. I was sure it was all Henry's idea. All his senility and health problems, it's mostly put on. Since his wife's death, he's been anti-social and people assumed he was an invalid and they left him alone. Except for Mrs Jessup. With her, he acts more naturally. When I started having suspicions he or someone he knew could be behind it, I decided to find out if he might be capable. The day we went back there, when I was talking to her, I sneaked in a comment about his health and she told me, sort of sideways and without realising what she was giving away or what it meant, he was more compos and healthy than he seemed. Then I knew for sure something was a bit off balance. Also, you told me in the plane he was laughing at the people who'd smashed his house and written the graffiti, saying they couldn't spell. How did an illiterate old man know? It wasn't much but it started me thinking. You know what I'm like once that happens.'

She looked embarrassed and stared at the floor as she went on. 'He has money, not a lot but enough. He bought his house cheap when he was working and nobody chose to live in Parnham. It's where he and his wife lived, and he's on a pension that's far more than he spends.'

She paused. Obviously, we were coming to the hard part. I smiled. She tried to.

'You're wondering how I found out and why I didn't tell you. How is easier, I'll start there. We were told by several people Fenwick's widow used to be a doctor but nobody gave it any importance. It seemed to be the one detail everybody was ignoring so, for the hell of it, I looked into it and found out the whole story. Took doing but you know I'm a bloody determined researcher and I got there eventually.'

'Got where?'

'All of it. Let me explain it in a non-sequential way, it makes more sense. If Henry went public earlier with what he blurted out in court no one would have taken any notice. An unknown old Aboriginal man living in a rural fuel stop accusing a beautiful and popular widow of a locally-beloved politician of murder. Page seventy if at all, unseen and ignored. A non-event. Did you see what happened in the court room?'

Oh bloody yeah, I did! By tonight, what he said would be front page, a leading television-news story, and the main topic of discussion across the whole country. The sort of publicity you can't buy. No one will be ignoring him after those shit-shovellers from the media start digging for the dirt on Veronica Fenwick and, knowing them, finding it.

'Everything he's claiming about Veronica Fenwick is fairly easily verifiable. It took me less than four hours to find it all. It's seriously bad for her, she's about to be even more famous but not in a way she'll like.'

I was now totally confused. 'Yes. I saw it. She wasn't expecting it, and the press saw her reaction and went off like hungry bloodhounds. Whatever there is will be uncovered. But what exactly is it? You seem to know, and obviously Henry Day and Mrs Jessup do as well, but I don't. And I'd like to. I'm still his lawyer, I think. To be honest, I'm not sure.'

'Van, I'm sorry I didn't tell you but I wasn't sure if your desire to get him off might not be stronger than your often-stated preference for moral over legal. We can talk about it later, if we're still talking, but for now, I need to tell you what this is about. Yes?'

'Yes. Sure. Even if all it does is put his next lawyer in the picture.'

'Mrs Jessup knew near to nothing. About his wife dying and how but that's it. And to be fair to her, if she knew more, she's forgotten it, so I can't be certain where she fits, to be honest. Anyway, Mrs Fenwick used to be Mrs Haddon. Her husband was also a doctor. About twenty-odd years ago they ran local clinics for the Flying Doctor service, staying in some of the towns overnight. Doctor Veronica Haddon, later to be Mrs and then the widow Fenwick, liked a drink. One night in the Parnham pub, her husband was somewhere else at the time, she was well and truly wasted and was carried to her motel room and put into bed. There were unconfirmed rumours she wasn't alone. The next morning, still half pissed and hungover, she ran a clinic. Two patients attended. Mrs Bolton, who was expecting a baby, took one look at the doctor and went home. Which left Mrs Day there alone. Amy Day was fifty-five and suffering from an infection. Not much of one and a few days in bed would have done the trick. But Doctor Haddon decided to give her an injection of penicillin. A full dose, given without referring to the notes which said the patient was severely allergic to it. Fifteen minutes later Amy Day collapsed and within minutes was pronounced dead. The Flying Doctor sent a plane and the other Doctor Haddon but it was way too late. The enquiry, if that's what such a slapdash cover-up can be called, found Veronica Haddon not culpable of any professional misconduct, that's near as damn it a quote, and Amy Day's death was officially declared an unfortunate mistake by a doctor concerned about her severe infection. Mrs Bolton's evidence was discounted due to the difficulties she was having with her pregnancy and her, quote, hormonally-influenced emotional state.'

I could hear the anger in her voice. Indigenous women's and children's health was a low priority for many governments and it was something Maya cared deeply about. In most urban environments, the issue was less problematical; in rural areas it verged on an epidemic. No wonder Maya had been eager to see Henry succeed; Veronica Fenwick wasn't only answering to him for her own blunder, to Maya, she typified all who failed to do what basic humanity and the Hippocratic oath demanded. She took deep breaths and her voice returned almost to normal.

'What happened at the clinic, the hearing, Veronica's drinking, it's all on record but I can't reveal where it is or even mention I know about it without getting into trouble for not putting it into evidence. I'd be accused of hiding it to allow Henry could do what he did in court.'

She was right, she was legally obligated to reveal everything germane to the case and keeping anything hidden permitting Henry to use the court to set off his fireworks would be viewed as a serious breach of ethical conduct. She was wrong about one aspect of it: we'd both be in trouble, no one would believe I hadn't known regardless of any protestations she made concerning my ignorance. It was vital that her, and now my, secret, remained ours only.

I told her she was right and she relaxed a little. On top of everything else, her unethical actions while trying to help Henry, despite not knowing what it was she was helping with, caused her concern. If I'd known then, concern wouldn't have been a strong enough word for how I'd have reacted. What she said showed she knew me well; I might have used it to take the heat off Henry. Then again, if I'd been convinced of the validity of his quest for justice, I might not, leaving his plan to run its course. And now I'd never know. I told her the last part and said to carry on. I was bursting with questions and she had the answers.

'The term cover-up seems to fit how it was dealt with, or perhaps not dealt with would be more accurate. Shortly afterwards, Veronica Haddon left in a hurry and disappeared. I found out where she went. Her husband divorced her, the drinking and her other issues were too much for him. She reverted to her maiden name, Corris, moved interstate and worked in a variety of non-medical jobs. Four years later, in Canberra, she met then married Fenwick and buried her past. New husband in politics, new name and appearance, homes in Adelaide and Canberra. It was all forgotten and everyone moved on.'

Forgotten, according to Maya, by everyone except for Henry. He didn't move on. He spent the next two-and a-bit decades mourning his wife while knowing there was nothing he could do about it. That much was obvious. How he found out was the mystery. Not to Maya.

'Henry's friend, Mrs Jessup, let it slip. She didn't mean to and wasn't going to tell anyone about it for Henry's sake, but I was paying more attention to what she was saying than she was. She's old and her conversation wanders. Henry was at the shop and noticed the front-page picture. He knew it was the doctor. Older, richer, different but recognisable. And recently widowed. With an unexplained death creating a mystery. Mrs Jessup was there when he saw it, she noticed the picture in passing and knew who it was but she doesn't read the paper and barely gave it a thought until later. She has memory lapses and tends to forget a lot of things. Apparently, Henry didn't forget. He pondered on it more and came up with a plan. Then, when she told him about it much later, he pretended to be surprised. We were all trying to find out who was accusing him and it turned out to be Henry all along. As I said before, the word of an old man against the country's most famous and beloved widow for whom everybody displayed nothing but sympathy, it would be ignored completely.'

She was right. I finished it for her. 'But stir up a public accusation by blaming an old anti-social Aboriginal man for a murder spiced up with allegedly-traditional magic, throw in the Chinese connection and the sacred site debate as distractions, and get a bunch of overreactive religious loonies involved and all the hard work would be done by everybody else. Sounds absurd saying it like that, but it worked. Fooled us all.'

Both Veronica Fenwick and Madison Rundle used the term Black Magic openly. One believing in its veracity and potency, the other purely in its psychological and academic values. The media, possibly restrained by contemporary negative connotations of the word black and the likelihood of ridicule for any direct claims magic existed, chose more cautious phrasing to broadcast their versions of the same idea. In a way, they were all correct. The old man was indeed a magician; only not the sort everyone expected him to be. A rabbit out of a hat and, as an encore, a woman being sawn in half. What a showstopping performance!

One I played an unwilling bit-part in. 'Was it Henry who wrote to the press telling them he and Fenwick met and he somehow put his signature in the book?'

If it had been him, and we seemed to be in agreement it had, he'd almost definitely posted those letters in Parnham the day I was flying in, addressing them to Sydney and Melbourne to cause a delay. He probably hadn't expected me to be ambushed on the ABC, but it certainly stirred things up, which would have fitted with his strategy perfectly.

He'd been playing mind games with the irony being the person he was accused of playing them on was the only one he hadn't sucked in because he was already dead. Twenty million hypnotised by Henry's Machiavellian manipulations. And I was one also, too fixated on attempts to counter the unreality of the accusations against him to suspect the reality behind them.

Thinking back on it, I could kick myself for missing the only thing he'd slipped up on. I could make excuses, I wasn't looking, I was distracted, too involved with taking in the bigger picture to focus on the minute details. All of which might boost my feelings but I was still going to be irritated for missing something so obviously out of place it should have rung alarm bells too loud to be ignored. For anyone who was listening closely.

Maya caught it when I told the story without realising its relevance. On the plane, that first day, he'd made a comment the people who trashed his house were stupid and couldn't even spell properly. A supposedly illiterate old man picking up on the commonly confused which-witch homophone we all learnt early in school life, given a glaring new lexical entry in the BURN THE WHITCH slogan sprayed on his house. For whom he appeared to be, it didn't fit.

'And I missed it. He made one error, only one, and I wasn't listening. It would have changed everything.' I knew why I'd given it insufficient attention; I was too busy focussing on the cross next to it and the possibilities it raised.

'Van, I missed it too at the time and I was listening as closely as you were. It was a long day, the ACA hassle and all of it was getting to both of us. Getting hung up over a small mistake now is a waste of time. As would mentioning it to anyone else be. We can feel stupid for not noticing it but we don't have to admit it. Our secret, yes?'

Definitely yes. We didn't shake hands or cut our wrists and mingle blood or anything dramatic; we looked at each other and our eyes made promises.

So, enough of the self-destruction, to be resumed later when I was alone and despite what Maya said, I'd tell Alex, to get my head straight about such an amateur blunder.

Back to the case. Where were we? Right, the name in the book. I pointed out breaking into a rural office then getting into a filing cabinet and adding himself into a meeting attendance record wouldn't have been all that difficult.

'No, it wouldn't. When I was trying to put it together, that was one small part of what I came up with. But it was all guesswork, Van. There was no real evidence, only me putting a pile of separate ideas together, coming up with a wild theory, thinking what if I were right? Then his outburst today showed I had been. That was a surprise. I suspected he wasn't as doddery as he looked but honest, Van, I didn't know he was going to turn into Superman.'

She stopped and the smile disappeared. Her head dropped and she went back to staring at the table. We sat silently. She was right, it worked as planned. I had to admire him; the cunning old bastard prepared it well. It wouldn't make up for losing his wife and there'd be legal issues for him to face, which is where I came in, maybe, but finally seeing the pointlessly, as it turned out, vindictive Ronnie Fenwick publicly brought to account and disgraced would more than counteract all of that. Right triumphed over might for once.

The idealistic law student I once was would have been totally stoked and the older worldly-wise version was feeling the same way. But I knew I'd contributed nothing much beyond acting as a figurehead; any credit given should be for Maya and, obviously, the master magician behind the misdirections. Her considered inaction permitted Henry, the real driver of our runaway train, the opportunity to find closure. And, as she knew it would, threaten our relationship.

'Van, you know what I do. I do what I can for my people. He's my people, he and his wife. They were done over by a malicious bitch who was looking for someone to blame and the accusations against Henry, as ridiculous as they were, appeared at just the right time in her grief cycle. She probably didn't know who he was and maybe didn't even connect him to the careless killing of an old Aboriginal woman. I saw a chance to make it right. Can you look me in the eye and tell me what I did, and all I've been doing, is immoral or wrong?'

I could not: I didn't even try. I might be experiencing serious negative emotions now but I knew they'd pass. Or fade. But what about us? Our friendship? I saw her point, morality over legality: I taught it to her. But there was a lot to consider. I sat there considering. She'd lied to me by omission, hidden things from me, not trusted me. The reasons she gave were valid but it still hurt. I thought for a while and realised under the circumstances there was only one thing I could do.

'Do I still work for you?' I barely caught it; she was speaking in a whisper and still staring at the tabletop.

'No. No, you don't work for me anymore.'

Her head whipped up and her eyes opened wide in shock. She went to speak but I beat her to it.

'You just made partner. Let's go and talk to our client.'

Author's Notes

Researching this novel benefited from my far-ranging studies, especially those in Criminology and Law where many topics focussed on the Indigenous communities' legal, cultural, and social issues past and present. My countless wanderings, actual and virtual, took me into unfamiliar territory, often well outside my comfort zones. Those experiences included the ABC studios in Adelaide, Parliament Houses in Canberra and Adelaide, working courtrooms, a nineteenth-century prison, a remand centre, an excellent pub in Murray Bridge, several outstanding eateries in Adelaide, Sydney, and Canberra, one roadhouse remote geographically and from acceptable culinary norms, a terrifying martial arts school, a cold windy airstrip, a hot windy airstrip, and one important location that stands out for not actually existing. Standing alongside a deserted highway in the outback constructing a fictional town from an amalgam of photographed and notated realities was a challenge. The only parts requiring no invention were the scorching heat, the red dust, the endless landscape, the monstrous road trains, a bullet-holed sign, and the clusters of huge blowflies, whose enthusiastic welcome meant I could not possibly leave them out of the book. All the science and law is inherently factual, the magic and superstition: conjure your own conclusions.

www.blossomspringpublishing.com